The Story began in...

The Kind of a Girl...

as Lorraine Innis, a man in disguise trying to avenge the death of his girlfriend, accidentally foiled the assassination attempt on Russian president Kropotkin.

It continued in...

The Girl in the Diamond Studded Heels...

as Lorraine, now famous, became an international symbol of peace!

Then came...

The Girl in the Aubergine Sandals...

where we met Lorraine's Aunt Elinor and started to learn about the tragic flaws in Lorraine's past.

Which led to...

The Girl in the Lime Green Wellies...

and the star-crossed love affair with Verity Goodhue.

Now get ready to learn the final pieces of the puzzle that resulted in the creation of Lorraine in...

The Girl in the Saffron Espadrilles!

ALSO BY G.C. Allen

The Kind of a Girl

The Girl in the Diamond Studded Heels

The Girl in the Aubergine Sandals

The Girl in the Lime Green Wellies

Coming Soon...

The Girl in the Blood Red Stilettos

The Girl in the Sky Blue Plimsolls

Visit www.iLorraine.com

The Girl in the Saffron Espadrilles

G.C. Allen

The Fifth Book in the
Lorraine Innis Series

Daley◆into◆Print LLC
Mundus Est Vestra Locusta

To All The Ones

We Have Ever Loved and Lost

Watch over your heart with all diligence,
For from it flow the springs of life.

- Proverbs 4:23

The Girl in the Saffron Espadrilles

– 1 –
Me, Two Stupid

Lorraine Innis was dreaming again.

It began after her hypnotherapy session with Clodagh Clott. Lorraine had been reliving the past of her alter ego, Chesney Potts. In the dream, Lorraine was falling, and all her departed loved ones, Aunt Elinor, Verity Goodhue, and Martina Fergus, were just beyond her reach. Though she was Lorraine in the dream, her loved ones still recognized her.

They waved to Lorraine, almost beckoning her to join them in death. She continued to fall. Plummeting faster and faster, but at the last moment, she would find herself again at the top of the abyss, starting the plunge all over again.

If she hit bottom, would she die? Perhaps then she would join them all in a happier place. She wondered if Martina and Verity had met there. That might be awkward. Martina knew all about Verity, but Verity had died before Chesney met Martina. How would Verity react knowing that her beloved had gone off and gotten engaged to another girl? Perhaps Aunt Elinor would mediate on his behalf. How would he face them? Would they even recognize him now?

It didn't matter. The dream never reached a conclusion. It repeated until Lorraine could stand it no longer and awoke.

Lorraine sat up in bed and put her hand to her face. It was clammy and cold. She waved the front of her pajamas to cool herself and then exhaled.

"I'm driving myself insane," she muttered, then reached for the telephone beside her bed. She glanced at the clock. It was half-past three in the morning.

"I can't call Clodagh now. No use ruining the sleep of two people," said Lorraine, "or is it three?" She never knew whether to count herself as two people or just the one.

Lorraine rose from her bed, slipped on her robe and went down to the kitchen to make a cup of tea.

As the kettle came to a boil, Lorraine stared at a magazine. Her face was on the cover. She was smiling and confident. The expression made her face hurt, and her mind ache. She couldn't remember the photoshoot. There had been so many since last October. Lorraine thought of all the other smiling faces she'd ever seen on magazine covers over the years. Were they all as confused as she was? Were they all living double lives?

She turned away and caught sight of her reflection in the glass front of a cabinet door.

"The goddess of peace," she murmured sarcastically, recalling one of the names assigned to her by the media. "You don't look like a goddess of anything." She glanced down at the magazine cover again, and then back at her reflection.

"Without your smile and your makeup, you look like any one of a million other tired…"

Lorraine paused before whispering: "…women."

She slumped into a kitchen chair.

"I'm gone, or I'm going," said Lorraine. "Is there anything left of me? Is there anything left of him? I'm losing myself in a complete fiction. And what am I asking Clodagh to do? Totally erase, Chesney for Lorraine? To become me, I mean, her, in the hope that this cardboard person, will be able to settle all his, I mean, my problems?"

Lorraine buried her head in her hands.

"I must be out of my mind. I've dug a pit for myself. The original plan was to bring Peter Liverot to justice. Now I find he wasn't responsible for Martina's death. But now, I'm in so deep I can't climb out. So what do I do? What's my brilliant sequel to my first brilliant plan?"

Lorraine stood up and started pacing the floor, stopping only when she found herself in front of the hall mirror.

"I'll tell you what you did," she said, pointing at the reflection before her. "You dug a hole and put yourself in it, Chesney Potts, and then when you saw that you couldn't dig it any deeper, you asked for me," Lorraine pointed at herself, "to jump in and dig you out."

She froze for a moment, her eyebrows knit in consternation. "Wait, that's not right, is it?" Lorraine's index finger waved back and forth, trying to sort out whether her male side was the problem and her female side the solution, or if it were the other way around.

"Oh, it doesn't matter, does it?" she concluded, throwing up her hands and walking away. "You're a stupid boy…girl…you're stupid people…both of you!"

She went into the kitchen, looked at the phone and then the clock. It was still too early. Lorraine picked up the receiver and began to dial the number anyway. She stopped and put the receiver down.

Why was she calling Clodagh? What would she say? When first she had woken up, Lorraine would have said they needed to continue their hypnotherapy immediately. Now, she wasn't sure. She had forced herself to live through the death of one lover, what would happen when she relived the second one? Would she clear her mind, or obliterate her remaining sanity?

What could she do? Who could she be? She wished she could run away from all of it. From Lorraine Innis, from Chesney Potts, from all of the mess she'd made.

Lorraine returned to her bedroom and looked out the window. The dawn was breaking. Off to the right was the city of Wilmington. To the left lay the surrounding suburbs, which quickly faded into the rolling countryside of the Brandywine Valley. In that area lay the full scope of humanity. There were poor, rich, virtuous, villains, the humble, and the proud; every type of person, every kind of individual. She suddenly felt terribly alone. Out there must be a representative of every segment of society, but she doubted there was anyone else like her. Was there another person in Delaware or beyond that was as famous as Lorraine Innis, as admired as Lorraine Innis… as totally screwed up as Lorraine Innis? She hoped not. She wouldn't wish the mess she was in on her worst enemy. She started to think of Peter Liverot in that last category, until she reminded herself that for all his villainy, Liverot was not her worse enemy. Who was that now? Albrecht Eckner? She didn't know. She was back where she started in regards to finding the person responsible for Martina's death. Why couldn't Martina's death just have been an accident, like Verity's? Why did she have to go looking for justice? She could hardly recall anymore.

She had cut herself off from the rest of the human race. If only she could…

"Why can't I?" said Lorraine answering aloud the question only half-formed in her mind. "Why can't I give it all up? I'll just disappear. I'll go back to being Chesney, him, that is me. I'll get rid of Lorraine Innis, and no one will know, and after a few weeks, no one will care. The world will find a new celebrity and forget I ever existed. Let someone else worry about peace, and charities, and all that. As for justice, whoever gets justice in this life? I've thrown my life away trying to sort this all out, but enough is enough. I'm going back to being a real person."

She picked up the phone and dialed the number. The sleepy voice of Clodagh Clott answered.

"Hello," said Lorraine, "I'm sorry if I woke you."

"It's okay," said Clodagh, "I had to get up in… I don't have my contacts in. What time is it anyway?"

"I just thought you'd want to be the first to know," said Lorraine ignoring the question.

"Know what?"

"You don't have to do anything else."

"Huh?"

"I'm not going through with it. We're done with the therapy."

"Uh, okay," said Clodagh, still sounding a bit dozy. "You mean you're not going to be Lorraine all the time, I mean, full-strength, I mean, oh, it was your idea, you know what I mean."

"No," said Lorraine. "Not even half-strength."

"Huh, but…what do you mean?"

"I'm not going to be Lorraine any longer, at any strength," she said. "I'm getting out of celebrity, out of charity, out of womanhood, out of all of it."

"But what…"

"I'm going to fade into the woodwork and rejoin the rest of faceless humanity. I'm going to rejoin the world."

"Yeah, okay, whatever," said Clodagh.

There followed a prolonged pause.

"Just one thing," said Clodagh with a yawn.

"What's that?"

"Next time you tell me you're not doing anything, don't wake me up to do it. Goodnight."

Clodagh hung up.

Lorraine looked at herself in the mirror behind her dressing table. She tugged at her shoulder-length hair.

"And you're the first thing to go," she said, "before anybody can talk me out of it, including me."

Lorraine opened the drawer looking for the scissors. She would cut off all of her hair, effectively killing Lorraine Innis.

The scissors were there, but there was something else there that stopped her cold.

Lorraine reached for the scissors, but at the last moment, grasped the small box beside them instead.

– 2 –
The Difference Between
"At" and "From"

ood morning, Valerie. I'm so happy to see you're back!"
Valerie Fierro suppressed the urge to tell Patsy Einfalt to find
a convenient lake and jump into it. Chirpiness wasn't a capital
offense, though, at 8:45 in the morning, it was close.

"Hello Patsy," mumbled Valerie.

"Oh, your arm's still in a cast," said Patsy. She made that "tsk tsk-ing"
noise and shook her head. "Does it hurt much?"

Not at much as it would hurt if I knocked you senseless with it, thought
Valerie.

"Are there any messages?" asked Valerie.

Patsy produced a folder containing all the messages from the last two
weeks. Valerie sighed and took the file in her good hand, then started for
her office.

"Oh," she said nonchalantly, "is Lorraine in yet?" It was a silly
question. Lorraine Innis had no life. She was always there early and
always left late. Being a wholly manufactured person, Lorraine had no
friends and no family. Lorraine had no real leisure activities. Her fame
made it impossible to enjoy any events in public. Lorraine was nearly as
dull as her alter ego, Chesney Potts. That's why Patsy's reply came as a
surprise.

"No," said Patsy, "Lorraine isn't in."

"Oh," said Valerie. "Well, she must be coming in later, huh? What does
she have… a doctor's appointment?"

Valerie smiled inwardly. The last place Lorraine would take her
"supplementary plumbing" would be to a doctor.

"No, Lorraine is…" Patsy stopped. Valerie eyed her suspiciously. Patsy
Einfalt was sweet and fairly dopey, but she was a good secretary. She
knew how to keep a secret. That was one more thing about Patsy that
annoyed the hell out of Valerie.

Valerie waited a moment on the off chance that Patsy would complete the thought she had dangled in front of Valerie. She tried to help it along.

"Lorraine is....what?"

Valerie could almost see the thoughts twisting beneath Patsy's spiral perm.

"Lorraine's...not here."

"I know. You told me that," said Valerie. "Where is she?"

Patsy's expression looked like a confused Labrador Retriever. It was cute in a dog. In Patsy, it was just irritating.

"Is Lorraine...home?"

"Yes," agreed Patsy. "Lorraine is home."

Valerie rolled her tongue against the inside of her cheek. While Patsy wouldn't volunteer confidential information, she would admit it if it was guessed.

"Is she sick?"

"No," said Patsy, "at least she didn't say she was sick when she called."

So, she called, thought Valerie. Until recently, Lorraine would have called Valerie and told her. Now she was only telling Patsy. This was a disturbing development. It had to be related to whatever Peter Liverot had told Lorraine on his death bed. Now Lorraine was home, but she wasn't sick. It was time for another guess.

"Oh," said Valerie, "so she's working from home."

"She working at home," said Patsy.

That was significant, thought Valerie. What was the difference in Patsy's mind between working "from home," and working "at home?" Of course, Lorraine and Chesney could provide a tedious grammatical analysis of both sentences, which would have supplied the answer.

"Oh, so... Lorraine is doing some work at home. "But not work for the Foundation?"

"I don't think so," said Patsy.

"Oh? Why not?" Valerie asked quickly, hoping to catch Patsy off guard.

"Because she's paying the consultant from her own..." Patsy stopped in mid-sentence. She gritted her teeth as if she had just stepped on a crack and was fearful of the consequences to her mother's back. "Forget I said that."

Valerie smiled and shrugged. "Oh, well, if it's not something for the Foundation, I don't need to know. After all, she's my cousin, but we're not attached at the hip. I'm sure Lorraine will tell me all about it later."

Patsy breathed a sigh of relief. "Good, I'd hate to disclose anything told to me confidentially."

Valerie resisted the urge to pat her on the head. "Just as it should be," said Valerie. "That's why you're such a good confidential secretary."

Patsy's grin broadened to reveal even more of her teeth. "Thank you for understanding," she said. "That means a lot. I'd just hate to give away any secrets."

"I wouldn't want you to betray the trust we have in you," said Valerie, especially when it was easy to trick it out of her.

Valerie entered her office and closed the door. If Lorraine was meeting with someone at home and paying for it out of her own pocket, Patsy wouldn't know the details. Lorraine was like a light switch. When Lorraine was "on," she'd tell Valerie everything, in fact, more than she wanted to know. When Lorraine was "off," it was total darkness. Lorraine wasn't "off" very often, but when she was, it was maddening. And the worst part was Valerie didn't know where the switch was. She had to sit in the dark and try to deduce the thoughts of Lorraine's all too moral mind.

What could Liverot have told Lorraine, she asked herself for the thousandth time? Wait, that question had changed. It was now: what could he have told Lorraine that she would need to meet with some private consultant about at home?

"Stupid bitch!" Valerie muttered as she sat behind her desk. Why did Lorraine have to be so honorable? Wasn't everyone out for themselves? It was how the world worked. She unconsciously fingered the pendant around her neck. Everyone takes care of themselves first. Valerie helped herself so she can help others later. So what if she got a generous... commission... for what she did. Liverot did. Liverot's backers did. Otherwise, they wouldn't have funded the operation and where would all those needy people be then? Everyone knew that's the way things worked, except idealists like Lorraine. She didn't even submit expenses for legitimate things like lunches and cars, and homes. Lorraine had naive ideas about good for the sake of good. That would be like running a motor without oil, it might run for a little while, but it would quickly seize up and be less than useless.

Those were good points, thought Valerie. That's what she would tell Lorraine when she was accused of making a lavish living while working for the Foundation. The whole stupid charity was Lorraine's idea. It was okay if Lorraine wanted to play Mother Theresa, but how could she expect her best friend to do the same? Selfish, unrealistic bitch!

But why would Lorraine need a consultant?

Valerie fished through the pile of mail that had built up over the past ten days. Most were requests for funding; for Lorraine to make personal appearances; for endorsements. Then one item caught her eye. It had a small catalog attached.

"Congratulations!" Read the outside of the silver envelope.

"All of us here at Fourth Fiduciary Trust congratulate you on your recent anniversary with the company," read the card. "We look forward to many more happy years with you as part of our family. Please select an anniversary gift from the attached catalog (appropriate to your number of years of service) and submit your selection on the reply form. (Allow four to six weeks for delivery). And thank you again for your loyal service!"

At the bottom, was the signature of Peter Liverot printed in blue ink in an attempt to make it appear that he had actually signed the card. Valerie knew he hadn't, not just because Liverot was dead, but also because she wrote that phony sentiment years earlier.

She recalled her first day at the bank and how she had gotten there. And that made her think of Martina Fergus.

A smirk crossed Valerie's lips. The blame for everything fell on Martina Fergus. Martina was very sweet, not Patsy Einfalt sweet, how did Chesney put it? Gracious? Yes, that was it, but Valerie never understood that description. She understood graceful, but Martina wasn't particularly graceful. She was nice, almost too nice: the type of girl who would do anything for you but with whom you couldn't party.

Staring at the anniversary card, Valerie reflected on her career.

– 3 –
Acceptable and Unacceptable "C" Words

Valerie Fierro had always worked in the financial service industry, just like most of the people in Northern Delaware. There was a good living to be made in banking and opportunities for advancement. That alone charted Valerie's course after she graduated from college. She was going to the top.

College was fun. It was a four-year break and helped her forget the traumatic days of high school after her father had died. Her father's death made it impossible to bask in the glory of being elected queen of the prom. College was a way to shake off the past, get a new start, and have a good time. This too, was no more than she deserved. Reality didn't reassert itself until after graduation, and it did so with a hard slap.

It was at her first job interview. She had worn her best suit. She had her resume in hand. It wasn't a very long resume, but it showed that she had graduated from college, and it was printed on linen-finished paper. And her suit was very impressive. It was silk and well-tailored to her figure. She sat up straight and noticed the woman behind the desk was round-shouldered. While the woman reviewed Valerie's application, Valerie thought that she should be interviewing this woman, and not the other way around. After all, Valerie had a better figure, a better suit, better posture, and better make-up: the whole package.

"We can start you on the phones," said the woman jarring Valerie from her mental inventory.

"The phones?" said Valerie, unsure that she had heard the woman correctly.

"Yes, we're a call center," said the woman. "That's what we do. We answer calls from our cardmembers."

"Cardmembers," repeated Valerie.

"The people who use our credit cards, the cardmembers."

Valerie knew that. She wasn't stupid. She had credit cards. She wasn't asking for clarification. She was more shocked that someone with her qualifications was being asked to answer the phone.

"Yes," said Valerie trying to reassert her superiority, "I know who the customers are…"

The woman raised a cautionary finger. "Not customers! They are never to be referred to as 'customers!' They are our cardmembers, or if you must, our members, but they are never to be called customers. We like to make them feel that by using our product, our cardmembers are entering into an exclusive club, one that they have been selected to join. They'll explain all that to you in your training. And whatever you do, don't ever, ever let someone hear you use either of the 'C' words, especially not on the phone."

Valerie thought she knew the "C" word, but doubted whether that was what this woman was talking about. "What are the 'C' words?"

The woman looked at her as if she were dealing with a slow child. "Customer and client," she said. "Of course you can use the other 'C' word; in fact, you should…"

"Cardmember," said Valerie.

The woman flashed a patronizing smile, followed by a sober stare. "It's important to remember that when you get on the phones…"

"Pardon me," interrupted Valerie, "but you keep mentioning the phones."

"That's correct."

Valerie stared at the woman. She obviously hadn't gotten a good look at who she was talking to. Perhaps she was worn out from a steady stream of mediocre applicants, the type of people who were suited to talking to customers for eight hours a day. Perhaps she hadn't noticed how well Valerie's suit fit, or how flawlessly she applied her cosmetics. The woman looked back at Valerie, and they shared five seconds of silent reflection.

"It's an entry-level position," said the woman.

"Yes, but…"

"And everyone starts on the phones."

"I understand that," said Valerie, "but…" she smoothed her lapel, and then looked at the woman's own polyester jacket and realized that appeal was futile. "…but, I have a degree…"

The woman looked back down at Valerie's application.

"Yes, well, I was overlooking that."

Valerie smiled.

"When I say I overlooked your degree," she said, "I don't mean that I didn't notice it. I mean I ignored it on purpose, as a favor to you. Having a degree isn't really necessary. In fact, it can be a hindrance. I'm not looking for the next CEO. I'm looking for someone to help the cardmembers. Here everyone starts on the phones."

Valerie just looked at the woman. The woman looked back at her.

"Like I said, we don't care about degrees. They just get in the way. But you seem like a nice kid, and if you want the job, it's yours."

The woman smiled again. Nice kid? Everyone started on the phones? Valerie doubted whether this woman started on the phone. This may have been just a call center, but the whole building didn't answer the phones. There were people in offices supervising the drones on the phone. Valerie didn't go to college to sit answering phone calls from confused customers. Didn't this woman realize that?

"The next training session starts on Monday," said the woman. "It's a four-week training…"

"Training? For the phones?"

"Yes, technically the title is 'cardmember service representative…'"

"On the phone."

"Yes, that's how our card members contact us in ninety-nine percent of the cases…"

The woman rattled on about schedules and training and benefits, assuming that Valerie would be honored to be on their silly phones 40 hours a week. Valerie half-listened to it all while trying to figure out the magic words to refute the declaration that "everyone starts on the phone."

As the woman rambled on, Valerie touched the pendant her father had given her.

"*Prima I denti, poi I parenti,*" she could hear her father saying. Literally, it was: "take care of your teeth, then your family," but it meant: "Look out for Number One."

She thought of her father. She was his *Piccola Principessa.* Valerie looked at the woman as she droned on about company policies. She had undoubtedly said it all hundreds of times before to hundreds of other employees, all of whom were shunted out of her drab little office and out on to the phones. She was no longer a Princess.

Or was she?

Princesses didn't work on the phones for eight hours a day, did they? No, they gave orders. They supervised. They didn't wait on others. They were waited on. They didn't listen to problems all day from customers who had to be treated like some exclusive club member. They were the exclusive ones.

Her father had understood that. She owed him better. She owed herself better.

"And we have a generous profit-sharing plan which employees are eligible for after…"

Valerie stood. The woman's mouth hung open.

"I'll say this just once," said Valerie. "I have a valuable degree. I am an intelligent young woman. I understand you probably have a set career track for the average applicant who falls in off the street, but I can assure you I am not that average person. Now, what positions do you have for an individual of my caliber?"

For effect, Valerie placed her hand on her hip two seconds after saying "caliber." It felt right.

The woman just stared at her for a moment. Then when she had recovered from the shock of meeting a genuinely determined young woman, she picked up Valerie's application and resume and tore them both in half.

Valerie smiled through pursed lips.

"And just so you know, there's another 'C' word," said Valerie as she walked out the door.

– 4 –
Standing Out from the Stretch Pants Platoon

S ix weeks later, she said the dreaded words for the first time.
"Thank you for calling Magna Card. My name is Valerie. How may I help you today?"

Five interviews at five separate credit card banks, all of which recited the same mantra: "everyone starts on the phone." She had not received a better offer. Take it, or leave it.

Valerie took it while making a solemn vow. She may be stuck on the phone now, she may be pushed down in the dirt, but she would regain the place she had once held. Her father had recognized she was special, and now, in his memory, she would show everyone else. Whatever it took, Valerie Fierro would rise to the top of the business world. She'd run one of those banks someday. Then she would take over those other four banks and demote everyone in human resources to phone reps.

For the first time in her life, Valerie detested talking on the phone. It was torture spending eight hours a day, five days a week with that stupid headset crushing her hair while whining customers spat their petty complaints into her shell-like ear. To add insult to injury, the company papered her cubicle with idiotic platitudes about the "card members being everything," and "let them hear the smile in your voice." Her co-workers may have had smiles in their voices, but most of them also had at least twenty excess pounds around their midriffs. Most of them seemed quite content to listen to the insignificant problems of customers all day between their three scheduled breaks. Those breaks, as welcome as they might be, were almost as bad as being on the phone. In herds of eight, they would shuffle off to graze in the cafeteria. There they would chat about their dull little lives as if they were actually interesting. And to make matters even worse, they were friendly. It was as if they were in some weird customer service cult into which they wanted to indoctrinate her.

23

"Be like us," they seemed to say every way but vocally. "Be happy on the phone. Eat a donut. Find a nice husband, maybe a plumber or a construction worker. Have some babies. After that, you won't need that cute figure anymore. You'll like stretch pants, you'll see!"

The subliminal message was seductive. They all seemed fat and happy. It almost worked. Then one morning, Valerie stepped on her scale and was shocked to learn that she had gained five pounds in a single month. She refused to become a clone of these women.

Despite the relaxed dress code, Valerie determined that she would exceed its requirements. She would dress as if her career were on the fast track to success. She wasn't going to be like those roly-poly reps. She was going to get off the phones. She was going to be in management. She wouldn't dress for where she was, but where she was going. While others in her phone unit casually sat as they spoke to cardmembers, Valerie made sure her posture was always perfect, imagining she was behind a desk in a private office speaking face to face with a client. In short, she cultivated an aura of sophistication and superiority calculated to get her noticed.

And it worked.

"Mr. Minear wants to see you," her unit manager told her one afternoon.

The reps in the adjacent cubicles grimaced as if this was the worst thing that could possibly happen. And for them, it would have been. Their only goals were to put in their time, go on breaks, gossip, get paid, and hurry to their average little homes and their dull families. Being called into a senior manager's office meant one had become visible, and being visible to upper management was not a good thing.

"What did you do?" asked one purple pair of stretch slacks as Valerie rose from her chair.

"Did a caller complain?" asked another pair in magenta.

"I got called into his office once," a third said hopefully, "when my husband broke his leg at the plant." But her optimism quickly evaporated. "But you don't have a husband, and he don't have a plant."

"I don't know what it's about," said her supervisor. "They just called down from the third floor and said Mr. Minear wanted to see Valerie Fierro…"

The third floor. The mention of the third floor made the women jump as if a dentist had just smacked a decayed incisor with his little metal hammer.

Valerie buttoned her suit jacket. Her supervisor walked her to the elevator, like a warder escorting a condemned prisoner to the electric chair. When they reached the elevator, she pushed the button for the third floor. Her mouth offered words of encouragement, though her eyes seemed to be saying a final farewell. As the door opened, her manager's body language betrayed that she was already distancing herself from the leper Fierro.

As the doors closed, Valerie began to question herself. Had she done anything wrong? She didn't remember arguing with a customer. As the elevator began its ascent, she recalled rumors about secret callers. Upper management would pose as difficult customers. Maybe she had been gotten one of these test calls. But she hadn't had any difficult calls. She rarely deviated from the scripts that they were provided with for dealing with customers. No, she concluded as a ding signaled she had arrived on the third floor, she hadn't abused anyone recently.

Minear: She had seen the name on memos. She had probably seen him walking around the building like so many of the nameless suits that seemed to drift through the customer service area on their way to more rarified climes on the third floor.

The secretary outside Mr. Minear's office gave her an odd look accompanied by an even more curious smirk before telling Valerie: "You can go right in... dear."

Valerie started to thank her, but that "dear" had a strange edge to it. Instead, she just nodded, and looked into the open door. The man inside was on the phone. So that was Mr. Minear. She had seen him. Valerie recalled him talking to her boss' boss' boss. He wore good suits. He had a nice haircut and a nice smile to go along with it. He had nice shoes, too, which she could plainly see because he was leaning back in his swivel chair with his feet on his desk. He was talking on the phone in a jocular way. He waved Valerie in, directing her to close the door behind her and sit down. When he wasn't talking, Minear made gestures to Valerie, mocking the person on the other end. Valerie found herself smiling as if he was including her in a private joke.

He had nice eyes, did Mr. Minear, blue they were. She glanced around the office. The furniture was richer looking than most of the other offices in the building. Those offices, the head of her cardmember service unit and the human resources office, only had metal desks. Mr. Minear's desk was made of wood.

"Yeah, well, I gotta go..." Mr. Minear took his feet off the desk and sat up. "Yeah, yeah..." The person on the other end of the line apparently was not giving up easily. Mr. Minear opened and closed his hand in a "yack-yack" motion.

"Look, someone just came in," he said, now with a bit more authority to his voice, though at the same time, he winked at Valerie to indicate it was only for show. "Yes, you get me that report, and we'll discuss it after I review it. Thanks."

He put down the receiver and shook his head.

"Nice guy, but he hangs on like bug guts on a BMW grille. Sorry."

Valerie just smiled.

"So, how do you like it?" Minear asked.

Valerie stared at him. How did she like what? The weather? His office? His necktie? Mr. Minear must have sensed her confusion, for he clarified the question.

"How do you like it here…at Magna Card?"

"Oh," she said, careful to smile, "I like it very much."

"How do you like the phones?" He asked.

She started to answer, but then realized she had forgotten to smile.

"Not so much, huh?" he surmised.

"Oh, no, it's not that…"

"Then, you like being on the phones?" He said it in a way that made the answer evident to both of them. They apparently shared the same opinion of customer service work. It was like asking a gourmet how they enjoyed the aroma of the deep fat fryer at Burger King.

"Well…" Valerie began carefully, "…we're here to serve our cardmembers. Without them, we'd be out of business."

He smiled. "A perfect answer," he said. "I couldn't have said it better myself." He stood up and looked out his window. "We're here to serve the cardmembers, no matter how stupid their questions may be, no matter how obvious the answers would be if only they'd taken a moment to apply logic to the situation, no matter how much they waste our time and resources with piddling issues. We're here to serve our wonderfully thick cardmembers."

"Oh," she said, "I wouldn't call them thick…"

He turned to her, lowered his voice and gave her a wink. "It's okay," said Mr. Minear, "they're thick, and that's putting it nicely. Why else would they agree to pay us exorbitant interest rates to go out and buy cheap crap they don't think they can live without and will no doubt throw away within a year if it hasn't broken first? They're as thick as the Great Wall of China. Without their impenetrable stupidity in matters of economics, not only our company but the whole American financial system would quickly be extinct. Don't get me wrong, I love them, bless every idiotic, self-absorbed cell in their bodies. But they're thick, and I love them because they're so dense. If they'd ever wise up, we'd all be selling used Buicks or scrubbing toilets."

He crossed back to his desk and craned his neck to read from an open manila file folder.

"University of Delaware, hmm? Business administration."

"Yes."

He looked her over again and then looked down at the file and shook his head.

"I don't know what they're doing down in HR," he said. "They should have never hired you."

Valerie felt a lump forming in her throat.

"Obviously overqualified…"

She didn't fit in, she thought. Valerie knew she didn't fit in with the fat and happy crew downstairs. But she thought that standing out was a good thing, not a prelude to being fired.

"They never should have hired you for phone work."

He looked her in the eye. After a long pause, his grimace dissolved into a smile.

"Relax, Valerie," he said, "I may call you Valerie?"

"Of course, Mr. Minear."

"And you call me Mitchell. It's not your fault, Valerie."

"No… Mitchell?"

"It's those nitwits down in human resources," he crossed to the front of the desk and sat down on the edge. "They've got some stupid notion that everyone needs to start at the bottom in customer service. Hell, why don't they just have everyone start by cutting the grass or picking up cigarette butts in the parking lot? That would make as much sense."

He laughed. Valerie laughed as well, thinking that was what was expected. Mitchell Minear stopped and leaned towards her. He was practically looking down her blouse. Valerie fought the urge to squirm. She was glad she stopped buttoning at the center of her décolletage.

"That's an interesting pendant," he said. He raised his gaze slightly as if that was where his focus had been all along.

"Thank you," she said, "it was a gift from my father."

The mention of a father seemed to give him momentary pause. "Oh, your father, that's nice. Are you and your father close?"

"He passed away when I was in high school."

"I'm sorry," though there was no remorse in his voice. They sat frozen for an awkward moment before he lurched the conversation forward. "As I was saying, you shouldn't be on the phones. Okay, yeah, it was good that you had the experience, but a few days of that are more than enough for a girl…excuse me, a young woman with your background."

"Oh?"

"You're obviously cut from different cloth than most of the girls down there in customer service." Valerie noticed he didn't correct that use of the word "girl" even though all of those women were much older than she was. "I can see that from the way you deport yourself."

Valerie sat up a little straighter and threw back her shoulders.

"That's what I first noticed," he said. "You don't belong down there. Anyone walking through the department should have seen that. Oh, nothing wrong with the other phone reps, but they're where they should be. They're a lot like the people they're serving, and that's how it should be. They're our frontline troops, but like privates in the army, there are a lot more of them than the officers, the leaders. You're not in that class, though, as I said, there's nothing wrong with them."

"Thank you," she said.

He shrugged his shoulders, and for the first time she noticed the well-toned muscles beneath his fitted dress shirt. Although he was older, at least forty, he kept fit. "No need to thank me," said Minear, "it's just an observation." He looked at her intently as if weighing options in his mind before speaking his next sentence. "What are you doing tonight?"

"Tonight?" The question caught her by surprise. Though she tried not to show it, her reaction must have registered on her face.

"Whoa, hold on," said Minear with a laugh, "let me rephrase that. I don't want you to get the wrong idea; after all I'm a married man. What I meant to ask is if you don't have any plans tonight would you like to attend a charity dinner? The bank gives donations to various charities, you know: good corporate citizenship and all that sort of crap. We gave to this organization..." he glanced at a piece of paper on his desk. "...some homeless shelter, or something, you know feeding poor people. Ironic, isn't it? A lot of businesses give them money to feed the homeless and they turn around and feed us. Anyway, it's how the non-profit racket works. They throw a dinner and all the benefactors go and eat chicken and listen to how much our contributions mean to the people who are eating soup in some shelter across town. Then we give them more money so they can keep up the good work for another year until the next gala dinner. We get a table of ten, and it doesn't look good if we don't fill it. It makes it look like the bank doesn't care, and we want the bank to look good, don't we?"

Valerie quickly agreed. Even though Mitchell Minear seemed to have a healthy cynicism about life, he was still upper management.

"Good, it's business attire," he said, scrutinizing her appearance again. "What you've got on is perfect. It's at 6:30. I can give you a lift, if you like. It will save you paying to park in town, plus we can talk...philosophy."

"Philosophy?"

"Yes, deep questions of existence like: is there life after the phones? Be ready down at the front desk at 6:00."

That was how it began. That evening, on the ride to the Hotel du Pont, Valerie was treated to a monologue on the two themes in the life of Mitchell Minear. The first was his career, to which he was devoted, despite his jaded view of the credit card industry. His second was his marriage to which he was less dedicated. Valerie had seen enough TV shows to recognize the familiar excuses a middle-aged man tried to pedal. What made it interesting, however, was the added twist: what he could do for Valerie Fierro.

Not long after that first night in public, there was a first night in private. Valerie knew he was using her, and she was fairly certain he knew she was using him, but no one had to spoil the façade by pointing out the arrangement. For his part, Mitchell Minear wanted sex, at least on the surface. If it just began and ended with sex, he could have gotten that at home, whether or not his wife "understood him." The frequently mentioned but never seen Mrs. Minear probably didn't understand him. What sane woman in her forties could understand her husband's need to be forever twenty-two when the calendar insisted otherwise? Valerie understood him, at least more than his wife did. She understood that Mitchell Minear appreciated a good young body. That it was her good young body was to Valerie's advantage. She would gladly trade what he wanted, sex, for what she wanted, a career. It did involve some role-playing, though. It wasn't anything kinky or even interesting. She just had to pretend he was young, virile, and desirable. In his early forties Mitchell Minear was nearly ancient. He had the beginnings of those squishy rolls of fat around his waistband that someone had mistakenly christened "love handles." His hair was thinning. And years of practicing his sexual skills had shaved several minutes off his time, which was a veritable boon if one was a downhill skier. But in regards to intercourse, it just made him a downhill lover.

But she played the part expected of her. She moaned at the moments he expected moans. She laughed at his stale jokes, even after he repeated them three or four times. She listened sympathetically as he described how nobody around him appreciated him. In short, she was kind to an aging male. When she was laying there, through yet another too-long monolog or a too-short sexual act, Valerie found consolation in rubbing her pendant and reminding herself that she was looking out for number one.

Mitchell Minear was true to his unspoken promises. Not long after their first private rendezvous, a job opened up in regulatory compliance. It was an area over which Minear had no responsibility, but that made it even better. It wouldn't look like he was giving her the job. All she had to do was post for it, and after a few charade interviews, she'd be sure to get it. And she did. She was off the phones.

He got what he wanted. She got what she wanted. No mess, no consequences. Valerie was on her way.

- 5 -
A Prescription for Life

It was a simple little box. It held the ring Aunt Elinor wore. The ring was silver, without any gems to distinguish it. Only once had Chesney given it any thought. It was when his aunt had taken it off to examine it.

It was in those marvelous days when Chesney had the world or at least all of it he ever desired. He and Verity Goodhue were engaged to be married. He had stopped by to see Aunt Elinor and found her in a pensive mood. Later he realized that must have been the day she had received the terminal diagnosis. However, she didn't burden him with that information.

He was buoyant that day. She was merely sitting at her kitchen table with a cup of tea, studying her ring.

He kissed her on the cheek and gushed about the wedding plans right down to his ideas on footwear.

"...and as it'll be a morning wedding, and I'll be wearing a morning suit, and I'll be wearing spats."

Chesney paused and waited for a response from his aunt. Instead, she kept sliding the ring on and off her finger.

"Aunt El," he said first subtly, as one might prompt an actor who had forgotten her lines and then again more sharply.

She looked up.

"Oh, yes, Chesney, dear, what you were saying?"

"Aunt El, I was talking about spats."

"Oh, you haven't been quarreling with Verity, have you?"

"Not fighting spats, foot spats, you know, like Fred Astaire wore. You know, morning suits, pearl gray spats over black shoes. Aunt El, are you all right?"

She nodded. "Oh, yes, I'm fine, I'll be fine..."

"Only you look as if you're lost in thought," said Chesney.

As if to confirm this statement, Aunt Elinor took several moments to reply.

"Lost...no, no," she said, "I know exactly where I am. I was just thinking about..."

Chesney looked at her ring. Had it been given to her by her college boyfriend, the one who wanted to marry her? Perhaps his wedding was stirring up melancholy memories.

"Thinking about the past?" Chesney asked.

She looked up abruptly. "The past? Good heavens, no. Why would I be thinking of the past?"

He nodded towards the ring. "I just thought..."

Aunt Elinor slid the ring back on her finger. "This, well, no, this is more about the future. This is my, well, it's my, you could call it, my prescription for life."

She glanced at the ring and then seemed to discard the mood which had hung over her. Aunt El once more was her usual self, and Chesney quickly forgot the incident.

Chesney didn't think about ring again until after her death. Looking at the ring now, and knowing its significance, Lorraine Innis placed it on her own finger. She then looked down at the scissors, still waiting in the drawer. Lorraine studied her hair in the mirror. Finally, she sighed and smiled grimly.

"Prescription for life," she said, and then closed the drawer. She picked up the phone to call Clodagh but reasoned she would just be falling asleep again.

"It will wait a few hours," said Lorraine, and then went to make another cup of tea.

– 6 –
Revelations Off
Coral Tiles

Valerie Fierro was in the third floor Ladies' Room, at Magna Card, minding her own business, literally and figuratively when she overheard it.

One woman had just left a stall and was standing by the sinks. Another woman entered.

"Oh, hi..." said the first woman. Valerie recognized the voice of Mitchell Minear's secretary. "Slumming?" she asked facetiously. The third floor was where the top executives worked.

"No, just coming out of a meeting with the empty suits."

Valerie bit her lip. The second woman was Betty Mullet, her supervisor. Maybe she'd find out something useful. Knowledge was power, and that's what Valerie craved, not the knowledge, just the power. At the very least, she might hear some juicy gossip. Valerie was glad she was in the furthest stall. She raised her feet off the floor to bring them above the bottom of the partition.

Valerie felt a pang of guilt about eavesdropping. She'd been working for Betty a few months, and she liked her.

"How's your refugee working out," said Minear's secretary.

"Refugee? Oh, right," chuckled Betty. "For a minute, I didn't know who you were talking about."

Valerie held her breath. Refugee? There was a new guy in the department. His name was George. He had an accounting degree, so he was dull and perfectly suited to regulatory compliance. He came to the unit a month after Valerie.

"It's working out," said Betty." But I didn't appreciate being the dumping ground."

"Don't blame me," said the secretary, "as if I had any input in what he does with his friends."

Now, that was curious. Valerie didn't know George had been placed in the department by Mitchell Minear.

"I'm not blaming you," said Betty, "you're the last person I'd blame after what you went through."

"Yeah, just the first in a long line of dumb..."

"Don't say that," Betty cut her off. Valerie punched the air. This was getting good. It was frustrating when the confessors weren't allowed to finish their confessions.

The secretary snorted. "Why? That's what I was."

"It's no sin to be young and deceived…"

Young? Minear's secretary was pushing forty. Betty was being kind. Apparently, the secretary had an office affair with George. Valerie smirked. You couldn't tell from the looks of either of them. One looked as dull as dishwater, the other was past her prime.

The secretary was mumbling something about love and mistakes. She sounded on the verge of tears.

"Now, come on," Betty continued, "dry your eyes, fix your face…"

"It's so stupid of me. I don't know why…"

"There's no shame in being fooled by a smooth line," said Betty kindly.

Valerie tried to piece together the half-spoken tale to create a full picture.

"If it's any consolation," said Betty in even more confidential tones, "they're not getting away with it."

Valerie strained to catch every word. George apparently had pulled some strings or finagled some shady deal to get his position. Perhaps they had dumped him in Betty's department to cover up some scandal.

"But they've got the job…"

"There's a big difference, honey," confided Betty, "between getting what you want and being able to enjoy it. I don't think they're going to like being on the bottom of the pile, especially not when I start shoveling all the shit jobs that way."

"Really?" The secretary sounded happy at the prospect. She must really detest George. Again, thought Valerie, you never could tell. George seemed like such a clean, boring type.

"New regulations are coming out. Someone's got to copy and collate them all for each unit and section in the building, and then go around and remove and replace them in every binder. And they have to do it personally to make sure the old regulations are shredded. It's a major pain in the ass. They're not going to enjoy it."

"It couldn't happen to a nicer person," said the secretary.

"They won't even realize it," said Betty. Valerie heard the door open. "I'll tell them it's a plum project, a real favor, and the fool will probably believe it until they're swimming in it."

The conversation faded away as the door closed. Valerie sat in silence for a moment, waiting to make sure that her presence had been undetected before leaving the stall. As she washed her hands, she thought about George. He must have done something to Minear's secretary. He was about to be handed the worst job and made to believe it was a reward; to be given a punishment wrapped as a gift. Still, that was his problem.

Valerie had her own career to care for, and towards that end, she had a rendezvous that night.

– 7 –
When I and Me Disagree

Lorraine Innis adjusted her dark glasses even though dawn was just breaking. She pulled her wide-brimmed hat down and the collar of her trench coat up, both as far as they would go. She rang the doorbell and pushed herself inside the doorjamb to keep even further out of sight.

After four rings, Lorraine could hear someone coming towards the door. The footsteps stopped, and it grew silent for several seconds. Then she could hear the footstep retreat.

She knocked on the door sharply. The footsteps returned.

"Who's there? I can't see anyone," the voice of Clodagh Clott said through the door.

"It's I," whispered Lorraine.

"Who? Oh, you…wait."

Clodagh threw back the deadbolt and opened the door.

"I thought it was you. Why are you cowering in the corned like that?"

"I didn't want anyone to see me," said Lorraine rushing inside. She motioned for Clodagh to close the door.

"Including me?" said Clodagh. "I couldn't see you."

"But you recognized my voice," said Lorraine.

"I recognized your anal-retentive grammar. You're the only person I know who says: 'it is I.'"

Lorraine pulled off her hat and her dark glasses and stared at Clodagh. "Well, you wouldn't say 'it is me.'"

"I would," said Clodagh, "so would everyone I ever met, except you."

Lorraine placed her hands on her hips. "Think about it, rephrase the sentence. What did you ask?"

"I said: 'who's there?'"

"And?" asked Lorraine.

"And the answer is 'it's me.'"

"No," said Lorraine, "if you rephrase the sentence, you would say: 'I am here.' You wouldn't say: 'Me is here,' would you?"

Clodagh stared at her.

"You're thinking that I'm right, aren't you?" said Lorraine.

"No, I was wondering if I'd be throwing out 'I' or 'me' when I chuck your pedantic ass out of my house."

"You would be throwing out me. You are the subject doing the throwing out."

"I should have let that big dog swallow you when we were twelve."

They stared at each other for five seconds, and then both spoke simultaneously.

"What are you doing?" asked Lorraine.

"What are you doing here?" asked Clodagh.

Both fell silent, waiting for the other to answer.

"You first," said Clodagh.

"I want to finish what we started," said Lorraine.

"You mean the hypnotherapy?"

"Of course."

"I thought you said you were going to end it all," said Clodagh, "not even be Lorraine any longer."

"Yes, I did. I changed my mind."

"Well, it's a woman's prerogative to change her mind," said Clodagh, walking toward the kitchen, "and as you still look like one, then I guess you're within your rights. Tea?"

"Will it keep me awake," she asked. "I mean, will it interrupt our session?"

"It might," she concluded.

"Then no, thank you," said Lorraine.

"So you want to do this here and now?" said Clodagh.

"You don't have anything else scheduled today, do you?"

"No, I had planned on spending it with you, tiptoeing through the verdant glens of your psyche." She forced a grin and fixed herself a piece of toast.

"Where do you want me?" asked Lorraine after Clodagh finished her breakfast.

"We can go in the living room," she said.

Lorraine followed her into the living room. And looked around. "I guess this will do."

"Shut up and lay down," said Clodagh.

Lorraine lay on the sofa. Clodagh put a pillow beneath her head and then covered her with a light throw. Lorraine closed her eyes and sighed.

"Are you comfortable?" Clodagh asked after several moments of silence.

"I do okay," said Lorraine. "Sorry, it's an old joke."

"Yes, I seem to remember you telling me that about twenty times in one week between the ages of ten and eleven," said Clodagh with a cautionary edge to her voice. "If you want to tell jokes…"

"No, no, I'm sorry," said Lorraine. "It just slipped out."

"All right, just relax and take a deep breath."

Lorraine inhaled and then exhaled several times. All she could hear was the sound of her own breath and the low hum of the heating system. She was just starting to relax when she suddenly felt very alone. Had Clodagh left the room? Lorraine opened one eye. Clodagh was still sitting there, staring at her, a look of concern overshadowing her brow.

"Are you sure you want to do this, Ches?" she asked.

"I told you I did," said Lorraine. "What's the matter?"

"I just want to be sure," said Clodagh. "I mean, the first session was pretty rough, but you said you wanted to continue. Then you call me in the middle of the night and say you not only don't want to go on, but you're completely giving up Lorraine, and then you show up here and are ready to go ahead full speed. I guess I just want to know that you're sure of your own mind."

Lorraine looked at her and smiled. "It will be fine," she said and held up her hand.

Clodagh leaned forward. "I've never seen that ring before."

Lorraine closed her eyes. "It's the reason I'm here."

"And I'm sure I'll find out what that means, sooner or later. I just want to be sure you can handle this," said Clodagh.

"I lived through it all once, and it didn't kill me."

"No, but look at you," said Clodagh.

"Which me are you looking at?"

"That's precisely my point. I'm a licensed therapist. I'm not some stage hypnotist doing tricks for the amusement of the audience. I've been around the human mind a little bit, and I'm concerned for you, Chesney… Lorraine…all of you…"

"I appreciate that," said Lorraine. "I know you're only looking out for me. And I realize that what you saw the other night wasn't pretty. Not many people know about what I went through in England when, when I lost…her…"

"See, you can't even say her name, can you?"

"I can say it. I just choose not to…"

"Verity, Verity Goodhue," said Clodagh firmly.

Lorraine winced, and a tear welled in the corner of her eyes. "I could say it. But just because I can, doesn't mean I have to."

"And that's my point," said Clodagh. "Why put yourself through the pain of reliving the past like this?"

"So I can get to the future," insisted Lorraine. "I need to be completely Lorraine Innis; all Lorraine, all the time. My Lorraine side is smarter than my Chesney side. Chesney's just getting in the way of working out this whole mess. Lorraine will straighten it out, I'm sure of it. She's made up of all the best parts of so many special women: my Aunt Elinor, Martina, and…well, a lot of women. Then once I straighten this all out, that is, once Lorraine does, you can snap me out of it and I can get rid of Lorraine once and for all. I've explained it all before."

"And I told you I want to be sure I'm not doing permanent damage to your mind."

"And I agree," said Lorraine. "Look, I know it's not pretty, but life isn't pretty, and death isn't pretty. But this is what I've got to go through to get out of where I am. Right now, I feel as if I'm neither dead nor alive. It was painful going through all that the other night. Seeing…her, loving her, and then losing her all over again. And I'll have to relive another death to fully explain this whole mess. I know it will be painful. If there was an easier way, don't you think I'd take it? But it has to be done, and the sooner the better. I appreciate all your concern. That's why I know I'll be okay. You're looking out for me. But I've got to go through this. I've got to do this. Chesney has to die, just for a little while, so Lorraine can live, so then Chesney can live again. Does that make sense?"

Clodagh shook her head. "If I were walking in on that statement, I'd have you committed, but yes, I know what you mean. Okay, if you have to do this, close your eyes…"

Lorraine took several deep breaths.

"So," began Clodagh, opening her notepad, "You just finished with the funeral of Verity…"

Lorraine grimaced again at the mention of her name.

"Take a deep breath," continued Clodagh in a soothing, comfortable tone, "and let's go back. When last we left Chesney, he was in London."

– 8 –
The Smokey Bacon Departure

Lorraine Innis felt her arms grow heavy with the same beckoning weariness that she'd encountered during the first hypnosis session. Almost imperceptibly, her friend's voice guided her back through the years, like turning the pages of a book. Then, as it had a few nights earlier, Clodagh disappeared. Lorraine Innis ceased to be; her thin frame taking on weight, until she was once again Chesney Potts, in body and mind.

Heathrow Airport was buzzing with early morning activity. Clerks in the concourse shops were tidying their shelves, brewing coffee and tea, setting out fresh newspapers and buns.

Chesney watched them humming, like so many bees in a hive, each working as part of a larger whole, nameless, indistinguishable one from another. And in his pain, he envied them. If he could be absorbed into the mass of humanity, perhaps it would dilute the pain tearing at his heart. He may not be happy in that role, but certainly, he would not be so miserable. He would no longer feel, and that now would be a great relief.

Just a short time ago, or was it ages past, he had rejoiced in his feelings. Back then, he had the love and understanding from the two most important people in his life: his Aunt Elinor and his beloved Verity. Now they were both snatched from him in the space of a few hours.

In his hand was the return ticket purchased by Lord Bagnold. Chesney wished he could have stayed on a little longer at Bagnold Hall. But Lord Bagnold preferred to suffer stoically in private. Also, he was sure most people around the estate blamed Chesney for Verity's death. They hadn't even attended her funeral. No, Chesney would have to take his wounded heart back to New Jersey and go on alone.

"I got you some magazines." A voice jarred Chesney from his dark musings.

He looked up. There was Mr. Postlewaite, one of Aunt Elinor's dearest friends. Behind him stood Li Gao, the lay preacher and lorry driver who completed his Aunt's British family.

"Thank you," said Chesney, taking the periodicals.

"I tried to get you an eclectic assortment," said Postlewaite nodding at the pile. "I'm not sure how your tastes ran. I just picked them as if I were getting some for myself and some for..." He choked back a sob. "...our Elinor."

Chesney nodded. He looked down at the magazines. There were copies of *The Beano*, a children's magazine, along with *The Radio Times*, and a magazine of knitting patterns. The kids' magazine and the media listings were of little use, especially as Chesney was traveling outside of the broadcast range of the BBC. That left the knitting magazine.

"I didn't know Aunt Elinor knitted," said Chesney holding up the last selection.

"She often said though that she wanted to," said Mr. Postlewaite. "Wait, no, her exact words were: 'Postlewaite, one of these days you'll drive me completely batty and I'll live out my life in a padded cell knitting tea cozies."

Li Gao gave Postlewaite a censorious look.

"Sorry," said Postlewaite. His comment was too close to the dementia to which Elinor Potoski had succumbed. He grabbed the knitting magazine back and crammed it in his coat pocket. "On second thought, she didn't say that, uh, someone else must have, and to some other person. I think I'll go get you some boiled sweets for your flight. My mum used to always give me a bag of boiled sweets before I went on a long train trip. I've never been an airplane to America, but I imagine..."

Postlewaite backed away from Chesney and retreated to a nearby newsagent. Li Gao sat down beside Chesney.

"That was very kind of him," said Chesney indicating the magazines.

"My old friend Postlewaite always holds the kindest of intentions," agreed Li Gao. "Unfortunately, there is frequently an absence of thought behind his kindness."

Chesney looked up at Gao, who remained emotionless for several seconds before offering a slight smile.

"No doubt now he will be selecting an assortment of sweets which are completely contrary to your personal tastes. I do not make that observation with any malice. It is merely the way of Postlewaite with which I have become familiar over the course of many decades."

Chesney nodded. "Still, I appreciate you both coming here today."

"It has been a very trying time for you," said Gao. "You have suffered a great loss. We have all grieved at the passing of your dear aunt. And your personal loss is greatly multiplied by the death of..."

"Yes, yes," said Chesney cutting him off before Li Gao said her name. "I don't know how to thank you for everything."

Li Gao smiled and nodded. "Chesney, we are never burdened beyond our ability to bear it."

"Thank you," said Chesney, he doubted the sentiment. "I just…" his voice wavered, and he dropped his head.

"Perhaps this will be of comfort to you," said Gao.

Chesney looked up.

"This belonged to your aunt. She would want you to have it, I am certain."

Li Gao placed a ring in the palm of Chesney's hand. He recognized it immediately and thought of the day several months before when Aunt Elinor had held it. Chesney looked at the ring and then at the engraving inside of it: "RXII2."

"Her prescription…" whispered Chesney, recalling her words that day.

"Excuse me?"

"Aunt Elinor's ring, she said it was her prescription. And here it is. 'Rx,' that the abbreviation for prescription, it's from the Latin word for recipe, which also means 'to take.' But I don't understand the number 112."

Li Gao's looked puzzled for a moment before brightening into a smile.

"That is just like your dear aunt," he said. "It is not a prescription, at least not in the literal sense of a physical remedy to be ingested. The 'R' and the 'X' do not belong together, and the 'X' is a numeral. That is her favorite verse of Scripture. The 'R' indicates the letter of Paul to the Romans."

Chesney looked at the inscription again more carefully.

"Yes, the reference is to Romans, Chapter 12, that is the "XII" and verse 2. '…do not be conformed to this world, but be transformed by the renewing of your mind, so that you may prove what the will of God is, that which is good and acceptable and perfect.'"

Chesney stared at the inscription.

"You find that odd," said Gao.

"Perhaps not odd, but certainly ironic," said Chesney.

"How so?"

"Well, Aunt Elinor died of a disease that ate away her mind. It didn't renew her at all. And was it good, or acceptable, or perfect?"

Li Gao nodded. "No, to what we may call 'conventional thinking' it is not."

They sat in silence for several moments. A tour group of middle-aged men all wearing fezzes rushed to answer the calling of their flight on the Tannoy.

"Elinor understood," continued Gao, "that conventional thinking is just what is meant by conforming to the world. She pursued a different perspective."

Chesney thought of his aunt and the way she faced her illness and death and sensed there was something that she comprehended in all her circumstances that he didn't understand.

"Well, thank you," said Chesney closing his hand over the ring. "I will cherish it."

"I got you these," said Mr. Postlewaite returning.

He handed Chesney a bag of potato crisps. "They were out of any sort of boiled sweets or hard candy, so I got you smoky bacon. I hope they're acceptable."

"Yes, thank you," said Chesney, "they're perfect. I mean, good, that is, they're fine."

– 9 –
Covert Friends from High School, Dupes and Garters

Valerie still lived at home. Mitchell Minear's house, which he shared with his wife, was also out of the question. So, Mitchell rented a rather lower-middle-class apartment for their rendezvous. Valerie suspected a lot of auto mechanics lived there with their shrewish wives and runny-nosed kids. The down-market atmosphere justified the means towards her end: she was Mitchell's playmate to advance her career so that she wouldn't wind up living in this sort of place. The CountrySide Villas were like purgatory. She was serving time there to avoid such a place becoming her permanent hell on earth.

CountySide Villas! They hastily constructed apartment blocks, each so alike that they required large letters bolted on them to distinguish one from another. And the only adjacent views offered by the "villas" had nothing to do with rural scenery. The complex would have more accurately named "InterstateHighwaySide Villas" or "ShoppingMallSide Villas," for that is what surrounded them.

Valerie was glad that the Mall was nearby. Malls meant shopping. Her little fling, aside from getting her off the phones, provided Valerie with an excuse to shop for affair essentials. Knowing that an upscale lover would see them was justification for buying nice lingerie. Another good reason was a sale. With no other motivation necessary, Valerie made her way to Macy's intimate apparel department. She was holding a sexy ensemble of black bra and panties, looking for the matching garter belt when she heard the voice.

"Valerie? Valerie Fierro?"

She turned and saw the young woman a few racks over.

"Yes?" Valerie said coolly, not wanting to be too familiar to strangers in the underwear section.

The woman obviously knew Valerie, but Valerie couldn't place her. Maybe she worked at the bank. She was dressed professionally, but not particularly stylish. Her reddish-brown hair was shoulder-length, her make-up simple.

"You don't remember me," said the girl.

"Yes, I do," lied Valerie, as she studied her face, "of course I do. It's just, well, you know how it is. I'm just not used to seeing you here."

"It has been a while," smiled the girl.

"Yes, it has," Valerie agreed. "Since…"

"High school," said the girl.

"High school," repeated Valerie quickly as if they had been her next words, too. "Yes, you haven't changed a bit."

"That's very kind of you to say," said the girl. "Though I did lose some weight since graduation…baby fat my mother says. But you haven't changed, Valerie, if anything you're even prettier than you were when you were prom queen."

Valerie smiled. What chubby girls did she know back then? Not many, she concluded. Why would she? She was about to confess she hadn't a clue to whom she was speaking when a glint of silver appeared on the girl's wrist.

It was an ID bracelet that read: "Martina."

"Martina!" said Valerie, and then realized her reaction sounded a little too surprised. "Martina," she repeated, more naturally. "I was just thinking about you the other day."

"You were?"

"Yes, I was thinking about school, and of course, I thought of you, and I wondered: whatever happened to Martina?" Actually, at the moment, she was wondering: Who the hell is Martina?

"Oh, well," said Martina, "There's not much to tell. I went to college and graduated and then went to work."

"Really?" said Valerie trying to sound interested while continuing to look for that errant garter belt.

"Yes, I work at Voila Card," said Martina.

"Really? I work at Magna Card," she paused for effect. "I'm in regulatory compliance."

"Me too! What a small world!" Martina seemed genuinely excited by the coincidence.

This Martina… whoever… was probably a lower level grunt, a junior compliance clerk.

"Isn't it a small world," Valerie paused for effect. "Actually, "I'm an assistant compliance specialist, Martina."

"Oh," said Martina. She cast her eyes downward.

Valerie suppressed a satisfied smile. Obviously, Martina hadn't done as well as she had.

"So, what do you do at Voila," asked Valerie, "in their compliance department?"

"Well," Martina bit her lower lip, "I'm the manager."

"Oh," said Valerie. Rather than concealing her own embarrassment, Martina had been trying not to embarrass Valerie.

There followed an awkward silence. In an attempt to return to more secure ground, Valerie looked down at Martina's hands.

"Buying underwear?" She said, with a nod towards the pack of plain cotton panties Martina was holding.

Martina blushed. "Yes," she said, "they're having a sale. I thought I'd stock up."

Practical, thought Valerie, not just buying on sale, but the cut and style was also very functional and not at all fun. She held up her own seductive selections.

"I'm trying to find the last piece of the set," noted Valerie waving her fancy lingerie. Martina looked puzzled. Valerie sighed inwardly. She may be a manager, but this Martina What's-Her-Name didn't know squat about anything important. "There's a matching garter belt that completes this set," she said.

Martina's cheeks, which had turned slightly pink at the mention of underwear glowed crimson now that the conversation had expanded to sexy accessories.

"Oh…" she said softly. Her awkwardness was palpable. It begged to be exploited. So, Valerie did.

"You should spice it up, Martina," said Valerie in confidential tones.

"Spice it up?"

"You know…" she raised her eyebrows and gestured towards the racier offerings around them. "Kick it up a notch. You've got a boyfriend?" From her barren ring finger, it was apparent Martina didn't have a husband.

"Well, there is a fellow I've been seeing…"

"You've been seeing him, but what's he been seeing?"

"Um, me?"

Valerie rolled her eyes. "I mean, are you giving him something worth seeing…you know… in the bedroom?"

Martina's eyes grew wide.

"But we're not married."

"So?"

Martina's jaw went slack.

"I wouldn't let him see me in my underwear."

She looked at Valerie unblinkingly for several seconds.

"Well, how…" Valerie was about to ask how they had sex but stopped as she realized that she was talking to a virgin, an actual virgin, a smart, good-looking woman, one who had a better job than she did who was a real, honest-to-goodness virgin, right there in the middle of Macy's intimate apparel department. She didn't know quite how to react or what to say. It was like meeting someone from another country or even another planet. At first, she thought how uncomfortable Martina must feel at having another woman standing there, holding sexy lingerie that was made to be seen, while she was standing there in her virgin state with plain, cotton panties. But as she looked at Martina, Valerie noticed she wasn't the slightest bit embarrassed. This girl, a manager, was standing there entirely at ease with admitting her total inexperience to another woman. After a moment, a feeling of uneasiness began rising within Valerie. This was stupid, she thought, why should she feel odd? But Martina just stood there looking at her. Damn this stupid girl without a last name, thought Valerie, why was she just looking at her, with her non-critical expression. Valerie flashed a brief smile, hoping that would change Martina's countenance. It didn't. Valerie had a sudden urge to put her racy purchases back on the rack but stopped. No, she thought, this wasn't about her. The creepy feeling she was experiencing must be sympathy, yes, that was it, or empathy, or whatever you called it. This Martina was oblivious to her backward condition, and so Valerie was feeling sorry for Martina since Martina didn't have the sense to feel sorry for herself. Yes, that must be it.

"Well?" said Martina.

"Well, what?" said Valerie.

"You started to ask me something," said Martina.

"Did I?"

"Yes, you started to say: 'Well, how...'"

"Oh, right..." Valerie wracked her brain. She was going to ask how she and her boyfriend managed to have sex without her boyfriend seeing her underwear, but she had already solved that riddle.

"Well, uh...well, how...how are your parents?" said Valerie.

"They're fine," said Martina. "And how's your mother?"

"She's fine," said Valerie. Apparently, Martina knew her father had died. She wished she could remember a little more about her, like her last name.

"I don't want to hold you up," said Martina. "I'm sure you must be very busy. I just wanted to say 'hello.' It really is wonderful to see you."

Martina seemed so damned genuine Valerie found herself agreeing that it was wonderful, and then not to be outdone in being pleasant, she went further than she had meant to go.

"We really should get together..." The words had hardly escaped Valerie's lips when she wished she could reel them back, especially after Martina's face lit up.

"Do you really mean it?"

Valerie would have given anything at that moment to say: "No, I'm lying," but, for some reason, she cared too much what this near-stranger thought. So, she said: "of course."

Martina fished a business card from her purse and handed it to Valerie.

Valerie scanned the card. Martina Fergus! She remembered the name, though it did little to add to any other recollection of the girl. At least this would save her the tedious chore of searching through her old yearbooks.

"I wanted to ask you," said Martina, "but I wasn't sure if you'd be interested. We're putting together a reunion for our class."

"Our class? Oh, yes, of course, our class." Martina must have been helping out at the prom as a junior.

"And who better to help organize it than our most popular girl?"

Valerie smiled and hoped Martina couldn't see past her grin. If she'd been toothless, there would have been nothing between her and her throat screaming in horror. Reunions? With those people? She had kept in touch with all the people from high school whom she actually liked: both of them. This Martina chick was one of those sappy girls who liked everyone and, worse, thought everyone liked her. Valerie was willing to waste five minutes in Macy's on practically anyone, but organizing a party for a bunch of losers was just too much.

"I'd love to," said Valerie, parting her teeth just far enough to be audible. Martina's shining face seemed to brighten even more. "But, I can't..."

"Oh," Martina's face dropped.

"It's just..." she scoured her mind: work, yes, work was always a good excuse. "I'm so swamped at work. In fact, I've got to go back to work tonight." Technically, sex with Mitchell Minear was work, she reasoned. It was advancing her career, so it was work.

"I understand," said Martina. "I admire your dedication. You've got to keep on top of it, I suppose."

"Yes. Someone's always got to be on top," agreed Valerie.

– 10 –
The Trail of the
Horny Hansel

Valerie had just enough time to rush over to Mitchell's seamy apartment. She almost surprised him in her new lingerie but was loathe to wear it without first washing it. Instead, she opted for waiting for him naked in bed, which was almost as good, she reasoned. It was like giving someone a fabulous Christmas gift without the fancy wrapping. The shiny paper was nice, but it was what was underneath it all that really mattered.

Valerie created a trail of discarded garments from her three-inch pumps just inside the front door, through the living room with her suit, ending at the foot of the bed with her underwear. Then, like some erotic Gretel awaiting her horny Hansel, she climbed atop the bed and struck a seductive pose. She glanced at the clock. Mitchell should arrive at any moment. The things she did for her career!

She held her pose for several minutes before she became uncomfortable and adopted a new position. Five minutes later, she moved again, and again a minute after that. Mitchell was late. She started to become annoyed. Soon she was contemplating getting dressed and waiting for him in the living room with her arms folded, signaling that he had forfeited his pleasure for that evening. Then she heard his key in the lock and reverted to Plan A: the seductive pose.

"Valerie?"

He sounded excited. She whetted her lips, wanting to look her most alluring when he came through the bedroom door.

"Valerie? What the…?"

She heard a noise and realized he'd just kicked one of her shoes across the floor. Take it easy, she thought, those designer pumps aren't cheap, especially on the salary of an assistant compliance specialist. He obviously hadn't noticed the path of seduction, the couture map leading to the treasure atop the bed. Valerie only hoped he wasn't trampling all over her clothes.

"Oh, there you are," said Minear as he appeared in the doorway. It was a stupid observation. Only the bedroom saw any real use in the tiny apartment. Where else did he think she would be? She tried to drive the annoyance from her face and put on a coy, enticing smile.

"Hello, Mitchell…" Valerie drew out each syllable for effect.

"Hi," he said as if he was entering a meeting room full of subordinates, "sorry, I'm late."

"I was getting…" she paused. Actually, she had been getting angry, but she still had to play the game. "…hungry." She said: "hungry," indicating an appetite for something other than food.

"Oh, right," he said, "well, we can order something in. You know I can't take you out to dinner, not in public."

"I'm not talking about food," she said, using her last vestige of sultriness.

"Right," he said, not seeming to hear or care. Mitchell was pacing back and forth at the foot of the bed, ignoring the naked body in front of him. "This could be it, this could be it," he muttered, "yes, this…what is this?"

Mitchell lifted his right foot. Valerie's panties were caught on the toe of his wingtips. He pulled them off and examined them as if he'd never seen a pair before.

"Mitchell!" she barked.

"Huh?"

"What the hell is going on?" Valerie's voice rose to a bitchy pitch of a shrewish wife. She hated to sound that way but he was walking on expensive lingerie! "Well?"

He examined the lacey garment for a second before tossing it nonchalantly over his shoulder as if it bore no relationship to anyone in the room. He then sat on the edge of the bed.

"I got the call," he said.

"What call?"

"The call…the call to headquarters, they want to see me. I've got to fly out there tomorrow morning. You know what this means, don't you?"

Valerie clutched her pendant. It didn't just mean his promotion; it also meant her promotion. If Mitchell went out to headquarters Valerie would profit too. He might be able to name his successor, and if she didn't get that, she expected at least a two or three rung jump up the corporate ladder. "Do you think it's your promotion?"

He nodded. "What else could it be?"

"Oh, Mitchy, this is wonderful," squealed Valerie, throwing her arms around him.

He returned the hug and then looked down.

"Hey, you don't have any clothes on," he said with genuine surprise.

She just looked at him with her sharpest "no-shit" glare.

Mitchell Minear stared at her blankly for a moment before it dawned on him.

"Oh, wait, I forgot, wait, I'm sorry, I totally forgot, what a dope I am, I'm sorry..."

She smiled at him. "That's okay, this is really important. You must have had a million things on your mind. This is what you've been waiting for."

"Hey, this is what we've both been waiting for," he said. "I won't forget... my friends... my best friends."

"Did you call your wife," asked Valerie without the least shred of embarrassment. She didn't want to steal her husband. She was only borrowing him as one would borrow a drill or some other tool.

"Yeah," he said uncomfortably at her mention, "I told her to pick up my gray suit at the cleaner and start packing my bag." He stood up and took a step towards the door.

"Well, I'm sure you have a lot of things to do. Let me know how it all works out," said Valerie, pulling the sheet up around her bare shoulders.

"Right, yeah," he said, "lots to do." He made it to the doorway when he stopped and turned. His eyes met hers.

Valerie smiled and winked. It was more of a "go get 'em" gesture. Mitchell was taking both their career aspirations with him on that flight.

Minear started to go, and then looked back at her.

"Oh, what the hell," he said, unbuckling his belt. "She knows what to pack for me. She's good at that."

– 11 –

How Does It Feel to Be One of the Dutiful Cushions?

It gradually became clear, like the dawn on a misty morning. The first glimmers of light came during the weekly meeting of Valerie's unit.

Her manager was explaining the latest regulatory updates, while the unit members took notes. Valerie made a half-hearted effort at jotting down the information. It was the same thing every week, she thought. The piddling little rules handed down from Washington may change, but the net effect was the same: boredom. Valerie wondered how her coworkers could pretend they were interested.

Next to her, George was writing furiously, hanging upon every word. The poor sap, he hadn't been in the ladies' room when Valerie overheard his fate. By the end of the meeting, Betty was going to hand him the crappy assignment. Ironically, he wouldn't even realize that she was dumping on him. Betty was about to serve him up a double-decker horse manure sandwich, and he was going to think it was a prime filet.

Valerie glanced at her watch as the meeting droned on. Mitchell would be at headquarters now. They probably sent a limo to pick him up at the airport. Headquarters was one hour behind Delaware. They'd escort him into the board room and give him the good news, and then they'd take him out for a fancy lunch. He wouldn't have a chance to call her until later in the day, probably not until he got back to his hotel. He'd call her at home, discreetly. No one knew about their relationship. To avoid any suspicion, Mitchell would have to wait a month or so until he could promote her. But Valerie wasn't worried. It would come.

Betty was now going on about the OCC, or the FDIC, or some equally boring acronym created to make her life tedious. Valerie wondered how many more of these meetings she'd have to endure before she was promoted out of the department.

"Time for recognition," said Betty after she'd finally run out of her dull alphabet soup of government stuff. Magna Card was always awarding little prizes and tokens of appreciation. Valerie thought it was nice until Mitchell pointed out it was just a cheap way to keep employees happy without raising their salaries.

"Our unit member of the month," said Betty, "is being recognized for going the extra mile in helping out the rest of the team."

That's what she always said about the winner. It was sincere as the photocopied certificate that went with the award. Four hours of personal time also came with it. The award got passed around so that everyone won at least once a year. It was probably Valerie's turn this month. She'd try to act humble, though it was a sham. Still, the four hours of personal time would be nice.

"Congratulations, George."

Valerie was surprised. George won? He seemed honored. Betty acted like she was happy to give it to him. Valerie almost dismissed Betty as a corporate phony, until she realized how shrewd her manager was. It only cost Betty: a photocopied certificate and half-a-day of personal time. In return, George would think he was doing a great job while being handed the dirty assignment of updating every regulation manual in the building.

"Now, I have an important assignment," said Betty. "It's the vital responsibility of updating of all the regulation binders, building-wide. So, I'm relying on this person to do an excellent job."

Here it comes, thought Valerie. She snuck a sideways glance at George, still beaming over his cheap award. This was going to be priceless.

"So..." Betty picked up the folder and reached across the table, "I'm entrusting it to you, Valerie."

Valerie had turned her head towards George. Upon hearing her own name called, she jerked her head back to Betty, and then to George, expecting that she had somehow misheard. He was looking at her, however.

"Congratulations," said George.

"What?" Valerie looked back at Betty, her arm extended towards Valerie holding the thick binder.

"Here you are, Valerie," said Betty.

"But, no, that's..."

Her eyes met those of the unit manager. She darted her eyes to her left as if to say: "no, it's George's assignment, you know the dirty job." She even flashed a slight smile, but Betty's eyes remain locked, unmoving, and deadly serious.

Valerie's mouth dropped open as she took the binder.

"The details are in there," began Betty, and then she outlined the "very important big assignment."

Her words faded into insignificance, replaced in Valerie's mind by the echoes of what she'd said in the ladies' room to Minear's secretary.

"A major pain in the ass...they won't realize it...the fool..." Valerie, not George, was the one that had been dumped in the unit.

Valerie sat calmly, but inwardly she was seething. How dare Betty hand her that rotten job and then try and pretend that it was an important assignment. She started compiling lists in her mind.

"Wait until I tell Mitchell," she thought.

"Wait until I tell him what his secretary, his soon-to-be former secretary, was saying in the ladies' room."

"Just wait until he makes me the boss of all of you!"

The meeting ended, but Valerie sat there for a moment as the others filed out of the room.

"Are you alright, Valerie?" Betty asked.

"Oh," said Valerie looking her in the eye, "I'm fine. I'll be more than fine, don't you worry about me."

She walked from the room, determined to settle a few scores as soon as Mitchell got back.

The illumination grew even brighter at lunch. After that embarrassing meeting, Valerie didn't want to go to lunch with anyone in her unit. Instead, she made an excuse of wanting to make an early start on her new "important" project.

After they left, she dialed Mitchell's cell phone to tell him about Betty's insulting behavior. She drummed her fingers impatiently. After several rings, all she got was an answer about the number not being in service. Valerie stared at her own phone. Either his battery's dead, she reasoned, or perhaps he's deep inside headquarters and the reception isn't good. Not having anyone to vent to, Valerie went to the cafeteria. Several voices called out to her as she started to sit down. It was the women from her old customer service unit, waving and calling her over to join them. She resigned herself to their company.

They were all wolfing down fatty burgers and greasy fries. Valerie looked at her sensible salad and consoled herself with her superior choice.

"So, what do you think about it?" One of the women asked her.

"Think about what?"

"Haven't you heard," said another woman lowering her double-chin to shove a handful of corn chips into her mouth.

"Heard?"

Despite the indignity of having to answer customer calls, the department did have the benefit of being in the most immediate contact with headquarters. Consequently, they heard all the good gossip before the rest of the building.

"About Minear," said another, from behind a slab of cake.

"Mi..." she nearly said: Mitchell. "Mi... Minear? Oh, yes, him, what about him?"

"He went out to headquarters," said woman trying to draw out her story for dramatic effect.

Valerie masked her interest behind a sprig of arugula.

"So," said Valerie, "bosses go to headquarters all the time?"

"Sure they do," said the first woman, jumping in on the story, "but not to be fired."

"Fi..." a swig of vinegar slid down Valerie's throat, sending her into a coughing spasm. While the other women offered her sips of soda and advice on choking, Valerie wracked her brain.

How could he be fired? How could someone get on an airplane to collect a promotion and wind up out on the pavement? People didn't go all the way to headquarters to get fired. They must have it wrong. Maybe the rumor was that his old job was now open because he had been promoted. That had to be it. Still, she couldn't appear to be too inquisitive.

"A bit of dressing...went down the wrong way," Valerie croaked. She wanted to ask for more details but didn't dare.

"So, anyway," said another woman, leaning towards Valerie, "he went out there and right into the big board room, and they fired him."

"Are you sure?" asked Valerie.

"It's all over headquarters," offered another one. "I got it directly from a friend of mine in customer service out there."

"They took his company cards, his keys, and even his phone."

"But why did..." before Valerie could finish the question, at least three women jumped in with the answer.

"...sexual harassment!"

"Sexual harassment?"

That was ridiculous. She was the only person who could complain about Mitchell Minear's escapades, and she wasn't about to pull the brake on a train she was riding.

"He had pincushions all over the place," said another woman with a shake of her head.

"Pincushions?"

"You know..." said another woman holding out the fist of her left hand while poking it repeatedly with her right index finger. "Pincushion."

"Some girls..." offered another.

"His secretary..." said yet another.

"He was..." said Valerie with astonishment, "...with his secretary?"

"Oh, that was years ago..."

Another woman, the veteran of the group, explained. "She was the first...back in the day. Not anymore."

"This is...I mean, that's terrible," said Valerie before adding, "I mean, for all those women."

The group fell silent for a moment. Valerie busied herself stabbing at a stray crouton. After a moment, she had the uneasy feeling that all eyes were focused on her. She looked up.

"You knew him," said one of the women. "Didn't you, Valerie, dear?"

"Me?" said Valerie feigning surprise. "No, I mean, well, once I had to go up to his office. But he, he didn't try anything, not with me."

"No, of course not, dear," said another woman.

"Pincushions," said one woman with a shake of her head.

The other hens clucked in agreement.

Valerie bit her lip. Pincushion indeed, she thought. How dare they sit there and judge her…if they were judging her. Did they know?

One of the women noted the time. They all rose like arms of some amoebic organism. Valerie smiled at them as they bid her goodbye. Her grin remained frozen on her face until the last bit of spandex waddled from view. Once she was alone, Valerie threw down her fork and stared out the window.

Mitchell Minear was gone. So what, she thought. She wasn't implicated, was she? No, of course not, if anything she was a victim along with all the other pin…other women. She could pretend she didn't know that he had been fired and rush down to human resources and make a claim against him. Yes, she could do that, she thought. She could even work up some tears. That was a plan.

A moment's reflection changed her mind. Human resources would know about Mitchell's fate, wouldn't they? They probably knew days ago. They probably had his office locks changed or his computer access codes revoked, or whatever they do when someone is tossed out on their ass. They also probably knew how Valerie got her job. She thought back to the conversation that she had overheard in the ladies' room. Mitchell's secretary knew and Betty, her boss knew, so it was obvious others knew. A wave of paranoia swept over Valerie. She looked over her shoulder. How many people knew about her and Mitchell? They had been so discreet, hadn't they? She searched her memory. Had anyone been looking at her oddly in the past few months? She tried to recall every smile offered to her in the hallways. Were they smiles or knowing grins? Was she the last one in the entire company to see that she was just another…pincushion?

Still, she thought, she had a good job, well, a pretty good job. She wasn't on the phones talking to stupid customers all day. No, she reminded herself, she was at the bottom of the compliance department, making copies of endless regulations and shuffling them around the building.

She looked up. Entering the cafeteria was Minear's secretary, the original pincushion, the mold from which all her successors had been cast. Valerie studied her careworn face. She was around forty, but she looked at least five years older than that. She wasn't unattractive. Had she actually been pretty fifteen years ago? Would Valerie eventually look like her?

She forced herself to think of something else. Who had made the complaint about him? She hadn't made a complaint, and she doubted whether the secretary had. That meant there were more women. Had he been two-timing Valerie? She felt the anger rise in her cheeks. She reached up to her neck and felt the small gold charm.

"Prima I denti, poi I parenti!"

She thought she had been looking out for number one. She had gone into her relationship with Mitchell with her eyes open. It wasn't anything long-term. She had enjoyed the sex. He was a good lover while he lasted. Still, that wasn't her main motivation. It was a career move, she thought. She had been looking out for herself. She had been careful. Valerie looked around at the faces in the cafeteria. None were looking at her, but that didn't mean they didn't know. She thought about the company's rumor mill, the gossip, and the tongues that were already wagging.

"Look out for yourself," Valerie muttered into her half-eaten lunch. "I'll look out for myself," she said a little louder, though still only to herself.

"I'm not going to stay here and be picked apart," she said. "And I'm not going to be made into some glorified secretary, old before my time, and some worn out...pincushion."

Valerie stood up and started to remove her tray, but then decided that someone else could bus it, someone who worked for the company. She grabbed her purse off the back of the chair and walked out of the cafeteria at a steady pace, one she hoped displayed every ounce of resolve that she felt inside. Not willing to cede her will to anyone or anything, Valerie shunned the elevator. Instead, she kept moving, taking the stairs down to the first floor, past the security station, and through the doors of the human resources department. There she stopped at the secretary's desk.

The woman looked up at Valerie and smiled.

Valerie unclipped her company badge from the strap of her handbag and slapped it on the desk.

"I resign," she said. She had almost said "I quit," but thought "resign" sounded more dignified, besides which, Valerie Fierro was not a quitter.

Then, before the woman could reply, Valerie walked out of human resources, out of Magna Card, out to her car, and drove away.

It was only when she was a few miles away that she afforded herself the luxury of pulling over to the side of the road and breaking into tears.

As she reached into her handbag for a tissue, Valerie saw her next move.

– 12 –
Music to Escape
Purgatory By

On its westward journey, the plane was almost perfectly synchronized with the rotation of the earth. The sun seemed to remain motionless. The ocean waves below were just dots. The voyage home was like a timeless purgatory.

Home: there was a concept. Chesney had no home. Anywhere where Verity was would have been home: England, New Jersey, even this damned airplane. He had built his life on the assumption that she would be there, that they would have a life together. He knew it would not last forever, but he at least thought he wouldn't have ended before it had begun, three weeks before the wedding.

He cradled his head in his hands. For the thousandth time, he tormented himself with a punishing round of "what if." What if he hadn't gone to London that day? What if she hadn't driven on that back road? What if her father hadn't given them those matching sports cars as a wedding present? What if he had waited a few weeks before asking to marry her? Then she wouldn't have been driving on that winding back road. The main road wouldn't have been dug up. She would still be alive, and he would be with her. He would be home.

He shook his head and fought back the tears. He must think of something else, or he would surely go mad. So what? Why not go mad? He had lost his Aunt Elinor and his Verity on the same day. They had been the only two people who had really loved and appreciated him. Now both were buried under Britain's verdant landscape.

He forced himself to think of something else. He looked at the Atlantic waves far below. Had they ever crashed against the British coast? Had she ever been near them, perhaps on a seaside holiday? Had their spray misted her face… that wonderfully average beautiful face…

Chesney caught himself again. What had Li Gao said? That this current trial was shaping him for some future purpose. He had likened it to being a slab of stone in the hands of a sculptor, creating a work of art. Li Gao had meant God, of course. Chesney didn't feel like a piece of marble. Marble didn't fight the artist. It endured the blows of the hammer. How could he submit when his heart was aching?

According to Li, Aunt Elinor had been in similar circumstances. Aunt Elinor mentioned once that she had been involved in the death of someone a long time ago. Had she been in love with that person? Was it the curse of the Potoskis? Chesney found it impossible to imagine that Aunt Elinor had been anything but the person whom he had known and loved. But she had once been in his place. Li Gao assured him of that. He took some comfort in that thought for a moment until the image of Verity came fresh upon his mind, and the agonizing cycle started anew.

Hours later, as if by sleepwalking, he returned to his apartment in New Jersey. Everything was as he had left it. All his possessions were there, though they were strangely unfamiliar. They had never known his beloved. She had never been there. She had never touched that portion of his life. Were they real? Had she been?

Almost as if it were left there on purpose, he saw a record lying on the turntable, its jacket sleeve resting nearby. The grinning face of Hugh Goode looked up at him from the album, and for the first time in days, Chesney smiled. He hadn't recalled leaving it like that, but he was glad it was there.

He turned on the stereo, and the needle slipped down into the groove. He sat down and allowed the cheery music to wash over him. Closing his eyes, he recalled this was the first Hugh Goode record that Aunt Elinor had ever sent him so many years ago. He opened his eyes again and studied the photograph on the album sleeve.

He couldn't have imagined ten months ago that he would not only meet that marvelous old gent, but that they would become friends, and that Chesney would assist in writing his biography. Gazing at the cover photo, Chesney noticed for the first time that Verity had her grandfather's eyes: soft and gentle, loving but playful, twinkling with the joy of life. Chesney smiled. It was almost as if he was looking into her eyes once more. Then he remembered that Verity was dead, Hugh Goode was dead, and even Aunt Elinor was dead.

As he listened, the room grew dark with the onset of twilight until, at last, the only light was the illumination of the dial on the stereo.

Then, as if it were a benediction, the last selection began to play, and Hugh Goode started to sing:

You got to keep calm and keep on,
That's the only thing to do.

When troubles pile up and the world is looking black
Don't make it blacker still by adding in the blues.
Remember, lad, others have had it worse,
Far much more worse than you,
So when yer back's to the wall, don't turn and run,
Just keeping on keeping calm, and keep on going through.

It was one of Hugh Goode's most popular songs, recorded in England's darkest hour when the nation stood alone against Nazi Germany. The simple tune with the optimistic message was a rallying cry. With his customary humility, Hugh had downplayed the importance of the song, when they were writing his biography. But Chesney could tell that the old man was extremely proud of the recording.

As the tune reached Hugh's ukulele solo, Chesney recalled listening to it with the old man.

♦

"'Ere, listen 'ere, lad," Hugh had told him, pointing into the air, as the song as it played.

Chesney listened, not sure what he was listening for. Then halfway through the instrumental solo, he heard a faint, barely perceptible thud he'd never noticed before.

"There, there," said Hugh, jabbing the air, "did ye hear that? That was a bomb."

"A bomb?"

"We recorded number late one afternoon," said Hugh. "We wanted to get the record out as quick as possible, you know, to help boost morale. The city, the whole country was taking an awful beating, so we wanted to get the song out to help keep up spirits, an' all. Well, we started the last take just as the sirens went off, you know, the air raid. The studio was in the West End, and that part of the city hadn't hardly been touched by the attacks, yet. So, we gave it one more go, and kept on, sort of like the song said, you know. And there, right when you heard that 'fump,' that was a bomb making a direct hit in the next block. It was a Hermann Goering."

"Hermann Goering? The head of the Luftwaffe?"

"Not fat Hermann himself," laughed Hugh. "That's what we called their biggest bombs, 'cause Hermann himself was so obliquely rotund. It went off in the next street. Came through on the record, even though we were in the basement, and the studio was all soundproofed, an' all. Didn't half make the building shake, I'll tell you. Still, notice, I didn't miss a strum or a stroke." He smiled and nodded. "Right afterwards I put on me ARP helmet, I was an auxiliary warden, and we went to dig out the folks in the next street."

He stopped and listened to the end of the song. "I always listen for that bomb," said Hugh softly. "It's me favorite part of the song. And it reminds me that no matter what I've ever gone through that was the worst. We were all alone with all the might of evil thrown at us every night, and we kept calm and kept on. If we could get through that, well, then all the rest was piece o' cake."

◆

The record scratched against the end groove, as Chesney recalled the old man's words. Even in his darkened room, a faint glimmer of light seemed to appear. He had lost them all, the support of his dear Aunt, the friendship of Hugh Goode, and, most of all, his beloved Verity. But he was still there, for whatever reason, to keep on as best he could.

He rose from his chair and sat cross-legged next to the stereo. For the next hour, he listened to the song over and over again. It was at least a scrap of consolation. He didn't have Aunt El or Verity, but he could still visit with Mr. Goode through his recordings and his films, and that was a bridge to them all. And, he recalled, as he grew tired, he did have Hugh Goode's book. Somehow, he would keep on through that.

– 13 –
Kismet and
the Reversing Mercedes

I'm so glad you could come, Valerie. It's so nice to have your help."
Valerie Fierro smiled, and hoped she looked sincere. Even so, Martina
Fergus had so much sincerity of her own the overflow just spilled on
everyone around her. It was tiresome, but Valerie agreed to help plan
their dumb high school reunion. It would give Valerie a chance to casually
mention she was looking for a job, a job Martina could give her at Voila
Card. Valerie couldn't just say she needed a job. She'd just have to pal
around with Martina and help her organize this idiotic reunion. That
would put Martina under obligation to Valerie. Martina couldn't turn her
down when Valerie asked her for a little favor. By then, Martina would
owe her. Then, Valerie could wriggle out of the reunion planning. After
all, it was almost a year away.

"I don't know what I'd do without you," said Martina. "You just seem
to have a flair for doing this sort of thing."

Valerie smiled. It was true.

"You just seem to know how to pull off an affair," continued Martina.

Valerie looked at her sideways as Martina drove. Had Martina heard
about her quitting Magna Card?

"You have a sense of style," Martina continued, keeping her eyes on
the road.

No, Martina didn't know. She was being sincere. Valerie doubted
Martina had a sarcastic bone in her body.

"I would have had the reunion at a fire hall," said Martina, "Do you
think we can afford a place as elegant as the country club?"

"You just have to know how to handle these people," said Valerie. "We
just have to find the hole in the schedule and then work out a deal. It's all
timing. And we can always charge a little more for the tickets."

"I hope everyone can afford it," said Martina. "I'd hate to price anyone out of the reunion."

The meeting with the country club's events coordinator was fun. Valerie enjoyed subtly reminding her that she was an employee and Valerie was a customer. It was like the All-Delaware Snotty Tournament – Women's Division. A pretentious lob was answered with a patronizing backhand. Valerie did all the negotiating. Martina seemed more interested in boring practical items like budgets and dates.

The coordinator excused herself, ostensibly, to check on the availability of a particular menu item. They were left on the veranda overlooking the golf course.

"Isn't it a glorious day," exclaimed Martina. Valerie studied her profile and thought about her sparse use of make-up.

"So, what do you think about the club," asked Valerie.

Martina turned and faced the building's impressive façade. "It's lovely, but do you think it might be a little too elegant for a simple high school reunion, Valerie?"

"What's wrong with going a little upscale?"

"I'm just thinking about our classmates. You and I might be able to splurge, but maybe not everyone else has been as blessed as we've been."

Valerie looked away. She was wondering how she could broach the subject of a job with Martina, but this latest statement made it all the more difficult. If Martina thought Valerie was doing well, why would Valerie need a job?

"Oh, I'm sorry," said Martina. "That was unkind. It's a beautiful location, and I want to thank you so much for taking the time to arrange this visit. You have such good taste."

Valerie resisted the urge to giggle. How did this girl ever become a manager? She was smart, but she hadn't the slightest idea about real life. Then came the inspiration. With just a minor adjustment, Valerie turned her giggle at Martina into a sob. For a brief moment, she stifled a tear as she waited to see the girl's reaction.

"Oh, no, don't cry, dear," said Martina, putting her arm around Valerie. "What do I know about these things? You said yourself that we might be able to afford it."

"It's not that," said Valerie. "You're right, and you don't know it."

"Right about what?"

"About affording it," said Valerie. She snorted a trickle of tears up her sinuses and rereleased them to great effect. It was a technique she had perfected years ago. "I…I mean…me! I can't afford it!"

In her ensuing jag, Valerie gave a sanitized version of what had happened to her at Magna Card, painting herself as the innocent victim. She wondered if perhaps she was laying it on too thick. Valerie's fears were allayed when Martina not only fished a hankie from her purse but then proceeded to wipe away Valerie's crocodile tears.

"Thank you," said Valerie, in between sobs, as she brought her well-orchestrated hysterics to a tasteful conclusion.

"That's what friends are for," said Martina.

Valerie smiled and pushed aside her last lingering teardrop. It was no longer needed. She nodded her head.

"Don't worry," said Martina. "Maybe I can help your most immediate need."

"What's that?" asked Valerie.

"A job," said Martina, "you need a job, don't you?"

"Yes, I suppose… I hadn't thought about it."

"Of course not," she said, "how could you? You've been through so much. I wish you'd told me sooner."

"I…I didn't want to mention it…" Valerie sucked back a sharp breath as if to staunch a fresh flood of tears.

Martina hugged Valerie. "You haven't done anything wrong. You're the victim here. Maybe you should sue for…" she lowered her voice to a whisper, "…sexual harassment."

"NO!" Cried Valerie. "I…I mean, I don't think, that is, I just want it all to be over with."

"I understand," said Martina. She fished a pen and her business card from her purse, and wrote a name and number on the back of it. "There," she said, handing the card to Valerie. "That's the name of our director of human resources. Give him a call tomorrow; better make it after ten."

"Why after ten?"

"So, I can let him know you'll be calling."

"Thank you," said Valerie softly.

"There's no need to thank me," said Martina.

"Well, said Valerie, "I really appreciate all your help and, and I appreciate… your friendship."

Martina smiled. Valerie was glad. Just as with Mitchell Minear, she liked to think the other person was getting something out of the deal. And if all it took were a few words to make Martina happy, that was all the better.

"I really mean it," said Valerie.

"Yes, I believe you," said Martina.

"Good…because I do." Martina was happy. Valerie felt like a car dealer throwing in cheap floor mats that were already in the price of the vehicle.

The events planner returned with a detailed price list. After a few more professional pleasantries, they agreed to look over the proposals and get back to her.

As they returned to Martina's car, Valerie had an annoying feeling that she had taken advantage of Martina. It wasn't as neat an arrangement as it had been with Mitchell. She disliked the feeling of being in someone's debt. The fact that Martina was doing it so willingly bothered her even more.

"Hey, how about going to have a drink," said Valerie. "A few Cosmos? My treat."

"That's very kind, but I don't drink," said Martina.

"Oh." This declaration made Valerie even more nervous about being in Martina's debt. Valerie didn't trust anyone that she couldn't get good and ripped. "Well, how about dinner?"

"It's a little early…"

"My treat, still," said Valerie. "After all you've done for me, you know… the job."

"But I haven't done anything yet."

"Yes, but, I mean, you said you're going to, tomorrow morning, right?"

"Of course, but you don't have to take me out to dinner."

"I know I don't have to," said Valerie. "I'd take you out to dinner even if I had a job. It's not a thank you, thing; it's a girlfriend thing, you know?"

"Well, if you really want to…" Martina began, but before she could finish her sentence, a voice called out from across the parking lot.

"Valerie? Is that you? Valerie!"

The voice was familiar, but Valerie couldn't place it. She turned around. The man coming across the parking lot looked familiar, too, but again not instantly identifiable. He was certainly worth remembering. He was tall with light brown hair. His body was tanned and toned beneath his short-sleeved golf shirt. He seemed eager to see her, and that was good because this was the sort of guy she eagerly wanted to be seen by. He was jogging closer. Valerie could now see that the shirt was a silk knit, not at all cheap, and that made him all the more attractive.

"Valerie, it's really you…"

She wondered if this were another person she'd have to pretend to know when suddenly…

"Bucky!"

"Valerie!"

Another moment and W. Buxton Dorning was holding her at elbow length and marveling at the small size of the world. It wasn't all that remarkable give the size of Delaware. Still, it was as good as anything else to say.

"You haven't changed a bit, Valerie," said Bucky. "If anything, you're prettier than ever," he said.

She thanked him. She could have told him that he was even more handsome. Back in high school, he was just cute. Now Buxton was a man. His lanky frame had filled out marvelously. His sunken chest was filled with gorgeous pectorals. His face looked as if it had been contoured by a professional cosmetician. Rather than voice any of these observations, Valerie just told him he looked well.

"You know, I was just thinking about you the other day," he continued.

"How sweet of you to remember me."

He shrugged his broad shoulders. "It wasn't that difficult. You're a girl worth remembering."

"Oh, you're embarrassing me," she giggled while trying her damnedest to blush.

"I'm sorry," he said. "I always regretted the way things worked out. We had a good relationship until the prom."

The prom, thought Valerie, the night she was abducted by that little pervert Albrecht Eckner, only to come home to find her father dying.

"Well," he continued, "I just wanted to you to know that I think about you, always fondly, and wonder how things might have worked out, you know… differently."

They stared at each other for several seconds amid an awkward silence. Valerie hoped he was going to ask her out, but he just stood there. She wanted to slap him upside his head. Bucky Dorning may have made great strides outwardly, but inwardly he was still a clueless teenager who didn't know when he had a free move staring him in his beautiful, chiseled face.

While she waited for him to say something, anything, another sound intruded.

"Hi, Buxton."

What? Who? Oh, right, Martina was standing on the other side of the car.

"Martina Fergus?" said Bucky.

"Yes, that's right," said Martina. "I didn't think you'd remember me. After all, you were a year ahead of us."

"Oh, sure, we were in the honor society together."

Valerie, who was not in any honor society, felt a little bit stupid, and more than a little bit annoyed with the two people who were making her feel that way. From a private chat between two old sweethearts, the conversation was degenerating into a reminiscence between two high school eggheads. She had to break this off now.

"Well, I'm sure," said Valerie sharply, almost jerking Bucky's arm from his shoulder, "we're keeping you from some important appointment."

"Huh?" He glanced down at his wristwatch, and then up at Valerie. With her back to Martina, Valerie made some subtle eye movements to Bucky, trying to convey to him that Martina had to leave. Fortunately, he picked up on the message. "Oh, yes, well, it was great to see you…both. But I don't want to hold you up."

While Martina said goodbye, Valerie turned her back to Bucky and made similarly surreptitious signals to Martina.

Though Valerie had asked Martina to dinner, it was much more important not to let Bucky get away. Martina only represented a job in the short-term. In the long-term, Bucky represented a husband who apparently had done well. He wasn't hanging around the country club, planning some lame reunion. He was either a member or hanging out with members. Besides, Martina didn't really want to go to dinner with Valerie. Even if Valerie ditched Martina, that is, if she postponed their dinner, Martina would still put in a good word for her. Her course of action was clear.

Bucky began to walk away. With no time to lose, Valerie ducked into the passenger seat of the car and waited for Martina to get in.

"Look, I don't have time to explain," whispered Valerie, "but we can't have dinner tonight..."

"That's okay, I..."

"Good, good, look, I'll explain it...some other time...but right now, I've got to go tell Buxton something...."

"Oh, I can wait..."

"No, no, I don't want you to wait," said Valerie, "I want you..." She almost told Martina to "get lost." When you told people to get lost they often took it the wrong way. Besides, she didn't want Martina to get lost entirely. It was still important that Martina talk to the head of HR tomorrow on her behalf. "I want you...not to worry about it...I...I don't want to hold you up or inconvenience you..."

"It's no trouble, Valerie, really..."

Valerie glanced over her shoulder. Bucky was approaching his car. It was a Mercedes!

"Martina, I just....do me a favor..."

"...anything, Valerie..."

Valerie climbed out of the car and stuck her head back in.

"Good! Go home!"

She hoped Martina didn't interpret that the wrong way. Valerie had tried to say it nicely, but she didn't have the time.

"Oh..." Martina seemed a bit stunned.

"I'm sorry, but..." fumbled Valerie. "It's about a very sick mutual friend. You understand. He'll be very upset and well, just, I'll, we'll talk... thanks..."

Martina's expression started to melt into one of sympathy, but Valerie didn't have time to confirm that. Bucky's Mercedes was starting up. She scurried towards it before she saw the tail lights glow red. She broke into a jog, just long enough to pull close to the car as it reversed from the parking spot. Valerie had another inspiration. Taking her handbag by the strap, Valerie flung it toward the back panel of the car, causing a dull thump. The car's breaks jammed on, and the power window whirred down.

Valerie raised her right knee.

"Bucky..." she gasped.

He yanked up on the parking brake and jumped out of the car. In a moment, he was supporting her as she leaned against him.

"I didn't see you," he said.

"I just...I needed..." she panted.

"Are you all right?"

"Fine," she smiled bravely. "You hardly grazed me…my knee."

He touched her right knee, she winced just a little, not too much. Then he looked at the car.

"See," she said valiantly, "hardly a dent."

"But what were you doing?"

"I had to…I need a ride."

"But Martina…"

"She's got a date, and we're running late, so…"

"She just dumped you?"

Valerie shrugged her shoulders as if it were her lot in life to be casually dismissed by friends.

Bucky Dorning gallantly helped her into the passenger seat of his car. He said something about having to cancel an appointment and used his cell phone to do so. She couldn't tell if it was a business appointment or a date, but it didn't really matter. He was doing it for her. Bucky kept his explanation to the other person short and discreet. As he hung up, Bucky gave her a concerned look.

"Are you sure you're all right?" he said.

Valerie rubbed her knee. "Oh, yes, it's much better…I feel so silly…"

"There's no need to feel that way," he said. The concern on his face melted into a warm smile, which she returned. "Do you believe in Kismet?"

"What?"

"Fate?"

She batted her eyes as if to indicate that was entirely up to him.

"Well," said Bucky, "maybe bumping into you, literally, maybe it was meant to be."

"Maybe," she said as she caressed her knee, this time more seductively. But Valerie knew that, like most of life, it was more a case of fakery than fate.

– 14 –
The Fire Hydrant Bidet and
the Nicotine Cudgel

The department manager opened the file, looked up, and smiled.
"Is it a month already?" she said in a chirpy voice. Her style was unique, not because it couldn't have been imitated, but because no one would want to do so.

"It's time for your 30-day review," said a second woman, the unit manager, not nearly as perky. If anything, she seemed cruel by comparison. Valerie Fierro preferred the approach of the second woman, though it took two weeks to discover that.

Francine and Dulcy, the pair conducting Valerie's review at Voila Card, were inseparable and proof that opposites attract.

Francine Bidet – Valerie had almost laughed out loud the first time she had seen it on the nameplate outside her office. Before that, she had only heard it spoken.

"You'll be working in New Accounts," the HR manager told her, "under Francine Bidet."

Only she pronounced it "Bide," as did everyone else. On the rare occasion when someone said "Bidet" in Francine's presence, she would make a sour face which she quickly buried under her aspartame smile.

"The 't' is silent," Francine would admonish, "it's pronounced 'Bide.'"

After she was there a week, Valerie asked a co-worker why Francine didn't use her maiden name professionally.

"Her maiden name is 'Crapper,'" whispered the co-worked.

It was fitting that Francine's husband was a plumber.

While she could try to improve on her married name, there was little Francine could do to improve on her appearance. She was a blonde fire hydrant: squat and compact to the degree that strangers wondered if she indeed was just short or if she actually had a congenital defect. Further blurring the line was her vague figure. She wasn't fat, nor could she be considered svelte. As a result, the only items confirming her femininity were her wardrobe choices (skirt suits, usually in a "power" red color), and her hairstyle (a straight, shoulder-length blonde bob). When Valerie saw her in jeans, on a casual Friday, Francine looked like a chunky eleven-year-old boy in need of a haircut.

If Francine looked like a pre-pubescent boy in search of a trim, her cohort, Dulcy Cudgel, looked like her uncle who might be escorting her to the barber for the same. Dulcy was only five-foot-nine, but standing next to Francine made her look much taller. She was also an exercise devotee, spending hours at the company gym on weight training rather than cardio. This gave her a well-toned, hard body. Her heavy brow line only added to her masculine appearance, which her wavy jaw-length brown hair did little to soften. Valerie couldn't help but think that despite all this, Dulcy Cudgel could be attractive if she only bothered to employ two things: a bit of make-up and an occasional smile. Instead, her sharply featured face seemed covered by a perennial scowl, even when she was happy. Despite this, Dulcy was a nice person; she only looked like she was running a deli that specialized in knuckle sandwiches.

Now they both sat across the table from Valerie like an odd version of good cop/bad cop. In the month she'd worked for the pair, Valerie learned that while Francine seemed friendly, she was the more dangerous of the duo. At the same time, the scowling Dulcy was more likely to give someone a break.

"Most department managers here at Viola don't bother to sit in on reviews," began Francine Bidet cheerily, before whispering, "unless it's for a discipline issue."

Valerie looked back at her with a puzzled expression. Having learned from her tactical error at Magna Card, Valerie hadn't tried parlaying sexual favors into a promotion.

Francine smiled. "Oh, don't worry, you're not being disciplined."

"I didn't think I was," said Valerie.

"As I was saying, most department heads don't attend ordinary reviews, but I like to sit in so I can know all my team better, and so they can know me. I just think it's nicer that way, don't you think?"

Dulcy Cudgel was wistfully looking out the window while she bit at a hangnail.

"So how are you getting on, Valerie?" Francine asked.

Valerie replied she was getting on fine. Fine, she thought for a dull job. New Accounts was nearly as dull as customer service. Thankfully she only had to review customer information rather than actually speak to the wretched applicants.

"New Accounts is the lifeblood of our little company," said Francine. It was a phrase that Valerie had heard her repeat at least twice daily over the past thirty days. Only Francine thought it was a fresh observation.

Valerie stole another glance at Dulcy, who was now studying the bottom of her shoe. She was struck by the rugged way Dulcy sat, her right ankle resting on her left knee. She doubted the woman had ever worn a skirt in her life.

"That's why I like to have as much contact with all my team as possible," said Francine, "I like to see that they're as interested in our brand's future as I am."

Valerie assured her that she was at least as passionate about new accounts as the other members of the department. This was an accurate statement since everyone she had met was already bored to death with the process of lining up more debtors to the company.

From here, Francine rambled on for at least ten minutes on the outstanding features of the Voila Card. Valerie had heard it all enough times that she could have delivered the speech herself, though not as passionately as Francine Bidet. Dulcy Cudgel was drumming her fingers against the breast pocket of her shirt in which the outline of a pack of Marlborough cigarettes was visible.

After she had exhausted her usual repertoire, Francine let slip her ulterior motive.

"So, you know Martina Fergus," she said as she read Valerie's personnel file, though that information was not in there.

"Uh, I guess," said Valerie, taken aback. Since she had been hired, no one had mentioned Martina to her, nor had they intimated she had gotten Valerie the job. "I mean, yes, I know Martina. We, uh, we went to the same high school."

"The same high school," repeated Francine.

"Yes, but that was years ago," said Valerie unsure why her connection to Martina, no matter how remote, would be of interest to Francine Bidet.

"Of course, years ago, but isn't that…interesting," said Francine.

Dulcy Cudgel, impatient for a smoke, interrupted.

"Can I do her review now?" asked Dulcy.

"She's a lovely person," said Francine ignoring her friend and underling. Valerie nodded in agreement, but she'd played this game enough to know that Francine held little admiration for Martina. It was evident that Francine viewed Martina as competition.

Francine locked eyes with Valerie. While her phony smile shone from her mouth, those eyes seemed to be searching for a potential ally in her professional struggles.

Francine Bidet was a pro. She didn't get to be middle management without knowing when to stick in the knife, who to kiss up to, and who to kick down. Valerie had learned the corporate world was essentially an extension of high school, and she had been a prom queen!

Valerie matched Francine's stare, unblinking, not hostile, but still unyielding. She was her own player. She wasn't going to sell-out someone, at least not cheaply, and she wasn't volunteering to be Francine Bidet's toady either.

"Hey, Francine, let's keep moving, huh?" Dulcy Cudgel interrupted. "I got another meeting, okay?"

"Oh, of course, dear," said Francine turning to Dulcy. "I'm sorry. I guess I got sidetracked with my chit-chat."

Chit-chat? If what Francine Bidet had been doing could be called "chit-chat," then a sharks' feeding frenzy could be termed "nibbling."

"Yeah, good," said Dulcy leaning over the table and pushing up her sleeves. Valerie noted her biceps were larger than most of the guys she knew. "Here's your review…"

Dulcy read off the checklist from the personnel form. Her pace quickened as her need for nicotine increased. Finally, she got to the end.

"And there's your increase," said Dulcy. She shoved the paper across the table to Valerie.

Valerie glanced at the figure. It was nothing to get excited about.

"You're doing a good job," said Dulcy rising from the table and reaching for her pack of cigarettes in the same motion. "Keep up the good work. I gotta go…to another meeting. See you all later…"

Those last words were spoken as she hurried out the door. For a moment, Valerie and Francine just sat in silence.

"Busy girl," said Francine with a smile, "one of my best team members."

"Yes," said Valerie starting to rise.

"I noticed," said Francine, "that you weren't too thrilled with your increase."

Valerie shrugged. "Oh, it's fine, for now."

Francine Bidet stood. She seemed even shorter.

"That's a good way to look at it," said Francine. "I can tell you're a smart girl." She paused, waiting for Valerie to comment. Valerie didn't, so Francine continued. "Dulcy likes you a lot, too."

Valerie said nothing.

"I'm always looking to develop my team's talent," she continued. "I like to help my people."

Valerie nodded while thinking: by helping yourself.

"Well," said Valerie, "I'd better get back to work. You know, New Accounts…the company's lifeblood…"

"That's right," said Francine as if it were a fresh analogy, "new accounts are our lifeblood."

Valerie agreed again and started for the door.

"Do you read?" said Francine as Valerie started out.

"What?"

"Do you read? I mean, do you like books?"

"Uh, sure, I suppose…"

"Oh, well, I've got a little club; it's like a book club."

"Oh, that's…nice," said Valerie trying to smile. It was more polite than saying "big shit" to your department head.

"Yes, well, maybe you'll have to join us sometime," said Francine, "in the future, of course. Dulcy's a member of our group, too."

Valerie reasoned to herself that she couldn't very well join them in the past. The way Francine said it, however, seemed to have strings attached. It was as if she were offering Valerie entry into her inner circle with the likes of the chain-smoking, iron-pumping, surly Dulcy Cudgel, but only based on future services rendered. It was bad enough working with this female homunculus and her pal without discussing boring books with them on her own time.

Valerie flashed her most insincere smile, one she thought Francine would fully appreciate.

"Yes, wouldn't that be fun...in the future."

Then she excused herself and went back to her cubicle to transfuse some more blood into Voila Card.

– 15 –
Love in a Pump

"Anything new at work?"

"No, well, yeah," said Valerie. "I had my one-month review today."

"I'm sure you did great." Bucky Dorning seemed more interested in the topic than Valerie. "You're so professional."

Valerie smiled. She cultivated the image of the corporate woman with Bucky, even though she planned on chucking it all after she married him. That was why Valerie didn't care about banking, Voila Card, or Francine Bidet and her little schemes.

Her real review, an unspoken one, took place last week: the one-month anniversary of her reuniting with W. Buxton Dorning. They went to his place for their first love-making session. Valerie smiled to herself. He had been okay, not exactly a rookie, of course, but still a journeyman lover. She, of course, had been spectacular. From the expressions of ecstasy on his face, Bucky obviously thought so. Valerie faked an orgasm and even intimated that no man had ever made her feel "that way" before. She threw that in to bolster his ego, and hopefully encourage his future performances.

Now they were going to have dinner with his parents. It was a good sign. The only other time he had taken her home to meet the Dornings was back in high school. That evening ended with Bucky asking her to the prom. Although she didn't expect it that evening, Valerie suspected this was another step toward a proposal.

Valerie recalled the horrid suit that she had worn back then. To fit into it, she had to bind her breasts so tightly that she wound-up fainting in the soup. It had all worked out well, since Bucky's mother, Abigail Dorning, had a figure as level as an Iowa cornfield. She thought Valerie was a kindred sister in the flat-chest society. Tonight, however, Valerie was in all her full-boobed glory. Mrs. Dorning would just have to get used to having a daughter-in-law with spectacular knockers. After all, Valerie couldn't go around wrapped in an Ace bandage for the next thirty years, or however long the old plank had left on Earth.

The Dorning's home hadn't changed much. She recalled promising to herself that one day she would be a queen of that world. While she smiled at her girlish naiveté, her plans had not changed. They had only matured.

Valerie raised her hand as Bucky helped her out of the car. He looked good in his ecru slacks and blue blazer, his open-collar blue pinpoint shirt contrasting nicely with his tan. She had broken her budget to buy her dress just for this occasion. It was a knee-length pastel number with diaphanous layers comprising the skirt and a bodice that accentuated her bust. As Bucky rang the bell, Valerie stood there, exuding the confidence that comes when you look your best, and you know it.

"Funny," Bucky said, "I only moved out a few years ago, but since I left, I feel like I have to ring the doorbell." His voice betrayed a slight nervousness. Perhaps he knew this meant their relationship was "serious."

Lately, Valerie detected a thoughtful dimension to Bucky. She would catch him looking at her when he thought she didn't know she was being watched. He studied her as if he were trying to reach a conclusion in his mind. She had passed the physical test, so it was evident that he wanted more items checked off his list of wifely attributes. Valerie did her best to feed him all the answers she thought he was looking for while pretending to be unaware she was doing so.

Valerie made a great show of tidying up his kitchen, being careful to hum contently as she did so. Only after ten minutes of this charade did she look up and feign surprise at being watched. He also asked innocent but transparent questions about motherhood, and family. It was too easy to guess the sort of answers he was looking for. Valerie only had to think of his mother and respond as she thought that woman would.

Even now, as they stood waiting at the front door, Valerie looked at the shrubbery and commented on how she loved to putter around the garden and create her own flower arrangements.

"You do?" He answered.

"Oh, yes, I've always enjoyed whatever I can do to make my house a real home. Why?"

"Oh, no reason…"

A satisfied smile played around the corners of his mouth, and she could almost see him ticking another item from his list. Valerie glanced back at the shrubs. She would hire professional landscapers.

"Well, look who's here!"

The door opened, and there stood Mr. Dorning. The years had intensified most aspects of the man. He had completed his work on his middle-aged paunch. His face had grown jowly. His eyes, once twinkly, were now nearly popping from his head, giving him the look of an aspiring lunatic. And his voice, which had before reverberated with a baritone gusto now bellowed.

Valerie extended her hand to Mr. Dorning. Instead of shaking it, he took advantage of the moment to give Valerie a hug and then relaxed enough to hold her at arm's length.

"I always thought you let a good one get away, Buxton," he said. He gave her a full-body scan, starting with her breasts, then up to her face, meeting her eyes for a brief "hello," and then darting back to her boobs.

"Yes, I always liked this girl," he said.

"Dad," interrupted Bucky, "you only met her the once."

"Well, yes," he admitted, "just that one time. Remember, she passed out in the soup?" He looked back at Valerie and laughed. "Remember, you passed out in the Penang Assam Laksa. Remember?"

It wasn't often that a girl forgot passing out in a bowl of atomic Thai soup. She smiled, but then noticed he was addressing the question to her breasts. Valerie wished she could throw her voice and let the twins answer for her.

"I think she remembers, Dad," said Bucky, "now, can we come in, or are you going to tell all the neighbors about the soup?"

Valerie was impressed that Buxton was no longer the quiet deferential son he had once been. He seemed more self-assured in his father's presence. Having a good career and one's own Mercedes tended to do that.

Bucky herded them into the house. It was much as Valerie had recalled it, and while she had admired and envied the Dorning's home back then, she was disappointed that it was unchanged. It was typical of couples once they reached the upper reaches of middle age. They tend to change physically while their surrounding remained static. She scrutinized the expanded figure of Mr. Dorning. Valerie wondered if Mr. Dorning was a prophecy of his son's future appearance. Again, she vowed she would fight against that outcome. Still, when she did marry him, and even if he did grow wide and flabby in the coming years, she would always be able to get new furniture and drapes.

Mrs. Dorning entered. Unlike her husband, she had maintained her figure or lack thereof. She was still elegant and unencumbered of the slightest curves. Still, she had to be admired for dressing up what nature had given, or rather, not given her.

"Valerie, dear," said Mrs. Dorning exchanging a warm embrace combined with a clutch of air kisses. "It's so wonderful to see you again. My, you've grown so lovely…"

These observations, based on Valerie's facial features, were abruptly halted when she took a step back and was confronted by the Fierro bosom. A look of betrayal crossed Abigail Dorning's face, which her gracious manners quickly covered up. Still, Valerie had seen it. They were no longer soul sisters. The assumed bond between them had eroded in inverse proportion to Valerie's cup size. Valerie had gone over to the enemy: the busty persecutors of the boob-less, a Star-Bellied Sneetch, looking down her rack at the unendowed.

The rest of the evening was a strange mixture of performances. It was as if three artists with antithetical styles were working on a single canvass. On the one hand, there was Mr. Dorning, who kept looking at Valerie in the creepiest way. She was used to being around men mentally undressing her. Mr. Dorning's leers weren't merely undressing her in his mind, but it was as if he were redressing her in a series of strange outfits. She would catch his eyelids rising slightly as if he had just imagined a new fantasy costume for her. She felt like some sort of kinky Barbie doll under his gaze.

If her husband had been arraying Valerie in a series of increasingly decadent outfits, Mrs. Dorning kept Valerie fully clothed. Then she was mentally burying Valerie under layers of scrap lumber, boulders, old refrigerators, whatever was handy in her imagination.

Fortunately, these two opposing forces had to live with each other. Their son, on the other hand, was looking at Valerie adoringly, shielding her from the effects of his parents.

In the five weeks that they had been dating again, Buck Dorning's attentions had grown more real, more permanent. She equated it to shopping for shoes.

When she first went into the store, Valerie knew she wanted a pair of shoes, though she didn't necessarily need them. Still, it was fun to look, pick up a pair, stroke the leather, and compare the colors and textures. Then if she was interested: try them on. That first moment, slipping on the shoe would reveal a lot. Sometimes, despite looking cute, it only took a moment of initial contact to know that it wouldn't work. The toe pinched, the heel scraped, the vamp was too short. It didn't even bear wasting time to try on the mate. But if that first contact was okay, she'd slip on the other shoe. With both shoes on, attention shifted not to just the shoes themselves, but how they looked on her. Did they make her feet look big in comparison? How did they make her legs look? If all that was okay, then it was time to stand up and take those first tentative steps around the floor. If that went well, it was time to pick up the pace and try them at a good stride. After confirming that nothing rubbed, they looked good, and looked good on her, then, and only then was the time to take the plunge, make the commitment, and close the deal. Then, after she'd handed them her credit card, and her purchase was given to her; then, as she walked out of the store came the feeling that Valerie equated to love.

As she looked up from her dessert of sorbet garnished with fresh fruit, Valerie recognized the expression on Bucky's face. He had been around the store and had felt the merchandise and had even worn it about. He was ready to close the deal.

With that look in his eyes, his parents didn't matter. Mr. Dorning would probably have a coronary in a few years, and that would be that. His wife would likely carry her bony frame into old lady-hood. Her animosity would diminish once Valerie had given her some grandchildren.

From the look in Buck's eyes, Valerie knew she'd be in control of the situation...once the deal was closed.

– 16 –
Extra Credit for Penmanship

I'm going to groom you," announced Francine Bidet.

Valerie just looked at her boss. As if she would take advice on style from a stubby little troll. Francine wore biker shorts under the skirts of her power suits that you could see when she sat down. And she didn't know how to apply makeup, when she tried to at all. And if a styling brush ever touched her head it must have been when an irate hairdresser threw it at her in a fit of pique. No, Francine Bidet couldn't teach anyone, least of all Valerie, anything about grooming.

It turned out that Francine wanted to instruct Valerie on management skills. Those weren't much better. Francine slathered meaningless praise on her underlings, while heaping obsequious adulation on her own bosses. Francine seemed to be begging for love or validation from both above her and below her.

"Sit here, next to me," Francine told Valerie, as they entered the conference room. "Dulcy tells me you're ever so clever."

Valerie flashed a phony smile knowing Francine wouldn't recognize it when it was served back to her. Ever so clever? If Dulcy Cudgel uttered such a cloying phrase, her head would pop off her shoulders like some escape pod.

"So," continued Francine with a crinkle of her nose, "I thought it would be good for you to meet with a client and see the workings of upper management."

Valerie resisted the impulse to laugh. Francine was middle management and not even upper-middle management. She more like middle-middle management. Valerie had known upper management and how they worked.

Francine spoke to Valerie as if she were a visiting elementary school student. She outlined their merchant program, which offered clients cut-rate loans in return for them giving preferred placement to the Voila card. Big deal, thought Valerie, another sucker for Voila.

As Francine continued with her primmer on credit card economics, Valerie's mind wandered to Bucky Dorning. They'd recently spent a weekend in the mountains. It was the perfect place to get engaged, but Bucky kept his proposal to himself. Still, she could tell he was getting closer, even if he was approaching cautiously.

"Your client is here," announced Francine's secretary, popping her head in the room.

"They're not clients," snapped Francine, "they're visitors."

"Oh, sorry, I mean, your visitor is here."

"Show him in," said Francine returning the syrup to her voice.

The girl ushered in a tall man. He was reasonably good-looking, Valerie thought, though he had a big nose which he tried to balance out with a thick brush of a mustache beneath it.

"Francine Bidet," said Francine, leaving off the final "t."

"Stosh Potoski," said the man. He looked down at Francine, who came up to the middle of his chest.

"And this is, Valerie, one of my valuable assistants," said Francine, "I hope you don't mind if she joins us."

Stosh Potoski said he didn't mind.

"We really appreciate you coming in to visit us today, Mr. Potoski, or may I call you 'Stosh?'"

Stosh was fine, assured Stosh.

Francine then gushed about the glories of the Voila Card and all the benefits that savvy merchants would receive by accepting the card. Valerie had heard it all before, though she tried to look as if she were paying attention. Stosh Potoski concealed his boredom poorly, only showing interest when the loan portion of the deal was mentioned.

"So, Stosh," said Francine after twenty minutes of Voila guff, "do you have a relationship?"

"Huh?"

"By that, of course, I mean, do you have a cardmember relationship with any of our competitors?"

"Oh, uh, yeah, I, uh…" Stosh squirmed in his seat. "I do, I mean, I did, but, well, I don't like to speak ill of people in business…"

"Feel free," encouraged Francine, "we need to have a full picture of your business needs so we can better serve you."

"Oh, well, yeah," said Stosh, "if you put it like that, yeah, well, I wasn't happy, that is, satisfied with the service your competition gave to my company. I mean, we're ready to grow, you know, really take off, and I think, that is, I'm sure they were holding back my expansion plans."

"I understand," said Francine.

Valerie understood too. This Potoski clown was a small-time operator with lousy credit who had been dumped by the other major credit cards.

Why else would he come all the way down to Delaware to try and become a Voila merchant? It wasn't that Voila was a bad company, but they weren't exactly the cream of the industry. In trying to increase their market share, they'd take just about anyone. The joke in the cafeteria was that kids with lemonade stands were taking Voila.

"What business are you in, Mr. Potoski?" asked Valerie.

Stosh Potoski tugged at his collar. "Uh, yeah, manufacturing... and, oh, yeah, marketing."

"And what do you manufacture?" asked Valerie, "and market?"

For a moment, Stosh Potoski rolled his tongue around inside his mouth as if he had a popcorn hull wedged between his molar and bicuspid.

"Um...novelties." He said with a curious mixture of pride and shame.

"I'm sorry, Stosh," said Francine handing Valerie a brochure, "I didn't share with my colleague the nature of your business."

Valerie looked at the publication. It looked expensive, but the professionalism of the printer's job was lessened by the items displayed in the booklet. There were fake dog turds, plastic ice cubes containing artificial insects, small electronic devices which promised large, rude noises, and dozens of other objects not nearly as elegant.

Novelties? Thought Valerie, these aren't novel, they're just gross! She resisted the urge to pick up the catalog between her thumb and forefinger and flick it across the table. EWWW! Who would buy these tasteless things? Disgusting little boys with too much pocket money. It was like pornography for boys who had yet to discover sex. EWWW!

"Interesting," Valerie muttered.

"Yes," agreed Potoski regaining some of his initial hubris, "we turn out some very neat little items."

Francine jumped back in at this point and resumed her sales pitch about the wondrous features of the world's most innovative credit card. As Francine droned on, he nodded his head faster and faster. It was evident that he didn't care about the customer service, the merchant fees, retailer discounts, or the prestige of being associated with such a marvelous financial network. He looked like a bank robber enduring the sales pitch of an over-zealous used car salesman before being allowed to buy his getaway vehicle.

"And those are just a few of the benefits of being a Voila merchant," said Francine.

"Sounds great, I'm in," said Stosh.

"Did I tell you about the..."

"Yes, yes, you did, or if you didn't, well, it couldn't be any better, where do I sign?"

"Oh, you are so eager," said Francine as she rummaged through the merchant portfolio. She fished out the necessary form, and he grabbed it from her hands. "Yes, but not as eager as we are to have your company join our family."

Potoski began jotting in the required information.

"Really, there's no need to do it right now, Stosh."

"No time like the present..." he said, not looking up from his writing.

"And, of course, you have the necessary statements..."

He stopped and looked up. "Statements?"

"Your company's most recent audits and your financial reports," said Francine, her tone turning ominous. "I did mention that when we spoke over the phone, didn't I? I did explain that this was not just a merchant agreement, but a loan product, a line of credit, didn't I?"

"Right, yes, I mean, you did, the loan, that's what I'm interested in," blurted Stosh. "That is, I really, really love your card and your loan program. I brought all the statements like you asked..."

His last sentence trailed off, leaving Valerie to wonder just how desperate Potoski must be. Anyone with good credit and good security would be better off going to a regular bank for a loan. Financing a business on a credit card was almost as bad as doing it through a loan shark. The only difference was the loan shark wasn't as boring. Francine Bidet's frozen smile thawed as she read Stosh Potoski's balance sheet. It was like witnessing a mudslide: it started out slowly but accelerated into a catastrophic mess as it gained momentum.

Stosh Potoski had his head down. He knew how bad his situation was.

As she finished, Francine Bidet stared at the statement, then drew a long breath followed by an equally long exhale. She closed her eyes and forced the smile back on her face, though there was little sunshine in her eyes.

"Well, this was... helpful," she said.

Potoski looked up without raising his head. Valerie could see the beads of sweat on his forehead. She glanced back at Francine. She knew Francine hated to lose a customer. At Voila, numbers were king, no matter in which department one worked. Francine looked back at the report, searching for a glimmer of hope amidst the gloom. Then, her face brightened.

"Mr. Potoski," she said, adopting a more formal form of address, just in case she would have to kick him out, "it says here your initial capitalization came through your family."

"Yes," said Stosh, "that's right. It was from my father."

"Ah," Francine's smile broadened, "your father."

"Yes, he left me an inheritance."

"Oh," her smiled contracted slightly, "then he's dead."

"Yes."

"And you've used up all the inheritance."

Stosh craned his neck to look at the document. "Yes, that's all of it. I put it all in the company...to start it up."

Francine chewed her lip for a moment. "So, that's it," she said, "I mean that's all of the inheritance."

Stosh nodded. "Yeah, I suppose. There's not much chance of the old man coming back to leave me another bundle."

"And that was all of it," muttered Francine. "It's just if you had a little more collateral, a stronger cash flow, then we could swing the loan…"

"And that's all I'd need," he said. "I mean, your loan would put me over the top. You see, I've got this stock all done up. It's sitting in Chinese warehouses. But they don't give credit as generously as you do."

"Yes, well," said Francine, "of course. And that was all the inheritance?"

"That was all of it," agreed Stosh Potoski, "or at least all I got of it."

Francine looked up. "There's was more?"

Stosh shrugged his shoulder. "Yeah, that's all I got." Then as he looked across the table a light bulb seemed to flicker on over his head. "Yeah, that's all I got, but my kid brother…"

"You have a brother?" said Francine, hopefully. "And he received an inheritance, as well?"

"Yeah, he did, same as me, only…"

"He spent it?"

"No, he couldn't not until he reached thirty."

"How old is he?"

"You mean now?" asked Stosh.

"Of course now!" snapped Francine Bidet before softening. "I mean, yes, how old is your brother… now?"

"I don't know," said Stosh. "I mean, I don't have much to do with him. I guess, wait…" Stosh Potoski rolled his eyes up into his head while he began counting on his fingers. Having completed his calculations his irises returned to view. "I'm pretty sure he's past thirty now!"

"Excellent," said Francine, "and do you think he would loan you the money. It would help re-capitalize your business, so we can give you the loan," said Francine.

Stosh shrugged. "I don't know why he would."

"Oh," said Francine, "you mean he has other plans for his money, perhaps his own business venture?"

"Him?" said Potoski, "I doubt it. He's just a…writer."

Stosh couldn't have said "murderer" or "rapist," with any more disgust. But the word had the exact opposite effect on Francine Bidet.

"A writer?" Her faced brightened as Valerie had never seen before, meaning sincerely. "What does he write?"

"I dunno, books, I suppose."

"Your brother writes books?"

"No, it's more like he edits books," said Stosh, "but, yeah, wait, Mom, you know, our mother, she said he just finished writing a book, too."

"So he wrote his own book?"

"I guess… yeah."

Francine Bidet nodded her head and then turned to Valerie.

"Valerie, dear," she said. "Could you… um, could you go to my office…and… ask Dulcy if she could… print out the new accounts reports for the third quarter of last year? Oh, and you might as well print up the fourth quarter, too, and wait for them, and then bring them to me. This is very important, so I'm trusting it to you."

Bullshit, thought Valerie. Francine was smiling like the cat that swallowed the canary. She practically had feathers sticking out from the corners of her mouth.

"Thank you, Valerie," said Francine, before saying to Stosh, "Valerie is such a valuable member of our team."

Valerie left, closing the door behind her.

"I suppose I could get my brother to loan me some money," Valerie heard Stosh Potoski say through the door, "if I had to."

"Do you suppose you could get him to do something else for you, as well?" asked Francine.

"Give me even more money?"

"No, this has more to do with his profession as a writer."

"You want him to write me something?"

"I was thinking more of me," said Francine.

"You want him to write you something?"

"No, he's already done that."

"He has?"

Valerie had heard enough. She hurried off for the reports that she knew weren't needed. When Valerie reached Dulcy Cudgel's office, she was on the phone.

"Hey, you called me," she said to the person on the other end of the line. "I don't appreciate this kind of happy horseshit when I'm at work, especially not over something like the club."

Valerie wondered if Dulcy's club was a social group or a weapon.

"Yeah, we're friends," continued Dulcy, "but this isn't the biggest concern in my life, especially not at work… it's not just Francine's fault, you know that… who the hell cares who started it, you know how those two are… yeah, well, it didn't help that Carol went out and got a real live author when it was her turn… of course, that raised the stakes, and with Francine's turn coming up, she's going out of her gourd trying to…"

Dulcy looked up and noticed Valerie.

"Hold on," she put her hand over the receiver. "Do you need me?"

Valerie relayed Francine's request. Dulcy rolled her eyes.

"I gotta go," she said into the phone, "she's really losing it. No, I'm not gonna call you back. Stella, it's a friggin' book club. It's not that important to normal people. Later."

Dulcy hung up the receiver and stared at it as if she wished she could beat it up. Then, she shook her head.

"Old reports, huh?" She said. Valerie agreed. Dulcy made a few keystrokes on her computer, entered a password, and then hit "enter."

"Okay," she said to Valerie, "you can pick them up at the printer."

As Valerie walked away, she heard Dulcy muttering: "Friggin' book club."

– 17 –
The Watercress Ambush

It was good to get out of the office, even for this. He'd been back at Marlton Press for months. He was not the same person who left a year earlier to ghostwrite the biography of Lord Bagnold. Chesney was certain his story had been whispered about throughout the company. The women in the office looked at him differently. Before they saw him as the fat, pedantic, harmless boy with the rigid routine. He returned as the hero in a tragic romance. Some women spoke to him as if they wanted to get closer to him. Still, Chesney couldn't think of any relationship with anyone, not so soon after…

So day blended into day behind his desk. Each night he went home and, more often than not, listened to Hugh Goode records in the dark. It was almost a relief to go out for lunch with his mother.

It was the sort of restaurant his mother would select: filled with other older ladies, most of them wearing hats. All the sandwiches had their crusts cut off before being sliced up into diagonal quarters and then placed on three-tiered trays. It was an uncomfortably fussy restaurant, which is probably why his mother chose it.

His mother was already seated at a table when he came in. She wasn't wearing a hat, and he was glad. Approximately eighty percent of the patrons were women. Chesney was the only man there under sixty. He felt out of place as he walked across the room. His age and his weight, which had ballooned up again, made him even more self-conscious. As he greeted his mother and sat down he could see the approving nods of nearby ladies. He could imagine them thinking: "What a good boy, having lunch with his mother," "such a nice husky boy, she must be so proud of him," and other embarrassing thoughts.

"Hello, dear," said his mother.

Chesney tried to smile. It felt more like a grimace.

"Is this such a darling little spot?" Mrs. Potoski asked.

Even though it was a rhetorical question, Chesney swallowed hard and agreed it was a darling little spot.

"That's what I thought, too," said Mrs. Potoski. "How are you?"

Chesney smirked and shrugged.

"Still not over that nasty business in England?" she asked.

Nasty business in England? He didn't know whether to laugh at her clumsy consolation or scream at her from the depths of his shattered heart. He merely shook his head.

She looked down at the menu. "These things take time."

These things? What things? The Quiche Lorraine? The watercress sandwiches? Surely she couldn't be referring to grieving over the death of his true love? These things?

"I'll be all right, mother," he whispered.

"Of course you will," she said. "Still, it's not like losing your father. You know, I still haven't cried about that. I must be a horrible person, but I haven't. I don't know what that says about me. Maybe it's because I think of all the happy memories we had."

Nearly all his memories of Verity were happy. The only problem was that they all ended with a grave in Staffordshire.

"And you have to think of Elinor as well," said his mother.

Yes, thought Chesney, when he grew bored with the untimely death of his fiancée, he could switch to the passing of his favorite relative. Wasn't eating lunch in this blue-haired sanctuary torture enough without his mother making his heart on a platter the special of his day?

He diverted the conversation in the best way he knew how.

"And how are you, Mom?"

For the next ten minutes, Mrs. Potoski cheerily recited every picayune event from the last six months. Only the arrival of the waitress interrupted her. Mrs. Potoski ordered a salad while Chesney settled on a selection of sandwiches, all tiny, all containing some sort of pink meat or fish paste. He could get something real to eat on the way back to the office.

"I suppose you're wondering why I asked you to lunch," she said after the waitress had left.

"To see how I was doing?" he guessed.

"Oh, yes, that, of course," she said with a dismissive wave of her hand. "I know you'll be fine. You're a survivor."

"I am." He was a survivor, not the way his mother meant it: "continuing to function despite a tragedy," but as "one who remains alive after the death of others."

"I've got such good boys," she said, taking his hand.

"Isn't he a sweet boy," he overheard a nearby woman in a flowered hat comment to her companion, a rheumatic gent with a paisley ascot.

Chesney sighed. It couldn't get any worse.

It then got worse.

"Hey, there's the big guy!" It was a voice that could only belong to one person: Stosh.

Chesney looked at his mother. Mrs. Potoski smiled twice: first, a little grin at Chesney, and then, as she looked up at her eldest child, her face broke into a beaming smile.

"Stosh!" she said, feigning surprise, but Chesney knew it was a setup. Stosh Potoski would no sooner wander into an old ladies' tea room than he would be the guest lecturer at a Mensa convention.

"Stosh," muttered Chesney. He wanted to say, "oh, shit," but couldn't given the surroundings.

Stosh slapped Chesney on the back and sat down.

"Sorry, I'm late," he said to his mother.

"Actually," whispered his mother, "you're a little early."

Ambushed…by his own mother.

"Can I get some lunch?" Stosh asked. A waitress handed Stosh a menu. In return Stosh gave her a salacious leer. "Okay, let's see what they got here," said Stosh scanning the bill of fare. His eyes raced up and down the two columns several times before he looked up at his mother. "Don't they have steak or something?"

"I don't think so, but they have some lovely items," she said.

He frowned. The waitress took out her pencil.

"I'll have what she's having," he said, nodding toward his mother.

"Yes, sir," said the waitress, "two watercress salads."

Stosh forced a smile onto his lips.

"That sounds good," he said to Chesney, as one would speak to a five-year-old. "Is that what you're having, too, Cheese… I mean, Chesney?"

"I'm having a sandwich," said Chesney dolefully. "I don't like watercress."

"You should try it," said Stosh, "I didn't use to like vegetables, but I tried them, and now I do!"

"And what a big strong boy you became," said Chesney.

A scowl darkened Stosh's already overhung brow, making him look even more like a Neanderthal. He forced a smile, then reached out and tousled Chesney's hair.

"Ha, big strong boy, that's a good one, Ches, old kid, yes sir. I always said Chesney's got a great sense of humor."

Stosh, who rarely saw the humor in anything, least of all when he was the butt of the joke, forced a chuckle from his mouth.

Mrs. Potoski commented on how nice it was to have her two boys with her.

Stosh remarked that he, too, was terribly pleased to be having lunch with his favorite mother and favorite brother.

They both then looked to Chesney, expecting him to make the motion of familial bliss unanimous. Chesney eyed both of them for a moment. Should he be polite, or should he say what he really thought? A glance at his mother called for the first impulse. But then a look at Stosh overrode that.

"Okay," said Chesney, "what do you want?"

"Want?" they replied in unison.

"Yes, somebody here obviously wants something."

"How can you say..." started his mother.

"Mother," interrupted Chesney, "I've been back from England for almost two months, and no one has even made the slightest overture to me. I've been through a tragedy. I don't expect people to put on sackcloth and ashes for me. It's my tragedy, and I don't expect anybody to mourn with me. But I've hardly heard anything from you, and nothing from this one." He jerked his thumb towards Stosh.

"Yeah, well, I wanted to say how sorry..." Stosh started.

"No, you didn't want to, or you would have done so before joining this ridiculous charade. I'm not complaining, but don't expect me to play games with you. I don't feel like playing now, and I've never enjoyed your games. So, please, just tell me what you want so I can give it to you before I have to eat a fish paste sandwich with the crusts cut off."

"You mean you'll do it?" said Stosh hopefully.

"Probably," said Chesney, "just to get out of here and away from you."

"Isn't that wonderful, Stosh, dear," said Mrs. Potoski. "And you thought he'd say 'no.'"

"Yeah," said Stosh, relaxing and reverting to more Stosh-like form, "you were right, Mom. I didn't think he'd go for it, but you said he would."

"What," asked Chesney, "what am I supposed to be doing for...him."

They looked at him as if it was self-evident.

"Why," said Mrs. Potoski, "you're giving Stosh money for his company."

"Giving?"

"Lending, lending," said Stosh jumping in. "It's not a gift, it's a loan, an investment."

"Investment," said Chesney. "You want me to invest in Whoopee cushions, and itching powder?"

"Oh, it's much more than that, Chesney," said his mother, "isn't it Stosh, dear? Yes, he's got dribble glasses, and hand buzzers, and onion gum. Your brother is very clever. Aren't you, Stosh, dear?"

"Thanks, Mom, thanks," said Stosh, though it sounded more like: "shut up, Mom, shut up." He then turned to Chesney. "It's not like that, kid, uh, Chesney. I've got this new line of high-class items..."

"Oh, velvet Whoopee cushions?" said Chesney.

"You little...ha, ha, velvet, yeah, that's good," said Stosh, suppressing a snarl. "Actually, I've got this stock waiting at the manufacturers just waiting for shipment. And I've got my new catalogs sitting at the printer, but, well, it's a cash flow problem. You know about cash flow."

"Yes, you want my cash to flow into your wallet."

"It wouldn't be for long, dear," interrupted Mrs. Potoski, "just until he can get all his merchandize out of China and his catalogs from the printer."

"And then he'll pay me back as soon as he gets his stuff?"

"Yes, of course," she said.

"Well, maybe not right away," said Stosh in a rare moment of honesty. "I mean, once we realize a profit and we've got a little extra to keep things going."

"You're forgetting something germane to this plan," said Chesney. "I'm just a book editor. I've been on half-pay for the better part of a year while I was working on an independent project. I don't know what kind of money you need, but I'm barely keeping my own cash flow flowing."

Stosh leaned back and laughed. "How do you like this guy?" He asked pointing at Chesney. "Can you believe him? Did you forget?"

"Apparently," said Chesney, "since I don't know what you're talking about. And if I can't remember whatever it is to which you're referring, then I must have forgotten it."

"Dad's moola. The dough, the inheritance he left you. You didn't come into it until you reached thirty. You are thirty, aren't you?" asked Stosh before turning to his mother. "He is thirty, isn't he?"

"Yes, I'm past thirty," said Chesney wearily.

"That works out perfectly then," said Mrs. Potoski. "You won't miss what you forgot you ever had, will you?"

Chesney sighed. These two not only had a better knowledge of his assets than he did, but they were poised over them like two buzzards over a carcass. He looked at the anticipation on Stosh's face, and the equally eager look in their mother's eyes, and suddenly he didn't care. What did he need money for? Everyone he would have spent it on was dead and buried.

"No, I won't miss it," concluded Chesney.

"Great," said Stosh.

"You always were a good boy," said his mother.

"I really appreciate this," said Stosh.

"Right," said Chesney laconically.

"Oh, and, I'm going to help you out, too," he added.

"Yeah, sure, you're paying me back," said Chesney, "eventually."

"Oh, yeah, that," he said, "but there's something else…"

"Oh, yes?" said Chesney warily.

"You wrote a book," said Stosh.

Chesney was surprised. "How did you know?"

"I told him, dear," said Mrs. Potoski. "I showed him that copy you sent me, though at first, I didn't know who wrote it. The cover said someone named 'Chesney Potts' wrote it. I don't know any Chesney Potts."

It was at least the third time his mother had brought up his name change. He had tried to explain why he did it. He had tried to explain that he had the blessing of Aunt Elinor, a real Potoski. No matter how he attempted to justify it, however, his mother was still offended by the move. She hadn't been born a Potoski, but then, he reasoned converts were often more zealous than natives.

Chesney just shook his head and decided to quit while he was ahead. He almost asked if either of them had bothered to read it, but he knew the answer. Stosh wouldn't read it on a dare, and his mother only read women's magazines and cheap romance novels.

"Anyway," said Chesney, "What about my book?"

"I'm going to help you promote it," said Stosh.

Images of Hugh Goode's biography displayed in Stosh's tawdry novelty catalog next to dissolving nightgowns and X-ray specs sent a shiver down Chesney's spine.

"No, that's not necessary," he said.

"Hey," said Stosh, "you helped me. I want to help you."

"No, really," said Chesney, "it's not the sort of book that would interest the people who get your catalog."

Stosh snorted. "Duh! No kidding! You don't think I'd put that in my catalog, do you? Besides, they're already printed."

"Then…"

"How would you like to do a book club? I know this woman, and she's got a book club, and they'd go nuts to have a real author show up and talk to them."

This was a surprise. Chesney didn't think Stosh knew any women who would actually read books, let alone be able to discuss them.

"A book club?" said Chesney.

"Yeah, and you know everyone in the club has to buy the book, you know, so they can read it," said Stosh rubbing his thumb and index finger together. "That's a few spondulicks in your pocket, eh?"

Chesney was caught off guard. He tried to think of a good reason why he shouldn't accept his brother's proposal. Perhaps Stosh was genuinely trying to be nice. After all, Stosh couldn't be a selfish, self-serving bastard all his life, could he?

"Where is this?" Chesney asked warily.

"Delaware," said Stosh, "just down the Turnpike."

It might be a good opportunity, Chesney reasoned, not to sell books; his royalty wouldn't amount to much. No, it would be a way to honor the memory of Hugh Goode. He had been thinking of a way to pay tribute to Hugh. He had struck upon the idea of recreating his ukulele act. This might be a good way to try out the performance before a small, uncritical audience. He could talk about the book and Hugh, play some of his songs, and tell some of his jokes. It would be like an evening with Hugh Goode.

"And it's really a book club?" asked Chesney.

"Yeah," said Stosh, "they're a club, and they read books."

"And what's in it for you?"

"Chesney, what a terrible thing to ask," said Mrs. Potoski. "Your brother's doing you a favor trying to help you promote your book. Be nice!"

"Sorry, Mom," said Chesney, not taking his eyes off Stosh. It was like being overruled in a courtroom by the judge. He'd rephrase the question. "How do you know this person in Delaware?"

"I met her in business," he said. Stosh reached into his wallet, pulled out a business card, and handed it to Chesney.

"Francine Bidet?" He read aloud.

"Chesney, I don't like that kind of talk," scolded his mother, "and in a nice restaurant!"

"That's what it says on the card," said Chesney holding it out to his mother.

"I believe it's pronounced 'Bide,'" said Stosh. "She's pretty sensitive about that. She's a very refined lady."

"There, you see," said Mrs. Potoski, "it's pronounced 'Bide.' I don't think that's funny, Chesney."

Chesney shrugged his shoulders. He didn't think it was funny either, nor did he believe that B-I-D-E-T was pronounced "Bide," no matter how sensitive or refined a lady might be.

"So will you do it?" asked Stosh.

Chesney looked at his brother, and then at the card. He nodded. He'd do the book club. Not for Stosh. Not for this Bidet woman. He'd do it in memory of Hugh Goode, and of course, for Hugh's granddaughter.

– 18 –
Where Do Biographers Get Their Ideas?

Standing there with his ukulele, Chesney was having second thoughts. Francine Bidet seemed very pleasant on the phone. She was enthusiastic when he told her about his plan to talk about the book and to portray its subject.

"Oh, that's perfect, perfect," she gushed.

"It's really okay, then?" asked Chesney. "Only I've never done it before. I mean, I've played the ukulele…"

"But not in public?"

"Oh, no, I've done it on stage, in England."

"Well, that's where the book takes place, doesn't it?"

"Yes, so you've read it?"

"Not quite yet," she admitted. "I wanted to be sure you could do my book club first. Oh, I'm sorry, that didn't sound very nice, did it? No, what I meant to say is that I always wait until a few weeks before the club meeting to read the book. That way, it's fresh in my mind. It's not a real long book, is it?"

"Really long?" he said, subtly correcting her grammar. "I suppose not. It's only 357 pages, not including the index."

"Any pictures?"

"Oh, yes, a lot of pictures, most of them are from Mr. Goode's private collection. Most have never been printed in book form before."

"Umm hmmm," she said as if she were weighing something in her mind. "Are those pictures in the text?"

"No, there are three separate photo sections."

"So, it's 357 pages of solid words, huh?"

There was a brief silence on the other end of the line before her voice bounded back with its initial perkiness, and then some.

"Well, I guess I'd better start reading now," she said.

"It's really very interesting," he said, though he felt guilty about apologizing for his book. "...I think."

"Oh, I'm certain it is, Mr. Potoski."

"Potts," he said, "Chesney Potts."

"I thought your brother's name was Potoski."

"Yes, well, his is," said Chesney, "but, uh, my name is Potts."

"Oh, well, it doesn't matter," she said, "and really it's much easier, isn't it? I imagine that's why you changed it, huh?"

He thought of Verity and sighed.

"Yes, it doesn't matter at all," said Francine Bidet, "so don't you worry about that. I think it will be just super if you play your...whatever it was..."

"...ukulele "

"Yes, of course, and I'm sure everyone will love the book and love the music, and I know they'll all love you. Even more than Lewis P. Granthamhall. Have you heard of him?"

"Uh, no, I haven't," said Chesney.

"Good! Oh, yes, that's good. If a real author hasn't heard of him, then he can't be all that good, can he?"

"Not necessarily, I mean, he probably hasn't heard of me, either. Mr. Granthamhall is an author?"

"I suppose technically you could call him an author," she snorted. "He wrote *The Urology Lab Murders*. He writes mysteries all based around different hospital departments. You could call him a writer, barely. He's not a real writer. He's Carol's husband's proctologist."

"Carol's husband's..."

"Maybe he's a good proctologist," she said. "I hope he's a better doctor than a writer, at least for Charlie's sake."

"Charlie..."

"Carol's husband," said Francine. "But I'm sure you're a much, much better writer, and I'm sure you're a better speaker, too."

"But you've never heard me speak."

"Oh, but you're so good over the phone. Besides, a stuttering mute would be better than Lewis Granthamhall.:"

Chesney was about to ask how a mute could stutter, but she continued.

"You're going to be great. I'm sure you'll show her?"

"Show who?"

"Carol! Carol Pollard," she said as if it should have been self-evident. "Okay, well, then I'll announce my book at our next meeting. It's next week, and then the month after that is my turn. Right? Thanks! Bye!"

Before he could answer, she had hung up.

Now, on a Sunday afternoon, five weeks later, Chesney was standing in Francine Bidet's driveway, holding his ukulele. He felt a bit of a fool. It wasn't just the uke, but his suit that gave him pause. It was a loud yellow and black hound's tooth check pattern, just like Hugh Goode used to wear. As was the style back in the thirties the trousers were plus-fours, meaning that they ended just below the knees. Long woolen socks covered the lower half of his legs. Completing the ensemble was a matching flat cap.

"Who are you?" a voice barked. Chesney gave a start. Turning around, he saw a burly man with at least a two day's beard stubble on his face. He was wearing a dirty button-down shirt that hung open, revealing an even dirtier T-shirt beneath it.

"I...uh, I'm Chesney P-Potts."

The man just stared at him with a look that was totally unsympathetic to ukuleles, plus-fours, and individuals named Chesney Potts.

"I'm, uh, I'm looking," croaked Chesney, "for the Bidet house. I mean the Bide house."

The man rolled his eyes. "It's Bidet," he said as if he didn't care if the name were "Cesspool" pronounced "Cesspool." He scanned Chesney again before concluding: "Oh, you're here for that!"

"That? Oh, you mean the book club, yes, I'm the speaker, that is, they read my book."

The man grimaced. "Well, they're all here," he said, nodding towards the door. "I'd get in there if I were you...before it's too late."

"Too late?"

The man rolled his eyes again and shook his head.

He then gave Chesney one more long look and then stalked towards an open tool shed on the side of the yard.

Chesney no longer felt a bit of a fool; now, he was a complete fool. What had he been thinking? He wasn't Hugh Goode, and even if he had half the stage presence of that man, he was out of his natural element. Hugh Goode was unknown outside of England. Not only that, the real Hugh Goode was skinny. Chesney was at least twice Hugh's size. He felt like a hound's tooth blimp in short pants.

"Oh, why..." Chesney moaned to himself. He was about to turn and make a dash for his car when the door to the house opened. A very short woman with blonde bangs smiled and called to him.

"Mr. Potts? Chesney?"

"Uh, yes..."

"Well, look at you!" she said cheerily.

He suppressed the urge to say he'd rather not and crept up the steps.

"I'm Francine," she said.

"Chesney Potts," he murmured, glancing back over his shoulder in the direction of the shed.

She craned her neck out the door. "Oh," she surmised, "you must have met my Barney, did you meet my Barney?"

Chesney agreed it must have been her Barney.

"That's my husband," she said. He couldn't decide if she said it with pride, or cheery resignation since everything out of her mouth sounded like the announcement of the grand prize winner in a raffle. "That's my Barney. He's a plumber."

Her Barney looked like a plumber, though if she had said he was a longshoreman or a diesel mechanic he would have fit those professions equally as well. He looked back at Francine Bidet and wondered how this tiny woman in the financial services industry, standing there in her sweater twin set, had ever made a suitable match with the plumber out in the shed. Chesney looked past her into the house which seem very neat and homey, and wondered if she allowed Barney inside. Perhaps Barney's shed was like some giant dog house.

"They can't wait to meet you," said Francine, beckoning him inside.

Chesney nodded and then remembered his glasses. Hugh Goode didn't wear glasses. He took them off and stuck them in his pocket. His nearsightedness left him with an effective focus of about six or seven feet. This was fine for reading selections from the book and playing the ukulele, but made most objects across the room a blur.

"Well, come on, come on," she insisted, pulling him inside. "The girls are all here, and they're dying to meet you." Then in a whisper, she added, "Except Carol Pollard, but I'll let you know which one she is." Francine Bidet added a wink.

"The one with the proctologist…"

"Shh, not so loud, but yes," she gave him another wink. "Don't worry…"

He had been worried enough about it all without even recalling Carol Pollard. Now he had that to add to his growing list of anxieties.

She towed him down the hall into the family room. It was just off the kitchen and separated by a half wall/bar upon which were various trays of food and several boxes of wine. Chesney had never seen wine in a box before. Aside from vegetable and cheese trays and the boxes of wine, the room was well-stocked with women. There were at least six of them in addition to Francine, all of whom seemed to be holding wine glasses, most of those seemed to be at least half-empty.

"Ladies," said Francine, while waving for them to be quiet, "Ladies, this is Chesney…oh, wait, no, that's not it…" She reached for his book from a nearby chair. "Ladies, this is…Hugh Goode, and he's here today to tell us about his life." She looked up at Chesney and smiled before announcing: "Mr. Goode, I'd like to welcome you to the monthly meeting of the Tipple and Lit Club."

The women looked at him the way group of school children do when a substitute teacher enters the room. They were annoyed at being interrupted, but at the same time knew they commanded the field of battle. Chesney smiled, and swallowed a lump in his throat.

"Hello…ladies…" he said, "I'm happy that you've invited me today."

"It was her choice," said a dirty blonde woman sitting cross-legged on the sofa. "We take turns."

Chesney looked back at Francine Bidet.

"Yes, thank you…CAROL…" She said. "I'm sure that we're very glad to have Mr. Potts…"

"I thought you said his name was Goode," said another woman, her nose stuck in her wine glass.

Francine held up Chesney's book and pointed at the cover. "Yes, well, technically he's Chesney Potts, see?" She indicated the "as told to" credit on the cover.

"Dr. Granthamhall didn't have to be an "as told to..." noted Carol.

"He told it to himself," observed a third woman.

"Is that like taking dictation," asked another of the brood.

Chesney started to explain the process of assisting in an autobiography when another voice interrupted him.

"I knew it wasn't him," she said, pointing to a photo of Hugh Goode on one of the book's plates. "He's got the same clothes, but this one's a lot heavier. I knew it wasn't him."

The women all started talking at once, causing Chesney's attention to dart around the room. He never got out more than half a sentence to any one question before being distracted by another one. Having never addressed or even attended a book club before, he didn't know if this was normal. This coupled with the fact that most of the women were out of focus only added to his feeling of confusion. After a few minutes of this, he felt as if his head was spinning. Francine Bidet, sensing the meeting slipping away from her, banged a cheese fork against her wine glass.

"Ladies, ladies," she said sharply through a frozen smile, "I think we're overwhelming Mr. Potts, uh, Goode...our guest. Why don't we let him have a seat, and he can answer our questions in a nice orderly fashion, all righty?"

"All righty" sounded more like an "or else."

The women adopted forced smiles mirroring that of their hostess, and sat up politely. It was as if the principal had arrived.

"Let's just go around in the circle," said Francine. "We'll start on this side, Janice?"

The woman name Janice glanced at the cover of the book and looked as if she were searching for just the right words to frame her profound question. She looked down again, bit her lower lip for a moment, and then after nodding to herself, looked up at Chesney, and spoke.

"Where do you get your ideas?" she asked.

"My ideas?" said Chesney.

"Yes, well, maybe not your ideas, but, well, to be more specific, like, where do you come up with the characters?"

"I'm not sure I understand."

"Well, like," she opened the book to the first page, "like how did you think up the name Hugh Goode?"

Chesney recalled he was supposed to be Hugh Goode, so she was asking him to recount the story of how Herbert Goodhue adopted his stage name.

"I guess," he began, trying as best he could to approximate Hugh's Northern English accent, "it started all the way back in 1932, I was playing on the bill in a music hall in…"

"Excuse me," interrupted another woman, "1932?"

"Yes," said Chesney, "well, it could have been late 1931, but I was playing the music hall circuit and…"

"But you're not more than thirty or thirty-five…"

"Pardon?"

"And why are you talking funny all of a sudden," asked another woman between sips of white wine.

"That's me accent," said Chesney in character.

"You couldn't have been alive in 1932," said the first woman.

Chesney looked at Francine, but before he could say anything else, the first woman interrupted.

"I meant, how do you think of the names of your characters, like?"

"My characters?"

"Your character in your book," she said as if he was horribly dense. "All of them." She held up the book and rifled through the pages.

"It's an autobiography," said Chesney in his own dialect.

The woman just stared at him.

"So, you want the reader to pretend it's a real story," said another woman.

"They don't need to pretend. It is a real story," said Chesney.

"What?" said another, "Like it's real people?"

"Of course."

"I never heard of any of them," said Carol.

"Yes, well," said Chesney, "I suppose that's one of the reasons that I wrote the book, so people in the United States…"

"What's with the weird little banjo?" interrupted another woman.

"Oh, it's a banjulele, a ukulele with a banjo-like resonator. Hugh Goode was famous for playing it, among other things." Chesney swung the ukulele into position and began to strum and few introductory chords.

"Can you play *Wannabe?*"

"What? Uh, no," he said, "I don't know…is that a song?"

Several of the members rolled their eyes at his ignorance.

"It was number one," said one.

"The Spice Girls?" said another

"They're from England," said a third.

"And they're real," chimed in another.

"Actually, no, I'm sorry," said Chesney, "I don't know it, but Hugh Goode had over twenty top hits, of course, that was before the modern pop charts, but I could play you one of…"

Before Chesney could strike the first chord he was preempted by a spontaneous a cappella rendition of The Spice Girls which drowned out his efforts on the uke. He put the instrument back down again and sighed.

"I'm terribly sorry about this," said Francine Bidet as her fellow club members continued to sing. "It's my fault. I should have told you to be here a half-hour earlier." She pointed at the boxes of wine. Chesney nodded. He understood the warning from Barney Bidet to get inside before it was too late. He also apprehended the meaning of the club's name: "Tipple and Lit." While the "lit" obviously stood for literature, tipple came first, and he surmised was given preeminence.

"Perhaps I'd better just go," said Chesney to Francine.

Francine looked at the club members, now deep into the second chorus of their Spice Girls medley. Her eyes locked with Carol's across the room.

"No, no," she said, "I can get them back. They just needed to vent a little. They're really very nice ladies, well, most of them are. But they don't get many chances to let their hair down…"

"I got the hot tub going," announced a voice from behind. Chesney looked up. There stood a person in a bathing suit. He almost said it was a well-toned young man, but the suit was a woman's bathing suit. Otherwise, the muscular body, the neck-length hair, the strong, insistent jawline, and the severe brow ridge cried out not only was this a man, but a man spoiling for a fight. Even Barney, the plumber in the shed, would have feared this person.

This person strode into the room almost as if she owned the place, or at least had been granted special rights and privileges. She grabbed a wine glass in one hand, a box of Zinfandel in the other, and then, eschewing the comfort of the upholstered sectional sofa, straddled an oak Windsor chair backwards, landing with hymen-splitting force. Once ensconced on the chair, her legs splayed apart in her one-piece suit, she poured herself a generous helping of wine, downed half the glass, refilled it, put down the box, retrieved a Marlborough from a nearby hard pack box, lit it with a black Bic lighter which matched the color of her suit, and took a mighty suck on the cigarette. Only then, having satisfied her deepest felt needs did the individual take notice of her surroundings. Her first focus fell on the singing women, whom she dismissed with a shake of her head. Next she looked at Chesney in his checked suit. She looked up and down him several times, while taking forceful drags on her cigarette, and finished her review by draining her wine glass. Then she looked at Francine, nodded at Chesney, and asked: "What happened to the rest of his pants?"

"Chesney Potts, author," said Francine with an embarrassed titter, "I'd like you to meet Dulcy Cudgel, my very dearest friend."

"I'm very pleased to meet you," said Chesney in a way that he hoped would keep her from beating him up.

"Yeah, hi," said Dulcy, extending her hand, but then pulling it back when she realized it held her lit Marlborough. She stuck the cigarette on her lip and then offered him her hand. Chesney shook it, or more accurately, she shook his hand. The firmness of her grip reminded him of the time Stosh had slammed a screen door on his fingers.

Having completed these pleasantries, Dulcy Cudgel turned to Francine.

"What's their problem?" she asked, nodding at the other women.

"Someone reminded them of the Spice Girls," explained Francine without saying who. Dulcy nodded and then threw a darting look at Chesney.

"Yeah, well, it doesn't take much," said Dulcy. After a deep drag which finished off the cigarette followed by a deep swig which finished off the glass of wine, Dulcy swung a long leg around the top of the chair back and stood before the other members of the club.

"Cool it!" she said in a sharp tone. The other women immediately fell silent and gave Dulcy Cudgel their full attention. "That's better. Now, this guy…" she cast a dismissive glare at Chesney, "…is here to talk about his book. He came all the way here from…"

"New Jersey…" said Chesney.

"Jersey, huh," said Dulcy, with a look that seemed to say "it figures." "Any way he came all the way here, so let's let him talk about his book, so we can get the meeting moving, and I can get back to the hot tub, okay?"

The women sat back to listen.

"Okay, go ahead," said Dulcy Cudgel, pouring herself another glass of wine, and lighting another cigarette as she re-straddled the Windsor chair.

Chesney looked at the women and then at Dulcy Cudgel, who was holding them hostage as effectively as if she had a shotgun leveled at them. While this was preferable to the Spice Girl medley, Chesney also felt the compulsion to finish his talk as quickly as possible or risk the wrath of Ms. Cudgel.

Taking a deep breath, Chesney began a short biographical sketch of Hugh Goode. Its brevity was secured by the assurance that no one in the room had wanted to hear it, and he wanted to say it even less. The women listened politely under the censuring eye of their warden. He managed to finish in less than five minutes, after which, instead of asking for further questions from the group, he merely looked back at Dulcy.

She nodded appreciatively at Chesney, presumably for keeping it short.

"Thanks," said Dulcy picking up a copy of the book, "you know, I almost want to read it now."

"Uh, you mean you haven't read it?"

Dulcy flipped through the book and ignored the question. Chesney looked at the other women, most of whom looked down at the book in their laps. He wondered if any of them had read it. He was about to ask who had read it when he noticed one young woman he hadn't seen before. She was sitting in the back, behind the sectional sofa. Though she was just a blur, this woman seemed different from the others, almost as if she didn't belong. He could make out through his squinting that she had raised her hand, a formality he had yet to observe in the meeting.

"I read it," she said softly. "I enjoyed it very much."

The others all turned towards her with resentment on their faces. It was as if they were being shown up by the one kid who did her homework. One of the women looked testily at Francine Bidet. Francine, in a magnificently schizophrenic reply, managed to placate and chide both women.

"What a wonderful observation," said Francine to the woman at the back, "but visitors really are only supposed to observe, and not...well, it's a club rule."

"So, this guy really used to dress like that?" asked Dulcy Cudgel.

"Uh, yes, that's right," said Chesney. "Not all the time, this is just what he wore on stage."

"Wild," she said, still looking through the book, "oh, yeah, here's a picture of him. Wild! He's a little trimmer than you, sport."

"Um, yes, I know," confessed Chesney.

Dulcy just nodded as though the truth was never a cause for offense. After flipping a few more pages, she closed the book and turned to Francine.

"Well, that's all I've got," she announced. "Bitchin' book, thanks, Francine."

"And we want to thank our guest, Hugh Potts," said Francine with her indomitable cheer. "We all appreciate your coming to visit us today, don't we ladies?"

The others gave their murmurs of agreement, all except one.

"I want to thank our guest, especially," snorted Carol Pollard, "for what was a thankless job that was foisted on him."

"Foisted?" said Francine. "Now listen, Carol..."

"No, you listen," said Carol standing up. "Why don't you just admit it?"

"Admit what?" said Francine confronting Carol face to face, although in her case, it was more nose to chin.

"Admit that you can't pick a book, admit," continued Carol, "that you can't run a club meeting, admit that you're jealous of me..."

"Jealous of you, ha!"

"Jealous that I know I real author, and that I didn't have to go poking around New Jersey for some poor schlub in a funny suit...no offense...."

This last utterance was mentioned in aside to Chesney, who began edging towards the door.

"At least I don't get my books out of my husband's ass," said Francine Bidet. "You don't know any real writers either. The only author you gave us came courtesy of your husband's piles!"

"Shut up!" demanded Carol.

"You shut up," replied Francine, "you're drunk."

"Drunk, that's a good one," snorted Carol Pollard. "I may have a glow on, but at least I don't get totally plastered and start crying about..."

"Don't you dare, don't say it," warned Francine.

Chesney looked to Dulcy Cudgel as if she would stop the rapidly escalating fight before it got ugly. Instead, Dulcy Cudgel calmly took a puff on her cigarette, as if this represented the standard agenda of a club meeting.

"Don't say what?" said Carol.

"You know what!"

Carol paused, smiled, looked around at the other members, and then picked up an empty wine glass. Then, in a mocking tone that Chesney took to be an imitation of the hostess, she continued. "Oh, poor me, oh, I work in a bank, but no one likes me, and I try so hard. Oh, and I'm just a little girl, and my husband's too big…"

"You bitch!" said Francine raising her nails for Carol's throat. Carol Pollard was too caught up in her performance to notice.

"Oh, my Barney's a biggie, my Barney's a biggie, and I'm just a little girl…"

Chesney heard this last bit from the hallway. He had snuck out unnoticed thanks to the diversion caused by the two combatants. As he opened the front door he heard what sounded like a scuffle. Then, as he closed the door behind him, he heard a voice shout: "STOP RIGHT NOW!"

He doubted whether the command was directed toward him. It didn't matter. Chesney Potts was running for his car. Only after he was several miles away, crossing the Delaware Memorial Bridge, did he realize he'd left his ukulele behind.

– 19 –
Support Your Local
Gear Shift

It was a good day, even for a Monday.

The day started well when Valerie leaned Francine Bidet wasn't coming to work. Valerie would be spared the irritating business platitudes from the yappy little blonde.

She surmised Francine had some personal crisis since she was repeatedly phoning Dulcy Cudgel. Valerie even overheard Dulcy telling Francine to "just suck it up."

Francine Bidet's misfortunes were just part of Valerie's good mood. Saturday night was Valerie's engagement party. She had hoped for a big party at the Dorning's country club but settled for a more modest party at their home. She promised herself the wedding would be at the club.

Abigail Dorning was priceless. After Bucky proposed, his mother's anxiety skyrocketed. The girl with the ample breasts and the Italian heritage was invading her flat WASP world and was stealing her son. The poor woman went around with a nervous smile frozen on her face, probably out of fear that if she relaxed, she would burst into tears.

Life was a game, Valerie concluded, and if Francine Bidet and Mrs. Dorning were losing, then Valerie was winning.

About two o'clock in the afternoon, Valerie decided to surprise Bucky after dinner with dessert: a double helping of Valerie Fierro with whipped cream on top. By the time she left the office, she had decided to be even more benevolent, and give him his dessert before dinner.

It was a warm day for late winter; the sort of day when she didn't need the coat that she wore that morning. Sitting at a traffic light, Valerie started to undo her long wool coat when a thought occurred to her. It was a naughty thought, and that made it even more delicious. She would surprise Bucky, all right. She would show up at his door stark naked... under her coat.

Valerie buttoned up her coat just as the traffic light turned green. As she drove, she plotted her disrobing. There were plenty of traffic lights between the office and Bucky's townhouse. Oh, this was going to be such fun!

At the next light she put the car in park, and slid out of her slacks. That was easy. She even had time to fold them neatly and put them on the back seat of her Altima. The next traffic light was trickier: she had to negotiate the removal of her blouse. Fortunately, her coat was roomy enough to allow her to get out of the blouse without removing the coat. Still, it was a challenge, like doing a stunt on a game show.

At the next light, she wiggled out of her panties and tossed them on the backseat. As she did so, Valerie noticed she was being watched in the rearview mirror of the car in front of her. She could only see the back of the driver's bald head, and his bespectacled eyes in the mirror. She knew he had seen enough of her wriggling to rouse his curiosity. What was even more amusing was that his passenger was an imposing woman, either his wife or his mother-in-law. Rather than feel embarrassed, Valerie felt as if they now shared a cute little secret. After all, what did she have to be ashamed of? It was no worse than touching up her lipstick at the traffic light. Valerie looked directly into the mirror of the car ahead of her and gave the little bald man a big smile and an even bigger wink. Valerie laughed as the man grew flustered and aroused the suspicion of the battle ax.

Two lights to go; she could feel her pulse quickening. Fortunately, the next light was a left turn lane. It was always busy this time of day, so she'd have at least two cycles of the signal to execute her final maneuver: the bra. She pulled into the turning lane behind ten other cars. Valerie flipped up her turn signal, and immediately her arms disappeared up the roomy sleeves of her coat. Then, like an escape artist in a straightjacket, she writhed underneath her coat until her arms were behind her back.

With her hands now poised around her back, Valerie heard horns behind her. She looked up. The line was moving. Oh, damn, she couldn't make the light, could she? If she did, she had no way of navigating the turn. Valerie eased her foot off the brake pedal and moved forward, steadying the steering wheel with her knees. There were four cars ahead, now three...

"Change, damn you, change," she swore through gritted teeth. "Yellow, come on, yellow..."

With one car ahead of her, the light changed. Valerie breathed a sigh of relief. She found the clasp of her bra and released it. Then in a series of quick moves and shoulder dips, she was free. She slid her arms back down her sleeves and reached into the coat and pulled out her black lace bra. It was a favorite of Bucky's and never failed to get him excited whenever he saw it. Still, she concluded as she glanced under her coat at her free and firm breasts, those were even more exciting.

Valerie flipped the bra towards the backseat to be reunited with the matching panties.

"Come on, change, will you!" she growled at the light. Now that she was ready, she had no patience for the traffic.

The light changed. As if she were taking a victory lap, Valerie stepped on the gas and roared up the road. Now it was clear sailing to Bucky's and…

At first, she ignored the flashing red light. It couldn't be meant for her. She hadn't done anything wrong. It wasn't like she robbed a bank. Hell, she worked in a bank, and for a measly salary. If anything the bank was robbing her. The flashing lights had to be for someone else. She was just in the way, that's all. She pulled over to the curb.

To her surprise, the police car pulled in behind her. A cop got out and started slowly towards her. She lowered the window. It didn't pay to be snotty to cops, at least not male ones under the age of thirty-five. Instead, she found it was best to play dumb. Most men, especially cops, fell for that.

"Hello, officer," said Valerie raising the pitch of her voice, widening her smile and opening her eyes to an almost painful degree of naiveté. "How are you?"

"Ma'am," said the officer, "do you know why I pulled you over?"

Valerie thought a moment. It was best to admit to something you knew you didn't do. That was usually disarming, especially when delivered in an innocuous tone. It proved to the cop that you were trying to help him catch you. Cops liked cute cooperative girls.

"Oh, is my silly tail light out again?"

"Ma'am?"

"I had that silly mechanic fix it last month, but I must have worn it out all over again."

The cop glanced back towards the rear of the car.

"No, ma'am, your tail lights are fine."

"What a relief! Well, thank you, that's so good to know…"

"No, ma'am," he said, "you were observed driving your vehicle in an erratic manner."

"I was? By who?"

"By me, ma'am. Have you been drinking?"

"Oh, no officer," said Valerie. "You're not supposed to drink and drive."

"Yes, ma'am," he said. "May I see your license and registration?"

The cop leaned forward. Valerie guessed he was trying to detect the smell of alcohol, but then he stopped and looked past her. His professional cop demeanor was replaced by a quizzical look. He almost seemed amused.

"What is it, officer?"

"Ma'am," he said, suppressing a grin, "is that yours?"

He pointed to the gear shift, which was being kept warm by one of her bra cups.

"Oh, shit…" Valerie began to mutter, before she caught herself. "Oh, that? Oh, why, yes, that looks like mine. I wondered where that had gotten to!"

She grabbed the bra and flung it into the backseat, but one of the shoulder straps was tangled around the shift lever. Several attempts at casually tossing it into the back were thwarted by the bra snapping back as if it had a mind of its own.

"Oh, shit," she growled. Valerie remembered the cop, and again raised her pitch. "Oh, these silly things! You boys don't have to wear them, do you? They're just always in the way, these silly things!"

After a great effort, she freed the bra from the gear shift and chucked it into the backseat. Only then did Valerie feel a cool breeze from the open window. This cool breeze, however, wasn't on her face. It was on her nipples. Without moving her head, Valerie cast her eyes downward to confirm what she feared. It was true. Her fight with the truculent bra had caused the top of her coat to open, exposing her bare breasts.

Slowly, Valerie turned back towards the front, moving her right hand across the top of her coat, bringing down the curtain on the free boobie show. She then placed both hands on the steering wheel and looked forward for several seconds, as if she were completely alone and without a thought in her mind. Only then, after counting to five in her mind, did Valerie look up at the policeman. A slight smile played around the corners of his mouth.

"Oh, yes," she said with a smile, "you wanted to see my license and registration; didn't you, officer?"

The cop stared at her. Under his sunglasses, it was difficult to tell precisely where he was looking.

"That's okay, ma'am" he said, "I think I've seen enough."

Valerie could feel the blood rushing to her cheeks. Had she not thought it would earn her a ticket, she would have told him off. Another moment's reflection rationalized that a flash of nip was worth avoiding a ticket. Another moment's reflection more, and she congratulated herself on making a good bargain.

"Have a nice day, ma'am," the cop said, offering her a parting smile. That smile could have been his official cop smile, or it could have been in appreciation for a glimpse of two magnificent orbs. Valerie preferred the later and left it at that. She thanked the cop and carefully pulled away.

– 20 –
The Fennel Deficient Fiancee

Valerie arrived at Bucky's townhouse, shut off the engine, took a deep breath, and checked her makeup in the rearview mirror. She slid out of the car. The satin lining of coat buffed her naked thighs as she moved, making her feel even sexier, if that were possible. On the doorstep she paused. Should she let herself in, or should she ring the bell, and flash Bucky right there on the stoop? Flashing him would be sexier, but then she thought about the cop. Valerie looked to the right and to the left at the other homes in the row. There wasn't anyone about, but that didn't mean that a door couldn't open, and a nosy neighbor's head pop out when she sprang her little surprise. They planned on living in this townhouse for at least a year after they were married. If prying eyes saw Valerie exposing herself on the doorstep, they would have to move immediately. It was never smart to sell real estate because one was forced to do so. It gave all the leverage to the buyer. Economics dictated she spring her surprise inside, even though it lessened the impact slightly.

She slid her key into the lock and held her breath as the deadbolt opened with a tell-tale "click." Then she slipped inside and gently closed the door behind her. With the stealth of a cat burglar, she placed her handbag on the floor next to the door and listened. She could hear Bucky back in the kitchen. Nodding to herself, Valerie decided to keep her shoes on. They were three-inch pumps... incredibly sexy, especially with a naked body over them.

Valerie tiptoed across the parquet floor of the hallway and onto the carpeting of the living room. Facing the back of the house, towards the kitchen, she undid the buttons of her coat and let it hang around her gloriously bare body. She opened her mouth about to call out to Bucky, but instead of her own voice, another sound was heard.

"Buxton, where do you keep your fennel?"

106

For a split second, Valerie thought she was a ventriloquist, save for the facts that: one, she never called him "Buxton," and, two, she knew where the fennel was. Her open mouth now fell agape. That voice, it couldn't be…

"It's over in that cabinet…" Bucky replied before adding the word that made Valerie's blood run cold: "Mom."

"Here it is," she heard Mrs. Dorning say. "You don't have many spices, do you, Buxton, dear?"

"Uh, I don't know, Mom. I thought we did. I sort of leave that area to Valerie. She's a good cook, Mom."

Valerie smiled. Bucky was sticking up for her to his mother.

"Yessss…" hissed Mrs. Dorning, "well, that must explain this inordinately large jar of oregano."

Bitch, thought Valerie. She almost stormed into the kitchen when she remembered that she wasn't nearly dressed enough to battle Abigail Dorning. Valerie buttoned her coat. She would have to sneak back out of the house, get back in her car, retrieve her discarded clothing from the backseat, and then drive around the block until she was fully clothed. Then she would drive to the supermarket, buy every spice they had, return, and shove them all up his mother's rear end.

No, wait, she thought, while it was easy to undress in a car, getting dressed again was much trickier. She would just have to find the nearest public restroom…Ewww… and get dressed there….EWWW! She hated public restrooms, but it was her only option.

Valerie took a step towards the hallway when another noise froze her in her tracks.

FLUSH.

Someone was in the downstairs powder room, the powder room that opened on to the hallway, the hallway she would have to sneak through to reach the front door.

"Wow, that's better!" The voice of Mr. Dorning was heard coming out of the bathroom. "Hey, when are we going to eat?"

Mrs. Dorning muttered some expression of disapproval.

"I only asked," said Mr. Dorning.

"Valerie should be here soon," said Bucky. "She said she'd be stopping by after work. I doubt she was expecting company."

"We're not company, Buxton, dear," said Mrs. Dorning. "We're going to be, ah, family."

Valerie curled her lip. "Yeah, well, I'm not thrilled to be related to you either, sweetheart," she whispered.

"I'm sure Val will be surprised to see us," said Mr. Dorning. He was still in the hallway blocking Valerie's retreat. "And Russell, too."

Russell? Valerie looked around. Who the hell was Russell? She hoped he wasn't in the house, too.

"She's never met Russell," said Mrs. Dorning.

"That's why it'll be a surprise for Val," said her husband.

Valerie shook her head. Bucky's father had taken to calling her "Val." Valerie hated it almost as much as the way he stared at her breasts whenever he talked to her. Valerie sidled to the entryway and flattened herself against the wall. Mr. Dorning was just on the other side between the hall and the kitchen. She could see the door but couldn't hope to reach it undetected. If he would only go into the kitchen she could make a break for it.

They continued to talk about Russell, who, she learned, was a cousin of Bucky's who had just transferred from downstate. All she could do was wait, stare at the door and...her handbag! She had left her handbag sitting by the door. Fortunately, Mr. Dorning hadn't noticed it. She would simply have to grab it when she broke for the door if Dorning would ever get out of the hallway.

Another thought occurred to Valerie. She had half her wardrobe upstairs. But she was stuck in the living room. Besides which, if she could reach the stairs, she could reach the front door, and at the moment, both were in Mr. Dorning's view.

The conversation returned to the items in the cabinets.

"You never used this brand of coffee, Buxton," she heard Abigail Dorning sniff.

"Oh, that's Valerie's," said Bucky. His mother just provided a vague hum in reply. Other brands and products around the kitchen were similarly explained away by Bucky.

"Valerie likes that," or "Valerie bought that," were his standard responses. Valerie wondered what this nosy biddy was implying when it suddenly came to a head.

"Buxton," said Mrs. Dorning, "you don't eat Special K."

"No, Mom, I can't stand the stuff," he chuckled. "It tastes like Styrofoam."

"Then what is this box of it doing in your pantry?"

"Valerie likes it," he said. "She eating it to fit into her wedding dress. You know how brides can get about that sort of thing."

"Hmm, yes," she paused. "So, she eats this for dinner?"

Valerie held her breath. She knew where this was going. She only hoped Bucky could see the trap, but she doubted he would, the poor sap.

"No, she eats it for breakfast," he said without thinking.

Valerie winced. There was a painful silence.

"So..." said Mrs. Dorning, "Valerie stays the night."

"What? Uh, no, I mean...what makes you say that, mother?"

"Doesn't Valerie live at home?"

"Uh, yeah, with her mother and sister..."

"Didn't you say they lived up Kirkwood Highway," offered Mr. Dorning from the hall.

"Yeah, but..."

"And she works for that credit card company…

"Yeah, but…"

"Well," concluded Mrs. Dorning, "your house is quite a bit out of her way if she was traveling from her home to work. It would be a long way to come just for a bowl of cereal. She wouldn't have time on a work morning, especially not with the amount of make-up she wears, would she?"

Valerie gritted her teeth. This evil woman had attacked her figure, her cosmetic skill, and was strongly implying that she had no morals.

"Buxton, Buxton," said Mrs. Dorning with a tinge of regret. "You know how much regard I have for Valerie, but I hope you haven't let your little urges get in the way of your judgment."

"My judgment?"

"Buxton, darling," cooed Mrs. Dorning, "Mother is just saying that you're marrying a girl who, well, I think you know you're marrying a bit below your position…"

Valerie clenched her fists.

"What are you talking about, Abigail," protested Mr. Dorning. His voice was finally retreating up the hall towards the kitchen. This could be Valerie's chance to escape, but she wanted to savor Bucky's defense of her.

"I'm just saying," continued Mrs. Dorning, "that Valerie, lovely girl though she is, had a more common upbringing…"

"Mom, you almost sound like a snob…"

Almost? Thought Valerie.

"Nothing of the sort," Mrs. Dorning continued, "I'm not saying you're better than her. But you do have more advantages, and you have more assets…"

"I dunno," interrupted Mr. Dorning with a chuckle, "that girl's got some pretty big assets of her own…"

"Don't be crass," said his wife coolly, "you know what I mean. I just wouldn't want her to get Buxton in trouble before the wedding and use it against him. I'm not a prude. But this sort of thing has happened before. It happened to the Hendersons…"

"That was their daughter, Abby," said Mr. Dorning. "You make it sound like Valerie's scheming to get him pregnant!"

"Don't be crude, you know what I mean," she said. "Reputations can be ruined in both ways."

Valerie wanted to scream. How dare this woman? She took a step towards the kitchen, but then realized that she couldn't very well defend her morals stark naked. She'd have to get out the door, get dressed and then…

"Buxton, Buxton, dear, Buxton," Mrs. Dorning said in soothing tones. "I forgive your indiscretions. Youth will do those sorts of things…"

"Ah, youth…" said Mr. Dorning wistfully.

"…Just promise me," she continued, "you won't do any more of that activity until after the wedding."

Valerie's mouth dropped open. She didn't know which was more outrageous: that his mother would dictate her adult son's sex life, or that Bucky would be able to go without sex for almost a year. Go on, Bucky, she thought, tell off this old bitch.

"I...I guess you're right," she heard her fiancée say.

"Promise me..."

"I promise...Mommy." He said contritely.

Mommy? Mommy! Valerie had heard enough. Mr. Dorning had gone into the kitchen. She could rush out, get her clothes, dress in the car, and then come in and start to straighten out this family. They wouldn't know she had overheard them and...

The door knocker rapped sharply. Valerie scurried back into the living room, her heart pounding.

"That must be Russell," said Bucky. "I'll get it."

"Hello?" said Bucky as he opened the door. "Can I help you?"

"Hi, I'm looking for Valerie Fierro. I'm her boss, Francine Bidet."

Valerie peeked around the corner. The little blonde toadstool was sprouting there on the doorstep. Francine hadn't been at work. Wasn't that like staying home from school? If you didn't go to work, you weren't allowed to go out and play later.

"Valerie's not here, yet," said Bucky, "but I'm expecting her."

Don't say it, please don't say it, Valerie thought.

"Please, come in."

Crap. He said it. And of course, being brought up as he was, W. Buxton Dorning wouldn't make a guest wait in the kitchen. Valerie dove behind the sofa. She was trapped.

"Please, have a seat, would you like something to drink?"

Valerie felt Francine's butt plop onto the sofa.

Valerie was stuck there, at least until Francine left. The Dornings would stay at least through dinner. While she was pondering these things, Bucky brought his parents into the room and introduced Francine as Valerie's boss.

"Oh, I'm not really her boss," chirped Francine.

"More like co-workers, eh?" asked Mr. Dorning.

"Yes, well, I like to think that all my employees are also my co-workers," said Francine, "but to be perfectly accurate, I'm Valerie's boss' boss...I'm two levels above her, actually."

Valerie imagined reaching through the sofa and throttling the neck of her boss' boss, actually.

"Bringing Val a little work, eh?" said Mr. Dorning.

"Well, yes, not really, it was more of a little favor," said Francine. "I was going to ask her if she would return this to the brother of a client."

What client? What brother? And why did she want Valerie to return whatever it was?

"That looks like some sort of an instrument case," said Mrs. Dorning.

110

"It's a mandolin case," said Mr. Dorning authoritatively.

"It's a ukulele case," said Francine. "Like I said, it belongs to the brother of one of Valerie's clients."

"I give you an awful lot of credit," said Mrs. Dorning. "It can't be easy dealing with a staff full of, well, it can't be easy."

Francine asked for clarification of what her staff was full of, when Bucky returned with a tray of cheese and fruit. Valerie rolled her eyes. He was going to feed Francine Bidet. She'd never leave. No one would ever leave. Years from now, they'd move the sofa and find her perfectly proportioned skeleton.

"You and Valerie have a lovely home," said Francine.

"This is Buxton's home," corrected Mrs. Dorning.

"Who?" asked Francine.

"Me," said Bucky.

"We can assume that Valerie will move in if, excuse me," said Mrs. Dorning, "I mean, when she and Buxton get married, but dear Valerie doesn't live here now…does she Buxton?"

"Uh, no,mother."

An awkward crunching of crackers filled the next ten seconds, interrupted by Francine Bidet.

"But this is the address she gave."

"That who gave, dear?" asked Mrs. Dorning.

"Valerie, of course," said Francine. "This is her address, her official address for work. This is the address in her personnel file, on her pay stub, and…"

"Yes, I see…"

From Mrs. Dorning's icy reply, Valerie could imagine her staring down her son, reducing him to a spineless puddle of pink liquid.

Another prolonged silence ensued, only without the accompaniment of crackers being munched.

– 21 –
Nude Descending a Staircase on Rollerskates

As Valerie hid behind the sofa, Mrs. Dorning and Francine Bidet overcame their awkwardness with each other as they found a topic of mutual interest: denigrating Valerie. Valerie seethed but cataloged every word for future use. Once she was married to Bucky, Mrs. Dorning's days of influence would be over. As for Francine Bidet, Valerie would get back at her sooner or...

Another unwelcome sound intruded. The smell of the nearby fruit and cheese reminded Valerie that she was hungry...very, very hungry. She could endure hunger. She had already dieted down two dress sizes for her wedding. Valerie Fierro Dorning would not be a tubby bride, that is, one with a waist measurement over 24-inches. Her mind was accustomed to being a little hungry. Now, however, her stomach overruled her mind and growled...loudly.

The first churning was so voluble that all conversation in the room stopped. No one said a word out of embarrassment for one another.

Valerie grabbed her belly to try and squash any further outbursts. Instead, her stomach snarled as if it were under attack, this second outburst even louder than the first.

"Clifton," snapped Mrs. Dorning.

"What?" said Mr. Dorning.

"You know what."

"No, I don't," he said, "or else I wouldn't have asked 'what.'"

"You can just..."

Abigail Dorning's rebuke of her husband was interrupted by a third stomach growl, and they weren't getting any quieter.

"You mean that?" asked Mr. Dorning. "That wasn't me."

"Well," said his wife, "if it wasn't you then..."

She stopped in mid-sentence and made a conscious effort not to look at Francine Bidet. You could chide your spouse for being a pig, even in public, but it was rude to accuse a perfect stranger of the same offense.

"It wasn't me, Mom," said Buxton, trying to placate his mother, until he realized that if it wasn't either of his parents or him, that only left the guest.

"Yes, yes, it was," said Mrs. Dorning, though it probably pained her to do so. It was better to make her dear boy the scapegoat than the stubby blonde stranger.

Valerie held her breath, but her stomach still let out with another gastronomic cry.

"No, it couldn't be him," said Mr. Dorning with an air of triumph.

"Yes, it could," said Mrs. Dorning, "and let's just let it drop. Buxton, go get a drink of water…"

"It couldn't be him," insisted Mr. Dorning. "He's standing over there, and the noise came from that side of the room. I know you think he's got talent, but I doubt if he's a digestive ventriloquist."

"You're so clever, aren't you," said Mrs. Dorning under her breath. "You watch all those detective shows, and you think you're another Sherlock Holmes…"

"Yeah, well, I think it came from behind the couch…"

"It's not a couch," insisted Mrs. Dorning, "it's a sofa."

"Well, whatever…"

Valerie closed her eyes and started breathing deeply.

"Hey, will you look at this!" said Mr. Dorning.

Valerie kept her eyes shut.

"It's Valerie," said Bucky.

"She's been asleep behind the couch all the time," said Mr. Dorning.

"That's ridiculous," said Mrs. Dorning, the sound of her voice growing closer. "And for the last time, it's a sofa!"

Valerie could feel herself being watched, but she wasn't going open her eyes, not at least until she thought of a good excuse.

"Valerie, Valerie…" Bucky said. He reached down and nudged her shoulder.

"Maybe you shouldn't wake her," whispered Francine Bidet. "It might be dangerous."

"Don't be ridiculous," said Mrs. Dorning, "that only applies to sleepwalkers. The girl isn't sleepwalking."

"Maybe she's a necrophiliac," offered Francine.

Valerie tried not to flinch at the suggestion that she slept with corpses.

"I think you mean 'narcoleptic,'" corrected Bucky, as he shook her again. "Valerie…"

"Oh, sorry," said Francine.

"Don't bother, dear," said Mrs. Dorning. "With some people, you never can tell…"

"Valerie..."

"Uh, wha..." Valerie batted her eyelids and looked around dozily. She waited a minute to recognize the faces staring down at her. "Oh, my, where I am?"

"I told you she was sleepwalking," said Mr. Dorning.

"You said no such thing, Clifton, be quiet," said his wife.

"Valerie, you're behind the sofa in our...uh, my house," said Bucky. "You were asleep. What were you doing there?"

"You just told her," said Mr. Dorning, "she was sleeping."

"Yes, deary," said Mrs. Dorning skeptically, "you were asleep... behind the couch..."

"Ha! Sofa," said her husband, triumphantly.

"Shut up, Clifton. Valerie, why were you sleeping behind the sofa?"

Valerie rubbed her eyes. She began to lift her arms to scratch her head, but then realized that might reveal her nakedness beneath her coat, and she quickly lowered her arms to her side.

"Oh, uh, it was a surprise," she said with an innocent grin.

"A surprise?"

"Um, yes, a surprise, I was planning to surprise Bucky, that is Buxton," she said. It was the truth. She had planned on surprising him.

"By hiding behind the sofa?" asked Francine Bidet.

Valerie looked at her boss in a way that communicated that Francine was not helping her situation. Francine smiled back, sweetly.

"Yes, yes," asserted Valerie, "I didn't know we'd be having company. I left work and got here before Buxton, so I came in and hid, and I fell asleep..."

"You have a key to Buxton's house?" asked Mrs. Dorning.

"What's so strange about a fiancée having a key..." said Mr. Dorning.

"You have a key to Buxton's house?" repeated Mrs. Dorning sharply.

"Uh, yes, I mean, no, no, of course, I don't," said Valerie. "That, well, that wouldn't be proper, would it?"

"Then how did you let yourself in?" asked Mrs. Dorning.

"I...I used the emergency key," said Valerie. Mr. Dorning helped her up as she clutching the front of her coat. "Yes, Bucky has a key hidden for emergencies, and I used that, and, I...I let myself in. I even...silly me...I almost spoiled the surprise. I left my purse in the hallway. Didn't you see it?"

"No, we didn't see it," said Mrs. Dorning skeptically.

"I did! I noticed it as soon as I came in," proclaimed her husband, who obviously was lying, but just as obviously wanted to be right about something.

"Here it is," said Bucky retrieving her purse, "huh, I guess I didn't notice it. I guess you didn't notice it either, Mother."

"We got here at four-fifteen," continued Mrs. Dorning. "Buxton, when did you arrive home?"

"I dunno," said Bucky with a shrug, "I guess about four."

Mrs. Dorning shot a sharp look back at Valerie.

"Well, there you have it," said Valerie. "I got here about a quarter of four. I hid behind the sofa, and I guess I fell asleep. I probably fell asleep just before Bucky got home."

The others sat down, except Bucky, who stood behind Valerie.

"Hey," said Francine Bidet, "if you got here at a quarter to four, then you must have left work early…"

"I took a half-day, personal time," said Valerie speaking through a clenching smile. Now she'd have to use time-off just to shut up Francine Bidet and Abigail Dorning.

"Now that's settled," said Bucky, "Let me take your coat, dear." He grabbed the shoulders of Valerie's coat.

"NO!" Valerie pulled the coat down around her, wrapping tightly about her body.

Everyone stared at her.

"I mean," said Valerie, "no, I don't want, that is, you don't need, I mean, I'll just keep it on, thank you."

Mrs. Dorning's eyes narrowed, and her right eyebrow rose.

"But Valerie…dear, you said it was warm in here."

"Well, it was, but, I mean, it was warm when I first came in, and I fell asleep behind the sofa, but now, I feel a little chilly."

Mr. Dorning scratched his head. "It's pretty warm in here, I'd almost say it was hot."

"Yeah," agreed Francine Bidet, "hot."

"Valerie, are you feeling all right?" asked Bucky.

"I feel fine," she said, "I'm just a little chilly, that's all. I wish you'd all just skip it. I'm sure people wear coats in the house all the time if they're chilly."

"I can turn up the heat," offered Bucky.

"You trying to boil us like lobsters, son?" asked Mr. Dorning.

"Well, you can't very well eat dinner with your coat on," said Mrs. Dorning.

"I'm… I'm not staying for dinner," said Valerie. "I'm not hungry. In fact, I think I'll go home and take a nap."

"But you just had a nap," said Bucky.

"Yes, but I didn't get to finish it, did I? You woke me up. I want to go home and have a nap. I've had a very tiring day."

"I thought you said you took a half-day," said Francine.

"Yes, well, but the half I worked, I worked really hard," said Valerie. "In fact, you go and check. I did as much work in the half a day as I usually do in a full day, and I usually…"

"You're not wearing any hose," interrupted Abigail Dorning.

"What?"

"Hose, stockings, you're not wearing any."

"Hey, that's a violation of the company dress code," said Francine.

"But I wasn't at work," said Valerie. Their nitpicks were coming furiously. It was like playing tennis against a top-ranked octopus. "That is, I was at work for half a day, and then I was wearing pantyhose, and then I left early, and I took them off because…"

"You were hot?" offered Mrs. Dorning.

"No, because I got a run in them," said Valerie to Mrs. Dorning, before adding in Francine's direction: "After I left work! Now is everybody satisfied, or do you want to call the cops and arrest me for falling asleep and wanting to keep my coat on?"

They just sat there staring at her. Valerie kept the annoyed look on her face to keep any more questions at bay. Now, she just had to excuse herself and go home.

"No more questions?" said Valerie, adding a trace of sarcasm.

"Actually…" said Francine Bidet. "I came here to…"

Valerie shot her a hard stare.

"Never mind," said Francine. "It will keep until work…"

"Good, well," said Valerie, "I wish I could stay, but…"

There was a knock at the door.

"That must be Russell," said Bucky heading for the hallway.

"Buxton's cousin," said Mrs. Dorning.

"Well, come on in," said Bucky out in the hallway. "Good to see you again, officer."

"Buxton's cousin is a county police officer," said Mr. Dorning.

"That's on his father's side," said Mrs. Dorning.

"He's a cop on both sides," said Mr. Dorning. "It's good to have cops in the family; helped me beat a ticket once."

Valerie was less interested in the details of Clifton Dorning's ticket than in the words being exchanged in the hallway.

"You should have seen the stop I made about an hour ago, Buck," she heard Russell say. "It was the funniest thing. There was this girl…"

"Come into the living room," said Bucky, "Mom and Dad are here, and so's my fiancée."

Bucky led his cousin into the room, and Valerie's blood ran cold. He was the cop who got a good look at her naked breasts. For his part, Officer Russell smiled and exchanged greetings as he looked around the room. It was when he got to Valerie however, that he paused and widened his grin.

"And this is Valerie, my intended," said Bucky.

"Hello, Valerie," said Russell. "I, uh, think we've met."

Oh, crap, thought Valerie.

"Really?" said Bucky.

"Yes, I think so," said Russell.

"Where was that?"

In a split second, Valerie realized she was cornered, with no way out. The only decision now was: would she allow herself to be slowly dragged down by this pack of hyenas, or would she go out guns blazing? She glanced at the smug puss of Abigail Dorning. She studied the artificial sunshine of Francine Bidet. She observed the other faces in the room. It was an easy decision, one that Valerie reached before Cousin County Cop Russell could respond to Bucky's question.

"Okay, that's it!" snapped Valerie.

Numerous individuals in the room began to speak.

"No, everybody just shut up," ordered Valerie. The stunned looks on their faces only fueled her righteous indignation. "JUST SHUT UP! I've got a few things to say."

"Valerie, I'm not…" said Mrs. Dorning.

"That's right, you're not," said Valerie standing over her. "You're not a lot of things. You're not a nice person, and that's just the start of it. You're a bitch…"

"Young woman…"

"A Bitch! And a snob. You're a snotty, stuck up bitchy snob…and you've got no boobs."

Mrs. Dorning started to stand, but Valerie pushed her back down.

"You're a hypocritical back-biting dried-up plank of a woman. And you make soup that's way too spicy. And what's wrong with oregano? I'll tell you what, nothing, that's what!"

"Now calm down, Valerie," said Mr. Dorning trying to be the voice of reason, "I'm sure…"

"And this man," said Valerie turning on him, "this man is so starved for a glimpse of a real woman that he mentally undresses me every time he sees me. He hasn't looked me in the eye yet, he's always looking down here." She slapped her breasts. "You want to see knockers, pal," said Valerie, "well, feast on these beauties!" Valerie undid the top button on her coat and thrust her breasts out. Mr. Dorning turned his head away, though his eyes stayed fixed on her chest. After a quick flash, Valerie put her accomplices away.

"Valerie, what's got into you?" said Buxton Dorning.

"What's got into me? Well, I'll tell you what not getting into me anymore, and that's you!"

Mrs. Dorning nodded her head with haughty satisfaction. "I knew you were having pre-marital sex, Buxton."

"Oh, lady," said Valerie, "it wasn't just pre-marital sex, it was wild, satisfying, incredible sex, and it wasn't just Buxton getting it, it was Bucky, and it was Buck, and it was the best he or anybody in this room will ever have. And you don't have to worry about your precious little Buxton getting trapped by the wicked woman, because he ain't getting any more of it."

"Buxton," said Mrs. Dorning, "the wedding is off."

"Do YA THINK?!" said Valerie. "Lady, you don't call off the wedding. It's not your wedding, it's MY wedding, and there's not going to be a wedding, because I wouldn't allow it. You're a spineless, weak-kneed little mama's boy..."

"Now wait, Valerie..."

"Mama's boy," continued Valerie. "I wasn't asleep. I heard you promise your 'Mommy' that you wouldn't sleep with me until after you were married. Well, you won't have to worry about that now, will you? And another thing, Buxton...in bed? I was carrying you."

Out of the corner of her eye, Valerie noticed Francine Bidet smirking.

"Oh, and while we're taking care of business," said Valerie, "I not only quit this bunch of upper-crust baboons, I quit you, too!"

"But..."

"No, I've taken quite enough of your sickly saccharine double-crossing, back-handed crap you little bleached blonde garden gnome. If I had to suffer through one more meeting with you, I'd go into diabetic shock..."

For the first time since she met her, Valerie saw the smile vanish from the face of Francine Bidet. The look that replaced it was horrible, bitter, and cruel. It was as if a happy elf had been possessed by a hellish goblin. But rather than respond in words, Francine jumped to her feet and took several menacing steps towards Valerie, the ukulele case in her hand. Valerie snatched the case from her hands.

"Oh, is this what you came here for?" said Valerie, mocking Francine's usually cheerful demeanor. "You wanted me to take care of this for a client? I'd be so happy to help..."

Valerie flipped the case open, removed the banjo ukulele, and raised it above her head. Francine flinched. At the last minute, Valerie remembered the cop in the room and dropped it on the floor. Then she brought her heel down on the instrument, popping the skin and snapping the strings.

Valerie scanned the assembled faces, satisfied that she had settled all her business. She walked over to cousin Russell and extended her hand.

"Hello," she said with mock pleasantry, "I'm Valerie, Valerie Fierro. And I'm going to stay Valerie Fierro." She tossed a sharp glance back at Bucky. "It's a pleasure to meet you. Now, perhaps you'd like to tell all these delightful people where we met."

The officer looked as if he had walked into the middle of a play that he didn't fully understand.

"Uh, yes, well," he said, "it was a few years ago, actually."

"What?"

"Yes, I was working downstate," said Russell, "in Dover, and we ran a workshop on bank fraud. You were one of the attendees...I think."

Valerie's jaw went slack.

"No, no, it's all right," she said, "you might as well tell them. I mean, there's no point now."

"No point? In what?"

"Come on," said Valerie, "you said it when you were coming in. You mentioned something funny that happened... about an hour ago?'"

Russell looked confused. "You mean that redhead?"

"Redhead?"

"Yes, the redhead that I stopped to help. She had a flat tire. And when I went to get the spare out of her trunk, it turned out she had taken it out to make more room for her shopping bags."

"What?" asked Valerie.

"Yes, and when I asked her why she did that, she said that she didn't need the spare tire because it was flat anyway, but she could always use more room for shopping."

Valerie stared at him.

"Funny, huh?" he murmured.

"But...but, you..." Valerie looked at his regulation haircut and then realized that when they were in uniform and wearing their sunglasses, one county cop could very well look like any other, and this was not the cop who had caught her practically naked.

She looked back at the Dornings and Francine Bidet, at the mutilated ukulele on the floor and at her now ex-fiancé standing beside her.

Valerie realized that her diatribe, while so satisfying, was unnecessary, and entirely beyond retraction.

Valerie's ladder to the top, version two, had just collapsed under her.

But she still had her pride. She hiked her handbag up on to her shoulder, raised her head high, and walked out the front door. A moment later, Valerie reopened the door, walked through the living room, into the kitchen, and then as the others watched in silence, she came back out carrying a box of Special K and a large jar of oregano. She placed the house key in the hand of W. Buxton Dorning and then paused to look at them all.

Then with a note of bravado, she proclaimed: *"Prima I denti, poi I parenti!"*

Then she went out to her car and drove away.

– 22 –
Dulcy Cudgel and the Fetching Foam Mustache

The handwritten letter arrived at Marlton Press on Tuesday morning. It was addressed to Chesney Potts, and it was marked "personal."

"Dear Mr. Potts," it began, "I was at the book club meeting you attended the other day."

It wasn't enough that he embarrassed himself in front of a group of drunken women. Worst of all, he let down the memory of Hugh Goode and his beloved granddaughter. Now, one of them was writing to tell him what a sap he was. Or perhaps they were asking for a refund on the book.

Chesney crumpled up the letter and threw it at the wastepaper basket. As usual, he missed. He snatched it up to shove it in the trash when three words caught his eye.

"I'm very sorry..."

He stared at the wad of paper, debating whether or not to unfold it and read more. The words looked sincere, but that could be deceptive. The whole sentence might read: "I'm very sorry you made such a fool of yourself," or, "I'm very sorry you tried such an idiotic ploy to sell your pitiful book." He began to toss the paper again but stopped. After a moment, Chesney set the wad on the corner of the desk. There it remained for several minutes, hanging in a sort of correspondence purgatory. He returned to his editing. After five minutes, he realized that he read the same sentence at least a dozen times, and he still had no idea what it said.

"Oh, this is stupid," he muttered. He grabbed the paper, threw it into the garbage, and stalked from the office. He was back thirty seconds later to smooth it out.

"I was at the book club meeting you attended the other day," he read again, "and felt compelled to write to you. I debated whether to write this letter, as I'm not a member of that book club, and was there, as you were, as a guest. I'm very sorry for the shabby way in which you and your fine book were treated…"

Chesney looked up from the letter. It was an apology. He turned over the letter to see the signature. "Yours truly, Martina Fergus," it said.

Martina Fergus? She must have been the woman at the back, the one who was just a blur, sitting apart from the others, as if she didn't belong. Yes, she was the one who confessed to reading the book when no one else had. She was the one who had not only read it, but she admitted that she enjoyed it. That must be Martina Fergus.

Chesney returned to the front of the letter and reread it. She expressed her empathy for Chesney during his appearance at the book club, and her admiration for his restraint at their rude treatment. She expressed shock at the behavior of the other women while mixing it with forbearance for their faults.

He read the letter again and felt he should reply to her. Chesney had just fished the envelope out of the wastebasket, when the phone rang. The voice on the other end was familiar.

"Chesney Potts? I was there the other day at Francine's house…"

"Yes, I just got your note," said Chesney.

"I didn't send you any note," the voice said crossly.

"Who is this?"

"I told you, I was there the other day, I got your banjo."

"You mean my banjulele," said Chesney.

"Yeah, whatever you want to call it," she said. "I got it."

"Thank you," he said glad to hear his instrument was safe but disappointed this person wasn't Martina Fergus. "Ms…"

"Cudgel, Dulcy Cudgel."

"Oh, yes," he sighed, "I remember you, Ms. Cudgel." How could he forget the woman with the muscular frame, the damp bathing suit, and the scowling expression?

"Yeah, well," there was a pause, and he could hear half a cigarette being inhaled, "I'm up in your neck of the woods, so, you want me to drop it off?"

"Where? Here? At work?"

"Yeah, well, I'm game if you are," she said. "I mean, I'm not holding it ransom or anything. I had to come up the Turnpike and Francine asked if I would drop it off. I mean, I can drop it off at your office, or anywhere you like."

"Wait, so you don't put yourself too far out of your way, why don't you meet me at this little restaurant, it's sort of a café, it's by the Turnpike exit."

Dulcy Cudgel agreed, got the address and, hung up.

Two hours later, Chesney sat at a table in the Pepper Mill Bar and Restaurant. Watching the door, he wondered if he would recognize Ms. Cudgel without her bathing suit. Though she was ten minutes late, she sauntered in as if she were early, alone, and preferred to remain so. She was wearing a tan pants suit, which though it had a feminine cut, did little to soften the hard lines of her body. Aside from her muscles, he recognized her from the ukulele case under her arm. She was carrying it like it was a rugby ball, and she was looking for a particularly rough scrum.

She scanned the room. Chesney caught her eye and gave her an impotent wave and a sheepish grin. She nodded and strode over in his direction.

"Hey," she said, "I almost didn't recognize you in normal clothes...well, regular clothes."

"Oh, yes, thank you...I think," he said. "That was a costume the other day..."

"I'll say it was."

"Yes," said Chesney, "uh, won't you sit down?"

She looked around the room as if she were trying to gauge the damage to her reputation for joining him, and then with a shrug sat down as if she were dropped from the height of several feet. She swung the instrument case into the empty chair to her right with almost equal force. Chesney flinched.

"Thank you for returning my banjulele, Ms. Cudgel," he said.

"Like I said, it was a favor for Francine."

"You work with Mrs. Bidet?"

"Yeah," she said, "but we go way back."

He nodded.

A waitress asked if they were ready to order.

"Ms. Cudgel, won't you have some..." he began.

"What kind of beer you got," she asked the waitress, cutting him off. After listening to the selections, Dulcy Cudgel settled on a bottle of imported beer. Chesney ordered a Coca-Cola.

For a moment, they sat in silence. Dulcy reached into her pocket, pulled out a pack of cigarettes, extracted one, stuck it between her lips, struck a match, and lit it.

"Mind if I smoke," she asked after the first strong drag. Though expressed in the form of a question, it sounded more like a dare.

Their order arrived. The waitress poured Dulcy's beer and set the bottle next to the glass. Dulcy thanked her and took a healthy quaff from the oversized glass. This left her with a foam mustache that suited her quite well.

"I needed that, thanks," she said.

"Uh, you're quite welcome," Chesney said. "I want to thank you again for going out of your way to return this. It holds quite a bit of sentimental value, my late aunt gave it to me."

"Oh, that's too bad," she said from behind her cigarette.

"Too bad?"

"Yeah, it was an accident, and it wasn't Francine's fault."

"What?"

Dulcy swung the case atop the table, almost upsetting his glass of soda, and opened the case. She jerked her head at the open case while flicking an ash on to the floor.

Chesney gasped and picked up the banjulele. The vellum, the skin that stretched over the head of the instrument like a drum, was pierced. All four strings were snapped, too.

"Oh," he said in a stunned whisper, "my vellum."

"Your what?"

"This part here," he said, fingering the skin, "it's ruined."

"Yeah, well, like I said, Francine didn't do it."

"Your club…"

"Nah, nah," she said, waving her hand as if she were shooing away a fly, "it was somebody else, this other girl who works for her. Still, tough luck."

He nodded his assent while examining the rest of the uke. Fortunately, the resonator and the neck were intact.

"I told her it was trouble," said Dulcy, "Francine gets these dopey ideas."

"What dopey ideas?" he asked.

"Like you."

"Oh."

Dulcy Cudgel shook her head. "Nah, I don't mean you're a dopey idea, well, maybe that get-up you were wearing wasn't the sharpest plan, but no, I mean Francine. She's got one of those complexes, you know, little guys get them."

"A Napoleon complex?"

"Yeah," she said, pointing at him with the lit end of her cigarette. "Napoleon."

"I thought that was confined to men," said Chesney. "I didn't think diminutive women could suffer from it."

Dulcy shrugged as she chugged another gulp of beer, and then smacked her lips.

"Well, maybe she doesn't have it," said Dulcy as if it didn't matter to her either way. "I've known her most of my life, and she always had this chip on her shoulder. You know, she always had to prove herself, always had to rise to a challenge even if it was something dopey… like books."

Chesney grimaced. "You don't like to read?"

"Sure I do," she admitted. "But you know, a book's a book. I like books. I probably read more of them than the rest of them put together, but I don't have a contest over them. I mean, it all started because Carol Pollard got a real author, doctor what's-his-name. Ha! Real author, some proctologist comes up with a book, and that makes him Tolstoy."

"You've read Tolstoy?"

"Some of him," said Dulcy as if she didn't consider it significant one way or the other. "Anyway, Carol gets an author, so Francine has to get one. Just too bad it turned out to be you, huh?'

"I suppose."

"Friggin' Francine," she said, shaking her head, "don't get me wrong, she's my best friend, but what a pain in the ass sometimes, you know…"

Chesney almost expected Dulcy to sum up her complaint with the dismissive snort: "women!"

"Well, sorry about your busted thing," said Dulcy draining the last of the beer in her glass. "Like I said, Francine didn't do it, and she felt pretty bad about it."

"Did she," said Chesney.

"That's not the half of it," said Dulcy Cudgel. "She's got the rest of the girls steamed at her. Some of them probably won't speak to her again."

"Because of me?"

"No, well, yeah, kinda," said Dulcy. Her strong brow line furrowed. "No, well, it wouldn't have happened if she hadn't invited you, but that's not your fault. No, what really iced it all was how it all blew up after you left."

Chesney almost pointed out that the metaphors of ice and explosions contradicted each other. Instead, he asked what happened after he left.

Dulcy emptied the rest of the bottle of beer into her glass and registered a look of disappointment that it only filled it by a third.

"After you left was when the fireworks really hit the fan," said Dulcy. "If you know what I mean."

Chesney nodded, though her mixed metaphors were becoming a distraction.

"She shouldn't have invited that other one," she said.

Chesney's ears perked up. "The other one?"

"One guest was enough, but she shouldn't have tried stacking the deck, you know, with…"

"Martina Fergus?" said Chesney.

"Yeah," said Dulcy through her raised glass. Then she stopped and lowered it again. "You know her?"

"No, but I, uh, I was introduced to her," he lied, "before you came in. It was just a guess that she was the other guest, uh, to whom you were, uh, referring."

She eyed him for a moment before nodding. "Yeah, that's her. She works with us; Martina does, not in the same department. Actually, that's another burr under Francine's saddle."

"Miss Fergus?"

"Um, yeah." Dulcy Cudgel extracted another cigarette from the pack and lit it with the end of the one she had just finished. Then, after an inaugural puff, continued. "Real bright kid. Martina's the kind of easy natural talent that drives someone like Francine nuts. You know?"

"So, she invited Martina…"

"Yeah, so she could get in good with her, you know get to know her, socialize, get on her good side so when Martina went up the ladder, you know, she'd give Francine a boost. Friggin' Francine and office politics, I hate it. Francine feeds on it like a fly on a pile of horseshit, you know?"

Chesney admitted he'd met similar individuals, and then asked what happened after he left.

"Ha! What didn't happen?" She paused for a deep quaff of her beer. "Martina let 'em all have it."

"Did she?"

"Man, did she!" Dulcy ruminated over another drag. "Yeah, she told them off for the way they treated you."

"She did?"

"Yeah, she said they should be ashamed to do that to a guest of their club. She told them they embarrassed themselves, and you, and just about everyone in Delaware. Like I said she was pretty hot about it. I never saw her like that."

"No?"

"No, she's usually, you know, all prim and proper, at least that's the way she acts at work. I never heard someone tell off anybody else like that, and she did without even using a bad word."

"No?"

"Not one cuss or swear," said Dulcy as if she somehow admired Martina Fergus' action without understanding it. "Wild! They'd never seen anything like it either."

"The other women?"

"Nothing like it. And I've seen those girls well-oiled, you know, after they get a few belts in them," she mimed the draining of a glass. "I've seen them swear like longshoremen and fight like sailors on shore leave. But they just sat there and took it."

"They did?" he asked. "Why?"

"Maybe deep down they knew that Martina was right."

"Oh," said Chesney. "Do you think Miss Fergus was right?"

She shrugged again. "Didn't have anything to do with me," she said as if she hadn't been there. Apparently, Dulcy Cudgel, though brandishing a rough exterior, kept a meticulously clean conscience.

Chesney thought a moment and had to admit that throughout the whole debacle, Dulcy Cudgel had been painfully truthful and forthright.

"Well," said Chesney, "I want to thank you for everything."

"Everything?" she echoed from inside her glass.

"Returning my ukulele," he said, "and explaining to me about it all… and Miss Fergus."

Dulcy Cudgel put the glass down, stubbed out the end of her cigarette, and scrutinized Chesney.

"You know," she said, with a squint that reminded him of Popeye, "you should hook up with that one."

"Pardon?"

"Martina," said Dulcy, "you should hook up with her."

"You mean, ask out Miss Fergus?" he said.

"Yeah, her."

Chesney opened his mouth but couldn't think of an intelligent response.

"You're not seeing anybody else, are you?" asked Dulcy.

The directness of the question forced him to admit that he wasn't.

"Well, then, why not?"

Chesney thought of Verity but didn't feel like baring his heart to anyone, even someone as honest as Dulcy Cudgel.

"You're not," she paused, searching for her misplaced supply of delicacy. "You don't play for the other side?"

"Other side?"

"You know," Dulcy made a circuitous motion with her hand, "use your key 'round the back door?"

"Pardon?"

"You like girls?"

"Uh, yes…very much so," said Chesney.

She shrugged. "Well, then, you should ask her out. You're probably her type."

"Am I?"

"Yeah, I mean, you're not drinking," she nodded towards his soda. "Do you drink?"

"No, not really," he squirmed, "that is, not much to speak of…no."

"Yeah, she doesn't either," said Dulcy. She eyed him up and down. "You look a pretty clean-cut sort. I mean, you're nothing to write home about, but then, she's no beauty queen either. I mean, nothing against either of you, but you both look like the type that spends a lot of time up here…" She tapped her forehead. "You know, nice people, but not party animals. You're a little weird, no offense…"

"Uh, none taken, I think…"

"And she's little straight-laced, you know what I mean?"

"Yes, well…"

"Okay," said Dulcy Cudgel, standing. She reached into her pants pocket and started to pull out a wad of bills.

"Oh, no," insisted Chesney, "please, be my guest. After all, it's the least I can do for…" he pointed to the ukulele.

"Yeah? Okay, thanks," said Dulcy. She reached down and shook his hand. Her grip was stronger than his. She eyed his hand for a moment after she released it. "Yeah, well, thanks again, and, sorry about your busted…"

"Vellum," said Chesney.

"Yeah," she said, "I hope you can fix it."

"I can replace a broken vellum," muttered Chesney as Dulcy Cudgel trudged out of the cafe. "I only wonder if there's anyone who can replace a broken heart."

– 23 –
Dork, I Hardly Knew You

Valerie Fierro stared at the phone for several rings before picking up the receiver.

"Hello?" she tried to sound upbeat. It might be a response to one of the dozens of resumes she had mailed.

"Hi, Valerie," the voice was filled with optimism and warmth. Valerie had lost all desire for either. "It's Martina. I didn't catch you at a bad time, did I?"

Valerie glanced at the clock. It was four in the afternoon. She was lying on the sofa. She was still in her pajamas.

"Well," said Valerie. "I was just on my way out the door."

"I can call you later…"

"No, no, that's okay. I've got a few minutes."

"Great, I know you must be very busy."

"You know how it is," said Valerie. "Delaware's a small place; everyone knows everyone else's business. Once they hear you're available…well, the phone hasn't stopped ringing."

Delaware was a small place. That much was true. Soon after Valerie's Monday Night Massacre, she was sure the story was all over the state. She not only blew up her social life courtesy of wimpy Buxton Dorning, his snotty mother, and his horny father, but she ruined her career in the process. She was confident that Francine Bidet shared the story of Valerie's professional suicide throughout all the banks in Wilmington. To top it all off, Valerie cringed every time she saw a police car in case an APB on the mobile stripper was circulated to every state trooper. Today was the first day Valerie dared answer the phone.

"Well, I'm glad I caught you at home," said Martina.

Valerie sighed. Might as well get it over with, she thought. "I…I suppose you heard what happened."

"That you resigned from Voila?"

"Uh, yeah," said Valerie. "What did you heard about it?"

"I heard… some things," Martina finally said after an awkward silence, "I'm sure it was just gossip."

"Well, yes, I'm sure they got it wrong."

"Gossips usually do," said Martina. "As those remarks were not said in kindness or concern for you, I refused to entertain it."

"Thank you," said Valerie.

"I'm sure," said Martina. "You'd do the same for me."

Valerie agreed with her and was certain she would; well, reasonably certain. Still, she couldn't imagine Martina telling off anyone, or being engaged. And as for taking off her clothes in her car, Valerie doubted if Martina ever took off her clothes, even at home, unless she was alone, with the doors locked and with the lights out. Dull people rarely had juicy gossip attached to them. They were just too…dull.

"I saw an old classmate of ours today," said Martina. "Patsy Zyobidinski…"

"Who?"

"Patsy…Patricia…Patsy Zyobidinski?" said Martina, "she went to high school with us?"

"Ummmm, nope, I don't remember her."

"Oh, that's strange. She remembered you. She asked how you were."

"You didn't tell her, did you?" said Valerie. "I mean, you and I haven't spoken for a while, have we?"

"I did happen to mention," said Martina, "that you might be looking for a job."

Valerie grimaced. Thanks a lot, she thought. Sweet Martina Fergus, she was making Valerie look like some sort of charity case, some needy loser. In some respects, she preferred being gossiped about, at least that made her sound feisty, sexy, and defiant.

"What did you tell…Patty?"

"Patsy," corrected Martina. "I'm, I'm sorry…"

"For what?"

"I lied. Actually, I called Patsy, on your behalf.".

Great, thought Valerie, now she was some object of pity.

"You didn't have to do that," said Valerie.

"I almost didn't," she said. "But, I thought that if I were in your situation, I'd probably want you to do the same for me. Well, I might not want to admit it, but deep down inside, I thought I'd be glad if someone did.

She sounded so sincere that all Valerie could manage was a soft: "thank you."

"I hope I didn't embarrass you."

Considering all that had happened recently, Valerie was getting used to embarrassment.

"No, well…uh, what did you say, to this Patty?"

"Patsy, Patsy Zyobidinski," said Martina. "I just asked if they needed a good, smart, hard-working employee."

"Oh, thank you…did you mention my name?"

"No, not right away," said Martina, "only at the end."

"And did she remember me?"

"Of course, everyone at school knew you. She wants you to call her."

Valerie squirmed at the thought of calling someone who knew her, but whom she couldn't pick out of a police line-up.

"It's okay," said Martina, "if you feel funny about it, you don't have to call. Or we can meet her for lunch, or you can come over to my house."

Suddenly, Valerie felt like an even bigger loser. As if she needed Martina to hold her hand.

"No, that's okay, you've done enough. So, uh, just jog my memory. What's this girl like? I mean, from school?"

"Well, let's see…" said Martina, "well, Patsy's very nice…"

Valerie rolled her eyes. Martina thought everyone was very nice.

"…she's about five-foot-four, and she used to wear her hair in a shoulder-length spiral perm. And she's cute…"

"Who were her boyfriends?" asked Valerie. That's was one sure way to remember a girl: by the boy she had on her arm.

"Boyfriends? No, none that I can recall, not a steady boyfriend, at least. But she was very popular. Everyone likes Patsy. She was in the band. She played the clarinet."

Figures, thought Valerie: a band geek. No wonder she couldn't remember Patsy what-ever-her-name-was. The band was comprised of shapeless, faceless people. Oh, of course, they had faces, but most of those were half-concealed by having a tuba, or a cornet stuck in them. And they all wore those horrible uniforms, none of which fit any of them. They all looked like formless blobs. Band zombies all moving forward in lockstep as if they were searching for the lost chord that would release them from their bondage and let them have real lives.

"The clarinet," repeated Valerie.

"Yes! That's it. So you remember Patsy."

"Um…no, not really. But, I'm sure I will remember her, as soon as I see her," said Valerie. "I'll look her up in the yearbook. So, where does Patsy work?"

"Fourth Fiduciary Trust," said Martina.

Valerie thought she knew every financial institution in Delaware, but that was a new one. Still, she told herself, she wasn't in a position to be picky.

"They're a fairly new bank," said Martina. "It's a great opportunity to get in on the ground floor of a new organization and make a fresh start."

"Make a fresh start," echoed in Valerie's head. It told her that Martina heard it all. "So, this Patsy, what is she in human resources?"

"No, she's secretary to the president of the company," said Martina. "She said if you're interested, she'll set up an interview with him. I told her you wouldn't want her to go to any trouble, but Patsy said it wasn't any trouble at all for an old classmate. Isn't that just like Patsy?"

Valerie agreed, but she still didn't remember the chick.

"Patsy said if you want to get into the company," Martina continued, "you might as well start at the top."

Martina gave Valerie Patsy's number, both at work and at home, and Valerie assured her she would call.

"Look at the time," said Martina, "I've got to go, I'm meeting someone for dinner."

"Oh, a date?" asked Valerie, automatically shifting to the confidential tone she used when she was digging for intimate details. As quickly as she said the words, she felt foolish. She couldn't imagine Martina socializing with someone of the opposite sex.

"Yes, I mean, no," said Martina, "it is a man, but I don't know if I'd call it a date, or at least a 'date' date. He's a writer."

"Oh, nice," said Valerie, but only because she didn't feel quite right saying: "oh, boring," after Martina had done her a favor.

After she hung up, Valerie dug out her high school yearbook. Patsy was the last person in the book, as was to be expected when your last name began with a "z," followed by a "y." She was just as Martina had described her. In addition to her spiral perm, Patsy had a toothy grin and apple cheeks. Valerie studied the photograph for a moment, took in the totality of her features, and affixed her own description.

"Dork," muttered Valerie.

Still, it was good to be nice to dorks, especially when they were useful dorks.

– 24 –
The Compassionate
Trauma Fingers

It was a good name, one with so many anagrams. Martina Fergus: Fruits Manager… Fungi Are Smart… Mafia Restrung… Fairer Mustang.

Chesney Potts ran through the possibilities in the vestibule of the restaurant.

He checked his watch. He was early. He was anxious. He hated first dates. He was always so worried about making a good impression that invariably he made a poor one.

He never thought he'd be on another date again. Married people didn't go on dates, not like a "date" date. They just went out. The pressure of the first impression had long passed.

After they were engaged, Chesney hadn't considered it a date when he took out Verity. It was just, well, wonderful.

He wished it was him planted beneath that headstone in Staffordshire. Why had he asked this girl out?

Martina Fergus… Fair Arguments.

It was a fair argument he was having with himself. Why did he ask her out? He wasn't ready. He would never be ready. He didn't want anyone, but… Verity. He felt as if he were being unfaithful to her. How could you be unfaithful to a… But this Martina seemed so kind. Her letter was so kind. She didn't have to write it. And then she didn't have to tell off the women of the Tipple and Lit Club. It wasn't her fault they were the way they were. She was only a guest like he was. She was probably the only one there who had read his book, and she wasn't even a member of their club. She didn't have to read the book. She didn't have to defend him. She didn't have to write to him. She didn't have to have dinner with him now. She didn't have to do any of those things.

But she had.

He wanted to meet her without being chaperoned by a room full of half-sloshed harpies. It was only right to meet her and thank her for her kindness to a stranger. He owed her at least that. That's how he justified it all, but deep down inside, part of him wanted a date.

As he sat there, winding his watch and fingering his collar, he tried to recall what she looked like. He hadn't worn his glasses at the book club, and couldn't see clearly beyond five feet. Martina was just a blur in the back. A quiet, polite blur.

He wanted to see what she looked like. He hoped against hope that up close, in focus, when he had his glasses on, she would look like...

Of course, she wouldn't look like her. There was only one girl like that, he told himself, though he hoped that he was wrong. But he couldn't help thinking about the girl he saw on that rainy London day, the girl that made him go weak in the knees. Could lightning strike his knees twice?

Martina Fergus...Fears Maturing.

Yes, the longer he waited, the more mature his fears grew. It was a stupid idea. What had he been thinking? It was too soon. It would always be too soon. He would never date again. He had his shot at love. It had been wonderful, more amazing than he had ever imagined, but it was gone. He should be glad for the happiness he had, no matter how brief. That was probably more than most people...

"Mr. Potts? Chesney?"

He looked up. There was the smiling face of a young woman. It was the restaurant hostess, he reasoned. She was there to tell him that there had been a phone call for him, he guessed. His date wasn't coming. She had stood him up. She had thought better of meeting a strange author who wore an odd suit to a book club. It was a relief. He would drive back to New Jersey. Go to work every day. Grow old. Remember the one love of his life and eventually die. Well, that was settled.

"She's not coming, is she?" said Chesney rising.

"Who?" said the girl.

"The person for whom I was waiting."

"Are you Chesney?"

"Yes?"

"I believe I'm the person you're waiting for," she said. "I'm Martina Fergus."

She stuck out her hand, he shook it.

"Trauma Fingers," he said, thinking aloud.

"Oh, I'm sorry," she said, pulling back her hand. "I didn't know."

"Know what?"

"About your fingers, did I hurt you?"

"No," he said.

"Did you injure them playing your ukulele?"

"Oh, no," said Chesney, "there's nothing wrong with my fingers. When I said 'trauma fingers,' I meant you."

She looked at her own hand. "There's nothing wrong with my fingers."

"No, no, of course not, or at least, I wouldn't think so. No, I meant you're 'Trauma Fingers.' That's an anagram of your name. If you rearrange the letters in your name, that's one of the combinations…Trauma Fingers."

"Oh, I see," she smiled at him.

It was a sweet smile, a kindly smile, but it was a disappointing smile all the same. She wasn't patronizing him. She wasn't looking at him with the kind of frozen smile one gives to a lunatic to keep them calm while looking for the exit. It was a genuine smile, but it wasn't a smile that made his knees buckle. It was a charming smile. It just wasn't *her* smile. That smile was buried. He would never see that smile again. Still, as one will usually do when smiled at, Chesney returned the smile.

"Silly little habit," he said, with a shrug, "anagrams."

The actual hostess appeared and led them to a table. They sat, and he examined Martina Fergus as she read the menu.

She had a pleasant face, a cute nose, pretty eyes, and the ugliest hairstyle he had ever seen. Her hair itself was very pretty, striking for its dark auburn hue, but it was pulled back with these odd hair clips.

"What's yours," she asked, looking up from her menu.

The question caught Chesney off guard. He looked down and fumbled with the menu. "Uh, I don't know…maybe burritos."

She laughed. "No, I meant the anagram of your name."

He stared at her for a moment until his mind caught up. "Oh, yes, I see…um, well, the best is probably 'Coke Hypnotises," using the British spelling of 'hypnotize,' with an 's' instead of a 'z.' I don't know if Coke has that effect on me, but I do drink it."

A confused look crossed her face. "Wait, surely that's not right. There's no 'k' in your name."

"Oh, yes, you're right. I hadn't thought about it," he said. "You see, my name originally was Potoski. I changed it to Potts."

"For professional reasons? As an author?" she reasoned.

"Uh," he looked down. "No, it was more a personal decision."

"Oh, I see," she said. She seemed content with that explanation, and he was glad. He didn't want to get into the whole story of trying to please Lord Bagnold, of Hugh Goode and…

"So, do you know the anagram for Chesney Potts?" she asked.

"Odd," he confessed, "but I hadn't thought of it. Very strange, seeing that I automatically do it for everyone else. It was a little game introduced to me when I was just a boy. Now it's a habit, I suppose, like I did with your name."

"Trauma Fingers?"

He agreed and shared the other combinations that had come to mind while he was waiting.

"I never knew I had so many interesting phrases hidden in my name."

"Not as many as Francine Bidet," he said.

"Really, like what?"

"Brain Infected, Bran Deficient, Rancid Benefit, Debt Financier..." recited Chesney, "some of those are rather appropriate, as I learned the hard way."

Martina looked down and blushed.

"I'm sorry," said Chesney, "that wasn't very nice, she's your friend, isn't she?"

"Actually, she's more a co-worker than a friend, and I'm sorry to say that you're probably right. She wasn't very nice to you. I'm very sorry you learned that the hard way."

There was an uncomfortable silence.

"But what about Chesney Potts," she said cheerily, "I mean your anagram."

He thought a moment and then grimaced. "Hmm... 'Psycho Tenets,' 'Snotty Speech'...no wonder I never thought of them. Sound sort of like my book club appearance."

"That wasn't your fault," said Martina, "you mustn't keep blaming yourself."

"It comes naturally, I'm afraid," he said and pretended to look at the menu. After a few moments of silence, he looked up to find Martina scribbling on a scrap of paper.

"What are..."

"Shh," she said without looking up, "this is fun..."

Chesney craned his neck over the table, but she shielded her paper with her forearm.

"There," she announced after thirty seconds, "Thy Top Scenes...Chesney Potts...Thy Top Scenes."

He smiled and admitted she had done very well on her first try.

"You have a very lovely smile," she said.

The smile dropped from his face. "I do?"

"Yes," said Martina, "it's the first time I've seen it. It's very nice, very open and inviting."

"Thank you," he said shyly.

He was grateful when the waitress appeared and asked if they were ready to order. Martina made her selection, and Chesney said he'd have the same.

"I hope I like it," he said after the waitress retreated to the kitchen, "I'm not very experienced with Mexican food. I'm afraid I'm not very experienced with most cuisines, though you can't tell that from the way I look."

"I'd don't know why I'd be able to."

He waggled his head back and forth, embarrassed at having to explain the obvious. "Well, I mean, I look like I know my way around food."

"Why would that be?"

"Uh, I meant," he said, "you know, most people think that I'd know a lot about food, because..."

"Because what?"

He leaned across the table. "…because I'm fat."

She looked at Chesney and then shook her head as if she disagreed with him, or if it didn't matter. Did she have even worse eyesight than he had, or was she really that nice? He thought of Aunt Elinor. That was the way she had looked at him, seeing him, obviously, but not judgmentally, not keeping a running tally of his weaknesses and faults. But Aunt El was that way because she was his aunt, and she loved him. Martina Fergus didn't know him, and he didn't know her. But there was something about Martina that made him want to know her better.

"Can I be honest with you," he said.

"Haven't you been?"

"Well, yes," said Chesney, "that is, I haven't been dishonest with you. But perhaps I haven't been entirely truthful."

"Oh."

"But I'd like to be."

"Thank you," said Martina.

He looked down and fiddled with cutlery. "I don't know why I asked you out to dinner. Initially, it was because you were so kind in writing to apologize for something that wasn't your fault."

"I didn't apologize. I said that I was sorry."

Chesney nodded. "Yes, you're right. There is a distinction there."

"Though it was my fault," she added.

"Excuse me?"

"I shouldn't have let it get so out of hand."

"But you were only a guest," said Chesney.

"Yes, but still, I sat there and watched them behave like that," said Martina. "At the very least, I should have gotten up and walked out."

"But you told them off."

She looked at him with surprise. "How did…"

"Dulcy Cudgel told me," he said, "when she returned my ukulele… broken."

"Oh, well, I should have told them off earlier," said Martina. "Edmund Burke said: 'All that is necessary for evil to triumph is for good men to do nothing.' I sat there and did nothing while those women made light of all your hard work. They were wrong and behaving very badly towards you."

"Oh," he said. Though her eyes were both the same color, Chesney could almost see Aunt Elinor in them.

"I'm sorry," she said, "I interrupted you. You said something about being truthful."

Chesney exhaled. "Yes, well, as I was saying, I didn't know if I was just asking you to dinner because I wanted to thank you, or if I had an ulterior motive."

"What would that be?"

He felt himself blush. "I…I didn't know if this was…a date."

"Oh," she said, "may I be truthful, too? I wasn't sure either, I mean about your motivation. You weren't entirely clear."

Chesney nodded. "And that's my fault because I didn't know if this was…"

"A 'date' date?"

"Yes," he said, "and I wanted to meet you tonight, so I could see you with my glasses on."

A puzzled look crossed Martina's face. "What in heaven's name for?"

"So I could see what you looked like," he said with a shrug.

Her bewildered expression only deepened.

He looked at her. No stunningly ordinary features leaped out at him and captivated him. There was no cute little beret, no green wellies, no glasses, nothing that rocketed bolts of lightning towards his heart. But given the same standard which she had applied to him, none of it mattered.

"So," she said, interrupting his thoughts. "Is this a 'date' date?"

"I don't know," he said, "but I know if you would, I'd like to have a 'date' date."

She smiled without answering aloud.

The waitress returned with their order. They started to eat.

"I did enjoy your book," she said after the first bite.

"Thank you," he said.

"You obviously cared very much about Mr. Goode."

"Yes, I did. He was an extraordinary person."

"There's only one thing I was wondering," she said.

"Ask away," said Chesney. She probably wanted to know something about Hugh Goode's films, or his work during the war.

"At the beginning…"

"You mean when he was a boy?"

"No," said Martina, "before that, in the book's dedication. Who is Verity?"

– 25 –
The Porcine Referral

"Valerie Fierro!"

The greeting was exuberant and genuine.

"Patsy! I'd know you anywhere."

That was true enough. Valerie had just seen her photo in the yearbook, and Patsy hadn't changed her hairstyle since high school.

"I don't know how many times I've thought about you since graduation," said Patsy. Patsy started rattling off the names of long-forgotten classmates. Valerie pretended to be interested. She needed a job, even at an obscure bank like Fourth Fiduciary Trust.

"And there's one more name I could mention, but I won't for now," said Patsy with a wink.

Patsy must be referring to Martina Fergus but didn't want to say the name out loud since Martina worked for a competitor.

"So," whispered Valerie, "your boss, Mr. Liverot, what's he like?"

Patsy's brow furrowed in thought. "He likes football," she whispered back.

"Football?"

"He went to a lot of games last fall. He knows someone with a private box. Oh, and he likes steak. And he likes these hoagies that the deli around the corner makes. But he…" she paused here, looked both ways, and continued in an even softer voice, "…but he likes me to sneak them in, so it doesn't look like he's eating them in his office. He…has a Diet Pepsi with them because he's afraid of gaining weight." She stopped here and put her fingers over her mouth and suppressed a giggle. "But you didn't hear any of that from me!"

"I would dream of telling anybody a word of that," assured Valerie. "But, I meant, is he a good boss?"

"Oh, yes," said Patsy. "I like him."

"Is he fair?"

"He's more what you'd call 'swarthy.'"

"Swarthy?"

"Yes, even though he's French," said Patsy, "I think his people come from the South of France, you know more Mediterranean, more, uh..."

"Swarthy," said Valerie. "Thanks, that's very good to know." Going into a job interview with the president of a bank, it was always essential to know his complexion. Valerie stared at Patsy, who was now beaming at her like a Labrador Retriever expecting a treat. She revised her opinion of Patsy. Patsy was no longer just a Band Zombie and a dork. She was a flaming dimwit, to boot! One consolation, she thought, anyone who would hire her as his secretary must be an even bigger idiot.

"Shh," whispered Patsy, "here comes Mr. Liverot, remember, nothing about the hoagies."

"Right," said Valerie. She didn't have to mention the hoagies, for as she turned around, she could see the effect of them approaching in an expensive suit.

"Mr. Liverot," said Patsy, "this is..."

"Patricia," he interrupted, "you didn't tell me we had fashion models visiting us today." He turned and took Valerie's hand daintily in his palm. She was afraid he was going to kiss it, but he merely held it. "I'm sorry, young lady," he continued to Valerie, "but this is a bank, not the offices of *Vogue*."

Valerie just smiled indulgently. If she hadn't needed a job, she would have told him to take some money out of petty cash and buy himself some new pick-up lines.

"Oh, no, Mr. Liverot," said Patsy, "this is your eleven o'clock appointment. Remember? Valerie Fierro?"

He exchanged a look with Valerie as if to say: see what I have to work with?

"Yes, thank you, Patricia," he said, "now that you mention it, I remember. It's nice to meet you, Miss Fierro, may I call you 'Valerie?'"

"Yes, of course," she said.

"Good," he said, finally releasing her hand. It was all clammy now from resting in the basin of his palm. She wanted to wipe it off, but the suit she was wearing was a silk blend and stained easily. As he escorted her into his office, she waved her hand behind her back to dry it off.

Liverot closed the door and motioned for Valerie to take a seat on the settee. He sat cattycorner to her in a wing chair. He smiled at her again. She smiled back politely. Valerie was careful not to offend, but at the same time not encourage him. She had learned the nuances of this game from Mitchell Minear and wasn't interested in playing again. At the moment, she just needed a job.

"So," he said as his eyes darted around her body, "you've worked for a number of my competitors."

"Yes, I was with Magna Card, and Voila Card," she said.

He nodded. "Credit cards, huh?"

She agreed.

Liverot made a sour face. "Credit cards are okay," he said.

"Everyone seems to have them," said Valerie, apologizing for the majority of Delaware's banking industry.

"Everyone in my fraternity had the clap, too," he said as if it were urbane quip, "but, hey, it doesn't mean it was always a good thing, huh?"

Valerie sat there for a moment, trying to dissect his sentence. First, there was the idea of living in a house full of men, all of whom had a venereal disease. This was only followed by Liverot's opinion that, in some cases, it was actually desired. Before she could answer, he continued.

"Hey, I got 'em, too," he proclaimed.

"You do?" Valerie was so stunned by his proud admission of having contracted VD that she automatically asked: "which one?"

"A whole bunch," he said, rising from his seat and reached for his belt. Valerie almost expected him to drop his pants and show her his battle scars. She was relieved to see that he was reaching for his wallet, from which he pulled a stack of credit cards.

"Yeah, I got 'em all, Visa, Magna Card, even Voila...," he shuffled them as if he were going to perform a card trick. Then Liverot returned them to his wallet and sat down. "I'm not knockin' 'em," he continued. "Hey, my competitors got an easy thing goin' with that plastic. Nobody ever went broke with a portfolio full of suckers. We got a card, too, of course, I mean, we'd be dumb not to have one, but that's not our whole Magilla, you know?"

"Diversity," said Valerie.

"Yeah," he agreed, "with money, oh, yeah, and all that other stuff that the government says you have to do with that sort of thing, you know in hiring and discrimination, and all that shit. We're a good place to work. We got all kinds of people here. I don't care what they are as long they got it here..." He tapped his head.

Valerie just smiled. Liverot was a less refined blend of Clifton Dorning and Mitchell Minear.

"Well, Valerie, you come very highly recommended. I don't usually interview people," he said. "I mean, you know, I'm a pretty busy guy. I've probably only done this before once or maybe twice."

That explained his lousy interviewing technique.

"Yeah, well," said Liverot leaning back in his chair and locking his fingers behind his head, "that's okay, it's nice to meet such a well-qualified candidate. So, I hear that you've gotten customer service and new accounts experience, huh?"

"Yes, and a little regulatory compliance, too," added Valerie.

Liverot's shoulder lurched forward into a slouch. "Yeah, well, less said about that the better."

"Did I say something wrong?"

"Wrong? No, you didn't say nothing wrong," he grimaced. "Tell me, will you?" He leaned forward. "Did you like it? I mean, compliance."

He looked as if he had smelled a rotten egg.

"No," she said, following his lead, "I hated it."

A grin beamed from Liverot's face.

"I think compliance is a... a racket," she added.

"Yeah?"

"Absolutely, Mr. Liverot..."

"Call me 'Peter.'"

"Absolutely, Peter," she said. "That's why I was only in it for a little while. I couldn't stand all those petty regulations."

"Damn straight," he said, "they only get in the way of a guy trying to make a living."

"Most of them are just a waste of time," she said, feeding him what he obviously wanted to hear.

"Just a way for the government to stick their noses into the honest affairs of honest businessmen!"

"I couldn't agree with you more, Mr. Liverot...Peter."

He leaned back again and studied her body, though now, in addition to admiring her legs and breasts, he took the time to stare admiringly into Valerie's eyes. Valerie returned the stare. She had read that this was the way two dogs determined which one was the Alpha Dog in the pack. After about ten seconds, he broke the glare with a laugh.

"Little lady, I like the way you think!" he said, slapping his hands together. "Yeah, you got your head on straight. Fierro... you Italian?"

"Yes, that is, my father came from Italy."

He nodded his head. "Good people, the Italians. Me, I'm French, well, not me personally, of course, but my grandfather was from over there. Ever been?"

"To Italy or France?" asked Valerie.

He shrugged. "Either."

"No, though I'd like to someday... to either, or both."

He nodded. "I've been to both on business, side trips. We're setting up an overseas subsidiary."

"Oh, that's interesting," she said, though she really didn't care unless it meant a trip to Europe on the company's dime.

"Yeah," he said as if his train of thought had reached the end of its line. Liverot sat in silence, glancing around the room for a moment. "You married?" he finally said.

He obviously didn't do much interviewing, or he'd know that question was illegal. Was he looking for some action? She didn't see a ring on his finger, but married or single, Valerie didn't want to repeat the mistakes she had made with Mitchell.

"No, but I'm in a very contented long-term relationship with my boyfriend," she lied.

"That's nice," he said. His bland response indicated that he was just making small talk. "Yeah, well," he said, looking at his watch, "I guess that takes care of what I had to say. Like I mentioned, you came with real high recommendations. I just had to meet you, you know, like a formality. You got a good head on your shoulders, Miss Fierro. I'm happy to welcome you to Fourth Fiduciary," he said.

"Thank you, Mr. Liverot…" He raised his index finger. "…Peter. But what exactly will I be doing?"

Liverot shrugged his broad shoulders. "Whatever your boss wants, I mean the person you'll be reporting to. I'll leave that up to them."

"And just who is that?"

"The person who recommended you, of course."

Valerie felt the blood rushing to her face. They expected her to report to Patsy, a secretary? She hadn't expected to start at the top. Still, she thought her experience qualified her for a better job than an assistant to a secretary. Liverot must have noticed the change in her expression.

"Is there something wrong?" he asked.

"Wrong?" she said. "I've had experience in a lot of different areas of several banks."

"Yeah? So?"

"So? So, doesn't that qualify me for a little better job than the assistant to your secretary?"

He stared at her with a puzzled look for a moment before bursting out laughing.

"Patricia? That's a good one, you being her assistant?"

"But you said…"

"She's not the one who recommended you," said Liverot. "That's a hot one! Like I'd let my secretary pick my staff. I don't even let her pick my lunch."

"But I thought Patsy…I mean, Patricia recommended me," said Valerie.

"Yeah, she first mentioned your name, but I don't hire people on her say so. You really don't know?"

He was interrupted by a knock on the door. Liverot looked at his watch, rose from his chair, and walked toward the door.

"He's late…"

"Who?" asked Valerie.

"Your new boss."

Liverot opened the door.

A shiver ran up Valerie's spine. Though she hadn't seen them for years, those piggy eyes hadn't changed; if anything, they'd grown more porcine.

"Hello, Valerie," he said in the same smarmy manner he'd used back in high school.

"Albrecht Eckner," she gasped.

"Welcome to the Fourth Fiduciary family," said Albrecht. "We're going to make a great little team."

– 26 –
The Truth About Hot Dogs

*I*first realized I was destined for greatness at the age of three. And while it may come as a surprise to my legion of admirers that I waited so long to have my personal epiphany, I can assure you that this was the only area in which I was a late developer."

Chesney Potts took off his glasses and massaged the bridge of his nose. What a load of tripe.

He was ghostwriting the autobiography of Gaston Boules, the popular TV chef. Beverly Marlton was eager to publish the book, but Boules' opinion of himself was more puffed up than one of his soufflés. Gaston Boules! That in itself was a fanciful concoction. For a man who insisted on only genuine ingredients in his cooking, he didn't demand the same standards of himself.

"I prepared my first soufflé at the age of five. It was a culinary monument to my perfect wedding of the ingredients into a marriage of delight, the consummation of which was realized in an orgasmic explosion on the pallets of my stunned family. Since then, each meal, nay, every morsel I have put my hands to has been described as 'love' experienced by those who have had the distinct privilege to dine on them."

Chesney closed the manuscript. If this was the first page, he didn't know how he would get through the… he flipped to the end …three hundred and ninety-seven pages that followed. The great Boules had dictated his memoirs on to a tape that was then transcribed. His egotistical style was bad enough, but it was all one long, florid lie.

Chesney had interviewed the subject's parents at their home on the Jersey side of the Hudson River across from Manhattan. While Gaston's mother bragged about him incessantly, his father remained silent. It was only when Chesney was leaving that the man finally spoke.

"Here," muttered Mr. Boules with a jerk of his head as he escorted Chesney to his car, "a grain of salt... about the boy."

Chesney thought that was an interesting way to start a conversation about a famous chef. "Yes, Mr. Boules?" said Chesney, moving closer.

"Balls!"

"Pardon?"

"Not Boules," said the father, "Balls. I'm Balls, she's Balls," he nodded towards the house, "we're all Balls, Gary's Balls."

"Gary's balls?" repeated Chesney.

"Yeah, that's our name, not 'Boules.'" He said "Boules" with disdain. "It's all a sham. His real name is Gary Balls. And all that stuff about learning in my kitchen and making his fancy dishes before he could walk, it's a load."

"A load?"

"Yeah, a load of old crap," said Mr. Balls. "I wasn't no fancy chef. I ran a hot dog cart in Jersey City. We lived in Jersey City. Gary used to help with the cart when he was little. That was his first 'culinary' experience. Culinary crap! He filled the mustard bottles, loaded the relish hopper, and stirred the sauerkraut."

Chesney just stood looking at Mr. Balls.

"Don't get me wrong," continued Mr. Balls with a shrug, "Gary's done good. He worked hard. He did go to school for chefing. And he's taken good care of his mother and me." He nodded at their beautiful home. "We didn't get that off a hot dog cart. And I know that you're being paid to make his story look good and say what his fans want to hear. I just wanted you to know the real story. You seem like a decent sort of guy. I just didn't want writing all that malarkey without knowing it was a load of crap."

"I see," said Chesney.

"It's like when I was back on the cart," he said. "I sold hot dogs. The sign said 'hot dogs.' The people got a hot dog. I don't know what they thought was in the dogs, but I knew. The guy I bought the dogs off wholesale didn't try and con me that they was made of filet mignon. I knew what was in them. I just wanted you to know what was really in the hot dogs you're selling. You know?"

Chesney shook Mr. Balls' hand, thanked him for the real story, and left.

The real story...

Chesney looked up from the first draft of the manuscript and sat there in his office, staring into space, his mind deep in thought.

There was always the real story.

He thought of Martina, sweet, lovely Martina. She was all those things and every other praiseworthy adjective he could imagine. Most people don't want to know the truth. From the start, Martina wanted the real story.

Chesney had almost choked on his food when she asked: "Who is Verity?"

Three little words, the proper noun of which he was unable to utter. There he was making his first tentative step towards moving on with a life without her. He was daring to date again. He had hoped Martina might help him in that process, but then, right out of her mouth was that name.

"Who is Verity?"

He wanted to run out of the restaurant. He wanted to brusquely change the subject. He wanted to give a curt reply that that was a locked room in his life, shut and barricaded, which must never be approached. All those impulses ran through his mind. But then he looked across the table at Martina Fergus, and he saw her eyes. They weren't inquisitive eyes, though she had just asked a question. Her look didn't pry, nor demand an answer. They weren't probing or insisting. He looked up into the eyes of love.

Not romantic love, for they had just met. Her eyes were even more loving than that. Her eyes bespoke a deep compassion and concern and a genuine wishing for the best for him. And not just him, he was sure that she would have held the same expression for anyone who had been sitting across from her. But it was him sitting there, and it was the most painful question that could have been thrown at him. But at the same time, those eyes made it bearable. It was a love that was innocent, and the question was unselfish; she sought nothing for herself.

Chesney sat there for a moment, trying to look away, but at the same time not able to for fear that when he would look back, her expression would have changed.

"Um…" he took a quick sip of soda, hoping she would say something to change the subject. She just sat there patiently waiting.

"Who is…V…"

"Verity." She said it again. He must have winced. Her eyes grew even more sympathetic. Still, she didn't look away.

"Uh, she…she is…that is, she was a girl…"

Martina smiled at him kindly, while Chesney cursed himself. Of course, she was a girl, he scolded himself. She couldn't think I was talking about a pet frog.

"You must have loved her very much," said Martina.

Chesney lowered his eyes, and nodded.

"And she's no longer with you," said Martina, "I'm so sorry."

Try as he might, Chesney couldn't help but start sobbing. The harder he tried to staunch the tears, the more freely they flowed. Finally, when it was impossible to stop, he buried his face in his napkin muffling his outburst as best he could. After a few minutes, he felt the jag subside, and he lowered the napkin to offer an apology to Martina. But when he looked up, she was gone. He closed his eyes, and then felt an arm around him.

"It's okay," she said softly from beside him.

"I'm really, really sorry…"

"For what?"

He snorted. "For breaking down in the middle of a restaurant, for embarrassing you…"

"I'm not embarrassed."

He looked at her. Her face was placid, her eyes still filled with compassion.

"You're really not embarrassed?"

"Why should I be?"

"Because…" he began, "because a guy asks you to dinner and then starts crying about some other girl."

Martina put her hands in her lap and looked down for a moment, as if she were gathering her thoughts. Then spoke.

"I doubt we're just talking about 'some girl,' are we?"

"No," he said, wiping a tear from the corner of his eye, "no, we're not."

"Obviously, she was a very special girl, Ver…"

He started to tense up. Martina must have noticed for she stopped, and began again.

"…this girl. You must love her very much."

Chesney nodded.

"That's nothing for you to be embarrassed about and certainly nothing for me to be embarrassed about." She glanced around the restaurant. "And as for anyone else, well, it really doesn't concern them."

They sat in silence for a moment before Chesney spoke.

"She… she died."

Verity placed her hand on his. "I'm very sorry."

"Car accident," he whispered.

"I see."

"We…" he took a deep breath and exhaled, "we were going to be married."

"That's very sad."

He nodded and looked down.

"I'm really sorry," said Chesney, "but I'm not really hungry anymore."

Martina said she understood, called the waitress over and asked for the check. Then she returned to her seat and reached for her handbag.

"No, I'll get this," he said, "I invited you, and well…"

She put her wallet away. The check came. He paid it, and they made their way to the front of the restaurant. Once outside, he fumbled for an apology. He stopped when she cocked her head to one side, as if confused.

"What's wrong?" he asked.

"It sounds," said Martina, "as if you're saying goodbye as if we're never going to see each other again."

"I just thought," he looked over his shoulder towards the restaurant, "I mean, after that…"

"Didn't you say you wanted to ask me on a 'date' date?"

"Yes, but, I mean, after…"

"After that?"

"Yes…"

She smiled a barely perceptible smile. "If we had gone out to dinner, and I had slipped coming out of the restaurant and broken my leg, would you still go out with me?"

"Well, yes, but…"

"Or," she continued, "if I had shown up this evening with my arm in a cast, would you still have gone out with me."

"Of course, but that's silly, I…"

"Or if I had a scar on my cheek, would you still go out with me?"

"That wouldn't matter, those are all things on the outside," said Chesney.

"And you're hurting on the inside," she said. "Isn't it odd how we can excuse each other's obvious outward wounds, while we ignore or worse, run away from the deeper hurts inside?"

Chesney shook his head. "That's very kind of you, but I'm damaged goods."

"We're all damaged goods," Martina said. "The only difficulty arises when we try to pretend that we're not. We stumble around, falling on our faces, and pretending that we're still standing. And we ignore the obvious, instead of helping each other to get through the hurts and heal."

"Again," he said, "that's very nice of you, but, but, well, maybe it's just too soon. Maybe I shouldn't go out. It wouldn't be fair to you. You shouldn't have to compete against…" His sentence trailed off.

"Would you have said that if I hadn't brought her up?"

Chesney confessed he wouldn't have.

"All right," said Martina standing face to face with him, looking into his eyes, hold his arms firmly, "forgive me for saying what I'm about to say. I know it hurts, but I promise, it will be the last time I will do this without your permission. I am not Verity. I am not competing with Verity. I will never take Verity's place, nor will I attempt to take her place. She was very special. I can't be her, and no one can ever be her. I can only be me. As for you, Chesney, I've only met you twice, but you seem to be a kind person. You have a big heart, and I suspect enough room in there for several people."

"You sound like my Aunt Elinor," he said. "Oh, that's a compliment, a very high compliment."

"I'm sure it is."

They stood silently for a moment. Finally, Chesney looked around.

"Would, would you like to go for a walk?" he said.
"Yes, I would," she said.

♦

Chesney threw Gaston Boules' manuscript, on the desk. It was almost four-thirty. He would go home in a little bit. Eat dinner, and then, at six o'clock as he had done every weeknight for the past two months, he would call Martina. They would discuss each other's days. Since it was Thursday he would ask her what she was doing this weekend. They would make plans to get together. Most weekends Chesney would drive down to Delaware. Occasionally they would meet somewhere in between.

At first, in their time together, and in the nightly phone calls Chesney was embarrassed even guilty to talk about the past, though Martina never seemed to mind. In fact, she encouraged him to do so, but only if it would help him. And though she kept her promise not to mention Verity by name, it was apparent Verity was the subject of many conversations. In time, with Martina's patient care, Chesney found the shadow of the past slowly being lifted. And though he reserved a special place in his heart for Verity, it was no longer a place of mourning. With Martina's encouragement, he recalled the happiness he had shared with Verity Goodhue, without the regret and sorrow overshadowing it. He also found himself looking to the future, a future that included Martina Fergus.

This coming weekend would be a big test of their relationship. For the first time they would be among a group of her friends. She had invited him to her high school reunion. If that went well, he was going to tell her he loved her.

He thought about saying it for a while, as her tender compassion had supported and healed him. Several times he nearly said it.

Martina must have sensed this, and she stopped him, almost as a nurse or therapist might restrain a patient from doing too much, too soon.

"I...I want to say something," Chesney said. He paused, looking deep into her eyes.

He wasn't sure what betrayed his thoughts, but a concerned look crossed Martina's face. She gently placed her fingers on his lips.

"Don't," she said. It was the way many girls might react to a physical advance, and in some ways he felt she would have allowed that liberty over what she sensed he was about to say.

"Don't," she repeated, "not now, not yet. 'Above all else, guard your heart, for everything you do flows from it.'"

He stopped, respecting her wishes. He would wait for the right moment. Now, he was stronger, thanks to Martina. If all went well, this weekend, he would finally say those words.

– 27 –
The Smorgasbord of Disappointed Souls

Institutional casserole. Valerie Fierro looked down at her plate. It sat there in a disgusting lump. It was a strange concoction, formulated from some mutilated pasta, an unidentifiable cheese substance, some vague protein, and a sauce that was rumored to contain tomatoes. There was nothing worse: except for all the other selections in the Fourth Fiduciary cafeteria.

"That looks good! Can I sit here?"

Valerie looked at Patsy Zyobidinski and nodded.

"I brought my lunch," said Patsy waving a bag.

"Want to trade?" asked Valerie facetiously.

"Trade?" said Patsy. "Oh, just like in school!"Patsy looked in her bag. "No, I've got a cupcake for dessert. I couldn't trade that. We had casserole like that in school."

"Could be the same one."

Patsy looked at Valerie's plate. She shook her head before realizing Valerie was joking and then laughed.

"Isn't this fun?" said Patsy.

Valerie agreed it was a veritable carnival, and took a forkful of casserole. She stared at the plate and shook her head. "I must need an eye check-up. Everything's blurry from a few feet away."

"Maybe you need glasses," said Patsy.

Valerie shot her a nasty look. Glasses? If anything, she'd get contacts. Or, she'd just not see clearly. But glasses? Never.

"My sister got glasses," said Patsy, "but only because she needed them," said Patsy. "Otherwise, she wouldn't have. She likes them."

"Oh, do they flatter her face?"

Patsy thought a moment then shook her head. Her hair danced around her ears, like dead leaves around an abandoned house on a windy day.

"No, not really, but she couldn't get contact lenses. I'm not sure why. Maybe her eyeballs are too big."

Another few moments of silence ensued.

"Did you get your invitation? I got mine," chirped Patsy.

"My invitation to what?"

"Our high school reunion."

Valerie grimaced.

"Weren't you helping Martina with that?" asked Patsy.

"Sort of," said Valerie. "At the start."

"Well, it's going to be a big shindig," said Patsy. Valerie marveled at how anyone could not only use the word "shindig," but do so with joyful expectation. There was only one word that would have been worse.

"Yes, a real big wingding!"

That was the other word.

"Martina's really done a super job planning it," said Patsy. "We're having it at the Elsmere Fire Hall. I expect everyone will be there."

Not me, thought Valerie. She vaguely recalled seeing the outside of the invitation before throwing it away.

"You're going, aren't you?" repeated Patsy.

"Of course she is," said a voice from behind.

Valerie cringed and turned around. There holding a lunch tray was her boss, Albrecht Eckner. Valerie would have asked how long he had been standing there. He'd never tell for fears that he would reveal his trade secret for slithering.

"Ladies," said Albrecht in a catty voice, and sat down, "I don't need an invitation, do I?"

"Didn't you get one?" asked Patsy, "I addressed them myself. I put the stamps on them, too."

"He meant an invitation to sit down, Patsy," said Valerie.

"Oh."

"I hope," said Albrecht eyeing Patsy while he prodded his salad, "I hope you didn't address those on company time and using the bank's stamps."

Patsy's mouth dropped open. "I would never do that!   That wouldn't be fair to Mr. Liverot, and besides which it wouldn't be nice either!"

"Patsy," said Valerie, "he's kidding."

"That wasn't funny," said Patsy. "I stayed up all night finishing those."

"Didn't Martina Fergus help you?" asked Albrecht.

It sounded like an innocent question, but Valerie had learned that Albrecht never asked an innocent question. He was always digging for information, which he then churned into gossip. Pumping Patsy for gossip was like teasing a puppy.

"Oh, yes, well, she's running most of the reunion," said Patsy, "but she's been a little busy lately." Patsy suppressed a giggle. Albrecht's right eyebrow rose almost imperceptibly.

"Busy?" said Albrecht pretending to be interested in his lunch, "oh, yes, she's very busy with her career, I imagine."

Patsy smiled. "No, Martina's got a boyfriend."

This was the sort of dirt that piqued Albrecht's interest. "A boyfriend?" he smiled. "Our Martina?"

Valerie rolled her eyes.

"Tell us all about him," whispered Albrecht. "I'm sure Valerie wants to know, don't you, Valerie?"

Valerie glowered at him. She wasn't in the mood to hear about anyone's love life, especially not Martina's.

"I've never met him," said Patsy, "and I don't know anything about him, only he's from New Jersey."

"All the way from there," said Albrecht nibbling on the morsel of information. "Did you hear that, Valerie?"

"Yeah, New Jersey, great," said Valerie.

"And he writes...like books," said Patsy.

"Really?" said Albrecht feigning fascination.

"Oh, yes, and Martina likes him very much. She says he's very sweet."

"Oh, I'm sure he is," said Albrecht with a prissy smirk. "And that's just what Martina deserves, isn't it, Valerie?"

"Sure," muttered Valerie.

Albrecht smiled and turned back to Patsy. "And are we going to meet this sweet boy at the reunion?"

A puzzled look overspread Patsy's visage. "Gee, I don't know."

"Oh, well, it doesn't matter, does it?" It was Albrecht Eckner at his most cheerily patronizing.

Valerie looked at Albrecht Eckner and then at the casserole. She didn't know which turned her stomach more. "I've got to get back to work," she said and excused herself.

As she returned to her desk, Valerie replayed the conversation in her mind. The only thing worse than Patsy's peculiar optimism was Albrecht's cynical imitation of it. He delighted in holding up a flexible mirror to everyone. At first, it only slightly distorted reality as he won people's confidence. Then, for his own amusement, he would twist and pervert their image into one closer to his own. The worst part was that Albrecht knew Valerie saw the game he was playing. He would give little conspiratorial glances and subtle nods, as if to say: "come on, it's fun, you can play, too." She never did, well hardly ever; it was difficult with Albrecht Eckner to resist at times. He was so slick, so accomplished at steering conversations, like some talk show host for moral degenerates.

She sat at her desk and looked at the pile of boring compliance work. Neither Albrecht nor Peter Liverot held a high priority on government regulations. Consequently, Valerie didn't have to work very hard. Her main chore was staying in her boss' good graces.

"You left lunch rather early."

Albrecht was standing over her desk, smiling.

"I was done," she said.

"You didn't finish your lunch."

Valerie pretended to read the latest FDIC update.

"It wasn't very appetizing," she said.

He nodded towards the door. "Wanna go get something? My treat?"

"No, thanks," said Valerie. "I've got all this to go through."

"Oh, come on," he said. We can go to the mall. You can get a pretzel or a smoothie, we'll walk around."

"I don't know…"

"Peter's up at a board meeting with his 'investors' this afternoon," he said. "I can always call it a team-building exercise."

She looked at him in disbelief. "Team-building? Just the two of us?"

"Small team," he said with a shrug. "Yeah, come on," he smiled. "You haven't really had anything to eat. And you're getting too thin."

"Excuse me?"

"Yeah, you need a little meat on you," he said with a mock sassiness, "I like you like that, with a little extra upholstery in those bottom cushions."

"I've got work to do," she said coldly. She looked down and tried to read the report in front of her.

Albrecht rarely left anyone on bad terms. If he offended anyone, he would feign shock that he had been misunderstood and apologize. With those closest to him, he would wait a moment and pretend the previous words hadn't been spoken.

"Looking forward to the great reunion?" he said with a smirk and a roll of his eyes.

"I don't know," she said.

"It'll be a hoot," he said. "I mean the Elsmere Fire Hall? And what kind of party would be thrown by Martina Fergus and Patsy Zyobidinski?" He made another mocking expression that was genuinely funny. Valerie laughed. "They'll probably serve cold pizza washed down with non-alcoholic beer. And you'll get to see all the former size sixes and eights now at least up to size fourteens and sixteens, trying to squeeze into size tens and twelves."

Albrecht was the only man she knew that understood women's fashion and wasn't embarrassed to admit it.

"And all the former jocks trying to hold up their sagging biceps and the beer bellies, trying to arrange their hair to conceal their bald spots!"

Albrecht noticed her looking at his own paunch.

"I may not have been an Adonis in high school, but at least I'm consistent," he said proudly. "I'm the same puffy size I was back then, and I have all my hair. You really should go."

"It could be interesting," said Valerie.

Albrecht snorted derisively. "Interesting, oh, you're too nice! It will be the hoot of the year, a hoot-and-a-half."

Valerie smiled and nodded. "It would be funny to see how everyone turned out ten years later."

"Funny? It will be delicious," said Albrecht. He was practically drooling over the prospect of feeding on the roomful of disappointed dreams and shattered aspirations. "How ironic that the people that usually put these affairs together are the biggest losers of all."

Valerie thought a moment. "I wouldn't exactly call Patsy and Martina losers."

Albrecht flipped his hand at her as if he were swatting away her argument. "Please! Patsy Zyobidinski. A secretary…"

"Administrative assistant… to a bank president," interjected Valerie. "And Martina is now a senior manager at Voila."

"Again…Voila? Do you have a Voila Card?"

Valerie admitted she did.

"Let me restate that," he said, "would you have a Voila Card if you hadn't worked there? And those two are the best of the lot. Can you think of anyone else who has done well since high school? Present company excluded, of course. It'll be a load of laughs," assured Albrecht, before adding: "just like reliving the prom."

Their eyes met for a moment in silent combat.

"Yes," said Valerie, with a smile just too sweet for him to ignore, "I'd love to go to the reunion. It will be fun reliving it all. Won't it?"

– 28 –
A Second Chance at
Frozen Pizza

The Fergus' house always made Chesney uneasy. Martina couldn't help that her parents built their home on the edge of a marsh.

"It's Eden," Martina had told her the first time he had picked her up there.

Chesney looked at the patchwork ranch house in its fetid setting and smiled politely.

"You don't get it, do you?" She nudged his arm.

He stared at her blankly.

"*Martin Chuzzlewitt?*" She asked with a laugh. "That was always my favorite Dickens novel."

"Oh, yes," agreed Chesney, though it was an obscure choice. He had read it but didn't recall much of it. He couldn't help thinking of Mr. Postlewaite back in England, who had appropriated Chuzzlewitt to be the imaginary partner in his shop. "Yes, *Martin Chuzzlewitt*, all about greed and Pecksniff and all that."

"And Eden," she continued. "When Martin goes to America and buys land in a place called 'Eden,' and it turns out to be a swamp."

He nodded. "Oh, right, the marsh. Yes, Eden, of course."

"I first read that book when I was twelve, and I imagined I was Martin," she continued. "You know Martin, Martina, and my middle initial is 'C.'"

"Not for Chuzzlewitt?"

Martina laughed. "No, for 'Christine,' but I used to pretend it was for 'Chuzzlewitt.' It's a lovely middle name, isn't it? A bit silly, but it's nice to have a middle name that's a bit silly, isn't it? You can use just the initial most of the time, for serious matters, but then you know you've got a silly little secret there hiding between your first and last names."

Chesney saw her in a fresh light. Until then, she had just been a kind girl who patiently listened to him pour out his broken heart and help heal it.

"I've never told anyone that before," she confessed.

"After all I've burdened you with, I'm honored that you shared that with me."

"You're welcome," she said and gave him a peck on the cheek. "And besides, you're not a burden. But still, don't tell too many people about Chuzzlewitt and me."

He looked in her eyes and understood. It wasn't embarrassing, just personal.

"I won't tell a soul," he vowed.

That was the first time he thought that Martina might fill the hole that Verity had left in his heart. Martina couldn't replace her. No one could, and it was Martina who had told him as much. But Martina might fit very well into his heart. He hoped he would be able to do the same for her.

These thoughts were running through his head as he picked her up the night of her high school reunion. Tonight he planned to tell her he loved her. Given Martina's serious approach to love, that was tantamount to a proposal of marriage.

She met him at the door with her wrap over her arm. "I'd invite you in, but there's grease all over the living room. Billy's got a double order, and the overflow went into the living room. Mother's fit to be tied."

Chesney nodded. Martina's brother had a home-based business repairing Yugos in the garage.

"He would have put it all in one of father's sheds," she said as he helped her on with her wrap, "but they're always filled, you know."

Chesney agreed. Mr. Fergus' hobby was building sheds out of odd bits of lumber and other found building materials. The new material would invariably go into one of the existing sheds until they could be used to construct another shed. That new shed would be appropriated for more odd bits of material.

"Mother warned Billy that if any of his carburetors chipped any of her collection, well…she didn't say what she would do, but she warned him, all the same."

It all made perfect sense to Chesney, now at least. Mrs. Fergus collected novelty cookie jars that were displayed throughout the living room. It seemed everyone in the Fergus home had a strange hobby except Martina. Perhaps her hobby was collecting odd relatives with weird hobbies. He also wondered if that was why she was so tolerant of his foibles.

Chesney escorted Martina to the car and opened the door for her, and they rode away. Martina was silent as they drove. Martina wasn't a chatty person, but given the importance of tonight, her silence preyed on his mind.

"Heh, heh," he said nervously, "I bet you're excited."

"Excited?" she said, "Excited about what?"

"You know, about the reunion and seeing all your old friends, heh, heh." He bit his lip. His anxiety was making him pretend to be amused by the mundane conversation.

"Yes, well," Martina said, "it's been a lot of work. I only hope everyone has a good time."

"Heh, yeah," he said, "uh, I mean, I'm really excited."

"Oh? Why is that?"

"Uh, well, heh, heh, I'm looking forward to meeting...all your old friends."

"Oh," she said, "I thought it would be boring for you."

"Uh, no," said Chesney, "why?"

"It's just that you don't know any of these people. And since I'm on the committee, I'll expect I'll be pretty busy. And then there will be all my old friends..."

Martina's last sentence drifted off.

"Old friends?" he said. "I suppose you'll want to see them all after all these years."

"Yes, I suppose," she said another sentence half-spoken.

"Yes, I can see that," he said after another interval.

"Turn up here. Here's the fire hall," said Martina before hurriedly blurting out. "I need to tell you something."

He parked the car and turned off the engine.

Chesney turned to her. She looked anxious.

They exchanged tense smiles.

"I'm nervous, and you're nervous," he said. "And, you've been great, more than great, you've been wonderful these past months. You've really helped me talk about my past. But you've hardly talked about your past. And now you're actually taking me to that past. Is that what's making you a little anxious?"

Martina looked down. The indirect lighting of the parking lot put her face in the shadows.

"Yes, that's most of it," she said quietly.

"I just want you to know," he started and then paused. The hairs on the back of his neck were tingling. The words "I love you" were waiting on his lips. "I..."

"I wanted you to know," she blurted before he continued, "that you'll meet a lot of people here tonight, most of whom I liked very much, and some..."

"That you didn't like?" he guessed, filling in her pause, though he couldn't imagine Martina disliking anyone.

"No," she said, "I...well, I'm not quite sure what I mean."

"Oh." Chesney sat for a moment in the dark. For months he had rambled on and on about his past, about his tragic love life, but he had never bothered to ask Martina about her experiences. He had treated her as if she had been a newly minted person the day he met her. How stupid could he be?

"I suppose what I'm trying to say," she began gingerly, "is that there are people here whom I liked very much, and some whom I liked very much who… aren't here…"

"Oh, " he said. Maybe Martina had lost someone, or at least they weren't going to be there tonight.

Martina reached out and gently touched his hand.

"We don't have to go in," she said.

Chesney almost said, "Good." He almost reached for the key to turn on the car. But then he thought about Verity Goodhue, and frozen French bread pizza. He thought about the time she had wanted to buy it in the grocery store, and he had said he wanted something else. And then a few weeks later she was dead. He recalled what Li Gao said: that love meant dying a little to ourselves and giving of ourselves to the one we loved. He thought about Aunt Elinor and the sacrifices that she must have made for him because she loved him. As much as he was afraid of walking into Martina's past, not doing so would be selfish. If he wanted to say, "I love you," he would first need to live, "I love you."

"Do you want to go? Is…is that what you really want to do?" He asked her.

Martina's eyes glistened in the pale light.

"I'd like to go in," she said softly, "but I don't want to if you'll be uncomfortable."

She turned away, and as she did, Chesney imagined at least two other women who could have been sitting there.

"No, of course not," he said. At first he was trying to sound brave, but as he spoke, he felt a genuine courage rising in his voice. "I want to do what you want to do."

She looked up at him and smiled tentatively.

"You won't feel uncomfortable?"

Chesney laughed. "I'd feel uncomfortable if I didn't feel uncomfortable. When you play the ukulele, you've got a head start on being a little odd. Besides, meeting new people is…" he wanted to say "frightening," but substituted "…fun. Just think of all the new anagrams."

Martina smiled.

"Thank you," she said and leaned over to kiss his cheek. "You're a very nice person, Chesney Potts."

"Let's go in," he said.

– 29 –
Of Giant Squid and Dragon Bites

Chesney's newfound bravery evaporated as soon as the first wave of former classmates engulfed Martina. He wondered which ones were ex-boyfriends. Which were his rivals? He also couldn't help wondering about the ghosts of those who were absent.

Chesney wanted to run, but when he saw how much Martina was enjoying herself, he took a deep breath and concentrated on her happiness.

The names started to run together as he was introduced to person after person. Almost every sentence seemed to begin with: "remember when..." Those which didn't started with: "I used to be..."

Martina was quick to introduce Chesney, though not many people were interested in him.

"Oh, Patsy," said Martina to a girl with a toothy smile who worked her way through the crowd, "Patsy, this is Chesney."

Chesney started to say hello, but the girl ignored him and pulled on Martina's arm.

"Martina, it's the DJ," cried Patsy. "The DJ!"

"Didn't he get here," said Martina.

"Oh, he's here, but he won't play," said Patsy. "He wants to get paid. He came in and set up his turntables and his glitter ball and everything, but he said that he wasn't going to start until he got paid."

"But we gave him a deposit," said Martina.

"Yes, but he said the hall was haunted by Moose."

"Moose?"

Patsy placed her hands on either side of her head to approximate antlers. "The Moose, you know, the Moose Lodge. The last time he spun records here was for a Moose dance, and he said the Moose shorted him. I told him we're not Moose, but he wants all of his money before he'll start."

"It's all right, Patsy. Where is he?" she asked.

"Up in front. He's the one sitting on top of that strobe light that isn't strobing."

"I'll talk with him," said Martina. She looked at Chesney. "Excuse me... Patsy, will you entertain Chesney, please?"

Patsy looked at Chesney now that the weight of the recalcitrant disc jockey was removed from her shoulders.

"Hello," she said, and then did a double-take, looked at Martina, then back at Chesney, and then at Martina. Each turn of her head seemed to broaden her grin. "Oh, yes, thank you, I'll take care of Chesney."

As he stood there, Patsy seemed to be studying him.

"So, you went to school with Martina," he said. Though that was obvious. He couldn't think of anything else to say.

"Oh, yes," said Patsy, "all four years of high school, and junior high before that, and grade school."

Chesney glanced at her name badge. "Zyobidinski?"

"Oh, yes, right," she exclaimed. "You said that very well!"

"It's not that difficult," he said. "Z-y-o-b-i-d-i-n-s-k-i... Zyobidinski. Besides, I'm Polish, too."

Patsy read his name badge. "Potts? That's not very Polish."

"No, you're right, it isn't. I...well, it was shortened. It used to be Potoski."

"Yes, that's Polish!"

"Yes, it is, uh, was," said Chesney. He stood silently as she stared at him. "So, Patsy," he said, "what do you do for a living?"

"I work for Mr. Liverot," she said.

"Oh, like the cheese?"

"Cheese? No, he's a man," said Patsy.

"No, I meant, Liverot is a type of French cheese."

"It is? Ha! Well, I am surprised. You think you know someone! I've been working for Mr. Liverot for five years now, and I just thought his name meant 'Mr. Liverot.' Wait until I tell him he's really a cheese. Isn't that funny. I wonder if he knows it."

"I would think he does," he said. "It is his name, after all."

"I don't know what Zyobidinski means. Do you?"

Chesney admitted that he didn't.

"Maybe," said Patsy, "maybe 'Zyobidinski' is a cheese, too, only in Polish. Wouldn't that be a funny coincidence?"

"Yes, I suppose so," said Chesney and started looking around for Martina. "Well, what sort of work do you do for Mr. Liverot?"

"I'm his administrative assistant," she beamed, before adding in a whisper: "That's a secretary."

"I see." He imagined Patsy answering the phone for a plumber or building supplier.

"He's the president of the bank," she said.

"Oh, you don't work with Martina, do you?"

"Yes, I don't," agreed Patsy. "I work at Fourth Fiduciary Trust."

"It must be very interesting," said Chesney.

"Actually, it's a lot of things that I don't understand," she said crestfallen, but then brightened. "But it's a nice job, and I like the people I work with, and it's a lovely office I'm in."

Chesney winced at the ending of a sentence with a preposition.

"Martina said you're a writer."

"Yes, I'm a writer of sorts," he said modestly.

"What sort of sorts?"

"I mean that I'm an editor, most of the time, at least. I did write one book."

"How exciting," she squealed. "Do you think I read it?"

"You never know," said Chesney. "Do you read much?"

"I read a lot at work," Patsy confessed. "I read all the letters that I type for Mr. Liverot, but I read outside of work, too. My mother subscribes to *Reader's Digest*, and my father gets *Sports Illustrated*. But I don't read that unless there's a story about hockey. I like hockey."

"Field hockey?"

"Ice hockey!" She said as if she'd been insulted. "Your book wasn't about hockey, was it?"

Chesney confessed it was a biography of Hugh Goode. Her blank expression spoke volumes.

"Well," said Patsy, trying to offer some consolation, "maybe you'll write another book someday."

"Actually, I'm working on a book. I'm ghosting it."

"You mean like vampires and zombies?"

"No," said Chesney, "that means I'm helping someone else write their autobiography."

"That's good," said Patsy, "I don't like scary books. They give me the creeps. Maybe I'll read that book. Who is it about?"

"Gaston Boules."

Patsy's mouth dropped in astonishment. "Gaston Boules, the chef on television?"

"Yes, that's right."

"I know him," she said, "I not only know him, I watch him. I watch him on TV all the time. I was watching him the other night when he made that soufflé, the one he did from the leftovers from the show before that. It was amazing! You wouldn't think that you could make a soufflé from leftover corned beef and cabbage, would you?"

"Uh, no, I wouldn't," said Chesney.

"And so, you've met him, I mean really met him in person."

"Sure."

"Is he as tall as he is on TV?"

"I guess that would depend on the size of your TV," said Chesney.

Patsy looked confused.

"Never mind, it was a joke."

"Oh."

Chesney scanned the room again for Martina.

"…Donny Osmond," he heard someone say. He looked and noticed it was Patsy who apparently had begun a new thread of conversation.

"I'm sorry, did you say Donny Osmond?"

"Yes," her face lit up, "do you know him?"

"Not personally."

"Oh, but you've met him then?"

"Uh, no, why do you ask?"

"I was just saying that he would make a good subject for a book, Donny Osmond would." Patsy paused a moment before adding: "He's my absolute favorite."

"Your absolute favorite what?"

"My absolute favorite, favorite," she beamed, "in everything."

Chesney smiled almost as broadly as Patsy was smiling at him in an attempt to show how pleased he was for her. After several seconds of this, his face started to hurt.

"Soooo," he said, relaxing his grin, "you've known Martina a long time, huh?"

"Only forever," said Patsy."

"I bet you two had lots of fun in school, huh?"

"Oh, yes, oh good heavens, yes!"

"Martina was popular, I imagine," said Chesney.

"Oh, sure, everyone likes Martina, she's so nice."

"I bet she was popular, uh, you know, with…the boys."

"Like I said, they all like Martina…"

"As many as that?" Chesney muttered. "Did she have many," he paused and scratched his head, "you know, friends… friends that were boys?"

Patsy tilted her head like a confused puppy.

"Uh, boy… friends… boyfriends?" said Chesney.

Patsy stared at him "You mean like boyfriends?"

"No, not exactly, yes, okay, boyfriends."

Patsy scratched her head. "Well, there was Eddie…"

"Eddie?"

"Eddie Fadden."

"Eddie Fadden." He generated an anagram. "Faded indeed…"

"Excuse me?"

"Nothing," said Chesney. "So, Eddie Fadden, huh?"

"Oh, yes, now that I think of it, Martina and Eddie went out together the summer between junior and senior year. They saw a lot of each other."

Chesney bit his lip and looked around, trying to guess which one of these Bozos was Eddie Fadden. "Is, uh, Eddie here?"

"Eddie? Eddie Fadden?" Patsy scanned the room. "I doubt Eddie would be here. He's kind of missing."

"Kind of?"

"It's very sad," said Patsy. "Eddie was very active, that is he was what you'd call an activist, and an active one, at that, so you could say he was an active activist. He was involved in a lot of very noble causes. He went to work fulltime for the ERF."

"You mean the 'Earth.'"

"No, ERF, the E.R.F. the Environmental Reclamation Foundation, they like to pronounce it 'ERF,' you know, because that sounds like 'Earth.' Well, he was working with the ERF people."

"Erflings?" suggested Chesney.

"Huh, oh, yes, that's clever," said Patsy. Ironically, she dropped her smile to say she found the comment humorous. "Erflings. Ha, that's funny!"

"As you were saying?"

"Oh, right, well, they had this ship, and they were on the ship, and so was Eddie, and they were off the coast of Japan trying to save the whales from the tuna fishermen."

"Whales from the tuna fishermen?"

Patsy knit her brow and then shook her head. "Maybe that's not right. Anyway, there were animals in the ocean. And there were people who wanted to take the animals out of the ocean. And then there was Eddie and his group wanting to keep them in the ocean. And there was a big fight out on the ocean, and they got Eddie."

"The fishermen?"

"No," said Patsy, "not the fishermen, the fish. He fell overboard, and the last anyone saw he was being dragged under by a porpoise or a whale, oh, wait, no, it was a giant squid."

"How horrible," said Chesney, "and they couldn't save him."

"No, the fishermen were too busy fighting the ERF people, and the ERF people were busy fighting the fishermen." Patsy shook her head. "The fishermen probably could have saved him, but the ERF people didn't want them to hurt the squid, or whatever it was. I heard the ERF people were mad at Eddie because he was fighting the giant squid. They said he was a traitor to animals everywhere."

"Even ones that were dragging him to a watery grave?" asked Chesney.

Patsy shrugged her shoulders. "I guess they thought he was disturbing the natural cycle of life. Sad."

Chesney agreed.

"I haven't been able to eat calamari since then," said Patsy, "and that was five years ago. Of course, I never ate it before then, either."

After such a harrowing tale, they both paused to exhale.

"There, that's settled," said Martina returning, "has Patsy been keeping you company."

"I was just telling him…"

"Oh, yes," said Chesney cutting Patsy short, "yes, you couldn't have left me in better hands. Did you get the DJ straightened out?"

Martina pointed upward, and Chesney realized music was playing.

"Oh, right," said Chesney. "Well, should we dance, or would you like something to drink?"

"I'd love both," said Martina, with a slight grimace, "but now, I have to excuse myself again… something about tuna puffs and the caterer. I'll be right back. Sorry." Martina gave him a swift peck on the cheek and was off again.

Chesney looked at Patsy and smiled, though he couldn't help thinking of calamari.

"Hello, Ms. Zyobidinski," said a man's voice, "who's your friend?"

Chesney turned. There was a prosperous-looking man in a well-tailored suit. His thick hair was impeccably groomed. A miasma of expensive scent arrived a split-second before he did.

"Oh, Mr. Eckner, I mean, Albrecht, I mean," Patsy rolled her eyes and looked at Chesney. "We work together, but I forget what to call him sometimes when we're not at work."

"We're not at work now, Patsy," said the newcomer. "And who's your friend?"

"He's not my friend," said Patsy, "no, wait, that's not what I meant. He's really very nice. He's Martina's friend, that is, he's Martina's boyfriend…"

"Chesney Potts," said Chesney offering his hand. The man smiled through pursed lips, and let Chesney's hand hang in mid-air. The stranger's eyes narrowed, as if he had suddenly grown myopic, or was trying to read Chesney's mind.

Chesney repeated his name, wondering if he hadn't been heard the first time.

"Oh, this is Albrecht, Albrecht Eckner," said Patsy hurriedly, as if it was her responsibility to announce him. Only then, did Albrecht Eckner relax his stare and shake Chesney's hand. It was cold.

"Albrecht Eckner," said the person of the same name. His look betrayed a thin veil of smugness. "So, you're the lucky fellow that landed our Martina?"

"Uh, yes, I don't know if landed is the right word…"

"Patsy," said Eckner abruptly, turning from Chesney, "have you seen Valerie? She promised me that she would be here. We certainly wouldn't want to start the fun without her, would we?"

Patsy looked around the room. "Valerie, no, I don't think…"

"You'd like Valerie," said Albrecht turning back to Chesney. "She's a lot of fun. So, where did you meet our Martina, Charley?"

"Uh, Chesney. I met her sort of by accident. I was at a book club…"

"A book club?" said Albrecht.

"Yes," gushed Patsy, "Chesney's a famous author."

"Really?"

"No, I'm not famous," said Chesney.

"But he knows famous people," insisted Patsy, "he's writing a book with Gaston Boules, the chef... on television!"

Albrecht Eckner gave Patsy with a patronizing smile and then glanced back at Chesney with one less condescending.

"You'll have to excuse Patsy," said Albrecht. "She gets so excited. We often have to tamp her down her at the bank. Isn't that so, Patsy?"

"Yes," said Patsy, "Mr. Eckner..."

"We're not at the bank now, Patsy..."

She rolled her eyes. "Sometimes I wonder where I am..."

"We all do," Albrecht muttered.

"First, I called you 'Albrecht' when we were at school," she explained. "And then when I went to work for the bank, and Albrecht was there, I had to get used to calling him 'Mr. Eckner.' But now we're here, and it's like we're back at school, and I guess I'm all mixed up."

Albrecht Eckner gave her a patronizing smile.

"Of course," she prattled on, "I can't call him by his first name at work. There's no one more important than Albrecht at the bank, after Mr. Liverot, of course. We're all very proud of Albrecht, Mr. Eckner, at the bank."

"Patsy, really, you'll make me blush," said Eckner.

"Yes, there's no one, nearly no one, as important at the bank," said Patsy. Then she looked at Chesney. "Of course, that's just at the bank."

Albrecht Eckner's face dropped.

"It's not like working with famous people, people who are on TV, people like Gaston Boules and other famous people like Chesney does. That must really be exciting!"

"No, not really," said Chesney.

"Now, don't be so modest," said Albrecht. "It's probably exhilarating, talking to a cook."

"A TV chef," interjected Patsy, "it's not like talking to someone at a bank."

Patsy's enthusiasm seemed to grate on Eckner's ego, though she was oblivious to it. Chesney feared for the hand of corporate retribution coming down on the bubbly secretary on Monday when Albrecht was Mr. Eckner once again.

"Still," said Chesney, "Albrecht, uh, Mr. Eckner has a very responsible position, and I'm sure it's an excellent bank."

"Oh, it's a wonderful bank. Yes, Mr. Liverot and Mr. Eckner have built it up to one of the top fifty banks in Wilmington."

"Really," said Chesney, striving to support Patsy. "How many banks are there in Wilmington?"

"Thirty-seven," muttered Albrecht Eckner, along with a withering look to Patsy.

"I think..." said Patsy softly, "I think I'll see if I can help with those tuna puffs." She excused herself.

For a moment, Chesney wracked his mind for an excuse to get away from Albrecht Eckner, as well. He scanned the thickening crowd, hoping for a glimpse of Martina, and then saw the refreshments at the far end of the room.

"Well, it was very nice to meet you," said Chesney, "but, uh, I think I'll get something to drink…"

"Oh, don't go," said Eckner, touching Chesney's arm. "I was just about to get something myself. Let me get you something. After all, you're Martina's guest."

Albrecht Eckner steered Chesney toward the bar.

"I'm having a Dragon Bite, what can I get you?"

"Dragon Bite?"

"Yes, you know, Bacardi, lychee, lime, pineapple, cranberry…"

"Oh, no, I don't drink," said Chesney.

"No?"

"Not really," said Chesney, "well, the occasional glass of wine, but I'm driving."

Albrecht Eckner nodded and smiled. It was his first honest smile. "Good for you," he said. "I'll get this."

He ducked through the crowd to the bar and returned a minute later with an ostentatious concoction in his right hand. He offered the drink in his left hand to Chesney.

"Iced tea?" he said.

"Oh, yes, thank you," said Chesney. He took a small sip. It was iced tea. "I was thirsty, thank you."

"Chatting with Patsy Zyobidinski can make anyone thirsty," said Albrecht Eckner, raising his glass to Chesney. "Your good health. Don't get me wrong, I love Patsy like a sister, and she's a good secretary, but, well…"

Chesney took a deeper draught of the tea.

"So, tell me all about yourself, and dear Martina," said Albrecht as he peered over his Dragon Bite.

– 30 –
When Monsters and Vampires Mate

D onny Osmond smiled down upon Chesney Potts as he opened his eyes. He started to sit up, but a sharp pain in his head warned him that such sudden movements were ill-advised.

He was in a girl's bedroom. The decorations and the style made him guess it was a girl between the ages of ten and fifteen.

Chesney looked down at the comforter. It too was emblazoned with the likeness of Donny Osmond. Donny Osmond? Where had he heard the name recently? Oh, yes, at the reunion. He closed his eyes. The reunion, what had happened at the reunion? Donny Osmond? He only recalled speaking to two people. Patsy... Patsy with the Polish last name. She was the one who told Chesney he should write a book about Donny Osmond.

Had she had him kidnapped to write the definitive biography of Donny Osmond? It was ridiculous. But his head was splitting as if he had been drugged. The last thing he remembered was drinking iced tea.

The rest all ran together in a blur.

He peeked under the comforter. He wasn't wearing any trousers. Slowly, Chesney lifted his head to see if his trousers were in the room. They were not, but he did see two framed certificates on the wall. The first was a high school diploma. The second was one from secretarial school. Both bore the name: Patricia Zyobidinski.

Chesney gasped. He was in Patsy Zyobidinski's bedroom. Worse than that he was in her bed! She wasn't there now, but had she been? Had he spent the night with Patsy? Had he bedded her on the night he had wanted to profess his love to Martina? What had happened last night, if indeed, it had been last night? Was this Sunday?

He heard a soft rap, which he first mistook for the thumping inside his head. On the second rap, he heard a soft voice ask if he was awake.

"Come in," said Chesney.

The door opened slowly, and a woman's head appeared. At first glance, Chesney thought it was Patsy. It looked like Patsy, but she was older. Still, her hair looked the same, and she had the same toothy smile. The thought occurred to him that he had married Patsy Zyobidinski, and now it was twenty years later, and he was just emerging from a bout of amnesia.

"Good morning, I'm Mrs. Zyobidinski, Patsy's mother."

Chesney breathed a sigh of relief. He hadn't lost twenty years of his life, but he still was waking up in a strange girl's bed and was being greeted by her mother.

"Hello?" he said.

"Hello," she said pleasantly. "I have your pants, or I will in a few minutes. They're in the dryer."

Chesney grimaced. They were dry-clean-only. "Uh, what happened?"

Mrs. Zyobidinski smiled awkwardly. "I'd better let my husband discuss that with you." Like a turtle retreating into its shell, she pulled her head out of the doorway.

Her husband? Mr. Zyobidinski was coming in for a discussion? That didn't sound promising. Chesney had never had a discussion with the father of a girl while lying trouserless in that girl's bed. He moaned and thought of Martina. He had wanted to tell her how he loved her. Now he'd have to tell her how he was being forced to marry her friend. His mental anguish was interrupted by a determined rap on the door. Chesney was about to say "come in" when the door opened without his permission.

Mr. Zyobidinski looked just like Chesney imagined a father would look like when coming to have a chat with a man in his daughter's bed. He looked stern.

"Morning," said the man as he neared the bed. From that vantage point, Mr. Zyobidinski towered over Chesney. Chesney would have preferred to meet the man standing, but a lack of trousers prevented that. The only thing separating Chesney from the wrath of Mr. Zyobidinski was Donny Osmond.

"Good morning," said Chesney.

"Had quite a night," said Mr. Zyobidinski.

"Had I? I…and this is no excuse…I don't remember much of it."

"Don't remember, huh?"

"No, sir, the last thing I recall was drinking…iced tea."

"Iced tea, huh?" said Mr. Zyobidinski with a slow nod, which then switched direction and became a rueful shake of the head. "Son, sounds like you got a Bayonne Bomb."

"It tasted like iced tea," said Chesney.

"I'm sure it did."

Chesney just looked at him with a puzzled expression.

"A Bayonne Bomb," said Mr. Zyobidinski, "a Weehawken Wallop, a Lodi Lollapalooza."

Aside from establishing that Mr. Zyobidinski must be from Northern New Jersey, the colorful string of geographical euphemisms did little to clear up Chesney's confusion.

Mr. Zyobidinski made one last appeal. "Somebody slipped you a Mickey."

"A Mickey? You mean a Mickey Finn?"

"Yep."

"You mean, someone deliberately poisoned my drink?"

"It rarely happens by accident," said Mr. Zyobidinski, "you ever been in the Navy?"

Chesney confessed that he hadn't unless he had happened to enlist last night.

"Take the word of an ex-sailor," he said, "it never happens by accident."

Despite the pain that ensued, Chesney shook his head. "At a high school reunion? Who would want to poison me?"

"Someone who didn't like you," said Mr. Zyobidinski.

"But I didn't know anyone there."

"Maybe," he said, "but maybe somebody knew you."

Chesney tried to wrap his aching head around that thought, but another question forced itself into his mind.

"What am I doing here?" he asked.

Mr. Zyobidinski sat on the edge of the bed.

"Everybody's got to be someplace," he said philosophically. "According to Patsy... Patsy, my daughter... this is her bed..."

"Yes, I remember Patsy," said Chesney, "I met her last night."

"Um, yes..." said Mr. Zyobidinski, "well, Patsy said you started behaving, well..."

"Erratically?" guessed Chesney.

"No, she said 'like a big jerk.'"

"Oh," groaned Chesney.

"She was surprised, too," said Mr. Zyobidinski. "She said you seemed like such a nice fellow, clean-cut, and you were going out with her friend, Martina."

"Martina," groaned Chesney.

"Patsy said you started acting up, and to cut a long story short, you passed out."

Chesney closed his eyes and tried to recall anything that had happened.

"I didn't drive here, did I?"

"Drive here?" Mr. Zyobidinski snorted. "You couldn't have crawled here."

"But my car?"

"Still at the Fire Hall. I'll take you to get it once your pants come out of the wash."

"Why are my pants in the wash?"

Mr. Zyobidinski smiled with the wisdom that comes from being an ex-sailor. "You wouldn't have wanted to wear them the way they were, son. When they brought you here…"

"Who?"

He scratched the side of his head. "Let's see, Patsy called us, said you had taken sick, and that one of the firemen was bringing you."

"Firemen?"

"You were in the Fire Hall," said Mr. Zyobidinski. "They wanted to clear the place out after the reunion. They couldn't just leave you there. You're not a fire truck, even if you did have a snorkel-full."

Chesney almost asked what had happened to Martina, but was afraid of the answer.

"So," said Mr. Zyobidinski, "they brought you here."

"Thank you," said Chesney quietly, "I mean, for taking care of me. I don't know what to say. I've never had anything like this happen to me before. I'm, I'm so ashamed."

"Being a sucker is nothing to be ashamed of…the first time," said Mr. Zyobidinski. "If it happens more than once, that's when you'd better start worrying."

Chesney agreed and went back to wondering who would deliberately poison him. Then he recalled what Martina tried to say before they went into the hall. Something that made him think he had a rival there.

"What happened to Martina?" he asked, rising.

Mr. Zyobidinski shrugged. "I don't know. You'd have to ask Patsy…" he pushed Chesney back on to the bed. "After I get your pants."

A quarter of an hour later and after much effort, Chesney wobbled downstairs to the kitchen where Mrs. Zyobidinski and her daughter were cheerfully preparing lunch.

"Oh, good, you can walk," said Mrs. Zyobidinski.

"Mom," cautioned Patsy.

"Well, it's the first I've seen him do it," she whispered, before turning to Chesney. "Please, sit down, Mr…"

"Chesney," said Patsy.

"Sit down, Mr. Chesney," said her mother.

He did so.

"I'm afraid you missed breakfast," said Mrs. Zyobidinski. "Would you like some lunch? We're having deviled ham?"

The notion of deviled ham was enough to turn Chesney's stomach when it was healthy. Now, with the residue of the previous night in his system, the mention of it triggered a gag reflex that he struggled to control.

"No?" said Mrs. Zyobidinski interpreting his convulsed reply. "Well, maybe some dry toast and tea?"

The mention of tea had an even more upsetting effect. Chesney shook his head. "Do you have anything carbonated? A Coke, maybe?"

"Ginger ale?" she counteroffered.

He nodded. He detested ginger ale, but at least it wasn't likely to attack him. She poured him a glass.

Chesney took a sip and then noticed Patsy studying him.

"That green color is almost all gone," she said. Last night you looked like Herman Munster," she said. "You know, from the TV show…"

"*The Munsters*," he said.

"Yes, that's the one," said Patsy. "When I say you looked like Herman Munster, I don't mean physically, at least not his size or his looks, or anything like that. For one thing, that actor that played him…"

"Fred Gywnne," muttered Chesney.

"Yes, him," continued Patsy, "I didn't mean that you looked like Fred Gywnne. What I mean is that you were all green, like Herman Munster. Of course, the TV show was in black and white, but when they did the movie…"

"*Munster, Go Home*," noted Chesney.

"Yes, that's it!" said Patsy.

"My, your friend certainly is well-read," beamed Mrs. Zyobidinski. "You certainly are well-read, Mr. Chesney!"

Chesney nodded and took another sip of ginger ale. He would have pointed out the distinction between being well-read and knowing a lot of pointless television trivia. Under the circumstances, his nod would have to suffice.

"Well, anyway," continued Patsy, "in the movie, you could see the color of them all."

"I remember that," said Mrs. Zyobidinski, turning from the deviled ham. "Wasn't that interesting to finally see them all as they really were?"

Chesney would have interjected that was not how they really were since they were all actors in heavy make-up, but all he could manage was a sigh.

"Wasn't it interesting how Lily and Grandpa and Eddie were all sort of bluish-purpley, but Herman wasn't?" said Mrs. Zyobidinski.

"That's because Herman was made in a laboratory, Mom," observed Patsy as if it were a scientific fact. "The others were all human, or sort of, Vampirey, you know…"

"But wasn't Eddie like a Wolfman or Wolfboy, I suppose?" asked her mother.

"Yes, I suppose that's what happens when Vampires and Frankensteins mate," said Patsy.

"Patricia," Mrs. Zyobidinski gestured towards their guest as if the topic of inter-species sex between fictitious creatures was impolite in mixed company.

Chesney just put his head down on the table as the debate continued until Patsy suddenly recalled the inspiration for her tangent.

"Green," she said, "that's what I was saying, you don't look as green. Last night you looked horrible; not when you first came into the reunion, but by the time you left, or when you were carried out, you were very, very green."

Chesney tried to smile. "Yes," he said, "I'm feeling a little better, thanks to you and your family."

"We'd do it for any boyfriend of Martina's," said Patsy.

"Martina is such a lovely girl," noted Mrs. Zyobidinski, as she used her knife to make swirls of deviled ham on slices of Wonder bread.

"Did Martina, did she…" Chesney paused, afraid of the answer, "did she see me…green, like that?"

"Everyone saw you like that, I expect," said Patsy.

"Oh," said Chesney.

"She was worried about you," said Patsy.

"She was?"

"Yes, it was Martina's idea that you come here. So, I called my parents, and one of the firemen helped bring you here."

"That was very kind," he said.

"The fireman was happy to do it," said Patsy, "he said it gave him a chance to practice his fireman's carry."

Chesney pinched the bridge of his nose. "No, I…I meant it was very kind of you and your parents to take me in when I was…green."

Green, thought Chesney. Yes, he was green, green with sickness. Apparently, Martina felt sick at the sight of him, as well, so much so that she packed him off on the back of a fireman to the Zyobidinski's house. Wait, he thought, maybe there was another explanation. He thought of one more question.

"How, uh, how did Martina get home?"

"Oh, yes," said Patsy, "remember I told you about Eddie, Eddie Fadden?"

"You mean the guy the squid got?"

"That right," said Patsy.

"But, how could he take Martina home?"

"Not Eddie," laughed Patsy, "His brother, Fred. He's the one who took Martina home."

"Speaking of home," said Mr. Zyobidinski entering the kitchen, "any time you feel up to it, boy, I can take you down to the fire hall to get your car."

Chesney nodded and stood. His legs were still wobbly, but he wanted to leave as soon as possible. His head ached, his stomach was still churning, and he was green all over again: green with envy.

– 31 –
We're So Sorry,
Uncle Albrecht

Y ou really should have been there. It was priceless."

"I told you before," said Valerie Fierro, "I couldn't make it; my mother was sick."

"Oh, yes," said Albrecht Eckner, "what was it?"

He was trying to poke holes in her story.

"Food poisoning," said Valerie. She glanced at the clock. It was only 9:05, Monday morning.

"Fish, wasn't it?"

"Right, fish," said Valerie. "and I couldn't leave her."

"No, of course not," cooed Albrecht.

"Yes, it would have been nice to see everyone," said Valerie. She lied. She didn't want to see any of them.

He leaned back in his swivel chair. "You know how it is. You go to one high school reunion, you go to them all."

"I haven't been to any of them. And this was only the second our class has held, so I don't know what the big deal was. You said it yourself; all the cheerleaders were bloated, and all the jocks were balding."

Albrecht waved his hand dismissively. "Yes, but you missed the best part. Even I didn't anticipate it."

Valerie sighed. Albrecht never just told a story. He had to make a Broadway production out of it. "Okay, what? What did I miss?"

His eyes narrowed, reminding her of an overfed feline. A smug smile broadened his lips.

"The Long Island Iced Tea," he said.

She rose to leave his office. "Big deal! I've had Long Island Iced Tea. Besides, I thought you drank that fruity sissy drink, the Dragon Belches."

"Dragon Bite," he corrected. "And I didn't drink the Long Island Iced Tea."

Valerie stared at him. "Okay, I give up, so who drank the Long Island Ice Tea?"

His satisfaction percolated every moment he withheld the answer. Finally, Albrecht could no longer contain himself.

"Martina's new boyfriend," he said.

"So what?"

"So," said Albrecht, "he doesn't drink. Nor did he know that Long Island Ice Tea is loaded with alcohol. It was priceless."

"Yeah, sorry I missed it," muttered Valerie. "You gave booze that doesn't taste like booze to someone who doesn't drink: hilarious. And you should have been there when my mother was puking up the bad fish. I know drunk puke is funnier than ptomaine puke, but my mother was really at the top of her game the other night. Grow up, Albrecht!"

"It wasn't the vomit," he said. "Give me more credit than that. The art was in how I gave a fat little narcissist his comeuppance. Martina's boyfriend; who did he think he was, sashaying into a room full of strangers and acting like some sort of big shot? Bragging about all the famous people that he knew. Pretending he was such hot shit."

"Really?" Valerie was surprised. "That doesn't sound like the type of guy that Martina Fergus would go out with. She's all sweet and goody-goody."

"Well, I did her a favor," he said.

"By getting her boyfriend drunk?"

"Yes," said Albrecht. "I'm sure Martina is thinking differently of him now."

"Why what did he do?" she asked.

Albrecht leaned forward and lowered his voice. "Oh, that was the best part. After that first drink, I became his best friend…"

"He had to be drunk to fully appreciate your humanitarian qualities?"

"Okay, if you don't want to hear about it," sneered Albrecht.

"No, sorry, go ahead," she said. "This is getting interesting… finally."

"After the first drink, his tongue loosened up and Mr. Big Shot writer…"

"Oh, he's a writer?"

Albrecht pursed his lips. "If you could call him that. He writes other people's stories, not impressive people unless your last name is 'Zyobidinski.' The hot shit writer has a few stiff drinks, and the closet door opens up."

"You mean he's gay?"

"Not that closet door," said Albrecht. "No, you know, the place where he hides all his fears and his secrets, pouring out his heart, telling his dear Uncle Albrecht all the little things that are bothering him. It seems that the poor boy was worried about his rivals for Martina's hand."

"Her hand?"

"I know it's quaint. The jerk wanted to start with her hand. Anyway, this sap was worried that there may have been some competition there, old boyfriends, smoldering flames waiting to burst up into hot passion."

Valerie knitted her brow. "You are talking about a guy going out with Martina Fergus: Delaware's Mother Theresa, only not as sexy?

"You know Martina, and I know Martina," he grinned, "and everyone at the reunion knows Martina, but apparently to this little snot rag, she's some hot babe. And so he asks me about Martina back in high school, you know, if she had any serious boyfriends."

"So, what did you tell him?"

Albrecht smiled. "I told him to have another glass of iced tea. After that, it was easy. Every person I casually pointed out to him became a challenger. After the third drink, he was blubbering something about some dead girl, some dried-up old Aunt, and some other people I never heard of. It was classic. Too bad your mother ate that bad chicken…"

"Yes, wait, no, it was fish," said Valerie.

"Oh, of course, fish."

"And what was Martina doing all this time?"

"That's why it all worked so well," he said, beaming. "She was busy with the caterer, and then when she started looking for him, he was at the last place she'd ever expect him to be."

"At the bar with his new friend, Albrecht," said Valerie. She almost felt sorry for Martina's boyfriend. However, as a previous victim of Albrecht Eckner, she felt vindicated that she wasn't alone.

"She got to see him just before he passed out," said Albrecht, "but by then, everyone could see him."

"Why?"

"He was standing on top of the bar. That was his stage."

"Stage? What stage?"

Albrecht gave her a look as if the answer were obvious. "Valerie, you need to have a stage if you're going to sing! And sing he did. It was so delicious."

Valerie just shook her head. "So, what do you think this guy is going to do when he figures out that you're responsible for getting him drunk and making a fool of him?"

Albrecht Eckner flapped his hand as if brushing away a gnat. "I don't know what you're talking about. It was just an innocent little mistake. I asked the bartender, for an iced tea, and being a bartender he assumed I wanted a Long Island Iced Tea."

Valerie just looked at him.

"Besides," said Albrecht with a tiny smile, "when you're doing something like this, you make sure you get your stories straight and pay off the bartender… generously… in advance."

– 32 –
The Agony of the
Delayed Anagram

The question kept running through Chesney's mind. Who had given him a Mickey? Eddie was 40 fathoms down inside some squid. That left his brother Freddie. Freddie must have slipped him that Passaic Pistol, or whatever Patsy's father called it!

Freddie Fadden, that was…Red, uh, fire…

Chesney was so upset he couldn't even think of an anagram for the guy's name.

And to make matters worse, he hadn't been able to reach Martina. The last time he had seen her, she was trying to fix some tuna puffs. The last time she had seen him, he was passed out on the back of a fireman.

When he called her house, they told him she was out. He called her three times that day and was told the same excuse by her father, her mother, and her brother. He would have called a fourth time, but he was afraid they'd put the dog on the phone. He couldn't bear to be lied to by a dog.

She could have been out. But if Martina was out, she might very well be out with Fred Fadden…Fred Fadden…Dad…Darn…no…

Chesney's mind churned as he drove up the Jersey Turnpike. He stopped three times, at the John Fenwick, the James Fennimore Cooper, and the Woodrow Wilson rest stops, throwing up at each. He would have thrown up at the Joyce Kilmer rest stop as well, but he got off at Exit 8.

That night he tossed and turned, unable to sleep. Several times he picked up the phone to call Martina, but he stopped. It was rude to call after ten o'clock. Besides, if she wasn't there in the middle of the night, he'd go mad.

By Monday morning, he was a wreck. He probably looked better on the back on the fireman. He downed several cans of Coca-Cola, took a hot shower, then a cold shower, shaved, and got dressed. Outwardly he looked better. Inside he was still a wreck.

At work, Chesney was of little use. He spent two hours reading the same sentence written by the egoistical illiterate: Gaston Boules.

"Cooking is to culinary science what rocket science is to the real kind of science, at least it is when I do it right, and I always do."

He stared at that all morning while thinking of Martina.

"Cooking is to culinary science what rocket science is to the real kind of science, at least it is when I do it right, and I always do."

What was that supposed to mean? What did it matter what it meant? Where was Martina? Where had she been all day yesterday?

"Cooking is to culinary science what rocket science is to the real kind of science, at least it is when I do it right, and I always do."

She had run off with Freddie Fadden, brother of the ERP freak. Or maybe he had taken her against her will.

"Cooking is to culinary science what rocket science is to the real kind of science, at least it is when I do it right, and I always do."

Finally, he banged his head against his desk. He had to get one of them out of his mind: either Martina Fergus or Gaston Boules' wretched sentence.

His futile editing effort, sparkled in comparison to his performance at the afternoon editorial meeting. It was as if he had just arrived from Croatia with a mastery of only three English words: "What?" "Pardon?" and "Huh?"

Finally, Beverly Marlton asked him point-blank if he was all right. He just stared at her, trying to craft an answer using anagrams of "Fred Fadden," "Gaston Boules," and "I'm losing my mind." Having failed this, he merely said: "Okay."

"Maybe you're working too hard, on this Boules book," she said. "This is a big one, a really big one, but I don't want you to get stressed out on it, understand?"

Chesney nodded.

"I don't need crazy editors."

"Right, crazy..." said Chesney

"No, not crazy," she said, looking at him sideways. "Are you sure you're okay?"

"Uh, yes, fine."

"And the book will be finished on time?"

"Quarter past one," he said, glancing at his watch.

"Chesney, look at me," said Beverly. "That has to be on the presses in two weeks. They need it in the shops in time to for the premiere of his new show in December. Understand?"

"Don't worry... I'll get it done."

176

"Good, like I said, relax, but remember, this is going to be a big seller, and I'm counting on you to get it right."

"I do it right, and I always do," said Chesney mouthing Boules' words by rote.

Beverly Marlton stared at him for a moment. Then she glanced around the table as if she were searching for another editor for the project. Finally, she returned to Chesney.

"Oh, Chesney, go home. Go home, get some sleep, have a drink…"

"NO!" he said, grabbing his stomach.

"Fine, just get some rest so you'll be fresh for the home stretch, okay?"

"Yes," he said, "I understand." Then he sat there just looking at her.

Beverly Marlton returned his stare for nearly thirty seconds before commanding: "Then…Go…Home…NOW!"

He went home.

Back in his apartment, he sat down and stared at the clock. It was only a quarter to three. He didn't know what to do at a quarter to three on a weekday afternoon when his life was in turmoil. He could try again to call Martina, but she was at work, or at least he hoped she was at work. He didn't want to call her at work with a crisis.

He walked into the kitchen. It was too early to eat dinner at ten minutes before three. Besides, he wasn't hungry. Instead he picked up a box of pretzel rods, and buzzed through them like a beaver going through an acre of virgin timber. Now he wasn't just not hungry; he felt bloated.

Chesney returned to the living room and lay on the couch. He closed his eyes. He couldn't sleep. His mind kept imagining what he could have done the other night. Each successive scene was worse than the one before it. He opened his eyes, reached for the TV remote, and turned on the set.

He hadn't seen daytime television since he was a kid. A cartoon was on. It was terribly drawn and depressing. He switched the channel. The characters on the soap opera were terribly drawn as well. They all were in the throes of slow-motion agony designed to make five minutes of dialog last a full hour. He switched back to the cartoon. The mouse dropping a bowling ball on to the head of the cat may have been immature, but at least it was quick. And he could relate to the cat. Chesney was just starting to bond with the cartoon cat, when the phone rang jarring him back to reality.

"Chesney, it's Martina."

He froze. As much as he had wanted to call her, he was surprised to hear her voice.

"Hello, Chesney? Are you there?" She asked after several seconds of silence.

"Uh, yes, I'm…here. Why?"

"Because I was worried?"

"You were?"

"Of course I was," she said. "Wouldn't you be concerned if I got sick and started behaving oddly in public?"

He tried to imagine Martina doing anything oddly, but couldn't. "I guess I would, I mean, of course, I'd be concerned…if you were sick."

"Well, I was concerned," she said. "I'm…very fond of you."

He wondered what level of commitment "fondness" represented.

"Thank you," he said, still uncertain of where he stood. "So, I mean, you still…like me?" Chesney winced. He sounded like he was in third grade.

"Like you? I…" Martina stopped as if she had hit an invisible barrier. Chesney remembered what she always said about guarding one's heart. Was she doing that now?

"You're my…boyfriend," she said.

"I am?"

"Yes, of course, you are," she said. "Don't you want to be?"

"I wasn't so sure you wanted me to be after what happened."

"What happened?" asked Martina.

"Don't you know?" he said. "Because I don't remember a thing."

She laughed, putting him at ease. "I know, but I also know it doesn't matter. I've forgotten it already."

"Oh? That's too bad," said Chesney, "because I wish I knew what happened. Patsy wouldn't tell me in front of her mother. Her father had a theory, but he wasn't there, was he…was he?"

"No," she said, "Mr. Zyobidinski wasn't there. What was his theory?"

Chesney exhaled, feeling more than a little ashamed of what he did know. "Well," he said, "someone slipped me a Mickey."

"What's a 'Mickey?'"

"It's something someone put in my drink to make me sick."

"Oh, I see."

"Why would someone do that," he asked. "Was there someone there who didn't like me?"

"As far as I know, nobody there knew you," said Martina.

"But they knew you."

"What does that mean?"

He didn't know how to say it without sounding paranoid. "Maybe they knew you and liked you… a lot, and because of that… they didn't like me? Maybe?"

Martina was silent for a moment. "You sound paranoid," she said.

"I know, I know," he said, slapping his head. "I'm sorry, I haven't had any sleep, and I was all upset, and I couldn't find you…" Chesney stopped.

"What's wrong?"

"If you were concerned about me," he said cautiously, "how come I couldn't reach you all day yesterday?"

"Because," she paused, "I wasn't home."

"Yes, I know," he said, "I mean, sorry, that sounded like I was accusing you, it's just that…"

"You don't have to say anything," said Martina, "I understand."

"You do?"

"You were upset and worried. But I knew you were in good hands," she said. "I couldn't very well bring you home. I didn't want my family to see you at your worst, especially when it wasn't your fault."

"Oh."

"And I knew the Zyobidinskis would take good care of you. Then when I called yesterday, Patsy said her father had taken you down to get your car and you were feeling much better. So I thought you were okay."

He almost told her about how he was sick all the way up the Jersey Turnpike rest stops but decided against it.

"I guess that's that," he said, "sorry."

"For what?"

"For ruining your reunion," he said. "After all your hard work, the last thing you needed was a boyfriend to act like an idiot. I did act like an idiot, didn't I?"

"You weren't yourself," she said. "And besides which, I told you I've forgotten it."

"I wish I could remember it so I could forget it."

He heard her sigh. Finally, she spoke.

"You were behaving like you were drunk," Martina began.

"But I don't drink…"

"I didn't say you were drunk," she said. "I didn't see much of it. I was dealing with minor crises, and trying to get back to you through the crowd. That's when I heard it."

"Heard what?"

"You were singing."

"Oh, no," said Chesney.

"You were singing something about twerps in love."

"Oh, no, and you heard it?"

"And I saw it." Martina hesitated. "I couldn't really miss it. You were on top of the bar."

"Oh…" he moaned, "I'm so sorry…"

"You weren't there long," she said.

"That's a relief."

"You fell off," she added.

"I'm sorry, I'm so, so sorry."

"You wanted to know," she said, "and now you know. And now you can forget it because I have."

Chesney sat in silent marvel. That she could forgive and forget after he humiliated her in front of all her friends. If he hadn't loved her before, he certainly did now. He wanted to say it, but not at that moment, not over the phone, not yet. Instead, he just whispered: "thank you."

Martina said nothing in reply.

"Would you like," he started, "I mean, can we go out, maybe to dinner?"

"Tonight?" she laughed. "I don't think that's a good idea."

"No, no, of course not," he said. "I mean you're down there, and I'm up here, and I haven't slept and I don't know if I could eat, or drive, I mean, drive, cause I'd have to drive first, and then eat, and then after I ate I'd have to drive again... and I'm very tired... and now I'm babbling, aren't I?"

Martina agreed that he was babbling.

"Well, okay," said Chesney, "yes, then I'll go to sleep, and we'll have dinner some other time... soon, right?"

"Yes, soon, dear," she laughed.

"That makes it all okay," he said.

"What does?"

"Your laugh," he said, "it tells me everything's all right, and I was all upset over nothing."

"I'm glad," she said. "So when will I see you again."

"Oh, I've got this book at work that I've got to finish. It's on a hard deadline. If I work every night, not tonight, of course. I've got to get some sleep. What day is it?"

"Monday."

"Still? Oh, yes, I mean, yes, Monday. Let's see, Tuesday, Wednesday...if I work extra hard...how about Saturday?"

"I can't Saturday," she said. "I'm meeting someone for dinner on Saturday. I promised. It's a classmate."

"From the reunion?"

"It's just an old friend. Actually, he's the brother of an old friend," she said, "Freddie Fadden."

He didn't say anything.

"You do trust me," she said, "don't you?"

Images rushed through Chesney's mind, emotions from his childhood, thoughts of Aunt Elinor, and... the girl in England, and finally back to Martina, and how she handled the incident the other night. Trust her? How could he not trust her?

"Chesney?"

"Oh, sorry, I...I must have nodded off, what did you say? Trust you? Of course I do. I... I trust you."

I trust you, he thought. I just don't trust Freddie Fadden.

He said goodbye, and he hung up the phone, Chesney took a shower, and then climbed into bed. As soon as his head hit the pillow and he closed his eyes, it came to him.

He sat bolt upright in bed.

"Freddie Fadden," he muttered, "Faded Red Fiend!"

– 33 –
Advice from One Half
of a Picture Frame

Chesney awoke the next day refreshed. As he fixed breakfast, he thought of Martina and smiled. She was still his girlfriend. He marveled at how it all worked out. There he was hoping that the reunion Saturday night would go perfectly and that he would end the evening telling her he loved her. Instead, he made a complete idiot of himself, passed out, and woke up in a Donny Osmond nightmare. After that, he threw up repeatedly on a major toll road, misplaced his girlfriend for more than 24 hours, and nearly drove himself mad. And he loved her even more than he could have imagined. If she was so understanding and steadfast despite of all that happened, how could their relationship not grow even stronger?

His sanguine outlook didn't survive the second piece of toast. Why would Martina ask him if he trusted her right after saying she was meeting Freddie Fadden on Saturday night? Chesney put down his teacup and stared into it as if an answer resided in its residue. He felt ashamed of himself. After Martina had been so forgiving and gracious, how could he question her motives?

Then he thought of the question he forgot to ask: where was she all day Sunday? Was she out with Freddie Fadden? Or maybe she was out with other ex-boyfriends. Perhaps she was at a post-reunion orgy…

Chesney slapped himself for entertaining such outlandish thoughts. Still, the seed had been planted.

Throughout his drive to work, he continued weeding his mind. Pulling up each errant thought as it sprouted, and tossing it aside, trying to plant healthy images in their place. Still, the nagging insinuations and accusations returned. Martina was kind. She was loving. She was patient and understanding. She had listened to him as he had poured out his broken heart. She never complained.

But why had she asked him if he trusted her? Was she doing something untrustworthy? What had gone on all day Sunday? Why did she have to meet someone else this Saturday night instead of him?

The back and forth continued as Chesney sat at his desk, wrestling with the unwieldy manuscript of Gaston Boules. His red pencil was sitting where he left it the day before, lying atop that sentence.

"Cooking is to culinary science what rocket science is to the real kind of science, at least it is when I do it right, and I always do."

He picked up his pencil, ready to strike and then thought again about Martina.

"No, this isn't going to work," he said aloud. "I've got work to do, and it won't get done this way."

He turned on his computer and opened the transcribed file of Boules' manuscript. It was almost criminal that the work existed in one form, but Chesney had it both in hardcopy and electronically. He scrolled through the file.

"Cooking is to culinary science what rocket science is to the real kind of science, at least it is when I do it right, and I always do."

He highlighted the sentence when he thought again about Martina. What was she going to do Saturday?

Not again! He had to get to work. He sighed and looked at the silver double frame on his desk. Verity had given it to him. Her picture had once been there. After she died, he removed it, unable to bear the pain of seeing her. On the other side was a photograph of Aunt Elinor.

"Oh, Aunt El," he said, "What the matter with me? I'm being...

"You're being a prat," the photograph seemed to say.

He nodded. He was being a prat, a dumbbell, but what else could he do?

"That's easy: stop being a prat," she seemed to say.

He smiled. He could almost hear her voice. What would Aunt El say? He recalled his Aunt's advice: when you're upset with a person, write them a letter; pour out your heart, the good and the bad, and then, when you've put it all in writing... don't send it. Chesney nodded. Writing it all down would help get it out of his head.

He looked at his computer. Even Boules' ghastly memoirs seemed less formidable now that he had a plan of action. The cursor was blinking where he had left off, just before:

"Cooking is to culinary science what rocket science is to the real kind of science, at least it is when I do it right, and I always do."

Chesney stared at it with a steely gaze. It remained there, unyielding. "Right, that's it," he said and began to type.

Cooking is a precise discipline, and while it isn't exactly rocket science, it still requires dedication to reach one's goals.

Not great, Chesney thought, but better. The trick to re-writing someone else's work was to improve it just enough to make them believe they were still reading their own writing.

He plowed through a few more sentences when the thoughts of Martina began to intrude once again upon his mind.

"Okay," he said, glancing at the photograph, "let's take care of this; right, Aunt El?"

He opened a new document on his computer and began to type.

"Dear Martina, I wish I could tell you all the things that are bothering me, all my fears and insecurities. You've been such a wonderful listener, but these are things I can't share with you because now you are the source of my anxiety."

Chesney paused. The next thought wasn't quite there. He switched back to the Boules book, his mind clear enough to knock out a few more paragraphs. Then, his next thought to Martina seemed to spring to life.

"I could share all these things with you, but only if I could be more open and honest with you. This isn't to say that I've lied to you, I would never do that, not consciously. But before I can tell you anything else, I first have to say what's on my heart."

He exhaled and felt the corners of his eyes moisten. There he had said it, or at least he had written it. Though he had thought it often, now his feelings were more solid. Having this moment of emotional release, Chesney was able to bang out two full pages in Gaston's story before returning to his more important work.

"I know you've cautioned me to guard my heart, and I appreciate that advice. But despite all my most vigilant defenses, you've conquered it, captured it, and made it your own. I love you, Martina! I love you!"

- 34 -
The Girl with the
Diamond Studded Hankie

I've missed you," he said, "terribly."

She smiled and looked down in that demure way that was part of her strength. Martina reached across the restaurant table and touched his hand.

"I've missed you, too," she said, stroking his hand. "You look tired."

Chesney confessed he had been up until four the previous morning working, so he could buy a few hours today to see her. She chided him, then admitted she was glad that he found the time for their date.

It was the first time they'd seen each other since the high school reunion. Chesney expected their first moments together to be awkward, but Martina had meant what she said: it was all forgotten. He had planned to make his great announcement after dinner, but now everything about her, her demeanor, her soft words, even the way she looked compelled him to speak now.

He took a sip of water in preparation for his announcement.

"I have something I'd like to talk to you about," she said while the glass was still raised to his lips.

He almost told her that he also had something to say, but just replied with a noncommittal: "Oh?"

"Yes," said Martina, "about last night, about my date."

"Date?" Chesney was stunned by the word.

"Appointment," she quickly amended.

"Oh?"

"Yes," she continued, "it was more of an appointment. That is, I approached it like it was an appointment."

"But this…the other person?"

"I found out that the other person, Fred, he thought of it as a date," she said, nervously picking at her napkin.

Numerous thoughts ran through his mind. He could accuse her of being naïve. He could tell her he knew that's what this Fred Fadden had in mind, and he didn't even know the guy. But he knew that was how guys like Fred thought.

Or, Chesney could ask Martina if it became a date. He could ask her if she fell for dishonorable intentions of the Faded Red Fiend. He thought of accusing her of toying with his emotions. He could ask her how she could go on a date with another man after telling him that she was his girlfriend. He could throw in her face the fact that she had been out with another man while he was working overtime so he could spend a few hours to be with her today.

Chesney didn't know if it was wisdom or cowardice, maturity or stupidity. Still, he felt that if he started down any of those paths, it might be impossible to find his way back to where they now were. Instead, he took a deep breath.

"Oh?" he said.

"Yes, he thought it was a date," she said.

"But," Chesney cautiously, "that's not what you thought."

"No, I thought he just wanted to talk."

Apparently, Freddy the Fiend wanted more than talk. A new road emerged in his imagination, one that led to him doing great violence to this fiend, this snake, this weasel! Instead of issuing threats prematurely, Chesney just urged her to continue.

"I saw him at the reunion," explained Martina, "he was the one who gave me the ride home. I didn't think anything of it at the time. You see, Freddie is the brother of a boy who I was once quite fond of."

Chesney rearranged the sentence in his mind to keep the preposition from dangling too close to the edge.

"He had a brother named 'Eddie.' We were friends in high school, nothing serious. We dated, but never steady."

Steadily, thought Chesney. Steady Eddie? Or was it Steadily Eddie?

"Eddie died," she said.

"Sorry."

"Last Sunday, the day after the reunion, I had to go to the hall to help clean up."

He winced. Of course, that was where she had been. How stupid of him not to think of that.

"At the end," Martina continued, "just as I was finishing, Freddie showed up and asked if we could talk. He wanted to talk about Eddie. He said he was having difficulty dealing with his brother's death."

Chesney almost cried: "that old ploy! Some guys take advantage of sympathetic girls that way all the time!" He was only stopped by the realization that was what had brought him and Martina together.

"Uh, yes," he said, "that must be difficult to deal with, losing a brother."

Martina smiled. "I knew you'd understand. I knew you wouldn't mind when you knew the whole story."

Chesney forced himself to return the smile, though now he felt like a fiend, a snake, and a weasel for being jealous. It was just as well to let the matter drop. This Fadden guy wanted to talk to Martina. He talked to her. He may have thought it was a date. He may have hoped it was a date, but she didn't think it was a date. Chesney was her boyfriend. She would probably never see Fred Fadden again.

The salad arrived, and they started eating.

"Well, it was very nice of you to listen to the fellow," said Chesney. "I hope it helped him get over his loss."

Martina kept her head down, seemingly fascinated by a bit of endive. Chesney watched her for a moment, and then an uncomfortable feeling started creeping up the back of his neck. Suddenly the air seemed charged as if lightning was about to strike.

"There is one more thing," she said, reaching into her purse and pulling out a knotted handkerchief. Martina untied it to reveal a diamond ring.

"He asked me to marry him."

– 35 –
Musings of a
Suffering Editor

He didn't know how he got through it.
Dinner.
The evening.
The ride home.
The next week.
The final work on Gaston Boules' idiotic biography.
But Chesney Potts survived.

He drank a lot of caffeinated drinks. He ate a lot of comfort food. He talked to the photograph of his Aunt. And he wrote dozens of letters to Martina, none of which he sent.

Chesney tried to console himself with the fact that he had been through worse. It was much worse losing... Verity... the same day he lost Aunt El. Yes, that was worse. That was horrible, he told himself. Still, he reasoned, it was little consolation to say that you'd once survived a shot to the chest right after taking a bullet to the head. What made so difficult was that the person who had nursed him through the first injury was responsible for the second.

How could she? How could Martina do it? He asked her in page after page of his unsent letters.

In her defense, how could Martina know how deeply he felt? How could she know that he loved her and was on the verge of asking her to marry him? Chesney couldn't ask her now. It would seem like he was copying Fadden's proposal out of desperation. He would just have to stay calm, at least on the outside. To do this, he kept pouring out his anxiety in the letters that she would never read.

Ultimately, the one thing that kept him going was that she hadn't accepted Freddie Fadden's proposal. She hadn't seriously considered it. She didn't even classify their meetings as dates. Still, Martina wasn't the type who would laugh in the face of a ridiculous proposal or offer a harsh rejection. She was patient and understanding to Freddie Fadden. His proposal hadn't scared her off. She still was meeting with him at least once a week. According to Martina she was just talking with him, just listening to Freddie, helping him through a rough spot. According to Martina, she was Chesney's girlfriend. But, Chesney reminded himself, Martina's "just listening" to Chesney's problems was how their relationship grew. He would need to be careful, not being too aggressive, nor too passive, or he would lose her.

He just kept writing.

Finally, after days that ran together, Chesney finished the Boules project.

He hit "enter."

And then he was done.

– 36 –
Regrets for a
Non-Purple Boot

Peter Liverot looked at this watch and then opened the portfolio on the conference table. It was empty. He stared at it for a moment, and then glowered around the table.

Albrecht Eckner shot a look at Valerie Fierro as if to say: "he's clueless."

"What's this meeting about, anyway?" asked Liverot.

"The upcoming compliance exam," said Valerie.

Liverot smirked, he was about to ask where his meeting notes were when the door swung open with a violent bang.

"Sorry, sorry," said Patsy Zyobidinski, "sorry, I'm a little behind. Sorry, here are your notes, Mr. Liverot, oops...sorry..."

The last "sorry" was in response to dropping the jumble of papers she was carrying.

They watched Patsy in stunned silence. Patsy, while scatterbrained in personal interactions, was an efficient secretary. It wasn't this professional lapse that caused their mouths to hang open. It was her physical appearance.

"Patricia," said Liverot, first to return his jaw to the upright position, "what the hell happened to you?"

"Just running a little late," said Patsy, as she struggled to retrieve the papers. "I'm sorry, Mr. Liverot."

"I'm not talking about the time," said the banker, "I mean, what the hell happened to you?"

Patsy looked like she had just been thrown from a train wreck. Her hair, which was always a confusion of curls, looked even more disorganized. But her hair was the least of her issues. Directly beneath her disheveled coiffure was a bulky brace that encircled her neck and disappeared down her back as part of some larger surgical appliance. Her right cheek sported a nasty purple bruise that would have complimented her green eyes had it not been so ghastly. Moving south, Patsy's left arm was bandaged from the elbow to the wrist and was supported by a sling. As impressive as the brace, the sling, and bandage all were, they were not her greatest impediment. Patsy's right leg was encased in a large plastic appliance that looked like the boot of a Star Wars Imperial stormtrooper.

"I'll have the papers for you in a minute," mewed Patsy, though it was doubtful that left to her own devices, she'd retrieve them in under an hour.

"Never mind the papers," snapped Liverot, "we'll get the papers. Miss Fierro, get the papers."

Valerie helped Patsy to a chair and then picked up the scattered paper.

"Thank you," said Patsy, catching her breath.

"What happened?" repeated Liverot.

Patsy glanced back to where she had dropped everything as if that were the start of the matter.

"To you," barked Liverot. "What happened to you, Patricia? Look at you! Who did this?"

"Uh…Donny Osmond," said Patsy.

"Oh, yeah, well, don't worry," growled the banker. "This Osborne character isn't going to get away with this."

"But, Mr. Liverot…" Patsy protested.

"Don't worry, I'll take care of this. I know people who can handle this sort of thing, nice and simple. They'll enjoy this. Nobody can go around busting up my secretary. Don't you worry; just be careful about choosing your boyfriends in the future, Patricia."

"But, Mr. Liverot, you don't understand," said Patsy.

The banker waved aside her protests. "I get it. So, what'd ya do, give him some lip? What is he some sort of hot head? Well, it doesn't matter. I know some fellas who can cool him down. He'll think twice before he does something like this again, this Osborne…"

"Osmond," said Patsy, "but…"

Valerie glanced at Albrecht, but Albrecht was just staring at Patsy.

"Osmond, Osborne, it don't matter," said Liverot with a sardonic grin. "Soon, his name'll be shit!"

"But, Mr. Liverot, you can't hurt Donny," pleaded Patsy.

"Oh, you don't think so? Well, when someone messes with my…"

"Mr. Liverot," said Valerie as she placed the papers on the conference table, "Donny Osmond is a celebrity, sort of. He's a singer. He had a TV show… Donny and Marie?"

Liverot brow knit in confusion. "Patricia, you going out with a TV star?"

Patsy sighed as if that would be the fulfillment of all her deepest wishes. Then she caught herself and returned to reality. "Uh, no, I went to see Donny. He was at the grand opening of the new warehouse club, down in Dover, on Saturday."

Liverot rubbed his finger under his nose as if doing so would help him understand. "Let me get this straight. You went all the way down to Dover to see this guy, and this is what happened."

Patsy smiled weakly. "There was sort of a riot."

The banker's eyes shot up. "Sort of a riot? I'd say it was an honest-to-goodness riot. Who is this guy? Frank Sinatra?"

"Oh, Donny Osmond is wonderful," she sighed. She caressed her bandaged wrist like it was a badge of honor.

"Well, you gonna be okay?" Liverot asked. "I mean, you can work and all that."

"Oh, absolutely," she promised. "I won't let this get in the way of my work."

"Good," said Liverot as he scanned the meeting notes. Patsy nodded and started limping toward the door.

"Now, this exam these bastards are giving us…" said Liverot.

"The FDIC," said Valerie.

"Yeah, them," said Liverot. "You handled them in the start-up, didn't you, Al? Al?"

Albrecht Eckner's attention was on the exiting Patsy. It was only as she disappeared on the other side of the door and it closed with a click, that he replied.

"What?"

"Come on," snapped Liverot, "this is a big f**kin' deal, Al. You, yourself, told me that these assholes could fine us if they don't like what they see, right?"

"Or shut down the bank entirely," noted Valerie.

Liverot shot her an anxious look.

"Could they?"

"Could who what?" said Albrecht.

"Hello, Eckner. What the hell's your problem today? You didn't go see this Elvis Osborne, too, did ya?"

"Donny Osmond, uh, no," said Eckner. "I, uh, just was worried about, Patsy, uh, Miss Zyobidinski. Do you think one of us should make sure she's okay? I could go…"

Liverot rolled his eyes. "She's fine, she's okay. She said she's okay, and she's okay. Can the Feds shut us down?"

Albrecht stared at him a moment and then as if a switch had been thrown, answered. "Shut us down? No, well, technically, yes, but that hardly ever happens, almost never."

"Almost? I don't want almost. If this bank goes down the crapper because of an 'almost,' unemployment is going to be the least of your problems. When the investors ask who let their dough get flushed into the Delaware River what am I gonna say? 'Oh, it was Al Eckner… almost.' And if that ever happened, Al, you might almost be lucky to end up in as good a shape as that one!" Liverot pointed in the direction of the departed Patsy. "So let's not have any more 'almost.' It better not happen. Right?"

Both Albrecht and Valerie agreed.

"Good," said Liverot, "I'm counting on you two. Do whatever it takes. Okay?"

"Well," Valerie started cautiously, handing Liverot a three-page list of recommendations. "Here are the most egregious violations that came up in our internal audit. If we could fix these…"

Liverot's eyes shot down the page. He flipped the page, then flipped it again, and then flinched as he realized the pages were double-sided.

"What? All of this," he asked.

Valerie smiled, hoping Liverot would smile in return. He didn't.

"You did say to do whatever it took," she said quietly.

"Yeah, but, you know, you don't have to go nuts. If we did half of this stuff, we'd be out of business."

"But," said Valerie, "they don't put you out of business for complying with government regulations."

"Not out of business by the Feds," said Liverot as if he were talking to a slow child. "We'd be out of business because we'd go broke. This bank is here to make money, not to keep a lot of Washington pencil-shovers happy." He glanced over the list once more before tossing it on to the table. "Oh, shit, do what you have to do, and by that, I mean within reason. I mean, make it look as good as you can without spending too much, you know?"

Valerie agreed to do what she could. Besides, Liverot's neck was on the line more than hers. If he wanted a cheap ticket to prison, that was his choice.

"Alright, you'd better get busy, thanks," said Liverot. "Do what you can. Don't forget the end-of-the-year bonuses are coming in a few weeks."

Valerie thanked him and rose to leave. Albrecht, who had been strangely silent, started to stand, but Liverot told him to stay behind. Valerie excused herself and left the room.

Outside, Valerie shook her head. Liverot expected her to deal with a fetid cesspool by hanging a few air fresheners over it.

As she started back to her office, Valerie passed Patsy's desk. There she sat, bruised, braced, battered, and booted. She felt sorry for her, but Patsy didn't have an FDIC exam hanging over her head.

"You okay?" asked Valerie. Patsy was trying to pivot from her computer terminal to the phone and had gotten her boot caught in the wastepaper basket.

"Oh, hi, Valerie," said Patsy cheerily. "Yeah, I'm fine. I just have to learn to get around with this." She nodded towards her foot. "I asked them if it could be purple. You know, like Donny's socks."

Valerie just stared at her.

"Donny Osmond always wears purple socks," said Patsy, as if it was common knowledge.

"Oh," said Valerie.

"Anyway, I've got that thing on my foot, not in purple," said Patsy with a sigh. Then she looked at her arm. "And this…oh, and the back brace, too."

Valerie didn't want to ask, but still, there was no way around it. "How did this happen?"

"Well, you know how I told you that Donny was going to appear at that grand opening in Dover. You remember?"

"Right, sure," said Valerie. She didn't, but then why would she remember a sentence that included: Donny Osmond and Dover, Delaware?

"Well, there was a pretty big crowd of fans," said Patsy.

Dorks and losers thought Valerie.

"He was going to sign autographs," said Patsy.

"But, he didn't?"

"Oh, he probably did," she sighed, "but I was on my way to the emergency room by then. Have you ever ridden in an ambulance?"

"No, is it exciting," asked Valerie, trying to imagine it from Patsy's point of view.

"It would probably be more exciting if I wasn't strapped to a gurney," confessed Patsy, "but, yes, it was pretty exciting."

"But what happened?"

"Well, all these people were there with Donny Osmond posters, and pictures, and books, and dolls, but nobody had what I had."

"Which was?"

"A full Donny Osmond bed sheet set," beamed Patsy, "including a fitted sheet, sheet, pillowcases… and the quilted bedspread."

Valerie nodded. "That's a lot of Donny, alright."

Patsy's smile dimmed. "A little too much, I'm afraid. You see, when the doors opened there was the big rush and my feet got tangled in the bedspread and I tripped and fell. That how that happened - torn ligaments," She pointed to the boot. "Then a bunch of other people tripped over me, and there was a pretty big pile up. That's how the rest of it happened."

"I see," said Valerie. She could imagine the announcement over the store's loudspeaker: Clean up in aisle 2, Donny Osmond Dorks. "Were many other people hurt?"

"No, thankfully, I broke everyone else's falls when they landed on me. I was the only one who went to the hospital." She looked downcast for a moment, before brightening. "But I'll be fine. The doctor says it's just temporary. I'll have it all off by Christmas."

"Good…"

"But not in time for the bank's Christmas party. You're going, aren't you?"

Valerie smirked. Just what she needed a party with Albrecht Eckner and Peter Liverot. "Oh, well, I don't know…"

"Oh, you won't want to miss it," said Patsy enthusiastically. "Nobody ever wants to miss the bank Christmas party."

"Why? Is it that good?"

"I don't know how good it is, but that's when the bonus checks are given out. The first year nobody came, and Mr. Liverot was standing there, by himself with $750 worth of food. So since then, if you don't show up, you don't get your bonus."

"I can't wait," muttered Valerie.

"Great," replied Patsy. "You can help me get around," said Patsy. The party's a few days before I get rid of all this."

"Can't wait," said Valerie.

– 37 –
No Matter How Many Copies You Make, There's Only One Santa

As Christmas approached, Albrecht Eckner was not himself. There were no snide comments, no lewd observations, no gossip. Valerie wondered what could be going on inside his twisted little mind, but she concluded that it was better not to know.

Now, the day of the Christmas party, Albrecht was practically skipping around the office as he whistled: *It's a Marshmallow World*.

"You certainly are in the spirit," said Valerie. "You must really like the company party."

Albrecht's expression dropped. "Oh, please," he sneered. "I'm going to help the Big Cheese pass out the dough. But I have to leave early."

"Lucky you," said Valerie.

"I don't think so! I had the chore of hiring a Santa Claus. Have you ever tried to hire a Santa Claus in December for a one night stand?"

"Why do we need a Santa at a party for adults?"

Albrecht smiled. He almost looked sincere. "Because it's Christmas. Santa Claus will make it all…special!"

Before Valerie could ask him if he'd gotten into the egg nog early, Albrecht had walked out of the room, whistling.

By eight that evening, the Fourth Fiduciary Trust Christmas party was in full swing. The men were wearing the same suits they had worn all day for work. The women, under Liverot's double-standard for the sexes, were told to dress in more party-appropriate finery. Many changed in the ladies' room. It looked like the dressing room of a second-rate Las Vegas casino, complete with patterned hose, dark eyeshadow, and too many sequins.

As head of compliance, Valerie refused to comply. She wore the same suit she wore to work. Her only concession was a darker lipstick for an evening look. It was more than Liverot's cheap food, and the watered-down booze deserved. Aside from some decorations and a disc jockey, it was the same cheerless cafeteria. All in all, it was a second-rate party for a third-rate bank.

Despite the cheap liquor, or perhaps because of it, the party developed a festive momentum by 8:30. This was quashed when Peter Liverot grabbed the disc jockey's microphone.

"Hello, hey, is this thing on?" Asked Liverot, and then proceeded to administer a series of loud whacks to the mike. "Yeah, well, uh, Merry Christmas, everybody. Except for you Jews, you know who you are, Happy Chanukah. Only you're not getting eight bonus checks, ha!" The three Jewish employees offered token laughter while rolling their eyes.

Liverot scanned the room. "We don't have to do that Kwanza thing, do we?" The banker looked at his handful of African-American employees.

"Alright, then that about covers you all," said Liverot, satisfied at his display of diversity and inclusion. "Well, it's been a good year for us, not that it couldn't have been better, you know, but still, you all did pretty good. And on behalf of the board…"

At the mention of the bank's board of directors, a shadowy group no one had ever actually seen, Liverot paused and looked over his shoulder. This was an odd reaction, Valerie thought, since he was standing by a window, and they were on the ninth floor.

"…uh, yeah," he continued, "on their behalf, we want to show our appreciation for all you do. Al, where are you?"

Albrecht Eckner sidled in behind his boss and tapped him on the shoulder. Liverot gave a start.

"Al Eckner, our vice-president," said Liverot. The employees clapped unenthusiastically. Eckner stood there, empty-handed. A puzzled look crossed Liverot's face.

"Where are the checks," he whispered, but into the microphone.

"Patsy has them."

Liverot looked around the room then bellowed into the microphone: "Patricia Zyobidinski! Patricia Zyobidinski?" He sounded like the riot squad. Valerie expected him to add: "the building's surrounded, come out with your hands up."

"Here I am," came a cry from the back of the room.

Liverot ordered his guests to get out of his secretary's way. They parted, allowing Patsy to hobble up to the front of the room in her heavily booted foot and back brace.

"Come on, come on," said Liverot glancing at his watch, and then realizing his overt boorishness, forced himself to chuckle amiably.

"Here are the checks, Mr. Liverot," she panted. "Sorry. Sorry, I'm so slow, only I've was putting up the decorations all day."

Liverot laughed nervously and ordered her to sit down and called for someone to bring Patsy a drink. Someone handed Patsy a large fruity-looking affair with a purple paper umbrella, a plastic pink flamingo, and a curly neon green straw sticking out of it. Liverot winced at the sight of the beverage,

"Okay, then, right," said Liverot, flipping his thumb through the stack of envelopes like it was a deck of card, "let's get this show on the road..."

He made a great show of calling out each name, and then as the recipient came forward, he made a short speech of thanks and then handed over the bonus. Valerie noticed the hesitation in Liverot's fingers as he relinquished each envelope. He looked like a crab pinching at the check, as if to grab it back. After about five checks, Liverot grew bored with his generosity. He glanced at his watch, pretended to be surprised at the time, and then announced that he had another appointment.

"Sorry, kids," he said, "but I gotta go see a guy. Al will hand out the rest of the checks. Okay? See you all on Monday..."

"Monday's Christmas Eve," someone shouted from the back of the room.

Liverot glowered towards the voice as if to warn them that he would have no problem firing anyone on December 24th. He shoved the remaining envelopes in Eckner's hands and hurried from the room.

"Well, well," said Albrecht, pursing his lips, "I guess it's all up to me...as usual." Albrecht glanced down at Patsy and nodded a signal to someone. Another ostentatious drink appeared. The secretary gratefully accepted it.

"Well," Albrecht said, "I'm not going to give you all a speech. What you really want is your bonuses." With that, he began calling names. When the recipient came up, he handed over the check without a handshake or any acknowledgment at all. After a few checks, Albrecht too glanced at his watch.

"I've got to go," he said, "I have a sick relative in the hospital. Miss Fierro?"

He waved the remaining envelopes in Valerie's direction. She stepped to the front of the room.

"What?" she asked.

"Give these out."

"Me?"

"Please, uh, I've got a sick relative."

"What? Who?"

He rolled his eyes as if to say: you know I'm lying, I know you know I'm lying, so why are we wasting each other's time.

"It's my mother," he said in a low voice.

"Oh, really, what's wrong?"

"She's having a hysterectomy," he said, "for Christmas."

"What?"

"Just hand out the checks," he said, shoving them into her hands. "Just keep everyone happy, you know, keep the party going." He glanced at his watch again. "I don't know where that shitty Santa Claus I hired is. He was supposed to be here a half-hour ago." Albrecht Eckner grimaced and hurried from the party.

"Santa Claus," muttered Valerie and then, forcing a smile on her face, proceeded to distribute the remaining bonus checks. She gave out the last bonus and then opened her envelope. It wasn't much, she observed, especially after taxes, but it was better than nothing... just. The disc jockey had started up again. With Liverot gone, the music was more contemporary in flavor. It was the first time Valerie had heard a rap version of *O, Holy Night*.

She looked down at Patsy, who was working through another drink. "Oh, hi! Valerie!" she squealed. "Isn't this a fun party? Did you ever have one of these? They taste just like Hawaiian Punch!"

Valerie leaned forward and was herself punched up the nostrils by the overpowering smell of the alcohol in the fruity concoction.

"You're not driving, are you?" she said, backing away.

"Not with this..." Patsy pointing down at her good foot, and did a double-take. "Where did it go?"

Valerie pointed to her other foot.

"Oh," Patsy giggled, "there it is! Well, I can't drive with this, so my father's going to pick me up."

"Good," said Valerie.

"In his carrrrrrr," said Patsy, she waved her hand in an approximation of a moving vehicle and then smiled. "I must be getting all better. I feel so good!"

Valerie was about to ask Patsy if she wanted some coffee when the doors at the back of the room flew open, and a voice boomed out.

"HO! HO! HO!"

Valerie looked up. Albrecht's cheesy Santa Claus had finally arrived, only he wasn't cheesy. In fact, he was actually a very good-looking Santa, with real white whiskers and flowing white hair, and his suit wasn't at all stained with the residue of pukey kids from a mall or booze stains from adult parties.

"Merry Christmas, everyone!" said Santa as he strode to the front of the room. He swung his big red velvet sack down atop the buffet table. Then he reached into the bag and pulled out a small, beautifully wrapped package and handed it to the nearest woman, a clerk from accounting.

"Have you been a good girl?" Santa asked the woman who was probably at least thirty years past her girlhood. "Well, I'm sure you have, Merry Christmas!"

The clerk unwrapped the package to reveal some perfume. It wasn't top of the line, but it wasn't junk, either. Valerie was surprised. Santa began handing out other packages to the other employees. The women received packages wrapped in gold paper, the men in silver. And none of them were cheap. There were earrings, perfume, and pendants for the women, and pen sets, wallets, and cologne for the men. Valerie estimated that the average price of each was in the twenty-five dollar range, which was quite surprising for Peter Liverot.

"And I'm sure you've been good," Santa said as he reached towards the bottom of his sack. "This is for you…"

"Thank you… Santa," said Valerie, holding the package.

"Aren't you going to open it?" asked the Santa Claus. His voice was deep and rather common.

Valerie looked down at the package. It was wrapped in gold paper like the others, but she noticed that it had a green bow, whereas the others had been tied with red ribbons. She unwrapped it, and her mouth dropped open. The box contained a beautiful pair of diamond earrings, not cubic zirconias. Valerie knew. She could spot a fake stone from across a dimly lit city block.

"T-thank you," she stammered.

The Santa looked puzzled, then leaned over and looked at the contents of the box. His eyes grew wide over his octagonal-shaped glasses. "Wow!"

"And they're real," said Valerie in hushed tones so as not to attract the attention of any of the others. "Who?"

"It was that guy, Mr. Eckhart…"

"Eckner," corrected Valerie.

"Right, Eckner," said Santa, "he just gave me them. He said the one with the green bow was for the woman with the brown hair and the dark suit." He glanced around the room to make sure that there were no other women there who fit that description. "I guess that's you. You know him pretty good?"

"He's my boss," said Valerie.

Santa jerked his head to one side. "You must be doin' a pretty good job."

"I guess…" she said.

The Santa Claus looked around the room. "He here?"

"Who?" asked Valerie.

"Eckhart, your boss," he said. "He was outside when I came in and handed me the sack. I just didn't know if he should want me to do somethin' else."

"He had to go," she said. Valerie closed her fingers over the diamonds, expecting Albrecht or Liverot to rush in and reclaim them along with the other gifts. She looked up and noticed Santa looking at her. She just smiled at him sheepishly and put the earrings in her pocket.

"Well, I have one last gift," he said, reaching into his bag and pulling out a package. "Which one is Miss…Zibilinski?"

"Zyobidinski," corrected Valerie.

"Right, Zyobidinski," he repeated. "Mr. Eccles said it to me a couple of times, but it ain't such an easy handle."

Valerie pointed to where Patsy was planted. Valerie was alarmed to see three empty drink glasses on the table next to Patsy, and a fourth cocktail in her hand. She escorted Santa to Patsy's side.

"Patsy, someone has something for you…"

"Hi, Valerie," she said even more happily than usual, "thank you, but I haven't finished this one yet."

"I think maybe you've had enough of those," said Valerie.

Patsy smiled broadly and put a waving finger to her lips as if to impart a deep secret. "I know. Don't tell anyone, but I think I'm a little bit, you know... smashed."

"Ho, ho, ho," interrupted Santa, eager to finish his rounds and leave. "I've got something for you, Miss..., uh, Miss..."

"...Xylophone," giggled Patsy.

"Right," said Santa Claus, and handed Patsy the gift.

"For me? Oh, Santa," Patsy cried, "oh, this is wonderful. This is just like the time you brought me my Barbie Dream House. I still have it, you know, in the box, and everything."

"Uh, okay," said Santa.

Patsy unwrapped the gift. It was a gold necklace.

"Oh, it's a lace nickel," she said. "Thank you, Santa, it's almost as nice as the Barbie Down Spout. I love them both. Thank you. Isn't it pretty, Valerie?"

Valerie agreed that it was and then suggested that perhaps now was a good time for Patsy to call her father.

"Okay, I'll..." she paused to suck the remainder of her cocktail through the curly straw, "...I'll go give him a call." She started to stand. The combination of four drinks and her booted foot caused her to sway. Santa Claus grabbed her and put his arm under her arms.

"I've got you," he said.

"Ooh, Santa, aren't you strong," giggled Patsy. "He's strong, Valerie. Must be all those reindeer you lift."

Valerie thanked Santa and started to take Patsy from him. But, the dead weight of an incapacitated and inebriated executive assistant proved to be too much.

"Never mind," offered Santa Claus, "I'm leaving anyway. I'll take her down to the office to call for her ride. It's no trouble, really. And I'll wait for them. I'll take care of her."

Valerie tried to protest, but the man in the red suit insisted. "Besides," he reasoned, "you're sort of the host of the party now, aren't you?"

Before she could answer, Santa was out the door with Patsy. Valerie stared after them. Something wasn't quite right. As the party continued, Valerie slipped out into the hallway. She looked to the right and then to the left. There, at the end of the hall, a sliver of light appeared from the door of the office's copy center. She sighed. It was probably some drunks making photocopies of their butts. Then she remembered that with Liverot and Albrecht gone, she was in charge. This was why she hated office Christmas parties: they were attended by people you worked with. It was bad enough that she had to spend eight to ten hours a day five days a week with them, but to pretend to enjoy their company when she wasn't getting paid for it was too much. And now she had to be the responsible adult and reign in their juvenile behavior.

Valerie's hand was on the knob of the copy room door when she heard it.

"Oh, Santa, you are jolly… OH, Santa!"

It was Patsy.

Valerie pulled back her hand from the doorknob.

"You've been a very good girl," said the voice. It was different than she had heard previously from the Santa Claus.

"Have I?" giggled Patsy.

"Very, very good," he said, "here, let me help you."

There was a grunt of exertion followed by another giggle.

Well, Valerie concluded, Patsy was an adult, and even though she was blitzed off her butt, she seemed to be enjoying herself. Valerie took a step away and would have left the couple to their pleasure when she heard Mr. Claus' plea.

"No, no, don't take that off," he said.

"But the doctor's going to take it off in a few days," slurred Patsy.

"No, leave it on, leave it all on. You don't want to take off your brace or the boot, either."

"But it's uncomfortable," she whined, "laying this way."

"Don't," he said, "just don't take it off, any of it. I'll make you comfortable."

Valerie suspected what was going on, but unsure of what to do. The copier room had a second entrance from the conference room.

Valerie hurried to the conference room. It was dark. Closing the door behind her, Valerie felt her way around the conference table by the ambient light coming from under the copier room door. She quietly turned the knob.

Inside the copier room, the action had progressed rapidly. Valerie was surprised to see Patsy on top of the big copy machine, but then she reasoned, it was the largest surface in the room. The lid that housed the paper feeder was raised in the upright position to provide a flatter surface. Valerie shook her head. Why didn't they just use the floor? For that matter, why use the copier room?

The hired Santa Claus had hiked up Patsy's skirt and lowered her panties, and now was dropping his own red velvet trousers. Valerie always thought Santa Claus, even a paid Santa, would wear boxers. This one was wearing very un-Claus like briefs, not even white, but electric blue. Upon consideration, Valerie realized that his choice of underwear was not the least Santa-ish aspect of the man. That distinction went to the fact that he was taking advantage of a drunk, temporarily handicapped secretary on top of a Xerox machine!

"Ow," said Patsy.

"What's the matter?"

"It's this neck brace…"

"Don't take it off," he urged her as if doing so would hurt him more than it would Patsy. "Not yet, not now…. here."

The Santa pulled a roll of bubble wrap from a nearby shelf and wadded it up under Patsy's neck. After a few initial "pops," Patsy rested her head.

"That's better," said Patsy."

"Yes, hold on," Santa said as he hurried out of his briefs.

"Is there a breeze in here," asked Patsy.

"No, no, hold on, hold on," urged Claus.

"Hey, what are you doing?"

"Hold on, hold on!"

Santa Claus assumed a position that Valerie had never imagined for that character, one that would forever poison every Christmas mall display and holiday TV special.

"Oh, Santa Claus, what are you doing? Oh! OOOOHHHHH!"

From the sound of them, Patsy's first "oh" seem to express surprise, the second an unexpected intrusion, and the final was drawn out in a prolonged cry of pleasure.

The ersatz Santa seemed focused on his own pleasure, though, for some reason, he kept fondling Patsy neck brace with one hand while massaging her foot boot with the other. What an odd… Valerie stifled a horrified gasp. Her mind raced back more than ten years to a night that she had tried to banish from her mind. The night of the prom, the night she lost her own virginity to…

Albrecht Eckner!

She closed her eyes and could see the floor of that horrible surgical supply store; that twisted little creep and his fetish for braces and surgical supports, and EEWWWW! No wonder Albrecht had been so preoccupied the last few weeks. Patsy's brace, and sling, and boot had been driving the big pervert out of his depraved little skull. And now, since she would be rid of all those appliances in a few days, he was using the Christmas party as his last chance with her. And even worse, he was using a Santa Claus disguise to remain anonymous.

She looked away as Santa completed his final delivery of the night. No, thought Valerie, it couldn't be him. It didn't look like him. That looked like a real beard sprouting from Santa's face. No, it was just a horny guy in a Santa suit who fancied Patsy and didn't want her to risk injury by taking off her braces.

"Oh, Santa," she heard Patsy say, "that was wonderful."

Santa Claus didn't say a word. Typical man thought Valerie. She looked back in the room. His deed was done, his passion slaked. Patsy was still splayed atop the copier, her one good hand twirling her perm. Santa was reaching down to pull up his trousers. It was then that Valerie saw it: the birthmark. It was Albrecht! That was his birthmark; that squiggle on his hip, the run-over snake, or the used condom, whatever it was, that was what she had seen that night, the night of the prom. It was possible to have two perverts with the same kinky fetish, but not two with the same birthmark. Albrecht Eckner had just done Patsy Zyobidinski on the Xerox machine in a Santa Claus suit. Ewww! How terrible for Patsy.

How interesting! Valerie could use this.

"Wait, Santa, wait," said Patsy, reaching out for Albrecht, who was now fully clothed and heading for the door. "Where are you going?"

"I've got to go," he said. Valerie could now detect Albrecht's mannerisms in his disguised voice. "I've got a lot of people to visit this time of year."

"But, Santa," Patsy smiled. "I'm a little drunk… but I know you're not really Santa…"

Even beneath the beard, Valerie could see Albrecht's expression drop as if he had just been discovered.

"You do?" he asked.

"Ah, huh," she said, "the real Santa doesn't do that…except with Mrs. Claus."

"Oh, yeah, right," he said and reached for the doorknob.

"Wait, wait," she pleaded. He paused. "That was wonderful. That, that was the first time for me…"

Valerie couldn't believe her ears. A shiver ran up her spine as she realized that both she and Patsy shared the distinction of being deflowered by Albrecht Eckner. Ewwwww! Major EWWWWWW!

"Yeah, well," said Albrecht fumbling for his escape, "I've got to go. I'll… I'll be back."

"I'll wait for you," said Patsy longingly. "I love you. Hold on, I don't even know your name."

Albrecht was standing in the doorway. He turned, stared at Patsy for a moment, curled his lip in the Eckner sneer, and muttered: *"Einfalt!"*

And then he left, closing the door behind him.

"Einfalt," said Patsy, and then repeated it several times.

Valerie shook her head and closed the door. She wished she hadn't witnessed that, but at the same time, she now knew something about Albrecht Eckner, something he wouldn't want anyone to know. And best of all: Albrecht didn't know that she knew. Yes, she nodded to herself, it could work out to her advantage. This was ammunition she could use. She could…

Before Valerie could complete her thought a hand reached from behind and covered her mouth, while another hand grabbed her around the waist and pulled her backward.

– 38 –
People Who Love on Glass Tabletops...

Valerie struggled in the dark against her assailant, but he was too powerful. Her first thought was that it was Albrecht Eckner. No, it couldn't be him. The hands weren't soft and doughy. Also, she was confident could take Albrecht in a fight.

Her attacker suddenly reached up and caressed her breast, causing Valerie to momentarily recoil. At the same moment, he flipped her around with his other hand, leaving her mouth free. Before Valerie could scream, she found herself face to face with the man who was now covering her open mouth with his own.

She struggled as best she could in lip-to-lip combat, but only for a moment. While Valerie had strong lips, they weren't always reliable. The man was a good kisser, and his gentle massaging of her breast only enhanced the effort. She closed her eyes and surrendered to his sensuous advances. The spell was broken only when he released her lips, nuzzled his nose into her hair, and murmured in her ear.

"You don't know how much I missed that."

She hadn't heard that voice for a long time. She pushed him away, and in the dim light, she saw his face.

"What the hell are you doing here?"

Though her voice was a blend of surprise and outrage, her lips still would have gladly kissed him again. Stupid lips.

"I had a little meeting with your boss, Pete Liverot."

"You know him?"

"Delaware's a small state," laughed Mitchell Minear. "You can't be in the banking business without bumping into just about everyone sooner or later, just like us, now."

Mitchell leaned forward to kiss her again, and while her lips were compliant, her brain interrupted. Valerie shoved him away and then punched him on the arm.

"Hey, what's the big idea," he laughed.

"You tell me," whispered Valerie, "and keep your voice down. I don't necessarily want to be seen in a dark room with someone like you!"

"Me? What did I do?"

Valerie rolled her eyes. "What did you do? Oh, not much. Just..." She stopped. She was going to accuse him of getting her fired from Magna Card, but she quit. He was the one who had been fired.

Mitchell Minear stepped back and leaned against the conference room table. Maybe it was just the ambient lighting, but he still looked good, perhaps even better than before. It was unfair that a bastard like Minear could grow better looking with age.

He studied her for a moment, and then as if he had read her mind, he said: "You look great, Valerie, you look even more beautiful."

For a moment, she felt her shoulders relax, and her arms began to reach for him until she caught herself.

"You didn't answer my question," she snapped.

Mitchell Minear looked thoughtful. "I thought it was a rhetorical question. Okay, what did I do? Well, let's see, I got on an airplane expecting to get a big promotion, and found that they brought me all the way out there to dump me."

"Yes, speaking of dumping...."

"I didn't dump you," he said. "I went back to the apartment. I left you messages on the answering machine. Apparently, you never went back there."

"Ya think?! Can you blame me? Do you have any idea what you did to my reputation?"

"Your reputation? Well, yes, I was considering that. I thought about that all the time I was trying to find a job while being dragged through a nasty divorce by a vindictive bitch of a wife. I knew it couldn't have been easy for you either. I wanted to explain things, but at the same time, I didn't want to cause you any more trouble."

Valerie smirked. "I did okay."

Mitchell nodded. "Apparently, we've both landed on our feet. I wasn't worried about you. You were always a smart woman. You were smarter than I was, though that's not very difficult. Still, we had some f..."

He put her arms around her, and Valerie yielded to his touch.

"...we had some...fun?" suggested Valerie.

"Mmm, I was going to say, 'fantastic sex,' but, yes, that was fun, too."

"Shut up," said Valerie, and then made it impossible for him to reply. His mouth was otherwise occupied.

♦

"So, what are you doing here?" asked Valerie a half-hour later.

"Aside from some more fantastic… fun?" he laughed. "Well, I hooked up with a bank servicing company out in the Midwest. I was meeting with Pete to see if he could throw some business our way. In fact, we sat around this same table not more than an hour or so ago. I must admit, I like the way you used the table more than he did."

Valerie snorted. "Watch out. He can screw you, too, if you're not careful."

"After the meeting, Liverot and I were walking out when I saw your nameplate on one of the office doors. Then I realized I'd forgotten my portfolio. I left him at the elevator, came back here, and then I saw you standing by that door. The rest is, well, you know what the rest is."

They were silent for several moments. Valerie's head rested against his chest and listened to his heartbeat. It was almost like old times. They were compatible, especially in bed, or on the conference table, as the case may be. She reached up and stroked the hairs on his chest, twirling them slowly around her fingernail.

"I just bought a house," she said, though she hadn't meant to. Was she offering him something? Was she trying to rekindle their relationship? Now that he was divorced and they had both moved on from Magna Card, why couldn't they get together? They both knew what they wanted. It could work.

"Really," he said, "a house? Good for you."

"Maybe you'd like to…" she hesitated, "come and see it."

"Yeah, I'd like that... one of these days."

A chill ran up her bare spine.

"I've got to fly back to Columbus in the morning," he said.

"Ohio?"

"That's home base, but I spend most of my time on the road, visiting clients, meeting with prospects…hooking up with old friends."

Hooking. Valerie wished he'd chosen a different word. She began to feel cheap and foolish. Against that feeling, she decided to try once more.

"Well, old pal," she said, trying to sound nonchalant, "it was terrific. We'll have to do this again soon."

Minear kissed her on the forehead as he climbed off the table and pulled on his shirt. "Absolutely. I think I'm scheduled to be back in the area in late February or early March. We'll hook up again."

There was that word again.

"I'll give you a call," said Valerie.

He shook his head. "No, let me call you."

Valerie sat up. He must have seen her expression in the dim light.

"I mean it," he promised, "that wasn't just a line. Only I wouldn't want you to call my office."

"Give me your home number then."

A burst of nervous laughter escaped his lips. "Home? That's even a worse idea. That's all my wife…"

"Your wife," she said, pulling her blouse around her naked body as if to shield herself from this latest piece of information. "I thought you said you got divorced."

He shrugged as he tied his necktie. "And I got remarried; the boss' daughter. You know how it is. She's okay, keeps a nice house, but, hey, she's no Valerie Fierro in the sack."

"Or on the table," she murmured.

He laughed and pointed at her. "Right, or on the table. Good one."

Mitchell Minear did up his trousers, pulled on his coat, and then leaned over to give Valerie one last kiss and empty promise before slipping out of the room.

"Bastard," she muttered as she climbed off the table and got dressed. She was about to leave when a reflection caught her eye. Valerie turned up the dimmer switch, just enough to see more clearly.

"Oh, great," she muttered.

They had put a giant crack in the protective glass on the tabletop.

"That's perfect," she said. "Is there anything else that can go wrong tonight?"

Valerie turned out the lights and silently stole from the building.

– 39 –
A Rejected Romance Novelist's Christmas Bonus

Chesney Potts sat outside Beverly Marlton's office nervously picking at a hangnail. She was going to give him his bonus for completing the Boules book on time, or at least that's what he expected. Ms. Marlton had even hinted at another bonus based on sales of the TV chef's biography.

There was nothing to be nervous about in any of that. Martina was making him pick at his hangnail. Several months had gone by, and he was no closer to expressing his love for her, at least not verbally.

Kind Martina was still seeing Fred Fadden. She insisted it wasn't dating. She said she was just listening to him work out his anxieties about the loss of his brother. She insisted that Chesney was her only boyfriend. She insisted that Freddie was just confused, that he didn't really mean it when he asked her to marry him, repeatedly. She said that Chesney was the most patient, kind, and understanding boyfriend ever.

He believed Martina, or at least he believed that Martina believed all those things she said. He wondered if one day, she would call him from her honeymoon with Freddie to insist that they really weren't on a honeymoon.

Poor Martina. He wished she would be a little less sweet and kind and wake up to Fadden's tactics. As long as she believed that Freddie's intentions were innocent, however, Chesney couldn't tell her otherwise without looking like a first-class heel. He couldn't tell her that he loved her, not without it seeming like a reaction to freakin' Freddie Fadden. She was seeing Freddie yet again that evening, while Chesney was fifty miles away in New Jersey. His girlfriend was meeting his rival without realizing he was a rival and having a date without knowing it was a date. They always met in public, usually at the cafe of one of those mega-bookstores.

Chesney would go mad if this went on much longer. He thought of Aunt Elinor and wondered what advice she would give him. A few weeks ago, he received a letter from Li Gao.

"Recall the example of your dear Aunt who loved you very much," Gao wrote. "When you go through times that try your resolve, remember that these trials are merely exercise, building up your endurance in life so you will have the strength to help others."

Trials, exercise, endurance, strength, patience, thought Chesney as he waited to see Beverly Marlton. Oh, well, at least he'd buy Martina a nice Christmas present with his bonus.

"You can go in now," said the secretary.

Chesney went into the office. He was surprised to see that Beverly wasn't smiling. He was also surprised to see Dennis Ullmer, the personnel director, and he was smiling, sort of. On the desk was a stack of books, the first printing of Gaston Boules' biography.

"Oh, they're out," said Chesney nodding towards the book.

"Yes, they're out," said Ullmer.

"Chesney, sit down," said Beverly Marlton grimly.

"You've always been a good employee," she began.

Chesney smiled. She neither looked at him nor smiled. Ullmer bared his upper teeth and scraped them against his lower lip. It made him look even more rat-like than usual.

"When you were promoted to full editor, you were the second youngest person ever to reach that position…"

"The first was Ms. Marlton, herself," interjected Ullmer.

Beverly shot Ullmer a cautionary look. "If put that way," she continued, "you were the youngest editor at Marlton Press who didn't have a father who owned the place."

"I appreciate the trust you placed in me," said Chesney.

"Trust," she repeated, "yes, it is a trust. You were given great responsibility, especially on this…"

She lifted a book from the stack and then let it drop to the floor. That wasn't a good omen.

"Ms. Marlton entrusted a huge project to you," said Ullmer.

Beverly raised her hand to silence him.

"Chesney, I realize this project had a lot of difficult deadlines…"

"Yes, it did," said Chesney. "After I completed the first draft and it was reviewed, Boules had those last-minute changes, the extra chapters to plug his new TV show. But, we got it done."

"You got it done," she said. "I know how many extra hours you devoted to that. That's why this is so difficult," she said.

"If there's anything I can do…" said Chesney, not quite sure what was wrong.

"Do? You've done quite enough," snorted Ullmer.

"Be quiet, Dennis," snapped Beverly, before she continued in gentler tones. "Chesney, look at chapter thirty, starting at page 261."

Chesney picked up one of the books from her desk and found the spot.

"Read it, please," she said, "starting at the bottom."

Chesney's throat had suddenly become very dry. He began to read.

"'And after that, I received the exciting honor of being given a new hour-long show which to display my culinary craft on.'"

He looked up.

"That was one of the chapters Boules submitted at the last minute. I… I usually would never have let a sentence end in a preposition like that," said Chesney.

"Keep reading, turn the page," said Ullmer.

"Shut up, Dennis," said Beverly Marlton.

Chesney looked down and continued.

"Uh, '…which to display my culinary craft on…'" He turned the page. "'Martina, I love you. I wish I could say it aloud to you, face to face, but for now, I can only bear my heart to this page that no other eyes, not even yours…'"

He stopped and closed his eyes.

"'…not even yours will ever see…'" recited Beverly Marlton from memory.

Chesney opened his eyes again and looked down at the book. All of pages 262 and 263 contained his private thoughts to Martina. He flipped the page, hoping that it was just those two pages, but pages 264 and 265 were also filled with expressions of his love for Martina. He rifled through the book, looking for an end.

"Page 275," said Beverly without looking up.

She was right. Over ten pages of the most private emotions of Chesney's heart were there in print.

"We had to pull the shipment," Ullmer said smugly.

"That's a relief," whispered Chesney.

"But some got out," he added.

"Oh, no," said Chesney. "How many?"

She looked at a nearby computer print-out. "Too many," she said. "Enough that it became a story in the media, enough that Boules' people found out about it."

"What can I do?" asked Chesney.

"It seems like you've done enough, Potoski," said Ullmer, before adding, "oh, I'm sorry, you're Potts now, aren't you?"

Beverly Marlton shot Ullmer a dirty look.

"It's not really up to you at this point," said Beverly sitting on the edge of the desk in front of him and placing her hand on his shoulder. "If we had caught it before the books left the bindery, we could have held back the shipment. We'd have caught hell from Boules and his lawyers and his network, but at least it would have stopped there."

"It was a letter to my girlfriend," said Chesney. "That file must have gotten into those new chapters, the ones added at the last minute. It was all so crazy. I'll pay for whatever the damages are."

Beverly smiled at him and shook her head. "That's very sweet, Chesney, but I don't think you could afford it. They've agreed not to sue."

"Oh, well, that's one consolation," he said.

"As long the person responsible is dismissed," she said.

"That's me," said Chesney.

"Yes," she said softly, "I'm so sorry."

Chesney sat in silence. His career as an editor was ruined.

"Fortunately, Boules has such a big ego," continued Beverly, "your name isn't anywhere in the book. Not even as the editor. And we told the media it was a printer's error. At least your name will be kept out of the papers."

"But not her name," whispered Chesney rifling through the unauthorized additions in the book.

"Her name?" said Beverly.

"Martina," he said. "I've made a spectacle of her. She'll never speak to me again, and I wouldn't blame her."

"You didn't mention the young lady's last name," she said. "We said the other pages were accidentally inserted from a rejected romance novel."

Chesney grimaced. How fitting, a rejected romance. He sighed. "I'll, I'll clean out my desk and be out of the building by the end of the day."

"I'm sorry, Chesney," said Beverly, "I truly am. Dennis…" She held out her hand. Ullmer grudgingly handed her an envelope, which she then gave to Chesney.

"Here's a month's pay," she said, "along with the bonus we promised you."

"But, I must have cost you…"

She waved away his protest. "It happened. We'll take the stock back, pay to have the erroneous pages cut out by hand, and put that up at a discount. Only a limited number actually made it out; in New Jersey and a few surrounding states. The rest were stopped in shipment." She pushed the envelope into his hands. "Take it. I'm sure it will come in handy."

Chesney thanked her and walked to the door. He had lost his job, but more than that, if Martina found out, he would lose her love. He suddenly thought of Li Gao. If Gao were right about trials and endurance, Chesney reasoned he'd soon be the strongest man on Earth.

"Oh, and Chesney?" said Beverly Marlton as he stood in the doorway. He turned to her. "This, too, shall pass. Merry Christmas."

– 40 –
Valerie Passes Tests 1 and 2

"Is there anything else that can go wrong tonight?" Valerie asked the night of the Christmas party as she saw the cracked glass of the conference table.

Her answer came one morning in early February in the form of vomit.

The chicken cutlets she had eaten the night before must have been off. By mid-morning, she felt much better.

The next day she was throwing up again. This time she couldn't blame the chicken cutlets. All she had eaten the night before was a bowl of cereal. She checked the carton of milk in the fridge. It smelled fresh. She felt sick, and not just to her stomach.

Valerie sat on the edge of the bed. She was a week late. She hadn't had sex since that night with Mitchell Minear.

She had had a period since then. It had been light, but it was a period. She couldn't be…

No, Valerie thought, she couldn't be. It was just a little stomach bug.

Valerie arrived at work to find Patsy Zyobidinski in a heightened state of excitement, even for Patsy.

"I'm glad you're here," said Patsy.

"It's a weekday," said Valerie, "where else would I be?"

"Only I've got to tell someone, and if I don't, I'll just burst, and I don't know who else I can tell, so I'm glad you're here so I can tell you."

Valerie just stared. Patsy had said all that on one breath.

"Can you keep a secret," said Patsy, "oh, yes, of course, you can. I didn't mean to imply that you couldn't. People just say that. You know. They say: 'can you keep a secret?' But no one ever says: 'No, I can't, so don't tell me what you wanted to tell me.' No one ever says that, do they? And nobody ever asks someone else if they can keep a secret unless they're already pretty sure that they can…"

Valerie grabbed Patsy's shoulders. "I can keep a secret. What is it?"

Patsy looked down and assumed a bashful expression, and then sat on her hands and then rocked back and forth sideways. Valerie almost preferred the jabbering.

"Well?" Valerie asked.

Patsy looked to the right and the left and then leaned forward until their foreheads almost touched.

"Guess what?" she asked.

"Patsy!"

"Okay, okay," said the secretary, "sorry, because you'd never guess. I'm going to have a baby!"

"What!"

"A baby," said Patsy. "You know, I'm going to be a Mommy. I'm going to be a Mommy to a baby, my baby, and I'll be its Mommy."

Valerie just stared at her.

"And you'll never guess how it happened," said Patsy.

No guesses were necessary. In Valerie's mind, she could see the exact moment it happened.

"It was at the Christmas party," said Patsy. "And you'll never guess who the father is."

"Who?" asked Valerie.

Patsy giggled. "Santa Claus."

Valerie closed her eyes. Poor Patsy not only believed in Santa Claus but believed he went around impregnating naïve girls atop office copiers.

"Santa…" repeated Valerie slowly.

"…Claus," said Patsy completing the name. "Oh, I know it's not the real Santa Claus. I'm not stupid. It was the boy in the Santa Claus suit."

"The boy…"

"Yes, he was so nice," said Patsy. "Of course, I was a little tipsy that night. I had some of those fruit cocktails, not fruit cocktails like you have before dinner with fruit. I mean those drinks, the fruity alcoholic drinks with fruit in them. Anyway, I had some of those, and I guess, well, I was naughty with the boy in the Santa suit. He was very nice. And I don't usually do that sort of thing, in fact…" Patsy lowered her voice even more. "I never did it before then."

"So, what are you going to do?"

Patsy just stared at her as if either she or Valerie didn't understand. "I told you. I'm going to have a baby."

"But…" Valerie looked at her trying to figure out how to explain the options to the girl, "but, the… it… you don't… the baby won't have a father."

"Of course he'll have a father," said Patsy. "He already has a father. I know who the father is."

Maybe Patsy wasn't so ditzy. Even drunk, she had seen through Albrecht Eckner's disguise. Albrecht would finally get his. "So, you know the father."

Patsy nodded. "His name is 'Einfalt.'"

"Einfalt?"

"Yes, Mr. Einfalt," said Patsy proudly. She pulled a folded piece of paper from her pocket. "See? I wrote it down. I asked him, and he told me, and I wrote it down so I wouldn't forget it."

"I see."

"And he's coming back for me, he said so."

"He did?"

"Yes, he promised," said Patsy. "And then we'll get married."

"You think so," said Valerie. "I mean, you will?"

"Of course," said Patsy. "We'll be a little family." She rubbed her still flat belly.

"What are you going to tell your parents?"

"Oh, I already told them. I told them all about Mr. Einfalt," said Patsy. "They weren't too happy, I mean, that I sort of got a little drunk, and did everything out of order. But they're going to help, at least until my husband returns."

"Your husband?"

"Mr. Einfalt," said Patsy as if were self-evident. "I'm sure he'll do the right thing and marry me when he comes back. And he promised he'd come back."

"And you're sure of that?"

"Of course, he said he would be. And I'm sure he'll marry me."

Patsy smiled as if she was now imbued with a depth of wisdom only imparted after a woman is knocked up by a jolly elf.

"Valerie, he was wearing a Santa Claus suit. Men who wear Santa Claus suits don't lie."

Valerie bit her lip. She wanted to shake Patsy by her shoulders until her silly head fell off. Since there was no such person as Santa Claus, every man who said he was Santa Claus was automatically a liar.

"So," continued Patsy, "Mr. Einfalt will come back, and we'll get married, and I'll have his baby. Simple, isn't it?"

"Isn't it," said Valerie. She wondered if she should say something to Patsy, ever so subtly, that she knew the true identity of her "Mr. Einfalt." If she were to tell Patsy, she'd have to…

Before Valerie could complete her thought, her stomach interrupted, and not at all subtly. Valerie dashed from the room and just barely made it the toilet for another round of sickness, the sickness that just happened to be in the morning.

◆

Two days later, after trying to deny it, Valerie resigned herself to a home pregnancy test.

"Another genius invention for women designed by a man," she muttered to herself in her bathroom. She had purchased two test kits. She knew if the first one came up positive, she'd want to take a second. Both were ill-conceived, no pun intended. One involved peeing on a stick. The other required peeing into a tiny cup and then immersing a stick in the cup. She cursed the geeky male scientists who had developed them. With both, she wound up splashing herself in ways that she would rather not. The indicator results of both were even more annoying. One had a little plus sign that magically appeared, the other a tiny strip on the stick turned a cheerful pink. More appropriate, Valerie thought would have been a picture of a toilet that materialized, indicating her life was now in the crapper, or a black band to signify mourning for her miserable existence.

"Freakin' marvelous," she muttered.

Valerie picked up the box to double-check the meaning of the indicators. The picture on the first box featured an annoying woman beside herself with joy holding up an equally ecstatic cherubic infant. Valerie pronounced baleful imprecations on them both and their progeny for at least four generations to come. No one having anything to do with pregnancy, birth, or procreation, had any right to be happy until further notice.

She couldn't be pregnant. She'd had a period. After checking a medical dictionary, she found the explanation: Implantation bleeding.

"Bleeding implantation bleeding! Bleeding wonderful!"

And she was on the pill! She flipped the pages and read aloud: "'Odds becoming pregnant after missing one or more doses of the birth control pill increase 30 to 80 percent.' Oh, freakin' wonderful!"

Valerie slammed the book and then looked at the picture on the test box again. The happy mother and happy baby morphed in her mind into a much more satisfying image. In that picture, she was the mother, and her hands were clutching the neck of Mitchell Minear in a death grip. Mitchell's eyes bulged out of his head while Valerie looked radiantly happy.

She flopped down on her bed. A whirlwind of faces appeared in her mind. She could see Patsy, carrying the baby of Albrect Eckner in blissful ignorance. Valerie imagined herself standing beside Patsy. They were both massively pregnant. Patsy cheerfully speculated which would be born first, not knowing that they had begun their natal race only minutes apart.

"Maybe you'll have a girl, and I'll have a boy," she imagined Patsy saying. "And they can grow up together, and go to school together, and fall in love and get married, and then we'll be grandmas together, wouldn't that be fun?"

Valerie pressed her fists against her forehead as if to drive the picture from her mind.

Patsy was lucky to be an optimistic simpleton with supportive parents. Valerie's mother and sister would be supportive, but at a price. Every grain of support would come with a sorrowful expression and a shake of the head. Valerie could hear lectures. They detailed how Valerie had wasted her life, how Valerie had always made foolish mistakes, how Valerie had the good looks, but none of her sister's good sense. The worst thing was that the lectures would never actually be spoken, but still, they would scream at her telepathically, and that would be far worse.

Valerie could see all the other women in the office, and all the women she had ever worked with, and all the girls she had ever known in school, and every female in Delaware. As soon as she started to show, as soon as she put on her first maternity top, their tongues would start wagging, and knowing looks would be exchanged. In some great estrogen-fueled mind meld, they would agree that Valerie Fierro, the girl who thought she was so much better than the rest of them, had finally gotten what was coming to her.

She could see, Mitchell Minear, running as fast as he could back to his boss' daughter of a wife, denying ever knowing a person named Valerie Fierro. The dirty bastard.

She could see the smug expression of Albrecht Eckner, offering patronizing lip service to Valerie's condition, while making snide comments on her forever-ruined figure. She could hear his catty remarks about the exponential growth in a woman's hips once she had borne a child. She could imagine him calling her maternity dresses "muumuus," while commenting that it would be impossible for a single mother to land a good husband. These observations, along with feigned sympathy for the derailing of her career, would no doubt end with Valerie spending the rest of her days breastfeeding in a trailer park. And, worst of all, when he had dashed her last shred of hope and dragged her down to a redneck abyss, she could imagine Albrecht offering to rescue her from it all by marrying her. And at that point, she thought, she would have no other choice than to say "yes."

Yes?

No! No, thought Valerie. She rose from her bed, faced her mirror, and pointed at her reflection.

"No, you won't," she vowed. "You won't let anyone say those things. You won't give any of them even a chance to think any of those things. You won't let them win. And I'd kill you before you had to sink so low as to marry... well, you won't even think that!"

A glint of gold around her neck caught her eye: her father's pendant. Valerie pressed the charm to her chest.

"Don't worry, Daddy," she said with a fresh resolve. "I will take care of number one!"

She would have to act quickly. And she knew where to start.

– 41 –
The Consolation Prizes of the Dumbbell Lottery

From the age of five, Valerie's eyes were trained to always see the ring, especially where one hadn't been before. Talk about rubbing salt in her wound. But that sting would make what she had to do a little bit easier.

"You're engaged," shrieked Valerie with the same false enthusiasm that unengaged girls always used when congratulating a graduate from their ranks.

"Yes, I am," said Martina Fergus, suppressing a tiny smile.

"So," said Valerie as she sat across from Martina in the restaurant. "Tell me all about it. Who is he?"

"Well, his name is Chesney…"

"Martina Chesney… Mrs. Martina Chesney… oh, yes." Valerie nodded her head.

"No, Chesney is his first name," corrected Martina.

"What kind of a person has the first name of Chesney?" Valerie blurted out.

"Chesney does, I guess," said Martina.

"Yes, of course, I'm sorry."

Martina smiled, indicating it had no effect on her happiness.

"Chesney what?"

"Chesney Potts."

Valerie pretended to ponder the name, to make up for her previous remark.

"Oh, yes," Valerie concluded, "Martina Potts, Chesney and Martina Potts, the Potts, oh, yes, it's charming." Actually, she thought it was pretty bad. Chesney Potts: that sounded a lot like "Chamber Potts." Ewww! Still, it wasn't her name, so who cared?

Although Valerie had an urgent agenda, she had to show interest in Martina's engagement a little bit longer. She asked how they met. Martina related some story about this Chesney guy writing a book and doing a book club for Francine Bidet and her crowd. Valerie smiled if only to keep from laughing. She pitied anyone who would have anything to do with Francine. She thought of Francine's part in her own engagement falling apart and was glad that she wasn't the only victim of the little two-faced rat. When Martina said that his appearance was a total disaster, Valerie nodded sympathetically.

"The poor guy," said Valerie, while thinking: what a dope.

"Yes," agreed Martina, "I'd never been to her club before, but I felt so sorry for him, that I had to apologize, and well, we started going out from there."

Valerie smiled. Inwardly she was shaking her head. Martina might as well collect injured puppies. "How romantic," she said while thinking it was nauseating, and just as her morning sickness was starting to subside.

"Yes, I suppose it was romantic," said Martina. A teeny grin played around the corners of her mouth, "but it wasn't nearly as romantic as how we got engaged."

Valerie forced a smile. "Oh, you've got to tell me. How did he ask you?"

"Actually, he didn't ask me," said Martina with a slight giggle. "Not directly, at least."

"I know," guessed Valerie, "you went to a basketball game, and he had the proposal put up on the scoreboard. That's so cute."

"No, it happened it a book store, and he wasn't even there."

Valerie was growing weary of this story, no matter how much she needed Martina's help. She was now practically propping up her smile with her fingers. "Oh?"

"Chesney was writing a book," began Martina, "that is, he was the ghostwriter for a book by Gaston Boules, the TV chef."

"I watch that show!" The story became slightly more interesting.

"Yes, that's the one. Anyway, Chesney and I had been seeing each other for some time. He took me to our high school reunion. Oh, that's right, you weren't there," said Martina. "That's probably just as well."

Suddenly Valerie recalled Albrecht crowing about how he'd made a fool of Martina's boyfriend. So it was that guy, thought Valerie. He must be a real winner.

"We had been going out a while, but I wasn't quite sure how Chesney felt about me. It was as if he wanted to say something, but for some reason, couldn't."

Valerie nodded. "Afraid of commitment."

"No, not at all. I think that was my fault. He was getting over a very tragic hurt, and I didn't want him to give away his heart too quickly. You understand."

Valerie assured her that she did, though, hadn't a clue what Martina was talking about. The image of the wounded puppy returned to her mind.

"And then there was Freddie Fadden."

"From high school?"

"Yes," said Martina, "he was at the reunion as well. I hadn't seen him for years, and he was going through some rough things, too."

Valerie tried to look sympathetic but wondered why Martina was getting married at all. Why didn't she just open up a halfway house for wayward losers?

"I realize now that Chesney didn't like me seeing Freddie."

"You were dating Freddie, too?" Valerie had a hard time imagining Martina dating one guy at a time, let alone two.

"No, we weren't dating," she said, "but I guess I was seeing him quite a bit, as a friend, you know, just to talk. And with Freddie being from around here and Chesney being up in New Jersey, oh, Chesney lives in New Jersey."

"That's nice," said Valerie trying not to sound bored, which was difficult when the subjects were Jersey, and Jersey losers.

"But Chesney was so patient and understanding and trusting. That had to be hard, especially after Freddie asked me to marry him."

"Seriously?"

Martina pursed her lips. "No, not really, that is, Freddie was serious, but I knew he didn't really mean it, even though he asked me quite a few times. I think he was just trying to fill another need and I just happened to be there. I was with him in the bookstore when it happened."

Valerie shook her head. This was getting confusing. "Wait, wait, you mean you were with Freddie when this other guy…"

"Chesney…"

"Yeah, him," said Valerie. "You were with Freddie when Chesney asked you to marry him, but he wasn't there."

"Yes, that's it. Oh, you do understand."

"Not at all."

"Freddie and I were in the bookstore café having coffee when there was quite a commotion. They were putting out Gaston Boules' book when suddenly they started pulling it off the shelves. This upset the people there to buy the book. When they asked the store staff why they couldn't buy the book, they were told that there was some big mistake in the printing."

"What sort of mistake?"

"That's what I wondered," said Martina. "I knew this was a very important project for Chesney."

"So was the book messed up?"

"Yes, I found the manager of the store and asked her. I explained that this book was edited by a close personal friend, and could she please tell me what happened. The manager was very nice, and she explained that someone had messed up, and there were about ten pages printed in the book that didn't belong there. It was some mushy letter to someone named Martina."

Valerie's mouth hung open. "You mean, he put your name in the book?"

"Yes," said Martina, "it was an accident."

"What did he write?"

"That's what I wanted to know, but they wouldn't let me see it. They said they had to return all the copies to the publisher. I pleaded with them, but they wouldn't let me see the book."

"So?"

Martina's cheeks turned crimson, and she leaned even closer. "I stole one."

Valerie smiled. About time, she thought, Martina Fergus finally did something bad. Welcome to the human race.

"So, what did he write about you?"

"Apparently Chesney had been writing his deepest, most personal thoughts about me, and somehow those found their way into Mr. Boules' biography. It was so romantic. I sat in the corner of the bookstore café, secretly reading the book, and I knew immediately how much he loved me. And I realized how much I loved him and that we would have to get married."

Have to get married, thought Valerie. She thought of Patsy Zyobidinski getting knocked up by Santa Claus and not getting married. She thought of her own current condition caused by Mitchell Minear, and she wasn't getting married. But Martina Fergus gets her name accidentally printed in a book because her sappy boyfriend is a peabrain and they have to get married! Any remorse Valerie felt for what she was about to do evaporated. Martina's sickeningly sunny view of the universe deserved to have a cosmic crap taken all over it.

"I sat in the bookstore with tears of joy running down my cheeks," said Martina, who was getting misty-eyed all over again. "Then I looked up and saw Freddie just staring at me, and I told him: 'I'm sorry, Freddie, I can't see you anymore. I'm getting married.' Then I went home and called Chesney, and told him I loved him and I knew he loved me, and it was beautiful."

"It sounds beautiful," said Valerie. Beautiful? No, she thought, it sounds like two grade-A dopes who learned they had just won each other as the consolation prizes in the dumbbell lottery. "I'm very happy for you. Sounds like everything is wonderful... for you." That was her transition, or so she had thought, but Martina wasn't done with her syrupy gushing.

"Yes, except that Chesney was fired because of it all."

"Oh, that is too bad," said Valerie. "I've got a little problem myself..."

"But he says it was worth it."

"What?"

"He said he'd gladly be fired from a job five days a week and twice on the weekend if it meant winning my love."

"Oh, yes, that's very…"

"Chesney says he can always get another job, but there's only one me," Martina blushed. "Sorry, that sounds awfully egotistical of me, but that's what he says."

"Yes, well, as I was saying…"

Martina beamed a giant smile. "What can you do with a boy like that, except love him?"

Valerie nodded. Love him or shove him off a cliff into the bottomless pit reserved for saps.

"Oh, but I'm sorry," said Martina, "you were saying…"

Valerie feigned that she had mislaid her own problems, in the wonderland that was the life of Martina Fergus.

"You said you wanted to have lunch," Martina reminded her. "Something you wanted to ask me?"

Valerie pretended to remember. "Me? Oh, yes, that's right. I did need a teensy little favor."

"Of course," said Martina, "what can I do for you?"

"I wouldn't dream of asking," here Valerie paused to cough and clutched her belly. "Only, I didn't have anyone else to turn to."

Martina took Valerie's hand, it was the one with the engagement ring on it.

"What can I do?" she asked.

"It's, no, I can't, it's too much to ask."

"Please, Valerie, I want to help," pleaded Martina.

"Can I, oh…"

"What? Don't be embarrassed. Ask."

Valerie wiped a tear from the corner of her eye. "Can I, that is… I need to…"

"Yes?" Martina was practically begging now.

"I need to borrow your credit card."

– 42 –
A Love Worth a Saffron Upgrade

It was a beautiful spring day for a picnic. The sun was warm. The soft breeze was gently playing with the folds of Martina's skirt as they walked. Martina looked as if she could have stepped from an impressionistic painting in her yellow dress, and matching broad-brimmed hat.

"You look beautiful," Chesney said as they walked.

"Really? I was afraid it was too much," she said self-consciously. "I don't usually go in for such coordinated outfits. Even the shoes..."

She pointed down at her feet.

"Yellow shoes," said Chesney.

Martina laughed. "Technically, they're called 'espadrilles,' and the woman in the store corrected me when I called them 'yellow.'"

"But they are yellow," he said.

"She told me they're not yellow, they're saffron."

"What's the difference between yellow shoes and saffron... what did you call them?"

"Espadrilles," laughed Martina, "I'd say the difference was at least ten dollars."

"You're worth saffron espadrilles," said Chesney as he kissed her.

Later, after their lunch, they sat beneath an elm tree. Martina cradled his head in her lap as she stroked his hair.

"Are you happy?"

He thought a moment.

"Yes, I'm very happy," said Chesney, closing his eyes. "I'm beyond happy."

"I'm glad; because I love you so," she said, "and I want you to be happy..."

With his eyes closed, Chesney couldn't tell if the sun had gone behind a cloud, or the breeze had suddenly turned chilly, or if the change was because he had completed her sentence in his mind.

"I want you to be happy," she said, though the ending was left unspoken. He imaged it was something like: "...after all you've been through."

As much as he cherished every moment with Martina, there was still that shadow. There was always the reminder of that grave in England filled before its time. Chesney gritted his teeth behind his closed lips.

"It's alright," she whispered.

He opened his eyes and saw her looking down at him so tenderly.

"You deserve better," he said.

She leaned down and kissed him. It was the closest Martina ever came to telling him to "shut up," though that was her intent all the same.

"Thank you," he said in response to her kiss.

"Thank you, too," she said and went back to making tiny swirls with his forelocks. Chesney closed his eyes again and sighed.

He was happy, he reminded himself. He was satisfied. Every day he told himself that he had more than he ever deserved. Still, he felt guilty for being unable to forget his past.

"It's okay," said Martina after several minutes of silence.

"Pardon?"

"You were thinking about England," she said without the least bit of criticism in her voice.

Since the first night they met and asked him who Verity was, Martina had never spoken the name again. Chesney couldn't speak it, still. Whenever the subject came up, it was just: "England." Odd how one person could come to represent an entire nation.

He opened one eye in a squint and looked up at her.

"How did you know?"

"Little facial expressions," she said, and then used her finger to trace the areas on his face that had betrayed him.

"Oh," he said.

"I love you, Chesney Potts."

"You must."

"I do, with all my heart."

He grimaced. "And you deserve the same."

Martina smiled softly. "I know I have all the love you have to give."

He sat up and took her hand. "Yes, you do. I only wish..."

She put her finger over his lips.

"No," she said, "never wish that."

"What?"

"You must never wish away your life, your past. It makes you what you are today. It makes you the man I love. It makes you good and kind. It makes you the type of husband you'll soon be, the kind of man who is loving, gentle, and strong. And, this is going to sound a little selfish of me, but it makes you the type of person I need."

Chesney looked into her eyes and seemed to be transported for a brief moment, not to other places, but to other people. Ever so briefly, he saw Verity, and then he saw Aunt Elinor. And he was reminded of Li Gao's consolation to him after they both had passed away; how that suffering would make him the type of person that his Aunt had been. And now it seemed, with great effort, but without actually trying, it was coming true.

"Then, I'm very glad," he said. "Then, it was all worth it."

She smiled and kissed his cheek, it was just the way someone else used to do it, and he smiled back at her.

Now, he thought, they could get married and live happily ever after: if he could only find a job.

– 43 –
Valerie Fails Test 3

A fter a few months, she rarely thought of it. It only came to mind at moments like this.

"Hi, Valerie," said Patsy, "you're early for the meeting. Mr. Eckner isn't even here yet, and Mr. Liverot is still on his overseas call."

Valerie watched as a very pregnant Patsy lowered herself into her chair with an unsteady plop. She rubbed her belly like some self-worshiping Buddha.

Valerie asked how she was getting along.

"I picked out some cribs from the Penney's catalog," said Patsy. "I can show them to you at lunch. What time are you going to lunch?"

"Oh, lunch... I've got to go out at lunch... for work."

"Maybe tomorrow," said Patsy.

Valerie smiled and sat down. She pretended to read a dull banking magazine to avoid further conversation with Patsy. She couldn't help looking at Patsy's progress and being reminded of her own lack of growth in the same area. It went well. It was the only option, she told herself. The radiant secretary was her only reminder of a brief mistake since corrected.

It went off perfectly.

She borrowed Martina Fergus's credit card. Explaining that she was strapped for cash because of the purchase of her house, Valerie told Martina she needed an emergency procedure that wasn't covered by the bank's cheap insurance. She relied on Martina's not asking too many questions, though Valerie intimated it was a "woman's issue." Valerie hadn't lied. She didn't have a lot of cash after she furnished her new townhouse. The bank's insurance was pretty cheap and wouldn't have covered the procedure. And you couldn't get more of a "woman's issue" than pregnancy.

With only a slight hesitancy, Martina handed her credit card to Valerie. There were no prying questions, and Valerie didn't have to use any of the little lies she had rehearsed. Martina hadn't asked. Valerie even felt that she almost overplayed it all, with ardent promises that she would pay her back as soon as her credit card bill came due. Martina just smiled and said she was sure that she would.

Valerie took a Friday afternoon off, drove over the border into Pennsylvania to the women's clinic; and, handed them the credit card upon checking in.

"Just fill out these forms, Ms. Fergus," said the receptionist.

"Thank you," said Valerie.

The next day she received a delivery of flowers. "Hope you're feeling well," said the card. It was signed: "Martina."

It was a lovely gesture, though Martina had already done more than enough.

By Monday morning, she was back at work. Easy. No muss, no fuss. At that point, Patsy wasn't even showing yet.

Valerie called Martina every week, asking if she had received her credit card bill yet. When it showed up the third week, Valerie was there immediately with the check. She even rounded it up to the next dollar. All done. Nice and neat. No harm.

The only reminder was Patsy. The usual glow of Patsy's personality was even more beaming. Ignorance is bliss, thought Valerie. Patsy thought she knew who the father was. She thought the man was coming back to marry her.

"Penny for your thoughts," murmured a voice in Valerie's ear.

"Nothing, Albrecht," said Valerie.

Albrecht Eckner had slithered silently into the waiting area. He smiled at her broadly without showing a trace of tooth, before looking at Patsy across the room.

"My, my," he said, adopting a southern, girly-sounding dialect, "our Miss Patsy is just getting a-fit to bust, ain't she?"

Valerie glowered at him. He smiled back.

"She's barely six months along," noted Valerie quietly. "She'll get even bigger."

Albrecht feigned surprise. "Laws! Do tell! Why our Miss Patsy is gonna look like a big ol' tick on an ol' bloodhound a'fore she's a-done."

Valerie bit her lip and tried to ignore him.

"You're looking nice and trim," he noted, dropping the accent. "Very nice and trim."

Valerie looked at Albrecht. What was that supposed to mean? What did Albrecht know? Did he know Mitchell Minear, or maybe Mitchell had talked to Liverot and Liverot had mentioned their brief escapade to Albrecht? No, she thought, even if Albrecht knew how the glass on top of the conference table got broken, and who did it, there was no way he could know that Valerie had gotten pregnant. She hadn't told a soul. Even the women's clinic thought she was someone else. No one she knew could have seen her.

The phone on Patsy's desk buzzed.

"Yes, Mr. Liverot," she said, "Right away…. yes, I'll tell them." She hung up the receiver. "He'll be with you in a few more minutes," Patsy told them before excusing herself and entering Liverot's office.

Valerie looked at Albrecht, who flashed another of his depraved looks wrapped in a smile.

He did know all about it, she thought. A ripple of panic overspread her mind. She caught herself and attempted a more placid look. It was too late. It was like an animal smelling fear. Once its prey had released that scent, it was impossible to take it back. Albrecht's smile broadened.

"Would you like to tell me about it," he said in soothing tones barely above a whisper. "Oh, wait, you don't have to, do you?"

Another imprecise statement that she could take one of two ways. Either he meant: "it's none of my business, and you don't have to tell me," or "you don't have to tell me because I already know."

"Who told you?" Valerie blurted out. "That damned M…."

She caught herself as she noticed Albrecht raise his eyebrows in anticipation.

"No," she said under her breath, "damn you."

"Me? What did I do?" Albrecht asked, feigning innocence.

Valerie nodded. "No, I fell for that back in high school," she said. "Little Albrecht going fishing again."

He shrugged his shoulders as if to say he couldn't be faulted for trying, after all, he was just amusing himself.

Valerie congratulated herself for not falling into his trap, especially on something so crucial. If Albrecht Eckner ever found out what she had done, her life would be over. She might as well publish it on the front page of the newspaper and deal with the rest of Delaware rather than the torture he would put her through. But she had been too smart for him. Her satisfaction lasted another ten seconds until she glanced at Albrecht. Instead of looking thwarted, he was actually pleased about something. Then Valerie realized. She hadn't told him what she had done, but she had let him know she had done something. She had a secret and now he knew it. Their eyes locked for a moment in a silent battle of wits. She couldn't let Albrecht…

Wait! Valerie knew Albrecht was the father of Patsy's baby. Still, it may not be the right time, yet. Valerie was saving that item for an emergency. It was such a potent weapon, like an atomic bomb, it would be a shame to use it when it wasn't necessary. Unlike a stockpiled nuclear arsenal, Valerie only had the one revelation to use. She thought for a moment as she stared into his eyes. Yes, the threat was enough. Yes, just the intimation that you had a weapon at your disposal, and you could use it: that was sufficient.

She looked at his smug little grin. No doubt, he was incubating his next little ploy, especially now that he knew Valerie had a secret to unearth. Well, two can play at this, she thought.

"Patsy looks so radiant," said Valerie.

A puzzled look crossed Albrecht's face.

"She's going to be such a good mother," she continued.

"I'm sure she will be," he agreed. Obviously, this wasn't his chosen subject, and he wanted to be done with it.

"They'll be such a happy little family," said Valerie. "Patsy, and the baby... and, of course, the father."

"Father?"

"Of course, there's a father," said Valerie, playfully slapping his wrist. "I haven't seen a star in the East. There's a father, and he's coming back. That's what Patsy believes."

"Really," Albrecht said in a non-committal way. "She thinks he'll be back?"

Valerie shook her head. "Of course, I know he won't be coming back."

"Oh?" Albrecht sat up a little straighter, as if he were regaining his advantage. "And how do you know that."

She shrugged her shoulders, picked up a magazine, and began to flip through it. After a few pages, and without looking up, she said: "He won't be coming back because he never left."

Valerie still didn't look up. She could hear Albrecht swallow hard. That should take care of him.

And just in time. The office door opened, and Patsy announced Liverot was ready for them. As they walked in, Valerie caught a glimpse of Albrecht's eyes. They didn't hold their usual confident focus. Instead, they were darting about. Good, she thought.

"Sit down," barked Peter Liverot, "shut the door."

Liverot wasn't happy. He looked through a scattering of papers on his desk, shuffling them as if doing so would somehow change their meaning. After a moment of this, he grabbed one and leaned back in his chair.

"The exit interview," he began.

"Is next week," said Eckner.

"F**ckin' Feds," said Liverot.

Valerie had been anticipating a poor result of the recent FDIC examination, but, as Albrecht had said, the exit interview wasn't until next week.

"They tip you off," said Liverot waving the paper. "It's all a big show. The examiners are already pretty sure what they're going to rate you when they walk in the door. Then they waste all our time before they get here, putting together all this data, and then they actually come in and spend... how long were they here?"

"Six weeks," said Valerie.

"Six weeks, wasting more of your time, going through all your files, all the stuff you already gave them copies of before they got here, and then they go write their report. And then, instead of just sending you their shitty report, they have to waste another day of your time coming in and giving it to you in person. But before they do that, they give you a preliminary final report that's almost exactly what they're going to give in the exit interview. They do that to tell you how deep in the crap you are. That way, they get to enjoy hacking off your balls twice.!"

Liverot chucked the paper on to his desk.

They sat in silence for a moment.

"How…" she began tentatively.

"How bad is it, Miss Fierro?" Liverot snapped.

It was never good when he called her: "Miss Fierro."

"It's f**ckin' disastrous," he said. Liverot leaned forward to retrieve the paper he'd just thrown down. He waved it in one hand while pointing at it with the other. "Significant… Non… Compliance!" He threw the paper down again. "Do you know what that means?"

Valerie figured it was a rhetorical question.

"Significant non-compliance," Liverot said. "This bank is in significant non-compliance! How did that happen?"

Valerie stole a glance at Albrecht Eckner, who wore a hidden but slightly discernible look of amusement on his face. He was enjoying this, the little shit.

"Don't look at him," said Liverot. "You're the compliance director." He then turned towards Eckner. "And don't you look so innocent. You're her boss. How are we in significant non-compliance?"

Valerie knew the answer. They all knew the answer. She almost wished she was pregnant. At least she could hide behind six month's worth of baby. No, that wouldn't help. She would be pregnant and fired, which would be even worse than just being fired, which she was now about to be. Three banks, she thought. Three strikes and she'd be out. What was there in Delaware once you washed out of the banking industry? Retail? She could always become a cosmetologist, but make-up was only fun when you were buying it for yourself and putting it on your own face. Showing some dumpy middle-aged woman how to transform her droopy lids into smoky bedroom eyes was a revolting prospect.

Oh, what the hell, Valerie thought, as long as she was going to be fired, she might as well tell him what he didn't want to hear.

"I said we needed to spend more on compliance," Valerie said. She wanted it to sound more forceful. Instead, an anemic kitten would have been more assertively.

Peter Liverot glowered at her. Had there not been a desk between them, Valerie felt as if he would have taken a swing at her. Then his face dropped.

"Yeah, you did," he said. "Fair enough. You told me, Valerie, right in this office."

She was "Valerie" again. She smiled, no teeth showed. It was more of a sympathetic smile, an "I told you so but wished it hadn't turned out this way" kind of smile.

Liverot nodded. "We're going to have to spend the money now," he conceded.

Valerie's ears perked up. Maybe, since she'd been right, she was going to get a bigger budget and a raise.

Liverot picked up another report and hefted it in his hand.

"At least they're not total bastards," he said. "They give you recommendations, which means that they essentially tell you what you're going to do so they won't shut you down. They gave us their recommendations, more like their orders. I want these put in place as soon as possible, especially the top one."

"Which one is that, Mr. Liverot?" asked Valerie.

He grimaced.

"Yeah, well, Val," he said, using his warmest form of address for her, "that's the kicker, ain't it?"

"Mr. Liverot?"

"Yeah, well, we need a fall guy for this all…"

"What?" Valerie shouted. He doesn't spend money on compliance. He ignores her warnings, and she had to take the fall for it all?

Liverot raised his hands. "Hold on, hold it, Val. It's for the Feds."

"I don't care if it's for the Pope," she said.

"You're getting a promotion," he said.

"What?"

"You just can't be the compliance director," he explained. "You gotta take the hit, at least to the Feds, but I know it wasn't your fault."

"Thank you," she said coolly.

"We just got to prove that we're taking this seriously, and we're going to kick it up a notch."

Valerie looked over at Eckner.

"Don't look at me," said Albrecht. "I'm not going to do compliance."

"No, not him," Liverot snorted. "No, we've gotta bring somebody in, you know, a compliance big shot. I've got a list of the banks in town with the best exam records." He pushed a paper across the desk to Valerie. "Know any of those?"

Valerie picked up the paper. First on the list was Voila Card.

"Yes," said Valerie, "I know this one, and I know their compliance person."

"Is he any good?" asked Liverot.

"She," corrected Valerie, "and yes, she's probably excellent."

"Get her in here."

– 44 –
Miss Fergus and the Blank Check

The elevator doors opened, and Valerie saw Martina Fergus waiting at the guard desk. She looked professional. Not stylish, but professional. Liverot would be impressed. Not excited, but impressed.

"Martina." Valerie shook her hand. She was still wearing that engagement ring.

"How's your mother," asked Martina.

"She's fine. How is your fiancee, Chauncey?"

"Chesney."

"Sorry," said Valerie.

Valerie signed her in and led her to the elevator.

"I really have to thank you for coming in on such short notice," said Valerie. "You're really a lifesaver, again."

"Again?"

"Yes, well, you loaned me that money awhile back for my... ladies' procedure..."

"You paid me back," said Martina. "Actually, you overpaid me."

"And now, I hope I can pay you back again, with interest," beamed Valerie.

Martina gave her a puzzled look.

"This job," said Valerie, and then lowered her voice. "Listen, between us girls, they need you bad..."

"Badly," said Martina.

"What?"

"Sorry, it's a habit I seem to have picked up from Chesney. He doesn't like it when people use adjectives in the place of adverbs."

"Yeah, okay," said Valerie, "anyway, they need you."

"For what?"

"To be their head of compliance, of course."

"You mean, this is a job interview," asked Martina.

"Of course."

"But I'm happy at Voila. I don't want to leave."

Valerie watched the buttons light up as they rose in the elevator. They were almost there.

"But they need you really bad, uh, badly," said Valerie. "You can write your own ticket. Whatever you want, you can get. They're about to have their exit interview on their exam. Liverot's looking at a 'Significant Non-Compliance'…"

"It's too late to fix that."

"Yes, but Liverot wants to prove the bank is being proactive by hiring the best, and that's you."

"There are plenty of good people…"

"This is no time for modesty," said Valerie. "Look, he's going to offer you the job. He needs you. He wants you at that exit interview, or at least to tell the examiners that he's hired you. You can get whatever you want."

The little bell went "ding," and the doors opened.

"Whatever," whispered Valerie as she escorted her to Liverot's office.

The meeting seemed to go well, at least what Valerie saw of it. Liverot was restrained, as he often was when meeting someone he needed to impress. This meant that he watched his language and was exceedingly polite.

"So, Miss Fergus, it is Miss Fergus," asked Liverot after about fifteen minutes.

"Yes, I'm engaged to be married," replied Martina with a smile. "But technically, you're not supposed to ask that question."

Peter Liverot lowered his head in mock repentance. "See? That's exactly why I need you as my Vice President of Compliance."

Vice President thought Valerie. They were upgrading the position to impress the government.

"Oh, and at the risk of breaking another regulation," added Liverot with all the charm at his disposal, "congratulations on your forthcoming nuptials."

"Thank you," said Martina.

"Now, if Valerie would excuse us," said Liverot, "I'd like to discuss particulars with Miss Fergus."

Valerie was a little bit surprised but then realized that Liverot wouldn't negotiate with Martina with her in the room. She rose to leave.

"If you need… anything," she said, "I'll be in my office."

"Thank you," said Liverot, "and Valerie, thank you for introducing me to Miss Fergus, very much."

Valerie closed the door behind her and lingered for a moment.

"Now, Martina," she heard Liverot say from behind the door, "what will it take for you to join our little bank?"

- 45 -
Chesney and the Coincidental Coincidence

He couldn't wait to tell Marti the news.

He didn't tell her about the interview. He didn't want to give her false hope, to say nothing of his own expectations.

He would have to move.

He already moved to Southern New Jersey. Now he was less than 20-minutes from the Delaware bridges. From that location, he could look for a job all over South Jersey, in Philadelphia, or in Delaware. And now he had found one. They would definitely live in Delaware.

Chesney Potts drove to Martina's parents' house and waited outside. She would be home soon. He wanted her to be the first one to know.

It was a good job. He would be making almost as much money as he had been making at Marlton Press, and though it wasn't editorial work, he would still use his writing skills.

Martina would be so surprised.

Chesney grew anxious when she was five minutes late. Maybe she had to work late. After all, she didn't know he was coming. That was the problem with surprising people. If they didn't know you were surprising them (and of course, they didn't because it was a surprise), they could surprise you by not showing up at all.

He didn't want to go to her office. They would be working for competing companies.

Where was she? Didn't she know he was waiting for her? Wait, no, of course, she didn't. Still, she would have to be home soon, wouldn't she?

His speculations came to an abrupt end when Martina's car rounded the corner. He nearly ran into the path of her car as she turned into the driveway.

"Chesney, be careful," said Martina as she got out of the car, "I almost hit you."

"That's okay, Marti, don't worry, you couldn't have hurt me," he laughed as he kissed her.

"Have you been drinking," she asked when he let her up for air. "Did someone slip you another Ricky?"

"Mickey, it's called a Mickey, and no, they haven't. And even if they had, I'm invulnerable. I won't wake up in Donny Osmond's bedroom ever again, my dearest Martina Chuzzlewitt Fergus soon to be Mrs. Potts."

He kissed her again, this one longer and even more passionate. She pushed him away and asked for an explanation.

"I got a job," he said.

"Chesney, darling, that's wonderful!"

"At Fourth Fiduciary Trust," he said. "I'll be their public relations director. It's a new position, they're a fairly new bank, that is, compared to some of the bigger banks, they're in Wilmington…"

"Yes, I know," she laughed.

"What? Yes, oh, right, of course, you do," he said, slapping his forehead. "You work in Wilmington, too, for a bank…"

"It is a coincidence."

"What? Oh, a coincidence, absolutely. Of course, I sent resumes to every bank in Delaware. That was your idea…"

"Yes, I remember, but that was months ago."

"And they called me up, their president called me up. The president of the whole bank, it's not a big bank, so I suppose it's not that big a deal, but still, it was the top man, the big cheese… that's kind of funny…"

"What is?"

"Big cheese, his name is Liverot." Chesney paused for her reaction. When he didn't get one, he continued. "Cheese, Liverot, get it? Liverot, it's a type of French cheese. I mean, it's not as popular as say, Roquefort or Gruyere, but it's a cheese just the same, French cheese… Liverot…"

"Yes, as I said, it's quite a coincidence."

"What? That he has the same name as some French cheese? He's probably French, well, I don't mean him. Actually, he sounded like he had a Philly accent. Still, his ancestors probably came from France with a name like Liverot, so I don't think it's too big a coincidence."

Chesney finally stopped to take a breath.

"No," said Martina, "I meant the coincidence is that I've also been approached by Mr. Liverot's bank."

"For what?"

"To work there."

"At Fourth Fiduciary Trust?"

"Yes," she said. "Is that so odd?"

Chesney thought a moment. "No, I suppose it isn't odd, but you'll have to admit, it is a coincidence."

"Yes, that is one way to put it," admitted Martina.

A thought occurred to Chesney. "Did Liverot call you, too?"

Martina looked at him for a moment before answering. "No, he didn't. I was contacted by an old classmate who works there. They want me to do their compliance."

Chesney stood there looking at Martina, wondering if it really was a coincidence. No, he thought. He'd been contacted by the president of the bank. And when he went in, he discovered that Liverot's secretary was Patsy Zyobidinski, whom he had met at the reunion. Liverot explained it all to Chesney: they had been looking to hire someone in public relations, they had his resume on file, Patsy had remembered him, and they called him in. Liverot liked him right away and hired him on the spot. That was all there was to it. There was only one question on Chesney's mind. He hated to be mistrustful, but it was better to ask rather than let his suspicion fester.

"Um, Marti, did you talk to Patsy Zyobidinski?"

"Darling, I talk to Patsy all the time," said Martina. "Can you be more specific?"

"Did you talk to Patsy about hiring me?"

"No, I didn't."

He looked Martina in the eye for a second. Of course, she didn't talk to Patsy. It must just be a coincidence. He laughed. She laughed.

"Well, then," said Chesney. "Do you know what I think?"

"What?"

"I think it would be great if you worked there, too."

"I think you're right," said Martina.

– 46 –
Poking Yourself in the Eye Practice

It was like poking yourself in the eye, thought Valerie. They told her it took practice; that she'd get used to it, but still, it was practicing poking yourself in the eye.

She needed contact lenses to see, and she was much too young and pretty to wear glasses.

She sat at her desk, hunched over the small mirror, the little piece of plastic balanced atop her fingertip. She edged the lens towards her eyeball. It was creepy and unnatural, she thought. It was almost there. Easy... Easy...

"You got something in your eye?"

The voice of Albrecht Eckner startled her.

The lens fell from her finger and curled up on her desk. She stared up at him. If myopic looks could kill, he would have been dead on the spot.

"I was trying to put in my contact lenses," she said, with all the malice she could cram into nine words. As usual, her venom bounced off Delaware's human king cobra.

"You never wore contacts before," noted Albrecht sitting on the edge of her desk and picking up the box they came in.

Valerie grabbed it from him and slapped it on the desk.

"No, I never did," she admitted.

"Why are you wearing them now?"

"So I can see!"

He picked up the box again to examine it further.

"Why don't you just wear glasses?" he asked.

Valerie moistened the lens with saline solution.

"As if!" she said, not bothering to look up. The question was ridiculous. Valerie Fierro? Wear glasses? Not likely! At least not below the age of sixty! She began inching it towards her eyeball.

"That looks like you're poking yourself in the eye."

"It's just what it's like," muttered Valerie.

"Is it hard to poke yourself in the eye?"

"Not as hard as it would be for me to poke you in the eye!"

Valerie gritted her teeth and made one quick jab at her eye in frustration. At the last minute, she blinked, and the lens wound up stuck to her eyelashes.

"Thank you very much," she spat. She squinted at the lens. "Oh, shit, now I've got mascara on it."

Albrecht picked up the other lens and examined it.

"Do you mind?" said Valerie. "I have to put that in my eye. Now I'll have to disinfect it."

"Ooh, pardon me," he feigned an apology. He put the lens back. "I thought contact lenses were supposed to be clear."

"You can get them in colors," she said before adding, "fashion colors."

"Hmm, never saw you as the blue-eyed type," he said.

"Well, you will soon, if I ever get the hang of... oh, never mind!"

Valerie put the lens back into its little holder, squirted some solution on it, and then screwed the top on it. Then she took a deep breath and looked up at Albrecht.

"Well?" She said frostily, "what do you want?"

He smiled prissily.

"You would have made a great old lady," muttered Valerie.

"Now, now," said Albrecht, only reinforcing her last statement, "no need to be catty, Valerie. I just came by to look at the office."

Valerie bit her tongue.

"You do know that you're moving, don't you?" he asked.

She gave him the evil eye and wondered if it would be more potent after her eyes were blue.

"Yes," she said, "Of course I know I'm moving. I have to move. The wonderful Martina Fergus needs my office!"

Albrecht shrugged his shoulders. "You wanted to hire her," he said. "A brilliant suggestion, I might add, filled with so many... delicious possibilities."

"What is so 'delicious' about Martina Fergus working here. I wouldn't think she was your type of playmate."

Again he smiled a catlike grin. "Playmate? No, not usually." Albrecht wrinkled his nose. "She's too... antiseptic? Yes, that's a good word to use concerning our Martina. And not antiseptic in the way that Patsy is. Patsy's fun. She's sweet and clean, but she's naïve as well. You can have a good time with Patsy without her realizing it."

"Copy that," said Valerie, looking down. Although she couldn't see his face, she knew the subtle reminder of Patsy, and the copy machine must have rattled Albrecht, if only for a moment.

"Yes…" he hissed like a bicycle tire with a slow leak. "But Martina, well, she's sweet, and pure, and smart."

"I would think," said Valerie looking up at him, "you wouldn't be interested in that combination."

He sat down in the chair opposite her desk.

"Normally, I wouldn't," said Albrecht with a growing smile. "That kind of person isn't much fun, normally, but she won't be alone." Albrecht leaned forward. "This is a secret."

Valerie leaned forward to meet him halfway. Dishing the dirt was Albrecht Eckner's only redeeming quality. He knew the best secrets, which was yet another reason to feel paranoid around him.

"Go on," she said.

He wiggled in his seat, like a hen about to lay an egg. "She's bringing her fiancée with her."

"Him? What's his name, Chutney?"

"Something dopey like that," said Albrecht.

"Does he do compliance, too?"

"No, he doesn't. He's never even worked in a bank. Probably doesn't even have a bank account."

"And Peter was okay with that?"

"Had to be, didn't he?" grinned Albrecht. "Or else Miss Fergus wouldn't have come to work at our happy little company."

Valerie tossed her head casually to one side. Big deal, she thought. Martina had them over a barrel and got her boyfriend a job. She told Martina she could get whatever she wanted, that's how badly they needed her. Valerie was surprised that Martina would have done that. Still it was a shrewd move. They'd pry two salaries out of Peter Liverot's tight fist.

"So, good for the both of them," said Valerie, "they got the better of Liverot."

"Only one of them did," said Albrecht with a wink. "He doesn't know his girlfriend got him the job." He raised his finger to his lips and winked. "That's the secret."

"Yeah? So what's this boyfriend do? I thought he was a writer or something."

"Something like that," said Albrecht. "Don't you remember? He was the one who had such a good time at the reunion."

"Oh, right," she looked at him sideways. "The one you sabotaged. Yes, I can see where you'd enjoy having him around. Another little playmate."

"More like your little playmate," he said with a knowing smile. "You'll be working with him, or at least next to him."

"Me?"

"Yes, you'll be cozy little cubicle mates."

Valerie shook her head. It was bad enough she was taking the fall for Peter Liverot's compliance cheapness. Valerie was also giving up her position to a person whom she had recommended. Far worse still was that person was probably making twice what she had been making. She was also surrendering her office for a cubicle. Now, as the cherry on top of the whole damn sundae, she had to sit next to some jerk who couldn't even get his own job. What had Martina told her? Oh, right, he had been a book editor, but he screwed up and got his ass fired. And that when Martina realized she loved him. Oh, please!

"Won't that be nice," teased Albrecht, "you'll be able to make a new friend. I'm sure you'll be such good pals with good ol' Chutney that when you go to their wedding, and the usher asks 'friend of the bride or friend of the groom,' you'll just stand there hopelessly trying to decide which you are."

I know which you are, thought Valerie, you're a silver-plated skunk, a solid gold vole, a 24-carat little slug.

"But then," continued Albrecht gleefully, "you may be asked to be a bridesmaid or maybe even the maid of honor. That is, of course, if Chutney doesn't have to ask you to be his best man."

I'd make a better one than you, thought Valerie. At least if I was a man, I wouldn't need a medical supply fetish to make my manhood function. That little unspoken insult, made Valerie smile. Albrecht, still unable to read minds, smiled back.

"So what?" said Valerie. "I'm just sitting next to him. I'll mind my business, and he'll mind his."

"Except when you're working together," said Albrecht.

"What do you mean? What is he going to be doing?"

"Public relations."

Valerie snorted. "Public relations? Peter Liverot is going to pay someone to do public relations?"

"Why not?" asked Albrecht. "We have an image to uphold."

"More like a reputation to live down."

"Have your little joke," said Albrecht as he crossed to the door. "But remember you're corporate liaison now. That means basically you'll do 'other duties as assigned.' And I'm the one who assigns those other duties. And who knows, I may be assigning you to help our dear Mr. Chutney."

Valerie flung a bottle of saline solution across her soon-to-be former office at the departing Albrecht Eckner.

– 47 –
The Exquisitely Elegant, Scrumptiously Sumptuous, Terribly Tortuous Lunch

This way to your table," said the maître de.

"I made a reservation," he said, nodding across the room, "that one there, by the window."

"Yes, sir," sniffed the maître de, "of course you did."

The restaurant was perfect. Valerie wondered why he had chosen it. She had been to lunch with Chesney nearly every day for months, but they'd never been to the Green Room before. The place reeked of elegance and class. The plush carpet cushioned her every step and even muffled Chesney's clumsy tread.

"Madame," said the maître de holding Valerie's chair.

She thanked him and sat down. Chesney plopped into his chair on his own.

Valerie smiled demurely.

Chesney grinned and fussed with his tie. They were both handed large leather-bound menus.

"I've never eaten here before," said Chesney.

"Oh, I've been here several times," she said airily.

"Really?" He said. With his broad, smiling face, he looked like a fat kid on Christmas morning. "I wouldn't normally eat here, not every day. But this isn't every day. This is a special occasion. Isn't it?"

Valerie was reading the menu. They did an exceptionally good Maryland crab cake here.

"I said: this is a special occasion," repeated Chesney.

"Oh?" said Valerie, still not bothering to look up. Seafood ravioli. Tempting.

"Yes," he said. There was a long silence, and Valerie realized he was waiting for a response from her. He probably wanted her to guess why this was such a special occasion. It wasn't her birthday. And she didn't think it was his. Was it? She glanced up from the menu. Chesney was sitting there like he was about to burst, and not just around his waist.

"I'm sorry," she said, putting down the menu.

"You don't have to apologize," he said gallantly. He was always that way with her. Valerie never had to make any excuses for his benefit, which was just as well, since she never offered any.

"Well, okay," she said, giving him her brightest smile, "what's so special about today?"

"Don't you know?"

"No," she said, making a concerted effort to keep the smile on her face. If she had known, she certainly wouldn't have wasted her breath asking.

"Well," said Chesney, his grin growing even broader, "today is exactly six months..."

Here he stopped. It was as if he expected Valerie to complete the sentence. Six months, she thought. What happened in the last six months? Patsy had her baby. But that was like three months ago. Six months? Chesney always remembered the stupidest things. She tried to imagine what he could possibly be thinking about. It was probably something about some old song, or movie, or something that nobody else would ever remember, but for some reason was monumental in his mind.

"Six months," said Valerie arching her eyebrows higher as if to coax the secret from him. "That long?"

He nodded. "Exactly six months."

"Sorry," she finally said, "I give up. Six months what?"

"Today," he said, "is six months since we became friends."

"Oh," said Valerie. Then she realized her response was somewhat subdued, especially when compared to the big deal he was making of it. "I'm mean, really! Six months?"

Chesney nodded. "It was six months ago today that I started working at Fourth Fiduciary, and we met."

Valerie smiled. She used the same demure smile she practiced in the mirror as a little girl when pretending she'd just been crowned Miss America and wanted to appear modest.

"You remember?" he asked, contrary to any evidence that she actually had.

Valerie tilted her head slightly and continued the smile from a different angle.

"Gee, I always loved the way you smile," he said. "I always thought it was so ladylike."

It was Valerie's favorite smile, too. It took so little effort.

"Well," she said, reaching out to pat his forearm, "it was very sweet of you to remember the six-month..."

"Anniversary..." he interjected, "...of our friendship."

Valerie nodded. Friendship? Well, yeah, okay, she thought. If that's what Chesney wanted to call it, fine. She wouldn't classify it that way.

It was a work friendship, which wasn't really much of a friendship, after all. Work friendships were okay. They filled a need to make the daily grind more tolerable, but they didn't belong to her real life. All she took home was the paycheck. Still, if made Chesney happy to think he was her friend…

"Six months," she said, "I'm always amazed how you remember those types of things."

"How could I forget," said Chesney. "That was the day not only found my new career but also the day I found my sister."

He was doing it again. Sure, Valerie enjoyed Chesney Potts' work friendship. He was sweet and attentive, though, at times, he was too needy, especially with this inexplicable desire to be a part of her family. He had tried to explain it to her once, something about dead family members, he had a baby sister that had died and something about his aunt.

"I remember the first time I saw you. Remember?"

"Of course," said Valerie, before completing the sentence in her mind with: "I don't." It didn't matter. With Chesney Potts around, she didn't have to remember anything. He would always fill in the blanks without being asked.

"The first time I saw you," he said, "my mouth fell open: like this."

"Oh, I remember," she said. And now she really did. "And, you pointed at me."

"It was as if I'd seen a ghost, well, the eyes of a ghost."

"Oh, right," agreed Valerie. It was all coming back to her now. How could she have forgotten? He repeated it often enough. "One of my contact lenses fell out."

"And you had one brown eye and one blue eye. Just like my Aunt Elinor," said Chesney. "She was heterochromatic. She had complete heterochromia iridium, which means the entire iris of one eye is a different color. Partial heterochromia is more common. That's where only part of "the iris is a different color."

Valerie just smiled. I know, I know, I know, please, please never explain that to me again. "Yes, well, I gave up wearing colored contact lenses. I wouldn't want to give you heart failure every time I lost a contact lens, would I?"

She laughed. He laughed.

"Thank you," said Chesney, then his expression turned serious. "I always took that as a sort of a sign."

Oh, no, she thought. Chesney was pretty good company, but when he got serious or philosophical, she wanted to ram her head… or better yet, his head… through the nearest wall.

"I know now that it was just a colored contact lens," he continued, "But it was like a sign that here was a very kind, very sweet person."

"Thank you," she said, and she meant it; she was very sweet and kind, after all.

"I've been very fortunate to know some wonderful people," he paused, "and I count you among them."

"Thank you," she repeated. Fortunately, the waiter arrived to take their order. Valerie knew just what she wanted, but Chesney had difficulty. It was amusing. Chesney had no idea what to order at a fancy restaurant and asked numerous questions about the choices confronting him. The waiter answered his questions politely, but he'd probably go back into the kitchen and tell the rest of the staff about the hayseed at the corner table sitting with the sophisticated girl.

After Chesney managed to order something, the waiter excused himself with a bow. Chesney gave a satisfied sigh.

"You know," he said, "I guess I'd been looking for a friend like you most of my life. I just never thought I'd wind up sitting next to them at work."

"Go figure," Valerie shrugged.

"Isn't life peculiar? You go through life looking for something without realizing that you're looking for something, and then you find it where you least suspect it."

Valerie smiled and nodded. She wondered if perhaps she should have had the ravioli after all. Still, the crab cakes were always excellent.

"It's like Marti and me," he continued. "How we met was really amazing."

Valerie's smile froze. She hoped he wasn't going to start rambling on and on about Martina. Once he went down that road, he could meander on about his fiancée for at least fifteen minutes. She got it, she got it: Martina was wonderful, Martina had saved his life, Martina was sweet, and all that crap! Valerie had known Martina Fergus since high school. She didn't need constant refresher courses in Martina. She knew more about Martina than he did. She knew Martina wore boring underwear. Well, she'd let him find that one out for himself. Happy honeymoon, she thought.

Their salad arrived. Chesney interrupted himself long enough to say that it looked "interesting." Valerie took her first forkful of arugula. She felt herself mellowing under the influence of the surroundings. Oh, well, Chesney was a nice guy. He was in love, and so was Martina. They were getting married, and they did both count her as a good friend. He invited her to this elegant restaurant to celebrate her friendship. The least she could do, she thought, was to listen to him. If only he wasn't so obsessive. When Chesney found something that interested him, he was unable to talk about anything else. Still, she could listen to him while she enjoyed her meal. Chesney was picking at his greens. It was a far cry from the burger and fries that he naturally favored.

While he rambled on, Valerie noticed a woman at the next table with a particularly good application of makeup. She had the most beautiful, natural matte effect. Valerie wondered what brand of foundation she used. She would have asked the woman if they'd been in an ordinary restaurant. She couldn't here, however, not in the Green Room of the Hotel du Pont.

"…and then when I went to the book club, dressed as Hugh Goode…"

Oh, now he was on that silly story of Francine Bidet, the day that he met Martina. Didn't Chesney realize how boring this Goode guy was? Still, more than once, Valerie bragged to others that she was actually a close acquaintance of a real author or a book that was actually published. That never failed to impress people. After all, she reasoned, anyone who wrote an entire book had to be pretty smart. And smart people who wrote whole books didn't hang out with shallow, vacuous people, did they?

Their main courses arrived. Chesney had selected what looked like beef tips. She detected a longing on his face for more pedestrian fare. Valerie took her first morsel of the crab. She allowed it to melt tantalizingly on her palate, and concluded that Chesney Potts was all right, a little boring at times, but all right. And, Valerie reasoned, she must be pretty smart and deep, too.

"Things always work out for the best," he rambled on.

Valerie had heard that one before, too. What was this? Chesney Potts' greatest hits? She sincerely hoped he wasn't going to bring up that dead girl in England. It was the one subject he never fully explained. The mention of it always was annoying because he never spilled the juicy details.

"…Li Gao told me…"

Oh, that one, some Chinese guy he knew somewhere. Valerie hoped he wasn't getting into one of his philosophical tangents. More often than not, they cropped up whenever Chesney mentioned Moo Goo Guy Pan, or whatever his name was. At least the restaurant was first class. This thought coaxed another well-timed nod and smile from Valerie.

What was he talking about now? Oh, he was back on the book club, and something about providence. She never admitted that she knew Francine Bidet. That was another reason to like Chesney. They had both been victims of the same nasty, selfish person. Chesney had been a victim of trusting Francine when she had just wanted to use him for that book club. Valerie had been a victim of deciding to strip off for her boyfriend when he had invited a houseful of people over. The only difference is that Chesney had just slunk off like a whipped puppy. At least Valerie had the satisfaction of telling off all those snots. But of course, Chesney didn't know about that, and he never would either!

"Then there was Gaston Boules' biography," he continued, punctuating his comment with an embarrassed grimace. Valerie had to smirk, too. That woman at the next table had just applied a ghastly shade of lipstick that totally ruined the effect of her flawless foundation.

"That was the blunder to end all…"

"Is everything satisfactory?" The waiter interrupted.

Valerie appreciated the break. She noted the crab cakes were delicious. The waiter made a servile nod and retreated.

"What was I saying?" asked Chesney.

"Can you believe that?" said Valerie in hushed tones.

"What?"

"That woman, over there, the one just leaving with that stockbroker," she said.

"By the door?" asked Chesney, looking around. "How can you tell he's a broker?"

"It doesn't matter," said Valerie, "he looks like a broker or someone in wealth management. Never mind him. See the woman with him?"

"The pretty one?"

Valerie rolled her eyes. "Well, yes, I suppose she's all right, to an untrained observer."

"Why? What's wrong with her?" asked Chesney.

"Over-plucked."

"Over-plucked? You mean her eyebrows?"

"Of course her eyebrows. You don't see a banjo in her hands, do you? She couldn't be more obvious if she hacked her foot off at the ankle while she was cutting her toenails."

"Really?" Chesney seemed mystified.

"The perfectly sculpted brow should begin at an imaginary line parallel with the center of the nose and the inside corner of the eye…"

"Do you mean the caruncle or the canthus?"

"What?" Valerie was rarely interrupted in the middle of a cosmetics lecture, and never by a man.

"Technically, they're the medial and the lateral canthi…"

"The inside corner of the eye," she repeated sharply enough for him to abandon his carbuncles and can openers, or whatever they were. "An imaginary line from the center of the nose, past the inside corner of the eye, and up to the brow. That's where the brow should start. Then in should arch slightly to the outside of the pupil, before tapering off gracefully just beyond another imaginary line; this one from the tip of the nose just beyond the outside of the eye. It's obvious. And that woman is horribly over-plucked."

She smiled. Chesney's face betrayed a look of awe.

"Hey, your eyebrows are exactly like the ones you described," he noted as if they had just turned out that way by some happy accident.

She gave him a benign smile. "It doesn't take that much effort to be well-groomed," she noted. Valerie only spent an average of two hours a day on grooming, but that included research and development.

"I guess not everyone has your beauty sense."

"That's true," said Valerie taking a moment to admire her own abilities, "I could make any woman beautiful." She paused and stared at Chesney and chortled. "I could even make you look like a beautiful woman."

"Yeah, well, right," he said, squirming uncomfortably in his seat. "Well, I guess we'll never know that! That's for sure!"

Valerie stared at him. The nose was a little large, not excessively so, and she'd had plenty of experience minimizing Italian schozzolas in her day, not her own, naturally. And of course, Chesney was way too overweight. She could make him look like a beautiful fat woman.

They both took another mouthful of their meals.

"Yes," he said, reboarding his train of thought, "if it wasn't for that disastrous book club, we wouldn't be here today."

"Well, there are other restaurants in the area."

"No, we would be at any restaurant."

"We'd have to have lunch somewhere."

"Yes," he said, "but we wouldn't have been having lunch together. We wouldn't know each other."

"Nope, sorry, you lost me." Valerie shook her head

"If I hadn't gone to that book club I would never have met Martina," he said. "And then I wouldn't have fallen in love with her, messed up that biography, gotten fired, found my job here…" He paused and smiled, "…and sat next to you. Not only would I have not met my Martina, I wouldn't have found my sister. And that's why we wouldn't have been having lunch today."

"Right," said Valerie, picking at her crab cake. It was an awful long route just to get to lunch. Still, it was a very elegant lunch.

There was a lull in the conversation. Valerie hoped Chesney had finished the interminable parade of thoughts that ran through his head.

"Do you know why you're my friend," he said with a serious look.

"Huh?" she looked up from her plate.

"Do you know what I like about you?"

Valerie pondered for a moment. At least the question was interesting. There were any number of things that anyone could like about her. She knew she had impeccable taste and fashion sense. It was also clear that she was intelligent, and interesting and fun to be around. That's how she would answer that question. But he was asking her why he liked her. That was trickier. Chesney would probably go all maudlin and bring up the dead baby sister, or the dead aunt with the weird eyes.

"We're friends," began Chesney after a short silence, "because you're one of the kindest people I know."

He was giving her the devoted look her dog Reggie used to give her.

"Thank you," said Valerie softly. She looked down at her plate. No one had ever told her that before. After mulling the idea over for a moment, Valerie conceded it probably was true. It was remarkable that no one had figured it out before this.

"You never judge me," he continued. "I know I'm a pretty odd guy, and I can be difficult. Most people don't try to understand. They just label me as some kind of nut. Even people who like me kid that I'm weird. I know they don't mean it maliciously, but it still hurts. But you've never

247

done that. You take me as I am. And that's why, after Marti, of course, you're the most important person in my life."

Valerie could feel herself blush. She tried to look up at him, but Chesney was still giving her that adoring dog gaze. Suddenly, Valerie felt a strange mixture of emotions. She liked Chesney, but not as much as he liked her. He was nice but he said it himself, he was weird. But she had never said so to him, or Martina, or even Patsy. She mentioned it to Albrecht, but only because Albrecht said that and much worse first, and he was her boss. She had to agree with her boss, didn't she?

Chesney, she thought, why are you doing this to me? You're a work friend. Don't you get that? It's like closet organizing. All her closets were neatly arranged. Everything was in their own appropriate storage bin: her sweaters, her shoes, summer clothes, winter clothes. Everything stayed in its own little spot where it was happy. Nothing got mixed up with anything else. Everything stayed in its own little compartment. It was the only way to organize closets or relationships.

She glanced up again. He was still giving her the Reggie eyes, even as he chewed his lunch. Once, she had considered opening up the compartments and letting Chesney into the rest of her life. He was so devoted, after all. Maybe he deserved it. Whenever she felt herself softening, however, she heard that inner voice telling her: "first your teeth, then your family." And she put the lid back on. It was better that way: nice and uncluttered.

Valerie thanked him, and then said how delicious lunch was. With her head bowed, she could sense he was sitting there waiting for her to say something else. She detested the feeling that she was expected to answer a compliment with a compliment. That was so trite. But now he had upped the ante. He had not just said: "you're a nice person," or "that's a pretty blouse." No, Chesney had gone and bared his soul to her. Now even though she wasn't looking at him, Valerie could feel him sitting there, expecting her to give him a glimpse into her innermost self. She had told him how great the crab was and what an elegant restaurant it was. What more did he want?

"Uh..." he started.

Valerie braced herself.

"Uh, how," he cleared his throat. "How... do you feel about me?"

"Hmm?"

"I said, what about me?"

"What about you?" she asked, trying to deflect the question.

"Why are you my friend?"

Valerie's eyes squinted into an anxious expression, like an escaped prisoner looking into a searchlight.

"Your friend?" She smiled, "of course, I'm your friend." She even reached out and touched his hand. There, that should do it, she thought.

"Yes, of course, you are," he said, "but why are you my friend?"

Valerie looked up and smiled. "Shouldn't I be?"

"I mean," he said, "what is it about me that you like?"

Valerie pretended to choke, just slightly. That, and the ensuing sip of water, gave her a few seconds to think. It didn't help. Even after she had cleared her throat, her mind was still clogged. She couldn't very well say: "You're my friend because you happen to sit next to me." That wouldn't satisfy Chesney. It certainly wouldn't match the tribute he had just given her. It also wasn't worth lunch at the fanciest restaurant in town. Another thought came to mind, and though it was nearer the truth it would have sounded even worse: "you're my friend because you're attentive to me and that makes me feel good." "You're my friend because I treat friendships much less seriously than you do. I don't think about them nearly as much as you do." That was closer to the nub of his question, but that was unutterable, as well.

"Uh, I don't understand," said Valerie, stalling.

"What is it that you don't understand?" he asked.

"What do you want from me?"

"I don't know," he shrugged, "I just sort of wanted to know why you like me."

She looked at him and smiled again. He smiled back, but he was still waiting for an answer.

She didn't *not* like him. She even liked him more than most people, but he probably wouldn't be satisfied being graded on the curve. She liked him more than most real people, but less than her dead dog or the characters on her favorite nighttime soaps. Damn it, Chesney, she thought, you think too damn much! That's why she liked dogs and fictional characters. They didn't ruin elegant lunches with stupid questions!

"Can you give me an example?" She said.

"I can't tell you how you feel about me," he said.

"Well," she said, trying to throw it back at him, as if it were somehow his deficiency, "you must know how I feel about you. I mean, we're having this lunch… celebrating our… our friendship. I wouldn't be sitting here otherwise. I… I just don't usually say those things, I don't put them into words. I let my actions speak for me."

"I know, I'm sorry," said Chesney. "I just thought you might like to say it, you know, this being a special occasion… *sorella*."

Oh, crap, he was using Italian on her. He wasn't Italian, but he learned key phrases in Italian because he thought she would like it. She thought it was cute. But now he was calling her his sister in Italian. She would have to say something. Every second she waited, she could feel herself losing stature in his eyes, slipping off the pedestal he had built for her. Usually, she liked it on that pedestal, except when she had to justify her place on it. Now she had to come up with a plausible reason why she liked him.

Valerie glanced around the room. Such a well-appointed restaurant should have the answers to difficult questions stenciled on the walls in gold leaf. But there were no answers to be seen, just the waiters. Wait – the waiters. She noticed the waiter at the next table taking an order.

"You're polite," she blurted out, glancing at the waiter.

"Polite?"

"Yes, polite," she said, "that's very important. That's a very important trait." Especially in servants, she thought.

"Oh, yes, I guess…"

"And, oh, you have a good memory," she added as she noticed the waiter was taking the order without bothering to write it down.

"Memory?"

"Well, yes, by that I mean, you're smart, really smart, and not just smart… you're wise. Yes, you're wise." Valerie remembered that Chesney was always going on about the importance of wisdom, so he would really like that one. "In fact, you're the wisest person I know."

"Really?"

She was about to add something about being prompt but decided against it. Instead, just outside the window she saw a policeman writing a traffic ticket. "And," she added, "I like your sense of… justice." The cop looked brave. "And you're courageous, too."

"Courageous? No one ever called me courageous before."

"Well, you asked my opinion," she said defensively, "and that's my honest opinion." Of course, it was her honest opinion about someone else, but he seemed to be satisfied, so why ruin it with the truth.

"Sorry, I didn't mean to question you," he said.

She tossed her head to one side. "Often, we have qualities we don't know we have until others point them out to us."

He looked down and blushed. "Oh, yes, well, thank you. I suppose that's why you didn't want to answer the question."

"Exactly!" Valerie snapped, before softening her reply. "I mean, yes, it's difficult to reveal the deepest feelings… from my heart."

They sat for a moment without saying anything. She wondered if he had bought it.

"Is that good enough," she asked.

"Yes, it was very nice," he said. "I'm sorry if I made you uncomfortable. I was just wondering."

Valerie exhaled. She felt like she did in school after faking her way through an oral quiz. She took the last bite of crab. Somehow it didn't taste quite as good any longer. Valerie was growing weary of this testimonial luncheon, and she wished it was over, or that he would at least start talking about something important.

The waiter arrived with a sample tray of desserts. Valerie usually wouldn't have indulged, but Chesney insisted. Besides, they had tiramisu, her favorite. After what he had just put her through, Valerie was owed tiramisu.

As they waited for dessert, there was a lull. Rather than leave it empty for Chesney to fill, Valerie hit upon a topic, one which she had expertise.

"Martina's shower is next weekend," she said.

"Yes, thank you for throwing it."

"It was my pleasure," said Valerie, and for the most part, it was. She excelled at running showers, and besides, Patsy was doing all of the grunt work.

Chesney promised he hadn't mentioned a word of it to Martina. It was his job to get Martina to the shower.

"And then there's the wedding," said Valerie. "I'm going to look for a dress when I'm out in Chicago in a few weeks."

"Oh, right," he said, "that seminar thing… with Mr. Liverot. I'll miss you."

"That's sweet," she said, though she wouldn't miss him. She liked getting away from the office, especially with an expense account, albeit a small one. "It's only four days. I'll be back late on Friday."

Chesney's expression darkened. "Yes, that's about three weeks before the wedding."

"Yes, I suppose it is."

"I'll be glad when it's two weeks before the wedding," he said cryptically, "I don't like three weeks before."

Whatever, thought Valerie. The dessert arrived.

"Martina's moved into the apartment," noted Chesney as he plunged his fork into his cake.

Valerie nodded as she savored the first mouthful of tiramisu. It was all rather quaint and old-fashioned. Martina had moved into their apartment, while Chesney still commuted every day from New Jersey.

"Everything's going smoothly," said Chesney, "all except for that credit card mess."

"What mess?"

"Someone got a hold of Martina's credit card numbers."

Valerie shook her head and clicked her tongue in disgust at the lack of integrity in modern society.

"It's probably identity theft," he continued, "you know, someone pretending to be Martina and making purchases in her name."

Valerie froze. Surely it couldn't be her little transaction. Martina knew all about that, well, not all about it, but enough about it.

"Well, uh," said Valerie, "at least they found out about it. Besides, Martina's liability will only be $50. The credit card company will have to eat the rest."

Chesney agreed. "Apparently whoever did it had been working the scam for over a year. They rotated their purchases between Marti's card and some others so it wouldn't be as noticeable. Martina ordered a detailed history of the account."

Valerie's hand stopped. A forkful of tiramisu was frozen halfway between the plate and her open mouth.

"Uh, a detailed history?"

"Yes," he said, "Martina's quite upset. She wants to go over every single transaction."

Valerie mind rewound to that day, months earlier, when Martina loaned her the credit card. Then she fast-forwarded to the clinic, where she handed the credit card to the receptionist. The woman then handed back to Valerie, smiled, and said: "Thank you, *Martina*, they'll be with you in a few minutes."

She wondered what a detailed record of the transaction would tell Martina. It wouldn't use specific phrases like "termination," or anything else, would it?

Valerie could feel cold beads of sweat popping out on her otherwise perfectly powdered forehead. She wasn't a thief. She paid Martina back. She even rounded up to the next dollar. It wasn't like she stole Martina's identity like those thieves. She may have borrowed it, but only that once. There wasn't any harm done, not by her. Despite the efforts of her mind to persuade her otherwise, Valerie's stomach remained unconvinced. Her bowel started rumbling.

"Is everything all right?" said Chesney, noticing she had stopped eating.

"It's... it's just a little, too... too rich," said Valerie before excusing herself and dashing off to the ladies' room.

– 48 –
Stand-Ins and Substitutes

W ill you still be our teacher?"
The little girl's eyes glistened as if she would burst out in tears at the feared reply.

"Of course, I will."

"Oh, that's all right, then!" The girl's face brightened.

"My mom told me we're getting a new teacher," offered a little boy.

"Well, not exactly…"

"Somebody named Mrs. Potts."

Martina smiled and pointed to herself. "I am Mrs. Potts, or at least I will be in a little more than a month."

"That's because she's getting married," said another girl.

"To who?" said the boy.

"To whom," said Martina gently.

"To Mr. Potts, of course," said the bespectacled girl.

"Whom's Mr. Potts," said the boy.

Martina pointed to the rear of the Sunday School room. "That is Mr. Potts."

All the children turned around with great anticipation, most of their faces fell at the sight of Chesney sitting on a chair made for a body at least half his size.

"And what's he gonna be?" asked the first girl.

"Very happy," said Chesney.

♦

"You don't understand, I told you I can't go on that trip," Valerie Fierro shouted into the phone in her bedroom.

"I heard you the first ten times," said the groggy voice of Albrecht Eckner. "It's quarter after ten, on a Sunday morning," he said. "You woke me up. Technically, I'm still on vacation."

"I waited until after ten," she said. "That was damned nice of me, seeing as I've been trying to get you since Thursday."

"You knew I was on vacation," he repeated.

"Where were you? Never mind, I don't want to know." The words "Albrecht Eckner" and "holiday" conjured up disturbing images of him and a disgusting variety of surgical apparatuses.

"I had a lovely time," he said. From his voice, Valerie could imagine his piggy eyes crinkling up and his mouth sneering. "But, can't this wait until tomorrow morning?"

"This will only take a second, only as long as it takes for you to say that I don't have to go to Chicago with Liverot."

"I'm flattered that you're all interested in Mr. Potts and our wedding," said Martina, "but let's move on to our lesson. It's about another man and woman. We talked about them last week. Can anyone remember their names?"

Several hands were raised. Martina pointed to one boy.

"Even Adam," he said beamed.

"Thank you, James," said Martina.

"That's Adam and Eve," said the girl with the glasses.

"They didn't have any clothes on," giggled another boy.

"You're right," said Martina. "Maybe Mr. Potts will help me with the Flannelgraph." Martina gestured to the nearby easel and held out a manila envelope to Chesney. He undid the clasp and fished around for the appropriate piece of flannel, then put it on the board. I was a flannel picture of a man and a woman standing modestly behind a shrub. Off to one side was a serpent and a tree.

"We saw that last week," noted one little girl. "When they ate the fruit, and it wasn't an apple."

"Well, the Bible doesn't say whether it was an apple or not," said Martina. "But, thank you for remembering."

Another boy raised his hand, and Martina called on him.

"How come?" he asked.

"How come what, Robert?"

"How come they always stood behind bushes?"

Martina suppressed a smile. "They didn't always stand behind bushes."

"Every time I see them that where they are," said Robert.

"It's because they don't have any clothes on," noted a girl.

"And they have bare heinies," said another boy. The other children giggled.

"Yes, that's enough," said Martina gently. The class began to settle down when suddenly they broke into even louder laughter. Martina turned around to see Chesney examining the back of the flannel as if doing so would reveal the subjects' backsides.

"You're not helping," she said, trying to be severe. "Are you going to be like this with our children?" He smiled sheepishly and shrugged. The twinkle in her eyes revealed that she hoped so.

"I thought you wanted to go to Chicago," said Albrecht. "You were going to go shopping on the Miracle Mile, and eat expensive meals on Liverot's dime."

Valerie grimaced. She had been looking forward to all that. "Yeah, well, I can't go."

"Why can't you go?"

"It's personal," she insisted.

"Oh, I'm sorry," said Albrecht softening his tone.

"Thank you."

"So, what is it?"

"Didn't you just hear me say it was personal," snapped Valerie. Now he was toying with her. "Don't you understand the meaning of the word: 'personal?'"

"Of course," said Albrecht. She could almost see his wicked grin over the phone, "it means you tell me, and I don't tell anyone else."

"What?"

"Or else you will go to Chicago."

"Fine, well, if you must know…it's my mother."

"Now, what did Adam and Eve do after they disobeyed?"

Several hands shot up.

"Yes?"

"They got scared," offered a girl.

"And they ran and hid," added another child.

"Why do you suppose they did that?" asked Martina.

"They knew they did something wrong," said a little boy.

"That's right," said Martina.

"My dog chewed up my brother's baseball mitt, and we found him under the bed with it."

"Do you think your dog knew what he was doing was wrong," asked Martina, "is that why he was hiding?"

"He does a lot of things under the bed," said the boy.

"My dog ate a whole roast once," said a girl. "But he didn't hide," she said. "He just was lying in the middle of the kitchen floor with a big belly. Then we got pizza for dinner."

Another girl raised her hand.

"My cat hid for a week but came back with kittens. Was that wrong?"

"I think cats can be expected to do that occasionally," said Martina. "Let's get on with our lesson."

◆

"Your mother?"

"Yes, that's right," Valerie added a tremor to her voice and threw in a sniff for good measure.

"Oh, I am sorry," said Albrecht. He sounded sincere.

"Thank you."

"So, what is it, an operation?"

"What?" She couldn't believe he was asking that, but then given his medical fetishes, she could. "I mean, yes, an operation."

"Oh...what kind?"

"What?"

"What's she having done? Your mother?"

"It's a woman's thing," she blurted out and immediately regretted her choice of words. Saying it was personal would have settled the issue with most people. Adding it was a personal woman's issue would have turned away the rest under normal circumstances. But this was Albrecht Eckner. He thrived on the indelicate and private.

"A woman's thing," he said slowly as if they were playing twenty questions. "Like a hysterectomy?"

Valerie started to agree but then noted the leading way he said: "hysterectomy." She recalled he had used the same excuse to duck out of the Christmas party.

"I don't believe you," cried Valerie, going on the offensive.

"Oh, then it's not a hysterectomy?"

"What does it matter?"

He feigned hurt feelings. "Just trying to be supportive."

Bullshit, she thought. Albrecht was enjoying this.

"Why do you need to know," she asked, "Are you going to send her a 'Happy Hysterectomy' card?"

"Oh, then it is a hysterectomy!"

"No, I mean, yes, I mean, it's none of your business. That is, I'd rather not say."

"You don't have to tell me," said Albrecht.

"Thank you."

He paused for a moment before asking: "Is it above or below?"

"Above or below what?"

"The belt," he said matter-of-factly.

"Are you serious?"

"Is it any region that would come in direct contact with a hygiene product?"

Valerie gritted her teeth. She just couldn't go to Chicago.

"Even though they hid," continued Martina, "God found them."

"He'd be really good at hide-and-go-seek," said a boy, realizing the benefits of omniscience.

"If God knows everything," asked another child, "how come he called their names and asked what they did?"

"Well, I suppose he wanted to give them the opportunity to come out and admit that they'd done wrong," said Martina.

"Is that like when my Dad asked my Mom and me who broke the basement window with the football?"

Martina smiled. "Yes, it's very much like that. Often someone asks a question to which they already know the answer. They do that to see if the person they're asking will be honest with them."

"So when is this mystery operation?" asked Albrecht.

Valerie paused. She couldn't tell if Albrecht finally believed her, or if he was just toying with her.

"The operation is next week," said Valerie.

"But, that's just when you're supposed to go to Chicago!"

"Yes!"

"Oh, that's why you said you couldn't go," he said sympathetically.

"Exactly!"

"Oh, well, then," concluded Albrecht, "it's plain that you can't go to Chicago."

"Thank you for being so understanding," said Valerie. And damn you for being such a pain in the ass.

"So, it says that God pronounced a curse on Adam and Eve and the Serpent," said Martina.

"I thought we shouldn't use bad words," objected one girl.

"It's not that kind of cursing," explained Martina. "Here it means pronouncing a judgment, that is, to make them see that their behavior has consequences and that often there is a punishment."

◆

"What else is new?" asked Albrecht. Valerie knew he was fishing for the real reason she couldn't go on that trip.

"Isn't my mother having an operation enough?" she snapped.

"Ooh, you don't have to be defensive with me," he said. I'm not giving you any hassle about the trip. I believe you."

"What's that supposed to mean."

"'It means I believe you," he said. "Your mother needs an operation, and you should be there with her, right?"

Now she was certain he didn't believe a word of her excuse. Valerie felt like a mouse in the dark: she could smell the cheese, she just didn't know if it was sitting on a trap.

"Well, someone will have to go in your place," noted Albrecht. "After all, we've already paid for your ticket, your registration, your hotel room."

"I suppose so," said Valerie. This was the critical moment.

"That leaves me with a problem," said Albrecht. "Who do I send in your place?"

◆

"Adam's punishment was that he would have to work hard for a living," said Martina. "And Eve's was that it would be painful while having babies. Yes?" She pointed to one boy with his hand raised.

"My Dad says my Mom had the pain when we kids were born, and he's had it ever since."

"I'm sure your father is just joking," she said, glancing down at her notes. "Then it says the Serpent would someday be crushed by a future offspring, a future child of Adam and Eve. Why do you suppose that God was going to send someone else to crush the Serpent?"

A few hands went up. She nodded to the first one.

"Because Adam and Eve were afraid of serpents?"

Martina smiled and shook her head. "Anyone else?"

"Cause, maybe they couldn't do it themselves?"

"Very good," said Martina. "Everybody needs help doing some things."

"My little brother can't tie his shoes," said James. "So, I have to do it for him."

"That's very kind of you," said Martina.

"I can't reach the top shelf in my closet," said one little girl, "but Daddy helps me."

"Yes, those are all good examples," said Martina. "Of course someday your little brother will learn to tie his own shoes, and eventually you'll grow taller and be able to reach the top shelf. But Adam and Eve were never going to get any better. They'd never be able to climb out of the mess they'd fallen into, not by themselves. So even after he had punished them, God loved them so much that he promised that he'd send someone who would help them out of that problem."

"Let's see," hummed Albrecht, "who can go to Chicago instead of you?"

Valerie had to be careful. It had to be Martina, but Valerie couldn't be too eager. "I haven't thought about it," said Valerie. "But, I can help you figure it out."

"Don't worry," he said. "This is my problem. You just take good care of your mother. I'll find someone to go to Chicago."

Damn him, she thought. "Well, I feel bad putting you in this spot. The least I can do is help you find a replacement. How about Chesney?" She knew the suggestion was ridiculous. The seminar included regulations; Chesney had nothing to do with that.

"Oh, well," said Albrecht pretending to mull over the suggestion, "no, no, I don't think so. Besides, I'd hate to tear him away from you. You've become such good little friends."

Valerie's eyes narrowed. Albrecht loved to tease her about Chesney's devotion to her as if she didn't deserve it.

"Thank you," she said, barely concealing her sarcasm. "Wait! I know!"

"Really? Who?" said Albrecht mirroring Valerie's fake astonishment.

"Martina," she said, "you could send Martina."

"Martina? Oh, you mean Martina Fergus?"

Valerie resisted the urge to tell him to cut the crap, but she had gone this far.

"Of course, Martina Fergus, she is head of compliance."

"Vice President of Compliance," he said, reminding Valerie of the title she'd never attained. "Yes, you know, that might just be the person to send."

"And there's one more important thing that God did for Adam and Eve," said Martina reading from the Bible. "'The Lord God made garments of skin for Adam and his wife and clothed them.'"

"Ewww, skin," said one little girl, her face contorted in disgust.

"It means animal skins," explained Martina, "like fur, or leather."

"Like the Flintstones," said one boy. "Did they drive cars with their feet, too?"

"I don't think so," said Martina. "Why do you suppose God gave them animal skins for clothing?"

"'Cause they were naked?"

"Actually, by then," said Martina, "they had made themselves some clothes out of leaves."

"Maybe the leaves weren't too good," said one girl, "I mean, for clothes."

"That's a good point," said Martina. "The leaves didn't really cover them up. Just like when we do something wrong and try to cover it up, it doesn't work very well, does it?"

The children nodded.

"But God could have given them anything to wear, made out of anything he wanted. Look at our clothes. None of us are wearing animal skins. Why do you suppose God used animal skins?"

The children sat in silence.

Chesney, who had been standing silently by the flannelgraph, spoke.

"I knew a truck driver," he said, "who told me about it once. The sin would have to be paid for with an innocent death."

♦

"Then it's all settled," said Valerie. "Martina is going to Chicago."

There was a brief silence on the other end of the line.

"You know," said Albrecht slowly, "on second thought, maybe I should go to Chicago."

"What?"

"It might be fun," he said.

"You can't go," insisted Valerie, not sure if he was serious. "Martina has to go… she… she wants to go."

"Martina wants to go?"

"Yes, she wouldn't want anyone to know it, but she does. Don't tell her that you know."

"That's odd," said Albrecht, "I would think with her getting married next month she'd have enough to do around here."

"That's why she wants to go to Chicago," said Valerie thinking fast, "because she's getting married. She wants to have one last fling."

"One last fling?"

"Okay, one first fling, and one last fling," said Valerie. "She's never flung and she wants to get in all her flinging in one shot. You know, uh, because she… loves Chesney."

"Please, don't mention love and Chutney Pot to me on an empty stomach," he snarled. "So you're telling me Martina wants to go to Chicago and run wild because she loves him?"

"Don't you dare tell anybody what I'm about to tell you," warned Valerie, "it was girl talk…"

"Oh, yes?"

Valerie could almost see Albrecht wiggling in his seat.

"Martina told me she was concerned, you know, about, well, being inexperienced…"

"A virgin!"

"Well, yes," said Valerie. "And she doesn't want to be inexperienced… on her honeymoon."

"So he wants to go to Chicago just so she can get some experience, so she can give Clumpy Potts a good time."

Valerie verified that was the case, and made him promise to keep the secret.

"Okay," said Albrecht, "so do you want to tell Martina she can go, or shall I?"

"Oh, no," said Valerie, wanting to put as must distance between her and the decision as possible. "You don't want to embarrass her. Why don't you get Peter to tell her?"

"Oh, what a good idea," agreed Albrecht Eckner.

"What Mr. Potts is saying," explained Martina, "is that when we're disobedient, there's always a price to pay. And if we can't pay ourselves, then someone else has to do it for us; an innocent substitute."

The bell sounded signaling the end of Sunday School.

"I'll see you all next week, children," said Martina.

– 49 –
Overcast with 100% Chance
of a Shower

C an you see them yet?" asked Patsy peering through the curtains.
"You're the one looking out the window," said Valerie.
"Rachel, where's Rachel?" asked Patsy.

"She back in her crib, where you just put her," said Mrs. Zyobidinski.

"Oh, right," said Patsy. "Isn't this exciting?"

Patsy had no idea what excitement was. Valerie engineered the change for the Chicago trip. Then she had to offer her condolences to Martina when Liverot told her that she had to go to Chicago instead of Valerie. Then she had to offer to run any little errands for Martina while she was away in Chicago, like picking up her mail. But, what if Martina wanted Chesney to pick up her mail? No problem; if Martina insisted on Chesney picking up the mail, Valerie could easily convince him that she should do it. Pliable! There, that was something she liked about Chesney Potts: he was pliable, reliable and pliable, reliably pliable… if only she had thought of those qualities during that awkward friendship lunch. Still, she couldn't very well have praised him for being a squishy lump of clay, could she?

"I think I see them coming," said Patsy. "Everyone hide."

The twenty or so women in the Zyobidinski's living room looked up but didn't move from their seats.

"Oh, wait, no," giggled Patsy, "no, you don't have to hide. It's not that kind of surprise. Just be ready…"

The women went back to their chatting. Valerie went to the door under the guise of helping Patsy, but she also wanted to get the credit for the shower. True, Patsy and her mother had done most of the work, but under Valerie's supervision. She glanced at the decorations. They were tasteful, and while she hadn't actually put up any of them, she had wisely vetoed a number of Patsy's suggested themes. These included various cartoon characters and old TV shows. A Scooby-Doo wedding shower just wouldn't work. Patsy's idea for an A-Team theme was also rejected.

"They're coming up the walk," whispered Patsy.

"What excuse did he give her for coming here?" asked Mrs. Zyobidinski.

"I told Chesney to tell Martina he wanted her to come over to see my Donny Osmond posters," said Patsy. "You know, to give them ideas for decorating their new apartment."

"I told him to say he just wanted to say hello to your parents," said Valerie.

"Oh, yes, that would work, too, I suppose," agreed Patsy. "Shh, I hear them on the stoop."

The doorbell rang. Patsy stood there, her hand hovering over the knob. The bell rang a second time.

A look of panic spread across Patsy's face.

"Open it," whispered Valerie, nudging Patsy's shoulder.

She did so, and despite no one hiding and very little shouting, Martina was surprised and delighted. Valerie felt a twinge of jealousy. Her envy disappeared when she considered that the source of her happiness was Chesney, an okay work friend, but certainly not the kind of man to marry.

Chesney smiled, apologized for lying to Martina, as if he had somehow maliciously deceived her, kissed her, and then left, allowing the shower to begin in earnest.

Martina was seated in her place of honor: a kitchen chair that Patsy and her mother had festooned with enough ribbons and bows to decorate a parade float. Patsy sat on Martina's left, Valerie on her right, the other ladies all around including Martina's mother and a few of her cousins and aunts. Valerie sat tall and proud with her head high, exuding an air of dignity over the event. Showers were okay, but aside from Martina, Patsy, and to a lesser degree, Patsy's mother, Valerie really didn't know any of the other women. This might be the first and last time any of them ever saw Valerie, and she wanted to leave a memorable impression in their minds.

The first order of business was the opening of the gifts. The room soon overflowed with a lot of vapid "oohing" and "aahing" over the presents, none of which really deserved those responses. What made it all even sillier was Patsy's insistence that Martina wear all the ribbons and bows that decorated the gifts as she removed them from the packages. Martina seemed quite happy to comply with this childish tradition. But then that was Martina, wasn't it? She appeared to be enjoying herself, which was another reason for Valerie to uphold the standards of dignity.

After the various kitchen implements, housewares, sheets, towels, and other similar items had been opened, one gift remained: the one from Valerie.

"Oh, it feels heavy," said Martina. She looked at the tag. "Oh, it's from Valerie," she said, "thank you, how sweet."

Valerie smiled.

"Oh, there aren't any bows," said Patsy.

That at least was a consolation, thought Valerie. Poor Martina's hair was already overcrowded with Patsy's handiwork.

Martina carefully unwrapped the paper.

"Oh, it's a case," said Martina, and then she held it up for everyone to see. The other women nodded. It was a case. Martina placed it on her lap, undid the latches, and opened it.

"Oh, it's... make-up," said Martina, looking inside. A puzzled expression crossed her face, and she looked up at Valerie as if to say: what do I do with it all?

Valerie smiled. "It's Facial Graffiti. It's the latest, hottest line," said Valerie, "...of cosmetics."

"It's very nice," said Martina. "It's lovely, thank you." She leaned over and gave Valerie a warm hug. Then she gazed into the case with a mystified look.

"I'll show you how to use it," said Valerie in a confidential aside, "it'll be fun."

Martina stared down at the array of cosmetics and then reached up and touched her own cheek. "Oh, yes," said Martina, regaining her natural cheeriness, "yes, you'll have to teach me. Thank you. You're very sweet."

Valerie nodded and smiled. She would have her work cut out for herself with Martina. She had potential, but Valerie wondered if she had ever owned anything beyond a lipstick and maybe a wand of mascara. Still, the cosmetics were safer than Valerie's first choice of a gift: a sexy negligee. Guiding Martina to her full potential would just have to be done in increments.

"Well, thank you," said Martina, first to Valerie, before turning to all the others, "thank you all so much. This is really so kind of you all, and I know I'll get wonderful use from all..." she glanced down at the case, "...from all of these lovely gifts."

With the gifts unwrapped, Patsy announced that it was time to play the shower games.

"Mom," she said, "will you help pass out the cards for Bridal Bingo?"

A smile froze upon Valerie's face. She didn't even care for regular Bingo, and a version based, not on numbers and letters, but on Martina herself was even more inane. Still, not wanting to be spoilsport, Valerie kept her mouth closed and pretended to play. She was grateful when one of Martina's aunts won, and the game ended.

Next, Patsy announced it was time to play "How Well Do You Know the Bride?" This involved Martina leaving the room, but still staying within earshot of the party. Then Patsy, as mistress of ceremonies, started the questioning.

"What color blouse was Martina wearing?"

"Blue!" shouted one woman. Actually, Valerie recalled, it was teal.

"Right," said Patsy, "give yourself one point. Next questions: was Martina wearing her hair up or down?"

"Up!" called out one girl.

"Down!" Insisted another.

Patsy seemed confused and asked for Martina to poke her head around the corner to settle the matter.

"It actually is a little of both," conceded Martina. "I'm wearing clips that pull it up on the side, but it's down in the back."

"I'll give you both points for that one," said Patsy, "in fact, everyone can have a point for that one."

With the basic questions on Martina's appearance answered, the bride was invited back into the room, and the game progressed into more challenging areas. Questions like: where Martina first met Chesney, where they went on their first date, and when they first kissed. Valerie knew some of these answers, but only answered them when no one else could. She had to keep the shower moving along. It was when Patsy asked a series of questions about Chesney that Valerie pulled into the lead. A cousin of Martina's named Renee tied the game because she just happened to know Martina's favorite flavor of ice cream.

"Well, the game is tied," gushed Patsy. "And there's only one question left...the bonus question that will decide the winner of the grand prize."

"What is the prize," asked the cousin.

"A spa gift certificate," said Patsy.

Valerie's brow shot up. It was actually a good prize, one she could use. Valerie glanced over at cousin Renee. She could be described as "roly-poly," though in truth, she was actually roly-roly-poly. What could a girl like that get out of a day at a spa? She'd need a mirror to see her pedicured toes and the image of her in a mud bath... well, it wasn't pretty. Valerie concluded she would be saving this girl certain embarrassment by winning the prize herself.

Patsy handing them each an index card and pen, "this will be a written answer."

"I won't have to write an essay?" asked Renee, a worried look creasing her chubby facial features.

"Oh, no," assured Patsy, "it's just a short answer. It's a shopping question."

Valerie suppressed a grin. Shopping question? She could have majored in shopping in college if they had had it in the curriculum. Hell, she could be a professor, the dean of the shopping university. She might as well book her appointment at that spa right now.

"What," said Patsy dramatically, "what was the last purchase... over $500... that Martina made... on a credit card?"

It was as if Valerie had just been gut-punched. She emitted a soft, but sharp gasp. Her mind went blank, save for one thought. Valerie could see

Martina's credit card in her own hand. She was handing it over the counter to the woman at the clinic. The one where she had had her procedure, the procedure she had on Martina's credit card, in Martina's name, in the name of Martina Fergus. Valerie felt her throat constrict. She heard a baby cry, and then a baby laughing. She looked up. Patsy's mother was carrying Patsy's daughter into the room and handing her to Patsy.

Everything seemed out of focus.

"I'm done," said a voice in the room. It was that fat cousin.

Valerie heard a nurse telling her it was all done.

"Mommy's here," said Patsy to the baby. The baby conceived that same night...

"Do you have an answer?" someone was saying something. Valerie wasn't sure who. The sounds in the room were competing with the sound of her own heart pounding in her ears.

"Aren't you going to write it down? Write it down..."

Valerie looked up, and then down at the card on her lap. She wrote in cursive as if she were signing her name. She turned the card over.

"Mom," said Patsy, "take Rachel, for a minute, I've got to finish the game. Okay... the question was: what was the last purchase that Martina made over $500 with a credit card? Renee, let's see what you wrote."

Patsy flipped over cousin Renee's card.

"Renee said: a wedding present for Chesney. I don't know if we can accept that. It's sort of right."

"It was," said Cousin Renee, "she bought him a wedding ring and a nice watch. She showed them to me. I saw them."

"Yes, I guess that's right."

"Then I win," said Renee.

"Wait, we have to read what Valerie wrote," said Patsy turning over Valerie's answer. "Valerie said..." she paused and, in a confused tone, said: "Valerie wrote... Martina Fergus?"

Martina Fergus. That's what Valerie wrote. That's what she wrote that day. The day she borrowed the credit card.

"That's wrong, I win," exulted Cousin Renee, though the sound of her voice and all the other noise in the room sounded strangely distant in Valerie's ears.

"Are you okay?" A voice said. It was closer, kinder, more directed.

A gentle hand reached out and touched her shoulder.

"Valerie?"

It was Martina. She was there, almost in Valerie's face.

"What?" said Valerie, suddenly snapping back to the present.

"I said, are you okay?"

Martina looked directly into Valerie's eyes. They seemed so compassionate, so understanding. And those were the last emotions Valerie could handle at the moment.

"I...uh..." Valerie felt like a cornered animal. She glanced around the room. The other women were looking at her as if something were wrong with her. All of them that is, except Martina. Martina kept looking at her so damned lovingly.

Valerie glanced down at her watch. "Is that the time? I'm sorry, I didn't realize...I've...I've got to go..." She grabbed her purse and stood up.

"But we haven't had the cake yet," said Patsy.

"I've got to..."

Valerie glanced back at Martina, who was still looking at her so caringly. Why did she have to be so damned nice? Why couldn't she be mean or selfish, just once? Why did she always have to be understanding? Why did she have to loan her that credit card so willingly? Didn't she realize what she had opened herself up to?

"I, uh...happy shower," said Valerie. She dared to look in Martina's direction one last time. "I'm sorry..." she said and then quickly added, "but I've got to go..."

And she ran out of the house.

– 50 –
Forever I'll Miss You

Chesney looked out at the waiting planes. One of them would be taking her away. Then he looked into her face. "I'm going to miss you," he said.

Martina leaned over and kissed his nose as they sat in the departure lounge of Philadelphia airport.

"I'll be back on Friday," said Martina.

"I'll come and pick you up."

"That's sweet," she said, "but it's still silly. I'll get a ride back to the office with Peter Liverot. Besides, you shouldn't waste your personal time picking me up. You'll need to save it for our honeymoon."

Chesney nodded. "But it's my fault you're going."

A puzzled look crossed her face. "How could it be your fault?"

"I wished Valerie didn't have to go. Now you're going instead."

"Be careful what you wish for," she said, "you may just get it."

"Benjamin Franklin said: 'If a man could have half of his wishes, he would double his troubles.'"

"I wish I wasn't going, either," she said, "but I doubt if my going on a short business trip would double your troubles."

They sat in silence for several minutes.

"I still don't understand the abrupt change in plans," said Chesney. "One minute Valerie's going to this seminar and the next minute you're going. Does it make sense to you?"

Martina tossed her head to one side. "Oh, I'm sure there's a good reason for everything. Besides, soon we'll be together forever."

He glanced at his watch. "I wonder where Mr. Liverot is. He is taking the same flight out as you, isn't he?"

"Yes, but I doubt he has such a devoted farewell committee. Besides, we are a little early."

They were very early. Chesney wanted to sit with her alone and enjoy their last minutes together uninterrupted by other distractions.

"How was the shower?" he asked. "Valerie never said anything about it,"

"Oh?"

"No," said Chesney, "she was very quiet about it all. I asked her about it at work the next day, and she seemed distracted."

"Well, Valerie must have had something else on her mind," reasoned Martina. She took his hand. "You are very fond of Valerie, aren't you, dear?"

"She's like the little sister I never had," he said. "Or like the one I almost had."

Martina squeezed his hand. "I know. We must be very kind to Valerie."

"Did you like her shower present?" he asked.

"It was very considerate," said Martina.

Chesney studied her face. "You know, I'm starting to read between your lines. I can tell when you're not saying something. Like just now, when you say how considerate Valerie's gift was, it's the closest you'll ever come to saying that you didn't like it."

"She gave me a case of make-up." Martina laughed self-consciously. "I tried putting some of it on. I didn't do very well, I'm afraid."

Chesney just looked at her admiringly.

"Are you disappointed," she asked, "that I don't know how to look sophisticated, like Valerie."

Chesney furrowed his brow. "You're you, and Valerie is Valerie. I love you both, in very different ways, but I'd never want you to be each other. She's like a sister to me. And you're going to be my wife."

"Still, it was a very considerate gift," said Martina. "Sorry, I'm giving you lines to read between, again. I suppose it's Valerie's attempt at making the world a little prettier one face at a time."

Chesney laughed. "Valerie once said she could make me beautiful."

"You are beautiful," she said, pulling him towards her.

"No," he said, "She said…well, never mind. Maybe that's why…"

"Why what?"

"I don't know," he said, "it's just that Valerie was acting oddly all week. First, I thought it was about the shower, and then they told her she wasn't going to Chicago. I don't know, she was just short-tempered. I thought maybe… well, you know, that it was… that time… oh, never mind…"

Martina smiled and kissed him on the cheek.

"You are beautiful," she said, "and very sweet. Just promise me one thing."

"Of course," he said. "What is it?"

"Promise me you'll never change."

Chesney looked into Martina's green eyes. He knew she would never change, and so neither would he, nor could he.

"I promise," he said in a soft voice nearly lost in the noise of the terminal, but the look upon her face told him that every word went deep to her heart. "I promise I'll always be for you what I am for you at this moment." He sighed. "I can't wait until you get back. And I can't wait until we're married."

"Oh, no," said Martina looking into his eyes, "no, don't say that. Those are all wonderful things, and I look forward to them, as well," she said wistfully. "But right now is wonderful and beautiful in its own way, too."

"But you're leaving, Marti."

"Yes, Chesney, but don't you see? This moment is bittersweet, but we're sharing it. And there's a touch of sadness to it, but only because we have each other. And we'll always have each other. And our lives will be made up of moments of joy but also sadness. If we didn't have the sad moments, the joyful one wouldn't be nearly as joyful.

"In a few minutes, I'll get on an airplane, and I'll go off to Chicago. And I suspect you'll go back to your apartment. And you'll miss me, and I'll miss you terribly, my dearest." Martina caressed his cheek. "But next to the ache in my heart for you, will be the anticipation of what's to come. And though I'm sad over being parted from you, even for four days, I know that my happiness when I'm in your arms again will be double that of the sadness. And I'm not just coming back to see you again. I'm coming back to marry you and to be yours forever, my dearest. So, yes, I look forward to that day, and all the days that will encompass the rest of our lives together… but I want to savor all that life has for us, one day after the other until those days in this world are all used up because I do love you so."

They kissed, even though the waiting area was now filled with other passengers.

"I didn't think you had it in you, kiddo," a gruff voice intruded from behind. "Way to go, Potts!"

Chesney looked up. There was the imposing figure of Peter Liverot. Chesney felt his face grow red, not for the public display of affection for Martina, but for Liverot's coarse approval of it.

"Oh, uh, hi, hello, Mr. Liverot…Peter," said Chesney sitting up straight.

"You're warming up for the honeymoon?" said Liverot.

"Peter," said Martina coolly but without hostility, "I'm sure you meant your kidding in the most innocent way. But I hope you appreciate the fact that this last-minute business trip has put unforeseen demands on the preparations for our upcoming wedding."

"Uh, yeah," Liverot looked down. Rarely was he chastened, but Martina had done it and without malice. Her gaze remained fixed on the banker until she was sure that he had received and accepted her message.

"Sorry, I was kidding," said Liverot. "I didn't mean anything."

"Of course you didn't," she said.

"Oh, yeah," he said, changing the subject, "I just wanted to make sure you got your boarding pass."

"Yes, I have it right here," said Martina touching her purse. She turned to Chesney. "You'll excuse me, dearest, I want to visit the ladies' room before we board the plane."

Chesney stood up, and Martina left.

"You got a good one there, kid," said Liverot.

"Yes, I do," agreed Chesney without looking at Liverot.

"Lighten up, relax," said Liverot. "It's only a conference."

"What do you mean?"

"Well," said the bank president, "you've got a look on your face like somebody just stole your lollypop."

"Lollypop?"

"It's a business trip," he continued. "You're hooking up with a smart dish."

"Dish?"

"Yeah, Martina's one of the sharpest skirts I've ever come across. You might as well get used to it."

Chesney faced Liverot. "Get used to what?"

"Conferences, seminars, business trips," he said. "I suspect she's going to be going on more and more of them."

"But Valerie was supposed to go on this one," noted Chesney.

"Plans change," said Liverot with a shrug. "If every time she goes off on business, you go around looking like a puppy who just got smacked on the ass with a rolled-up newspaper, you'll drive yourself nuts, and you'll lose her respect. Be a man. No dame wants to go away and come back to a dishrag when she goes on a trip."

"What dishrag?"

"You, kid," said Liverot poking his sausage-like finger into Chesney's chest. "Man up, get some lead in your pencil."

Chesney shook his head. Lollypops, skirts, puppies, dishrags, and now lead pencils: was there no end to Liverot's parade of disjointed metaphors?

The banker leaned forward. "Don't worry, you'll get your turn. Business trips are a great opportunity."

"For what?"

"Action," he said with a knowing nod. "You know, a little out of town R and R. Some of my best scoring comes on the road. You're doing some pretty good work for us, Ches,"

"Thank you."

"I didn't see the point of putting much effort into advertising, at first, but you've put together some nice PR stuff for us. 'Go Fourth,' that was pretty clever."

Liverot was referring to the slogan Chesney had created for the bank. He thought it was a fairly obvious one for a bank named "Fourth Fiduciary Trust."

"They got conferences for PR guys," said Liverot with a wink. "Keep up the good work, and you'll be on your way to some of them. No telling how far you can go if you use your noodles. Look at Al. Oh, wait, you didn't know about that. We've only just decided, but you'll need to throw up some of those press releases and some new ads. We're opening an off-shore bank, a subsidiary, in Gibraltar," said Liverot in a low voice. "... near Spain."

"Why does a Delaware bank need another bank there?"

"It's all legal and tax stuff," murmured Liverot in even more private tones.

"And Albrecht Eckner is going there on business?" asked Chesney.

"He's going for good. Al's going to run the whole off-shore shooting gallery."

For the first time during their conversation, Chesney was hearing some good news. Albrecht Eckner would be wending his slime trail across the ocean. Delaware's gain was Gibraltar's loss.

"Hey," said Liverot with a jab to Chesney's side, "you never know. After the honeymoon wears off you might need to go over there yourself for a few weeks, you know, a little marketing trip. Eh, spice things up with some hot tamales?"

Chesney thought of informing his boss that tamales were originated in America and had been consumed by the Mayans, the Aztecs, and even the Incans long before the first Spaniard set foot in the New World. But since the tamales to which Liverot was referring had nothing to do with cuisine, it would only confuse things further.

"I don't speak Spanish," noted Chesney, trying to dissuade any business trips on his part to Gibraltar. He knew it was a British territory but hoped the excuse would be good enough for Liverot.

"*No hablas usted*, eh?"

"I could do it all from Wilmington just as easily," said Chesney. The thought of finding himself four thousand miles from Martina with Albrecht Eckner the only familiar face around was enough to inspire a leap from the famed rock. "And it would save you money."

"Yeah, maybe you're right," said Liverot. "Here comes Martina. I think I'll DMV, too..."

"Huh?"

"Drain the main vein, you know, take a leak," said the banker, chuckling at his own euphemism. "I'll be right back."

"Where is Peter going?" asked Martina as she returned.

"Uh, to...the little boy's room," said Chesney.

"He'd better hurry up," she said, "they've started boarding our flight."

Chesney took Martina in his arms, and they kissed.

"I'll miss you so much, Marti," he whispered in her ear.

"Me too," she said. "It will be such a short time, and then we'll be together again."

Chesney kissed her, and she returned the kiss, which was only interrupted by a tap on his shoulders.

"Okay, break it up, you two," said Liverot.

"Yes, we'd better get going," agreed Martina giving Chesney one last quick kiss on the cheek as Liverot pulled her down the boarding way.

"I love you, Marti," called Chesney after her.

"I love you, too," said Martina as she disappeared down the ramp.

Chesney stared at the empty gate until the door was shut, and then he watched as the plane taxied from the terminal and joined the other airplanes in the queue for takeoff.

The sun had now set, and he stood alone by the large windows. He thought of driving home to his apartment in New Jersey, but the colored lights of the runway shining in the darkness seemed to mesmerize him. Their spell was only broken as a departing plane zoomed past on its ascent into the sky. Finally, it was the turn of Martina's plane. It gained speed, broke free of the lights of the runway and Earth, and took its place among the lights of heaven, fading away until it was gone.

– 51 –
In the Dark Room

He couldn't recall who had first told him or when or where.

Had it been an hour ago? A day? A year? Longer?

Had he been sitting in that darkened room a lifetime? It seemed possible. There were so many thoughts racing through his mind between the dark voids.

Chesney Potts thought about her eyes, her smile, and her loving, compassionate spirit. He closed his eyes tightly as if to imprint her in his mind, like an impression in clay, preserving the details of Martina Fergus forever in his memory.

She was crossing the street. She was in Chicago. She was struck by a bus. It was quick, he was told. The phrase "never knew what had hit her" was used, though he couldn't recall who said it. He sat in the conference room with the lights off. Occasionally the sound of a bus on the street below would intrude. If he were certain that he would join Martina, Chesney would have rushed downstairs and hurled himself under one of those buses. But the deadly accuracy of Chicago transit drivers could not be guaranteed in their Delaware counterparts. He stayed where he was.

It was not long before memories of Verity Goodhue flooded his mind. He wondered if they already met in eternity: the two prospective Mrs. Pottses, the two would-be brides both taken three weeks before their weddings. If there was any consolation, he thought, at least there was no more Aunt Elinor to lose on this day. No, there was no Aunt El, but...

He thought of Valerie. Was Valerie to Martina what Aunt Elinor had been to Verity? He hadn't seen Valerie that morning. He couldn't place her in the day.

Patsy. Patsy told him. He recalled now. He was sitting at his desk. He looked up and smiled at her. Patsy was always cheerful. Only today, for the first time since he met her, she was not smiling. Her eyes were filled with tears.

"Chesney, there's been an accident."

Accident. That was the word that Lord Bagnall used when he told him about Verity. Verity and the car in England. Martina and the bus in Chicago. It was like some macabre game of Clue: Martina in Chicago with the bus, Verity in England with the sports car. If they lived one hundred years before, perhaps they'd have survived. Or would fate have taken them despite the lack of technological advances? Would Verity have been thrown from a horse? Would Martina have been run over by a steam engine? Was he going mad?

Patsy led him into the conference room. She hugged him. She got him some tea, which still sat untouched. He asked to be left alone. She did so reluctantly.

Was this his fault? Chesney asked himself repeatedly. No, he hadn't wanted Martina to go. Who had?

Did he have regrets? He thought of Verity and the French Bread pizza. Had he done that to Martina? Had he denied her anything? He couldn't recall, though she was the least demanding person he ever met. Had he made her happy? Had she at least died happy? He hoped so.

It must be late afternoon now. The room was darker.

"I'm sorry. I'm so sorry."

There was a figure standing in the shadows. The silhouette and the voice were familiar. History had not fully repeated itself. Valerie was not a counterpart to Aunt Elinor.

He rose, and she approached him slowly. Reluctantly, it seemed she came closer, almost as if they were underwater. Finally, they embraced, and the tears flowing from his eyes in torrents.

"I'm so sorry," she kept repeating.

He wanted to say it wasn't her fault, and of course, it wasn't, was it? Valerie had wanted to go to Chicago. It wasn't her fault. She was just being a good friend, a good sister. She was just sympathizing. She wasn't apologizing. Why should she?

Chesney just held her tightly until someone came, he wasn't sure who it was, and drove him home. It was dark by the time they reached his apartment in New Jersey. They drove him home in his own car with someone else following. As they unlocked his door, he stood on the doorstep, looking up at the stars. High in the sky, the blinking wing lights of an airliner flew by.

– 52 –
The Warm Letter
Grown Cold

A day from hell," muttered Valerie Fierro as she tossed her keys on the kitchen counter.

It wasn't as bad as the day before. She spent most of that day avoiding Chesney. She didn't know what to say to him.

She arrived at work late. Peter Liverot and Martina were in Chicago. Albrecht Eckner was having meetings somewhere about that new subsidiary. There was no one there she was accountable to, so she took her time going into the office. She arrived at about eleven, or maybe eleven-thirty, armed with a good excuse for anyone who asked.

Patsy told her. Martina had been hit by a bus crossing the street in Chicago. Peter Liverot had seen it all. An hour later, Liverot called.

"I tried to stop her," said Liverot, shaken by what he saw. "I...I called out to her. I yelled: 'Hey, watch out,' but I guess she didn't hear me or see the bus. Jeez, it was horrible. You ever see somebody get smacked by a bus?"

Valerie quietly confessed she had not.

"You don't want to either if you can avoid it," said Liverot. "We were coming out of the hotel, that's when she saw it."

"Saw what?" asked Valerie.

"The mailbox, the mailbox across the street," he said. "She wanted to mail something, a postcard, you know, a postcard to Potts. She was going to see him in a few days anyway. Why the hell she had to send him a postcard, I don't know. Anyway, we're coming out of the hotel. I was hailing a cab when she sees it, the mailbox. And she says: 'just a minute, I want to mail these.' And before I can say anything, she takes off."

"And the bus hit her," said Valerie.

"Not yet," he continued. "She makes it across the street mails her stuff, and then, she sees I got the cab, and it's waiting for her. Well, she looks one way, but didn't look the other way and she steps out and, well, you ever see somebody…no, you said you didn't. Anyway, that was it. I doubt she ever knew what hit her."

There was a moment of silence before Liverot continued.

"Anybody tell Potts?"

"Patsy," said Valerie.

"Yeah, good," he said. "Sorry, Patricia had to do that. That's gotta be tough, but it was tough for all of us. Hope the FDIC don't hold it against the bank."

"The FDIC?"

"Yeah, well, no, not for the bus," said Liverot. "I didn't mean that. Nobody could be blamed for the bus. That was an accident. I didn't mean that. No, I just hope that the Feds don't bust my balls. I mean, we hired the best compliance person we could find. It's not my fault she gets hit by a bus."

"No, it's not your fault," she whispered.

"Oh, I know what's bothering you," he said.

"What?" she snapped.

"You're thinking, 'Hey, that was supposed to be me,' aren't you?"

"What?"

"I don't mean getting hit by the bus," said Liverot. "I doubt you'd be running across the street to mail a postcard. But still, you were supposed to go on the trip until Al changed it and said Martina should go."

"Yes, that's right," she agreed. "Albrecht changed the plans, didn't he?"

"Yeah, well, it just goes to show," said Liverot philosophically, "when your number is up, your number is up. And if your number is on the front of a Chicago bus, well, that's when your number is up."

"I suppose," she said.

"You're pretty good friends with Potts, aren't you?"

"Sort of," said Valerie, "we sit next to each other."

"Yeah, well, just go make sure he's okay, all right?"

Valerie agreed, said goodbye, and hung up. Martina was dead, and all Liverot can think about is the regulators. She looked at the clock. It was one. Patsy said Chesney was in the conference room. She didn't want to intrude on him. She'd give him some more time. She'd check in on him after lunch.

She looked in on him later that afternoon. Even though the room was dark, she could see he looked terrible. She tried to comfort him as best she could and then arranged for someone to give him a ride home. Actually, Patsy arranged that, but she helped escort him to the car.

After she saw Chesney off, Valerie went to Martina's apartment to check the mail. That really didn't matter now, did it? Martina's detailed credit card transactions hadn't shown up yet, either, but again, what did it matter now? The empty apartment gave her the creeps. It was half put together, and many of the gifts from Martina's bridal shower were sitting on the dining table. There was a list of all the gifts, the givers, and an opened box of thank you notes. Martina had already put a checkmark next to each name that she had sent a thank you. Valerie had already gotten her thank you note.

Valerie walked into the bedroom and looked at the new queen-sized bed. Valerie was sure that only one person had slept in it. She shuddered. How horrible: to die a virgin.

There on the dresser, she saw the cosmetic case she had given Martina. She considered taking it but decided against it. It wouldn't be right, would it?

After a fitful night, Valerie came in the next day. It was almost as difficult as the day before, but at least Chesney stayed home. She'd have to call him later. Albrecht Eckner was still out of the office. Not much got done, except by Patsy, who was busy making all sorts of arrangements and acting as the liaison between the bank and Martina's family. The body was coming back that evening. The funeral would be Saturday. Valerie would get her black suit cleaned.

"A day from hell," she said, as she kicked off her pumps, and flipped on the lights. In her hands was the day's mail. She poured herself a ginger ale and started looking through the pile. This month's *Cosmo*, some supermarket circulars, some clothing catalogs, and then…

"Ms. Valerie Fierro."

It was Martina's handwriting. It was the wedding invitation, was her immediate thought, until she recalled she already received that.

She looked at the postmark: Chicago, IL.

"Oh, shit," said Valerie.

Martina hadn't crossed the street just to mail a postcard to Chesney. Valerie put both her hands over it as if to feel the bodily warmth of the person who posted it, the person who was now cold. Then she held up the letter between her fingers. A shiver shot up her back as Valerie realized this was the last thing that Martina had held, the last thing she had touched before she…

Valerie put down the letter and covered it with a catalog. Then she looked down. It was a lingerie catalog. She thought about the time she ran into Martina at Macy's buying boring underwear. Somehow it was disrespectful to cover Martina's last letter with pictures of racy lingerie she wouldn't have thought to wear while she had been alive. Valerie took the letter back out and looked at it. She almost threw it away, but then thought that wouldn't be quite right. After all, it must have been fairly important if she lost her life to mail it.

Valerie sighed and walked upstairs to her bedroom, leaving the letter on the kitchen counter. She changed into her pajamas and robe, cleaned her face, came back downstairs, poured a large glass of wine, and only then sat down on the sofa with the letter. She took a swig of wine, closed her eyes, took a deep breath, and then opened her eyes and the letter.

"Dearest Valerie," it began, *"although I've already thanked you for the shower and the thoughtful gift, I wanted to write to you about that day. I didn't know when to bring this up, if ever, and I only do so now to hopefully make things easier for you.*

While that game was being played, I noticed your distress over the last question about the credit card. No one else knew, but I knew at once what was troubling you. I knew because I had known for quite some time. The clinic called me a few days after your procedure."

Damn, thought Valerie, looking up. She hadn't counted on that. How could she have been so careless? It was a good facility. It certainly wasn't cheap. Of course they would follow up. But she only gave Martina's name and a fake phone number. She took another drink and continued to read.

"They said I had put down the wrong phone number and looked my correct number. Before I could explain that it hadn't been me, it became clear what procedure had been done, and that it had been carried out in my name. I was shocked, to say the least. And I must confess that my first reaction was one of anger. Life is very precious ..."

Valerie closed her eyes for a moment at the bitter irony of that statement and then continued.

"Life is very precious, and any life that is not allowed to reach its potential is a great loss. As I said, I was angry. But I soon realized that mine was not the only hurt in the whole affair. You must have felt quite desperate and alone to do what you did. I often wanted to reach out and comfort you, but I wasn't sure that you would have sought or appreciated it. That is until the shower. That is when I fully realized the weight of the feelings you were carrying.

I cannot condemn you, for we all make mistakes. The best we can do is to forgive each other, and love each other, and bind up each other's wounds. Please realize that you have my forgiveness, my love, and my friendship.

I decided to write these things to you because I thought this way would be less uncomfortable for you. I hope it helps the distress you've been feeling. If you ever want to discuss it all privately, I'd be glad to do so with you. If not, it never need be mentioned again.

Forgive me if I've handled this indiscreetly. Chesney and I love you very much, and we want to be even closer friends with you after the wedding.

With Love,
Martina"

Valerie looked at the letter with tears in her eyes and then noticed a postscript.

"P.S.: I have not mentioned this to anyone, least of all, Chesney. He loves you like a sister, and I don't know if he would fully understand. This is our secret. Love. M.C.F."

Valerie placed the letter back in its envelope and poured another glass of wine.

– 53 –
The Guilt Burger

I'm leaving early," said Valerie as she unpacked a box. She was reclaiming the office that had belonged to her, then Martina, and now was her's again. "I promised to help Chesney clean out Martina's apartment."

"Isn't that nice," said Albrecht Eckner with a sincerity that would have sounded genuine in anyone else. "Don't forget to take personal time."

Valerie gave him a dirty look.

"I'm sorry," said Albrecht, "that was unfeeling of me, wasn't it. We're all about helping each other out here at Fourth Fiduciary, aren't we? Forget personal time. You just help good ol' Chauncey and don't worry about whose time it's on."

She stared at Albrecht before realizing he really meant it and was giving her the afternoon off. "Thank you."

"We're like family, aren't we?" He said, "one person needs a hand, we pitch in. One person can't make a trip for some reason, and someone else takes the trip in her place."

Valerie shot him another nasty look but then realized that Albrecht Eckner was impervious. Even her dirtiest looks would bounce off the Man of Slime. Instead, she left the room and went back to her cubicle to retrieve another box. A moment later, she returned to find Albrecht nonchalantly nosing around her belongings.

"Do you mind?"

"Not at all," he said and made room on the desk for her to place the carton she was carrying.

"That's not what I mean," she said, "I...oh, never mind."

Albrecht smirked. He was like a cat. He would never take offense unless a shoe was hurled at him.

"I always thought this was a cozy office," said Albrecht wandering around the room. He stopped and felt the seat of the swivel chair behind the desk. "Certainly didn't let it get cold," he muttered.

Valerie took a deep breath. Albrecht told her to move into the private office. Now she wondered if he only did it so he could deliver snotty one-liners.

"When are you going to Gibraltar?" she asked pointedly.

He turned and smiled. "Oh, in another week or two. I'm sure you'll miss me."

"Oh, you have no idea," she murmured.

"Yes, a lot of changes around here," said Albrecht. "I'm leaving. You're moving in here. The poor little fat kid will be lost without you sitting next to him..."

"I wish you would try and show him a little kindness."

"Oh, that's sweet," said Albrecht, "especially coming from you. But then, being an only child, I never did understand the special dynamic between brothers and sisters."

"Drop dead."

"Now, now, there's been enough of that around here," said Albrecht. "Oh, yes, and I forgot the happiest change around here. The re-christening of our little Patsy Zyobidinski," he said, "or I should say: Patsy Einfalt." His smirk widened into a grin.

Valerie shook her head. Patsy had legally changed her last name to "Einfalt." She had done it to match her baby's last name, which she had given at the hospital because she believed that was the father's last name.

"You're despicable," said Valerie.

"Me? You're the one who made Patsy's erstwhile lover... whoever he may be...feel so guilty that he wrote her that note."

"You did that to cover your tracks," she said.

"Again, you're assuming that was me," he said. "I'm sure you're mistaken, but then, you see, I'm not taking your nasty accusations personally because I'm a bigger person."

"Bigger rat..."

He clicked his tongue at her. "There, there, and just because the real Mr. Einfalt, whoever he may be, wrote her a note of encouragement... from Europe, I remind you..."

"Where you've been recently..." she added.

He feigned shock. "A lot of people are in Europe. The continent is full of them."

"Never mind," she sighed. It was bad enough that "Mr. Einfalt" sent Patsy a note filled with hope for his imminent return. What made it worse was that now Albrecht had the whole Chicago affair to dangle over her head. He still didn't know why she wanted Martina to go in her place, but Martina's death was enough. Thankfully he was going to Gibraltar. They had lots of buses and mailboxes there. Maybe Albrecht would get run over.

That afternoon, Valerie drove to the apartment. She picked up Chesney's favorite lunch along the way. It was the least she could do to cheer him up. She hadn't seen him since the funeral, and then he looked horrible. She resolved that she would be a good friend to him, at least until he got back on his feet. Hopefully, that wouldn't take too long.

Arriving at the apartment, Valerie knocked on the door.

"It's open," she heard Chesney call from inside. At least she thought it was Chesney. The voice sounded more like a moan.

Valerie edged down the darkened hallway towards the living room. The only light was provided by the windows, which had their blinds down, and one lamp without a shade. The effect, she thought, was creepy, though not as creepy as the figure she saw there.

Sitting cross-legged in the middle of the floor was Chesney Potts. If she hadn't known she was supposed to meet him there, she would have had a hard time recognizing him. The well-worn phrase "death warmed over" sprang to mind, though he didn't even rise to those standards. No, he looked like death, under-cooked, then warmed over, and allowed to sit on the kitchen counter until the fatty bits started to congeal and turn nasty. Ewww!

His hair looked like it hadn't met shampoo or even a comb in days. His face was all stubbly and nasty. His mustache, which he had used to keep so trim, was now hanging over his upper lip. She wondered if strands of it got into his mouth when he ate. Ewww!

It was hard to tell in the glare of the bare light bulb, but he looked puffy and swollen. Chesney was never even remotely what she would call trim. By her kindest assessment, she would have called him "plump" or "chubby." He had lost a little weight for the wedding. Now he just looked bloated.

Chesney sat there in the middle of the floor amidst a hodgepodge of papers, and personal items, wedding gifts, and knickknacks. There seemed to be little organization to what he was doing. While she stood there, he picked up a piece of paper, put it down, reached for a box, rummaged through it for a moment, and then pushed that to the side to fold a dishtowel.

"Chesney?" she said softly. She tried to put a coaxing tone to her voice, the kind a mother would use when trying to gently wake a child. "Chesney, I... brought you some lunch."

He looked up, in a jerky motion as if he didn't know where the noise had come from. Then he turned and looked at her. His eyes looked bleary, as if he had been crying. She prayed he wouldn't start crying with her there. She couldn't stand men crying. He cried on her shoulder the day Martina died. That was understandable. She just hoped he wasn't going to make it a habit.

"Thanks," he said, and he reached up and took the bag from her.

"Your favorite," said Valerie, "cheeseburger..."

He stared in the bag.

"I'm really not hungry."

She looked at the trash can behind him. It was filled with fast food containers and junk food bags. Then, as if he weren't even paying attention, Chesney unwrapped the burger and started eating it automatically. He chewed methodically. Valerie watched him until he was finished and then he balled up the wrapper and threw it into the trash.

She found a folding chair in the corner and sat down. He glanced up at her.

"We were supposed to have the furniture delivered this week," he said. "They canceled it."

Valerie nodded. "Who canceled it?"

He looked at the blank wall. Then he shook his head. "I don't know," he said, "somebody."

"That was nice of them," said Valerie.

"Yes, they've all been very kind," he said, again without offering a clue as to who they were.

They stared at each other for a moment. Chesney's face was oddly expressionless.

"What can I do for you?" she asked.

"For what?"

Valerie gestured to the general confusion around him. "For this," said Valerie. "What can I help you with?"

He looked around for a moment as if he were looking for a suitable chore. Then a glimmer of focus came to his eyes.

"Oh, yes," he said, getting up from the floor, "I know." He motioned for Valerie to follow him and led her into the bedroom, grabbing an empty cardboard carton along the way. The room looked like it hadn't been touched since Martina left it.

He opened the closet. Martina's clothes were hanging neatly there.

"Only half full," he said, pointing out the sharp demarcation between her clothes and the empty space. "Mine would have gone there."

"Do you want me to pack them up?" asked Valerie.

Chesney nodded. "That would be nice. I just...I wouldn't know how or what to do with it all." He gestured towards the clothes. His hand brushed against a sweater. Chesney pulled back his hand, and then tentatively reached out and stroked the sleeve. A faraway look captured his gaze, and she could imagine he saw himself holding Martina's hand for a moment. Then Chesney looked up into Valerie's eyes, breaking the spell and letting go of the garment.

"Anyway," he said, "if you could pack up her things, that would be a great help. I don't think I could."

"I understand."

"Thank you," he said, "and if you see anything you'd like..."

"Oh, I couldn't," said Valerie. The clothes were of good quality, but not Valerie's style. Besides, they had been worn by a dead girl.

He stared at the clothes for a moment. "You're right," he said, "that's not a good idea. I don't think I could bear to see those things without her in them…"

"Yes," agreed Valerie, "it's better…"

"Yes," he said. Stepping from the closet he pointed at the bureau. "Oh, and there are clothes in there too."

"I'll take care of it," promised Valerie. He smiled wanly, and started back to the living room. "What are you going to do with it all?"

A blank look crossed his face. "I have no idea."

"Well," asked Valerie without thinking, "what did you do last time… with the other girl?" She grimaced as soon as she said it.

A wince of pain crossed his face.

"I…I really don't know," he said. "She, that girl, the girl in England, had a wealthy father. I suppose the servants took care of her clothes and things. It's odd, but I never thought of that before."

"Servants," said Valerie, "well, at least that must have made that easier than now."

Chesney surveyed the room for a moment and then shook his head.

"No," he said softly, "that was worse." He glanced around again. "As bad as this is, that was much worse."

Then he turned and shuffled back into the living room.

Valerie started cleaning out the closet. If she had died in Chicago, who would be cleaning out her closet now? Probably Patsy, or Martina, she guessed, or her mother, or Rose. Would they be as sad as Chesney was now? She wondered. It must be nice, Valerie thought, to have someone love you so much that they were so sad when you died. She thought of her recent boyfriends. They were all a lot more fun than Chesney, but she couldn't see them moping around after her if she died. Martina and that English girl were lucky to die and leave behind someone who was so miserable at their passing.

Valerie caught herself. The stream of consciousness running through her mind slowed to a shallow trickle. She couldn't think those thoughts. If she had gone to Chicago she wouldn't have died. That was stupid. It wasn't like that ticket to Chicago, came with a free upgrade to the grave. It wasn't like death hovered over the boarding pass waiting to pounce on the first person who used it. No, it was just Martina's time. She had told herself that repeatedly over the last two weeks. That's just the way it was. It was Martina's time to go, and it wasn't Valerie's fault. If Valerie had gone to Chicago Martina probably would have died at home. They do have buses in Wilmington, she told herself. No, it wasn't anyone's fault, certainly not Valerie's. Soon, if she allowed herself to do so, Valerie would be blaming herself for everything bad that ever happened. If she was going to blame herself for Martina, she might as well blame herself for that English girl. English girl? Valerie didn't even know that one's name. If it all was anyone's fault, it was Chesney's. He was just bad luck;

that was all. Guys like that should come with a warning label: caution – entering into a permanent relationship will be hazardous to…

Valerie's thoughts were interrupted by a sharp gasp and thud from the living room.

"Oh, shit," she said, dropping a blouse and running from the room, "he's killed himself."

– 54 –
Who Am I to Contradict Your Delusion?

Valerie raced into the living room, there was Chesney his mouth agape. In his hand was the detailed record of Martina's credit card transactions.

The game was up. She would just confess it all to him. She would tell him that it was her procedure, not Martina's.

But, he would blame her for Martina's death, wouldn't he? No, not necessarily. No one else knew. Well, Albrecht knew she didn't want to go to Chicago, but he didn't know why, and besides, he was going to Gibraltar. Valerie could confess it was her procedure, and that Martina…

Valerie remembered the letter from Martina. It proved that Martina knew and forgave Valerie. She would show Chesney the letter. Valerie almost destroyed Martina's letter, now she was glad she hadn't. Martina forgave her. Chesney would have to forgive her, too.

"Chesney…" began Valerie.

"Termination…" he muttered.

"What?"

Chesney held up the papers. "It says here 'pregnancy termination.' Martina had…"

His mouth hung open the words caught in his throat.

"Wait," she said, "I've got something for you in my purse."

Valerie went to her handbag to retrieve the letter. She would have to show it to him. It would be difficult. There would be a lot of tears and maybe some shouting, but it would be much better in the long run and…

It wasn't there. She rummaged through the handbag. The letter wasn't there. It had to be there. It was a simple envelope with papers inside of it. It couldn't hide, not in that small space. Valerie ransacked the purse. She saw her lipstick, her wallet, her mascara, her comb, her mirror, her tissues, her work ID card, her phone, and a half-dozen other items. It was all there except Martina's letter.

"What is it?" she heard Chesney say from behind her.

"What?" She turned to look at him.

"You said you had something for me…" he said.

Valerie looked back into the handbag and grabbed the item closest to her fingers. She turned and held it out to Chesney.

"Mint?"

"What?"

"You look like you could use a… a mint."

Chesney took the small plastic container from her and stared at it for a moment, and then looked back at Valerie with a confused look.

"That's okay," he said and handed back the mints.

Valerie returned the mints to her purse. "Well, if you need one, just let me know."

Chesney nodded and looked at her with that pathetic look of his. She sat down on the floor near him, not too close. She didn't know if he was going to fall to pieces on her. Still, she was near enough to reach out and provide a reassuring pat on his shoulder.

He looked down at the paper again. "Pregnancy termination," he repeated.

Valerie craned her neck to look at the paper.

"Did… did you know about that?" he asked.

Valerie thought a moment before nodding solemnly.

"Oh," he said. "The date…" he said, pointing to the numbers beside the description.

"Yes?" she asked.

"We were going out then," he said.

That was a handy explanation. She grabbed it before it got away.

"Was it?"

"Yes," he said, "it was after we got engaged."

Valerie reached out for his hand and patted it. "Well, maybe she wasn't sure, yet, you know, about your future together."

"What do you mean?"

"Well, you know, when a woman gets pregnant… so I've heard… their hormones can go a bit crazy. Maybe she wasn't sure that your relationship was going to last. Maybe she didn't want to have your baby, or that's what she thought at the time. Remember, like I said, hormones can make a pregnant girl nuts… or, so I've been told."

Chesney's eyebrows knitted in consternation.

"But it couldn't have been mine," he said.

"Oh, uh, you mean you hadn't, you know, had… I mean, you hadn't been intimate before that?"

"Nor after that," he said. "We were waiting."

Valerie would have guessed that they hadn't had sex. But now, Chesney was admitting it like it was the most normal thing in the world. It was hard for Valerie to believe that a young, healthy couple a few weeks before their wedding hadn't taken a test drive. Then she recalled Martina's dull underwear, and then looked at Chesney sitting there like a lump of vanilla pudding. Then it wasn't hard to believe. It was sad, it was unusual, even odd, but it wasn't hard to believe.

"Oh, sorry, I didn't know."

"But I thought she was a virgin."

"Did she tell you she was a virgin?"

He thought a moment. "No, not in so many words."

Valerie smirked inwardly. She couldn't imagine Martina saying the word "virgin" aloud.

"Well, then…" concluded Valerie holding up her hands.

"Who?" he asked.

"Who?" repeated Valerie. "What who?"

"Who was the… I mean, who did she…"

Valerie shook her head. "I have no idea," she said, and she was quite confident that she was telling the truth. She rarely thought of Martina Fergus and sex in the same sentence or even the same paragraph. She could truthfully say that she hadn't the slightest notion.

"You think you know someone," said Chesney. There was a quiver in his voice like he was about to burst into tears.

"Hey," she said, "don't let your imagination run away with you. Remember what you know to be true. Martina loved you a lot, she loved you very, very much."

Chesney sighed and held up the paper in his hand. "I know that," he said, "but what I didn't know is that apparently, she loved someone else, too… at least once."

"That? That doesn't mean anything," said Valerie. She didn't want to get this personal with Chesney, ever, but she had no choice.

"Look, Ches, I'm going to tell you something I didn't think I'd ever tell you…"

"But you're like my sister," he said.

"Yeah, well, it's nothing a sister would usually tell her brother, but, well, sometimes you just got to say things that you don't want to say."

A concerned look crossed his face. "What?"

"I just don't want you to think any less of me, okay?"

His worried look intensified. He looked like a kid who had just learned that Santa Claus wasn't real, and was about to find out an uncomfortable truth about the Easter Bunny.

"You can have sex," she said, "without love."

He just stared at her.

Valerie rolled her eyes. "I know. I've done it."

He continued to stare.

Valerie didn't know if he were that naïve about life or about her. "Yes," she admitted, "once… maybe twice."

She didn't say what span of time in which that "once or twice" had occurred.

Chesney's face turned red, and he looked away. It was apparent he was embarrassed, and what made it worse was that he was embarrassed for her. Valerie would have slapped some sense into him, but he had just lost his fiancée, and she had just had a manicure.

"The point is," she said, "that Martina loved only you."

He looked up, hopefully. "You mean, she didn't love…whoever it was who…" He again held up the piece of paper.

"No, of course not," she said.

"Then, why?"

He was getting ahead of her. Valerie hadn't thought this all through. She just stared at him. The first excuse that came to mind was that Martina wanted to lose her virginity so she could enjoy Chesney better on their wedding night. No, she thought, even he wouldn't believe that one. What else could she possibly tell him? There was just one possibility, but before Valerie could approach the subject, Chesney was already there.

"Unless," he said slowly.

"Unless what?"

"Unless she didn't want to have… you know… but it had been forced on her…"

Valerie forced a pained expression on to her face and hoped it was convincing, and then lowered her head.

"You knew?" he said.

"Not at the time," she said. "I only found out recently." Technically that was true, Valerie reasoned. She only found out the possibility that Martina had been raped a second ago. It also didn't matter that the story wasn't true. If that's what Chesney wanted to believe, she wouldn't argue with him.

"How horrible for her," said Chesney. "Why didn't she tell me?"

Valerie shrugged her shoulders. "It's a difficult thing to admit," she said, especially when it didn't occur.

Chesney sat motionlessly. She could almost see the wheels spinning in his head as if he were sorting it all out.

"Do you think…" he started, rising to his feet.

"Ches, *fratello*," she appealed to him, "please, don't, you'll drive yourself crazy. It's over. It won't bring her back."

"Do you think… no, you're right; that doesn't matter."

"Good," said Valerie.

"But, that explains a lot."

"What?"

"How she died…"

Valerie didn't know where he was going with this. "She got hit by a bus."

"In Chicago... running..." he said, drawing out the words as if doing so would bring her to the same conclusion.

"To mail a letter," she said, "I mean, a postcard... to you."

"Or..."

"Or what?"

"Maybe she was running away."

"From who?"

"Whom," he corrected. "From whom was she running? Who else was there?"

"Nobody, just Peter..." she said.

"...Liverot, exactly."

"Liverot?"

"Don't you see," he said. "It all makes sense. She was running away from Liverot. The evening I took Martina to the airport, Liverot bragged how much he liked business trips and how they were the perfect venue for his little escapades."

"Escapades?" Valerie could never hear the word "escapades" without thinking of the Ice Capades. Now all she could think of was Liverot's naked chunky body wobbling on a pair of skates.

"He boasted about going on business trips and all the action he could get. And he used all kinds of disgusting metaphors, talking about the lead in his pencil and lollypops."

"Well, he's a pig, that's not news," said Valerie. "So?"

"So," said Chesney, "he was obviously making advances to Martina. And after what she went through previously, poor Martina was obviously even more sensitive to that sort of unwanted attention."

Valerie chortled involuntarily. "You really think Peter Liverot was trying to attack Martina in the middle of Chicago, in public?"

"Not initially," he said, "but what if that was just the final straw? What if he had been making his lewd comments and suggestions all the way out on the plane? And then throughout the previous two days? Then finally, who knows, he said just one more thing, or touched her inappropriately, on the street corner, thinking he could get away with it there. But that one little gesture drove her over the edge, and she had to get away, and..."

Chesney threw his arms up and froze at this point, approximating the stance of someone being hit by a bus.

Valerie shook her head. "I don't know..." she began slowly. "Why would he try that with her?"

Chesney's raised his index finger. "Ah, that's the point."

"What is?"

"Who was supposed to go on that trip?"

"Um, I was..."

"Right, and who went?"

"Martina, of course." Valerie could feel her pores tingle as tiny beads of sweat began to fill them. He was getting too close to the truth.

"So," continued Chesney, "we just need to answer the question, who wanted Martina to go instead of you, and we know who is responsible for her death."

"Uh, who?"

He smiled, but it wasn't a pleasant smile. It was a knowing smile, it was a smile filled with retribution.

"It's obvious," he said, "Peter Liverot changed the plans."

"Why?"

"Because he knew that he couldn't try that sort of thing with you," said Chesney. "You've, well, you're a little, well…worldlier than Martina, no offense."

Valerie waved her hand. "Uh, no, that's okay."

"So, he wanted some 'fresh action,' as he so crudely put it. He practically bragged about it to me. He all but rubbed his plans in my face, knowing that either I was too naïve to understand his twisted appetites, or that I was afraid to stand up to him. Liverot wanted Martina in Chicago."

Valerie Fierro stared at him. Chesney was so convincing, she nearly believed him. In any event, he believed it, and what was even better was that his theory didn't mention Albrecht Eckner, or the next step in the progression: Valerie herself.

She looked at him a moment as he stood there waiting for her response. Finally, she nodded her head.

"Yeah," she said, "that sounds plausible."

– 55 –
A Turned Table for One

A month after Martina's death, he finally returned to work. Chesney Potts felt as if he had no home. He had attempted to make people his home. The first was Verity, next came Martina, and now they were both gone. If anything, he thought, his homes were graves, and he felt as if he were staggering about the Earth, waiting for the day that he would join them.

Valerie had been wonderful. She had been patient and kind. She had helped him sort out what had happened. Without Valerie's counsel, he would have confronted Peter Liverot directly for Martina's death.

♦

"He's got to be held responsible," Chesney had said.

"Yeah, you know that," reasoned Valerie, "but the police reports into the accident didn't implicate him. The police, the bus driver, eyewitnesses, none of it implicated Liverot. He was just there."

"But you agree that he's responsible," said Chesney. "Granted, I can't prove that he was sexually harassing her. You can't prove a lion is necessarily stalking a particular gazelle, but it's still the lion's nature, isn't it? You said that yourself."

"I never said anything about lions."

"About Liverot," said Chesney. "He's a natural predator. He stalks the weak and vulnerable, any one of whom he thinks he can take advantage. I wouldn't expect him to attack her in the open, but given what we know about the man, it's within the low standards of his character. You said so yourself, didn't you?"

"Yes, well, I did," she said, "and don't get me wrong, all that is true…"

"And Liverot changed the travel plans," he reminded her. "He purposely picked what he thought would be a more vulnerable target. You said that, too, didn't you?"

Valerie grudgingly agreed.

"What's wrong?" he asked. "You always seem to hesitate whenever I talk about how Liverot changed the travel plans."

Valerie looked away.

"I think I know what it is," he said.

"You do?"

"Yes, you feel guilty."

Valerie's eyes widened.

"You feel that you should have gone," he said, "that you should have been in Chicago."

"Well, I was supposed to go, originally."

"But you can't blame yourself. That's what I'm talking about. Liverot is walking around without a care in the world. He's driven Martina to her death, and innocent people like you are the ones who feel guilty about it." Chesney patted her shoulder. "I don't want you to carry around that guilt. You didn't send Martina to Chicago."

Valerie wiped a tear from the corner of her eye.

"Now, what's wrong?" he asked.

"I..." her voice caught in her throat, and she looked nervously around. "I, uh, I'm...I'm just worried. I don't want you to go in and start saying all these things to Peter Liverot. You said it yourself, the man's an animal. He'd rip you to shreds. If you went after him and started accusing him of all those things..."

"But they're true," protested Chesney.

"You know that, and... so do I, but I don't want to happen to you what happened to Martina and all the others."

"Others, you mean Liverot's responsible for the death of other people?"

Valerie rolled her eyes, he assumed at his naiveté. "Peter Liverot did not get where he did because he has an MBA from Wharton or Harvard Business. Come on, Chesney, don't tell me you never wondered how a crude ape, like Peter Liverot, could become a bank president. He's got... friends."

"Friends?"

"Not just friends... friends... friends and family."

"Family?"

Valerie gave Chesney another look of incredulity.

"Yes," she said, "friends... in the family."

Chesney's brow furrowed.

"How can you be so smart and so stupid in the same day," asked Valerie. "The family!"

"You mean organized crime?"

"Yes, of course, organized crime. Shady partners, cooked books, the whole thing."

"But, Liverot," said Chesney, "he's French."

"You've seen too many gangster movies," she said. "So Liverot's French, so what? He's got partners who are all nationalities. I'm Italian. Do you think I'm in the mob?"

"No, of course not," he said. "I suppose it's only logical that villains come in all nationalities."

"Exactly," she said, "which I why I want you to be careful."

"You're a good friend and a good sister."

"Thank you," said Valerie.

Valerie was right, thought Chesney, as he walked back towards the executive suite. He had only been at his desk an hour when he was summoned. Chesney passed Martina's old office, which was now Valerie's office. The door was closed.

He stood in front of Patsy's desk. She greeted him with her usual warm smile.

"Yes, can I help you," she said.

"You called me, Patsy."

Her mouth dropped open. "Chesney? I didn't..."

The secretary stopped herself. In his month away, he had regained the modest amount of weight that he had lost and then some. Added to that were a beard and the chronic need of a haircut.

"...it's good to...have you back," said Patsy, regaining her cheeriness.

"It's good to see you, Patsy. I appreciated all you've done."

Her expression dampened. "You know how much I love you and Martina, and how sorry I am."

Chesney bit his lip and nodded. "Yes, I do, thank you."

"If there's anything..."

Her offer was cut short by the buzz of her phone.

"Oh," said Patsy, "Mr. Liverot is ready for you."

"Thank you," said Chesney, and he walked to the closed door and knocked once. From inside, the voice of Peter Liverot bade him enter. This was it, into the beast's lair. Liverot's demeanor was positively avuncular. Chesney was glad that he had been schooled by Valerie in Liverot's ways and his background, or he almost would have believed Liverot's act.

"Come on in, kid," said Liverot. He was studying papers on his desk. He looked up and blanched. "Whoa, you look like crap. I mean, you don't look so good."

Chesney smirked. He no longer put any value in Liverot's opinions.

"Sorry, sorry," said the banker. "Have a seat."

They stared at each other for a moment.

"Been through it, huh, Potts?"

"Yes," said Chesney, purposely leaving off: "sir."

"Gotta be tough," he said. "Patricia said you had this happen to you before, too, huh?"

"Almost exactly the same time before," said Chesney.

"Hot shit," muttered Liverot. "I gotta hand it to you! You can take it."

"I suppose."

"Still," conceded the banker, "you could clean yourself up, you know…" he gestured to Chesney's hair and beard. "And once you get a grip on it, you know…" here he patted his stomach, "lay off the comfort chow. Catch my drift?"

Chesney glowered at the man giving him diet and grooming tips. Had Valerie not advised him against it, he would have his hands around Liverot's throat by now.

"Yeah, well," said Liverot, "I just wanted to let you know…"

Chesney leaned forward. Was Liverot going to confess, or at the very least apologize?

"I wanted to let you know how much we liked Miss Fergus, me especially."

Chesney sat back in his chair. He wasn't going to do it. This skunk in a double-breasted suit, this snake with a manicure and an expensive haircut, wasn't going to take the least bit of responsibility. He thought of what Valerie had said: that Liverot had mob connections. Liverot could probably order Chesney squashed like a bug with just a short phone call. Still, what did it matter at this point?

"Is that all?"

"What do you mean?" asked Liverot.

"Is that all you have to say? That's it?"

The Liverot's face began to darken into a scowl.

"What do you want me to say?"

"I've written speeches for you in the past," said Chesney, "but you'll have to supply your own lines this time."

Liverot rose from his desk. "You fat little shit," said the banker. "Who do you think you are coming into my office with that crap?"

"The question is not: who do I think I am," replied Chesney, "the question is: who do you think you are? I'm fairly confident I know. Now I just want to see if you do."

Liverot's face turned a bright scarlet, and his jaw tightened. "I know who I am, you greasy little turd. First, I'm your boss, and the kicker is that I'm only your boss out of sympathy."

"Sympathy," snorted Chesney. "You?"

"Not me, you little shit, your girlfriend's sympathy."

Chesney's mouth dropped open.

"Ha, yeah, that's right, asshole," laughed Liverot. "You got this job, not because we needed you, but because we needed her. You were part of the deal: two for one. What do I need public relations for? That's a laugh. And part of the deal was that we didn't tell you. Now you come in here acting like I owe you something, or like the bank is somehow responsible for your girlfriend's death. You're trying to hold me up for some big payout because she died on a business trip? Good luck. I suppose you want me to say I'm sorry. Yeah, well, I'm real sorry she died because she was doing a hell of a good job. I'm sorry that bus didn't have your name on it. My advice to you is to get the hell out of here before I kick your ass up and down Rodney Square."

Chesney sat in stunned silence. Martina had only gone to work for this monster so that he would be hired? He looked up at Liverot.

"Yeah, that's right, pal," said the banker, as if he had read his mind. "If you don't believe me, ask Al Eckner. She wasn't going to come here. She had a job. Only her loser boyfriend didn't."

As if he were somehow another person, Chesney felt himself rise to his feet and stagger from the office. Liverot may have said something or not, he couldn't tell. He must have walked past Patsy, she may have spoken, but he couldn't have sworn to it. The next thing he knew, he was driving back to New Jersey. Liverot's words echoing through his mind. The bank president didn't need to threaten him with the violence or hitmen. He had just had to hurl the truth back at him. What bitter irony. Chesney had gone into Liverot's office to make the banker take responsibility for Martina's death, and Liverot had turned the tables on him. If it weren't for Chesney needing a job, Martina never would have gone to work for Fourth Fiduciary. She never would have been on that trip to Chicago. She never…

By the time he arrived back at his apartment, there was only one thing left to do.

– 56 –
Portrait of a Cereal Killer

Chesney had made up his mind by the time he entered his apartment. "I have nothing left to live for," he said aloud.

He took a step towards the bathroom, then stopped and hung his head in shame.

"…nothing left for which to live," he said with disgust. "This is lowest: ending a sentence in a preposition."

Chesney opened the medicine cabinet looking for the means with which to end his miserable existence.

"Aspirin," he sighed, "and Pepto-Bismol."

Not much help there. The bottle of aspirin was nearly empty, not enough for a fatal dose. Even if there had been more, he didn't want to risk the kidney and liver damage too much aspirin could cause if he wasn't successful. He'd never committed suicide before but didn't want to make a mess of it. A botched suicide attempt could leave one with side-effects that would last a lifetime. He'd rather be dead.

Chesney examined the bottle of Pepto-Bismol. "Warning…" Ah, now he was getting somewhere. A warning held out hope for a fatal consequence. "…may darken stool." He returned the bottle to the shelf. He could not recall a single case of a person dying from a darkened stool. Nor, he thought, would he be likely to have a quick end from terminal constipation.

Toothpaste, cotton swabs…

Chesney closed the medicine cabinet with the realization that he had a very safe and dull bathroom. He looked at his electric razor. Martina had given him that. Perhaps in her wisdom, she knew that one day, given that he was such a loser, Chesney would try to kill himself. Or maybe she just thought it was a good gift.

Electric razor? Well, he may not be able to slit his throat with the thing, but maybe he could electrocute himself with it. No, he thought. It would be the height of ingratitude to kill himself with a present from Martina.

Chesney walked into his bedroom and glanced around. There was nothing fatal there except the cords on the venetian blinds. Those were both too short versus his height, and too thin versus his bulk. He'd only tear down the blinds and get a nasty bump when they landed on his head.

He headed to the kitchen. Ah, now, here there was potential. Why hadn't he thought of it before? There, underneath the sink, were cleaning supplies. One of them had to be toxic, he reasoned.

"Dish soap..." he muttered, pushing through the bottles, "no, that would just give you diarrhea, which, if left untreated, could dehydrate you, but that's not quick and is very unpleasant. Ah, scouring powder... nasty, but still, it would more than likely tear up your insides. Wait, ah yes...toilet cleaner!"

Chesney stood up, clutching the bottle of toilet cleaner in macabre triumph. Then he stopped.

"Why is this in the kitchen?" he asked himself. "I never use it in the kitchen. I have space under the bathroom sink. I keep the toilet brush in the bathroom. Why didn't I store this in the bathroom?"

Chesney marched back into the bathroom and placed the toilet cleaner under the bathroom sink and returned to the kitchen.

There were always knives, he thought. But that wasn't fair to Mrs. Spottlefore, his landlady, who lived downstairs in the duplex. The mess would be terrible. Mrs. Spottlefore would have all that blood to clean up. He could do like he saw in that film, and take a warm bath, slit his wrist and slowly bleed away. That way the only clean up would be the bathtub. No, that wasn't any good. He couldn't bear the thought of being found naked by his landlady. It would be very embarrassing for both of them.

Chesney plopped down on the sofa. His home wasn't sufficiently dangerous. It could make him sick, but it wouldn't kill him. Lying on his back he looked up at a bug crawling across the ceiling.

"A short but uncomplicated life," he sighed while watching the bug. "You'll only live a few days. You will mate in an unemotional but satisfying manner, live your full span of existence, and then expire. You've probably never unintentionally caused the death of those whom you love if you even love at all. From where I am, bug, you may have the last laugh. You may be better off where you are crawling across the ceiling of a New Jersey apartment, safe from the world except..."

Chesney sat up. Chesney had always taken a laissez-faire approach to the bugs around his apartment. Not so, his landlady. Mrs. Spottlefore couldn't abide two things in her house: ex-husbands and insects. She had had two of the former, and, if she had her way, none of the latter.

She had given Chesney a large jug of insecticide with orders to use it if he saw any of the detested crawly things about. He had stuck the stuff in the back of the hall closet and forgotten about it: until now.

Chesney rushed to the closet. There, behind a bowling ball and an old slide projector, it lay. He took it to his kitchen table, sat down, and examined the label of BUGZ-KILLA, the name in all capital letters. According to the extensive warning label, BUGZ-KILLA would not only end the lives of insects, but would also bump off just about any other living creature if not handled in the right way.

"EXTREMELY TOXIC – USE RUBBER GLOVES WHEN HANDLING!"

Foiled again! He didn't have any rubber gloves. Then he realized how ridiculous this was. This and all the other warnings on the label were for those who intended safely using BUGZ-KILLA. It would do the job, and quickly. He needed no further advice from the manufacturer.

Chesney examined the spray top of the plastic jug.

"I'll get rid of that," he said. "It would take forever to squirt myself to death, and I'd probably get quite ill before that happened." He stopped. "Why am I explaining this to myself? And for that matter, why am I asking myself rhetorical questions?"

The thing to do, he concluded, would be to pour a big glass of the stuff, drink it and go lie down, presumably to be found in days to come on his back with his legs in the air like some dead insect. Unscrewing the top of the jug, Chesney was repulsed by the noxious odor that filled the room. He quickly resealed the bottle.

"That's very nasty," he said.

He stared at the jug of poison, pondering it for a moment.

"I'd never be able to drink that, not straight anyway. I'll mix it." He opened the refrigerator. He was out of Coca-Cola. The only other liquid in the house was a container of milk that he kept for his breakfast cereal.

"Yes, cereal," he hummed.

He hadn't eaten since breakfast. It was mid-afternoon, and he was hungry. He would have a bowl of cereal before killing himself. In fact, he could pour the poison and mix it with the cereal. Fortunately, he had a fresh, king-size box of Raisin Bran in the cupboard.

Getting out a large bowl, Chesney filled it with Raisin Bran, spooned several heaping teaspoons of sugar on top, and then covered it with milk and placed it on the table. He started reaching for the BUGZ-KILLA but decided to enjoy one last bowl of cereal before ending it all. It would be his last meal or at least the last one he'd enjoy. His last meal would be the second bowl.

As he ate, he wondered if he was being heroic. He caused the death of two fiancées. He hadn't meant to, but neither of them would have died if he hadn't come along. Would his beloved Verity have that little red sports car if it hadn't been given to her as a wedding present? Well, maybe, but all the people around her blamed Chesney. At least that's what her father implied.

Then, there was Martina. She wouldn't have died if she hadn't met him. She had only taken that job so he would also be hired.

He had to commit suicide before he inadvertently caused another death. Yes, this was the only course left to him: the fatal bowl of Raisin Bran.

He refilled the bowl with crunchy bran flakes interspersed with plump raisins. Then he sprinkled, one, two, three, oh, why not, four heaps of sugar on top, before pouring in the remainder of the milk. Chesney Potts took a deep breath. He unscrewed the top of the insecticide and poured it over the cereal. It was a putrid, fetid mishmash, but then lethal breakfast cereal shouldn't look appetizing. If it did, everyone would be killing themselves over their morning corn flakes.

Chesney stirred his spoon through it once. The BUGZ-KILLA made shimmering rainbows atop the milk, like oil slicks on blacktop. There was something almost artistic about it.

He filled the spoon with the fatal mixture and raised it to his lips.

- 57 -
The Incredible Hulk and
the Lifesaving Anagram

The noxious mixture was under his nose. His lips parted to greet the first spoonful of poison.

There was a knock at the door.

"Go away," Chesney muttered. "Come back when I'm gone."

He lifted the spoon back towards his mouth.

BAM! BAM! BAM!

Now it seemed like someone was kicking at the door.

Chesney shoved the spoon back into the bowl and got up. If that lunatic didn't stop kicking like that, they'd damage the door. It would be bad enough for his landlady to find his corpse without having to spring for a new door too.

From the top of the stairs, he saw a massive shadow on the shade drawn over the door's window. From the size of the shadow and the violent banging on the door, Chesney wondered if the Incredible Hulk had gone into door-to-door sales.

BAM! BAM! BAM!

"Hold on," shouted Chesney, "I'm coming! Stop kicking the door down!"

"I got my hands full," replied a muffled voice.

Chesney scrambled down the stairs and opened the door. There was a large crate with a pair of legs under them. They were brown legs, with heavy socks and work boots at the end. The owner of the legs was either wearing shorts, or he was naked. There was a brown delivery truck in the driveway.

"Delivery for Potts," said the driver.

"I'm Mr. Potts," said Chesney.

The crate and the man holding it stood motionless.

"Uh, I'm sorry," said Chesney, "please, come in."

Chesney guided him up the stairs.

"Please, just put it down right there," said Chesney.

"Where?" asked the driver. "I can't see."

"Oh, right," Chesney put a guiding hand on the crate. "Just let it down; here, slowly, don't hurt yourself."

"Thanks," said the driver setting down the crate.

The wooden box stood almost four feet high. Multiple labels and routing tickets were stapled across the top.

"Where in the world did this come from?" said Chesney.

"England," said the driver, mopping his brow with a bandana.

"England," said Chesney. His heart leapt at the name with a mixture of excitement and pain. He then looked back down at the crate. There, in the corner, was the return address. It was unfamiliar, though the name over the address was unmistakable: "Postlewaite."

"Mr. Postlewaite," said Chesney.

"You know him? Good," said the driver. He picked up his clipboard, removed a pen from his shirt pocket, and began writing on the manifest.

"Yes, he's a friend of my late Aunt," said Chesney. "He's a funny kind of fellow. The first time I met him, he pretended to be a haberdasher."

"Uh-huh," said the delivery man, not looking up from his writing.

"Can I get you something," said Chesney, and then he remembered that he had nothing to drink except for tap water and insecticide. "Would you like a glass of water? I'm afraid that's all I've got at the moment." It was all he'd have forever, too.

The driver looked up. "Sure, that would be great."

Chesney nodded and went to fetch the water. The driver followed him into the kitchen and was staring at the table.

"Raisin Bran," said the driver wistfully, "I haven't had that for, oh…" he paused and looked into the air, apparently retrieving a fond recollection from the distant past. "…two days."

"Two days? I thought you were going to say something longer. You know, like 'ten years.'"

"No," said the driver, "it's been two days. My brother-in-law came over, and he finished off the box. He ate it all. Sign here, please."

He handed Chesney the clipboard and the pen.

Chesney signed it.

"And there," said the driver, flipping up the page. Chesney did so, and did so once more on yet another page. "This thing's been rerouted all over the place," explained the driver when he was handed back the clipboard. "One place in England, then over to Colt's Neck, New Jersey…"

"My mother's home," said Chesney, "but she moved…"

"Then to a place called Marlton Press…"

"I used to work there…"

"Then, Hightstown…"

"I used to live there…"

"Then this address in Delaware…"

Chesney winced. "Yes, I…I was supposed to live there."

"Then finally to here," said the driver, clicking his pen triumphantly.

"Yes, well, thank you again," said Chesney.

"Is that stuff any good?" said the driver nodding at the jug of insecticide.

"Uh, well, I don't know, yet," said Chesney. "I mean, it's supposed to be good."

The driver reached over and picked up the plastic bottle and read the back of it. "My wife has been bugging me…."

"No pun intended," said Chesney.

"Huh? Oh, yeah, I get it, bugging me," said the driver with a grin, "anyway, she's been after me to spray around the house. She hates bugs."

"So does Mrs. Spottleford," said Chesney.

"I thought your name was 'Potts.'"

"Mrs. Spottleford is my landlady," said Chesney pointing towards the lower half of the duplex.

The driver read the label aloud, reciting the various insects the product vowed to annihilate.

While the driver read in a monotone voice, Chesney couldn't help noticing the yellow embroidery on the man's shirt: United Parcel Service.

Chesney automatically rearranged the letters in his head.

"United Parcel Service," murmured Chesney, "Prevent Clear Suicide."

"Huh?" said the driver looking up.

"Prevent…I mean, nothing," said Chesney. He glanced at the crate. It was probably something belonging to Aunt Elinor. He looked up at the ceiling. "Thank you, Aunt El,"

The driver looked up at the ceiling. "I thought this was just a two-story house."

"Yes, I mean, it is," said Chesney, "I just meant, I mean, it's just probably from my Aunt."

"Oh," he looked down at his manifest, "only I thought you said some guy name Popplewitt."

"Postlewaite," said Chesney, "but never mind, and thank you. Thank you and every one at your company. And thank them for having the forethought to name their company the name they named it."

"Uh…you're welcome?" said the driver handing back the jug of BUGZ-KILLA.

Chesney pushed it back into his hands. "Please," he said, "you keep it. Give it your wife… to take care of her bugs."

"Yeah," the driver hefted the jug in his hand. "Are you sure? It's almost full."

Chesney glanced over his shoulder at the deadly bowl of Raisin Bran.

"I'm sure," he said.

– 58 –
Aunt Elinor's Legacy

ortunately, given the meandering route it had taken, the crate was
well constructed. It took a claw hammer to open the thing. Inside
were two items, side by side, in a bed of excelsior: Aunt Elinor's
familiar old suitcase; and a large trunk.

The old trunk looked like a child's idea of a pirate's treasure chest. It
was the trunk his grandfather left to Aunt Elinor, a bequest that rankled
Chesney's father. Alexander Potoski was a highly decorated hero of the
First World War. Chesney promised Aunt El that he would never let his
father see the contents. An envelope addressed to Chesney was affixed to
the lid.

"Dear Chesney," began the typewritten letter inside.
"I hope this finds you well…"
Chesney turned the page over to see the signature of Mr. Postlewaite.
*"Please excuse the tardiness in executing my duties (along with Li Gao) as
the executor of your dear Aunt's estate. There have been various and seemingly
unavoidable delays.*

*"According to the desires of our dear friend, Elinor Potoski, you are her primary
heir. The contents of this crate represent the bulk of her remaining worldly goods.
As I'm sure you will recall, your Aunt knew of her coming demise and settled
the disposition of most of her personal effects before her passing. Aside from the
enclosed, your Aunt has left you a financial sum, which after legal costs, was, as
of this writing, approximately 15,500 pounds sterling."*

The letter went on to detail where the money had been deposited in his
name, and the account number.

"I want again to express," the letter concluded, *"my deepest fondness and regard for your dear Aunt. She loved you deeply and considered you one of the great joys of her life. If there is anything I can ever do for you, I am at your disposal. Li Gao probably would be, too, but I've also mislaid him, or his address, in the move."*

Chesney folded the letter and returned it to the envelope. He stared at the packing crate, uncertain if he would even be able to lift the trunk from it. The trunk's curved lid was secured by two thick leather straps on either side of a metal catch with a keyhole in the center. He pulled on the catch only to discover that it was locked. He would have to pry the lock open, but that could wait. He was more interested in the suitcase anyway.

The suitcase, though smaller, was also heavy and took a bit of effort to lift from the crate. Chesney placed it on the coffee table and undid the latches. Carefully, he examined the contents of the case. There were some books, apparently favorites of Aunt Elinor's: *A Tale of Two Cities*, *Jane Eyre*, an early novel by Evelyn Waugh, and a collection of P.G. Wodehouse's Mr. Mulliner stories. Next, there was a bundle of papers tied with a ribbon containing letters from Chesney going back to his childhood. She had kept every letter he had ever sent her. Not surprising, he thought, since he had all her letters, as well. He felt his cheeks blush red as he reread the sentiments he had written as a child. A separate bundle included pictures he had drawn her.

Next, were several clothing items, including two sweaters, one cardigan, one pullover, and one of Aunt Elinor's jumpers that she favored.

"One cardigan, two jumpers," said Chesney holding up the items. He thought it ironic that the British would refer to the pullover sweater as a jumper and call the dress a pinafore. Americans would call the pinafore dress a jumper. The dress was gray wool, sleeveless, and buttoned up the center. It was similar to the one she'd given Verity the last time they had all been together. He laid the clothes aside, not knowing what he'd do with them, but vowing to treat them with respect.

Under the clothes was a well-worn leather Bible. A cursory rifling through its pages revealed Aunt Elinor had made many notations in the margins. The different inks and degrees of fading seemed to indicate this had been the habit of a lifetime.

Next, there was a group of maps and guidebooks tied together with string. The maps were all street maps of London, while the guidebooks were all of London attractions. All were yellowed in appearance, and the copyright dates placed the most recent one from the mid-1960s. Besides these were a few figurines wrapped in tissue paper.

Chesney next pulled out a small quilted bag closed with a silken cord that wrapped around it. It unrolled, almost like a tiny sleeping bag, and contained a series of padded pouches. It was Aunt El's jewelry bag. While none of the jewelry was cheap, neither was it expensive, not that he would dream of selling it. Instead, like most of the things in her life, Aunt Elinor had collected these not because of their intrinsic value, but rather the worth she ascribed to them. That made each piece, indeed, all the items in the suitcase, precious to him.

Then, at the bottom of the suitcase, he saw a key, presumably to the trunk. It was taped to an envelope.

"For Chesney," it said, in Aunt Elinor's handwriting.

His hand trembled as he held the envelope. He turned it over. She had sealed it with wax. Chesney broke the seal, took out the letter, and began to read.

"My Dearest Chesney,

"By the time you read this, you will have learned that I have deceived you in regards to my illness, of which you were not even aware at our last meeting. Please forgive me. I just didn't want our last days together to be marred by sadness and that maudlin sentiment that loved ones have when they know they are experiencing their final parting here on Earth.

"I also didn't want to spoil my last moments with your lovely Verity. One of the great joys in these last days has been to see you with such a lovely young woman who loves you and whom you love so very much. Knowing that you have that dear girl to look after you (and I'm sure you will look after her) makes my separation from you that much easier. I only hope my inevitable outcome does not mar the happiness of your wedding day. In any event, bless you both, and best wishes for a long and happy life together."

Chesney wiped the tears from his eyes. It was a consolation that Aunt Elinor didn't know that the girl they both loved so dearly had followed her into death by less than 24 hours. He blew his nose and continued reading.

"Don't mourn over me, dearest. I've had an interesting and rewarding life, and I can sincerely announce that I leave this world, having experienced practically everything I ever hoped to experience. My only regret is not having more time with those I love: yourself, and your future family, the foremost of those. I have learned the hard way that it does very little good to look backwards in life. It is especially futile to look back and mourn over past mistakes. We all make mistakes, and I speak as one who has made them, the worst of which were fatal. I hope you never have to go through the pain of causing the death of another person. I have lived with that guilt, even though the death was accidental and inadvertent on my part. I don't mention this for any other reason to remind you to look ahead. God can forgive even the most grievous sins, that his stock-in-trade and there's none better at it. If you ever find yourself in a situation that you think so horrible, so unforgivable, please remember that. My worse errors in life were holding on to things like that for too long until I ran the danger of making them a permanent part of me.

"*Remember to show mercy to those around you, because you need it from them, too. And to that mercy, be sure to add grace. By that, I don't mean the little prayer you say before you eat, but those wonderful bits of favor that none of us deserve but all of us need so much. Don't ever look for revenge, because that never works out the way you want it. They say revenge is a dish best served cold, but hot or cold, I've found it bitter to the taste. At the same time, always seek justice. And as much as it is in your power to right a wrong, do so with all your might.*

"*Here I am, rambling on, probably telling you a lot of things you already know. You were always a good boy, and now you're a fine young man. I suppose I'm just saying these things as my final reminder of things, of which I'm sure you're aware. It's sort of like telling you to shut the windows, feed the dog, and don't leave the water running as I'm going out the door on holiday. And in a way, I'm going on holiday, though of quite a permanent duration. I truly believe that we'll meet again when you join me in the land where there will never be another parting or sadness. I hope that will be in far in the future and that you will enjoy a long, happy, and most of all useful life.*

With all my love,

Elinor

"*P.S. – Chesney, your Aunt really is losing her faculties due to this wretched disease. I nearly forgot, attached to this letter is the key to your grandfather's trunk. You are, of course, released from your promise not to share the contents with your late father as he is now your late father. I relinquish the contents of the trunk to you to do with as you wish and deem fit. I never knew what to do with it, not that any of it matters to anyone anymore. The contents used to be a terrible secret and a horrible burden to the one who kept it. Time has a way of turning those sorts of things into boring old stories. At times I came close to just chucking it all, which you are certainly free to do. Anyway, there you have it.*

Always, Your Aunt El."

Chesney Potts folded the letter and pressed it to his heart. He glanced back over towards the table where the poisoned bowl of Raisin Bran festered.

"Thank you, Aunt El," he said. "You got here just in time."

He walked over and poured the bowl of cereal down the sink, letting the water run over the bowl, flushing it out, and then throwing the bowl in the trash for good measure.

Then he returned to the living room and reread Aunt El's letter several times over, each time drawing deeper strength and conviction from her words. His mind drifted back to the last time he'd spoken with Li Gao, and how Li had told him not to waste his sorrow, but to let them mold his character into something better. He recalled how Li Gao assured him that Aunt Elinor had gone through similar hurts to become the person she became. He wondered if it was even truer, now that he had gone through this not once, but twice.

Another thought from Aunt Elinor's letter kept jumping off the page to challenge him: "always seek justice, and as much as it is in your power to right a wrong, do so with all your might."

He may have been partially responsible for Martina being in Chicago. But now Chesney saw that Peter Liverot had put Martina there, and for all wrong reasons. He could forgive Liverot because he too needed forgiveness. But Liverot denied doing anything wrong. Worse than that, he had tried to throw all the responsibility on Chesney. And like a fool, Chesney had almost killed himself under the weight of that misplaced blame. It was clear, Liverot wanted neither forgiveness, mercy, or grace. So what was left? Revenge? Chesney looked down and realized his fingernails were digging into his palm beneath his tightly clenched fist.

"No, no," he said aloud, relaxing his grip, "no revenge. But as much as it is in my power to do so, I'll seek justice."

Chesney took a deep breath and looked around the room.

"Justice… but how?"

- 59 -
The Comely Faux Girl Had
Just Won the War

The next day Chesney Potts was still pondering justice and how to achieve it. The authorities cleared Liverot of any complicity in Martina's death. The Chicago police even commended Liverot for his cooperation. No one else saw or heard anything that would suggest her death was anything but an accident. But they hadn't asked the right questions.

"Was this young lady originally supposed to go on this business trip?"

"Was the star witness a disgusting lecher?"

"Would any decent woman risk their lives to get away from this beast?"

Chesney imagined several ways to get to Liverot, but they all crossed the line between justice and revenge. Besides, kidnapping Liverot and torturing him slowly and painfully was a difficult undertaking. Also, there was Valerie's firm suspicion that Liverot was a front for some criminal syndicate. Chesney couldn't go directly for Peter Liverot. It would take cunning and subterfuge.

Fourth Fiduciary Trust was probably a front for all kinds of illegal money operations. If he could get the evidence on what was really going on at the bank, he could deal Liverot a decisive blow. But how could he do that? Had he thought of all this two days ago, Chesney would have been in a good position to poke around for information. Now, however, he couldn't show his face in the building without having it permanently rearranged.

He could ask Valerie to do it. But if Valerie was caught, there's no telling what Liverot and his cronies would do to her. He wouldn't be responsible for another loved one's death.

Patsy was privy to more sensitive information than anyone. Unfortunately, she was too innocent to be of use. Patsy thought the best of everyone and viewed the world through a filter as bright as Donny Osmond's socks. That's probably why Liverot valued her as his personal assistant. It was just too bad he couldn't climb into Patsy's head for a few weeks.

Who else was there? Albrecht Eckner was probably just as crooked as Liverot, and with a perverse nature added to his larceny. Besides, Eckner was on his way to the new bank in Gibraltar, probably to launder more of their ill-gotten gains.

Chesney's mind raced in circles, arriving at the same conclusions, but never approaching a solution. With nothing else to do, he decided to clean up the packing crate. He placed Aunt Elinor's suitcase in the hall closet. Then he wrestled the trunk from the box. He stared at his grandfather's trunk. What would he do with that? It was now a cumbersome artifact rather than a treasured heirloom. His father probably would have given anything to examine its contents. To Chesney, it was just an old trunk.

Chesney remembered his grandfather as a scary old man with a wooden leg. Maybe the trunk held his wooden leg. He doubted whether the truck's secret was relevant any longer. It probably was something his grandfather had once thought very important, but now was just an old story.

Chesney pushed the trunk in front of the couch. With a feeling of reluctance mixed with obligation, he put the key in the lock. After some initial stiffness, the lock gave way, and the latch dropped down. He undid the leather straps on either side of it and lifted the heavy lid.

A pungent miasma emanated from the trunk, and Chesney wondered when it had last been opened. Thankfully, there were no artificial limbs inside. Chesney had never thought about it before, but now wondered: did you bury a man's wooden leg with the rest of him? The first thing he encountered was an old Army uniform. The tunic was heavy wool, brownish-green in color with a high collar and brass buttons with an eagle stamped into them. All the buttons were tarnished with age.

Underneath the tunic was a pair of matching trousers. They looked like type worn for horseback riding, though he knew his grandfather had been in the infantry. They had an excess of fabric around the hips, like jodhpurs. Along with these was a pair of puttees, heavy wool wrapped around the legs between the boots and the trousers. Under these was an overseas cap, also with a brass insignia button.

Next came what looked to be a shaving kit made out of canvas, including a metal mirror and a safety razor.

None of these things was the least bit mysterious. Chesney could not imagine why any of it would have been kept a secret from his father.

A tin biscuit box came next. It held a series of commendations along with the corresponding medals and decorations.

"For Conspicuous Courage..." began one dated from July 1918.

Though short on specifics, it cited his grandfather, Alexander Potoski, for showing great bravery in saving his unit during an enemy attack at the cost of his own limb. Other citations seemed to reference the same incident without giving any insight into exactly what had happened or why his grandfather had never mentioned it. As a boy, Chesney had heard his father boast of Alexander's exploits. When Chesney had pressed him for details, his father could only shrug his shoulders.

"That's all I know," Rodney Potoski would say. "My father never talked about it much. In fact, he never spoke of it at all. Everything I know was told to me by my mother."

Chesney closed the tin. Beneath it was a scattering of mothballs strewn over some yellowed newspapers. He started to lift the papers, to see if they represented anything more than the bottom lining of the trunk, but they crumbled around the edges when he began to lift them.

He was about to give up and repack the trunk when something caught his eye. There was a slight bulge, a small lump under the newspapers. Chesney prodded it with his index finger. It was hard. Carefully he lifted the newspapers. There were several layers of papers, beneath which he found a layer of older papers. The lower tier was from the early 1920s and from New York. The top layer was British and from the 1960s. These must have been set there by Aunt El, after her father's death. As far as Chesney could guess, his grandfather secreted something underneath the layer of newspapers, while his daughter, had similarly covered it with a fresh layer of newspaper. Presumably, both had done so to keep the item hidden from prying eyes. It was only the deterioration of the papers that made it stick out.

Underneath the final layer, there was a manila envelope. Inside was a small pocket-sized book bound in black leather. For a moment, Chesney thought it was a Bible or prayer book, but as he picked it up, he could see it was a notebook or diary. He opened the book to the inside front cover. There, in faded ink, was written: Property of A. Potoski. Albany Street, Oswego, NY.

The handwriting was distinct and easy to read. Chesney recalled his father relating how penmanship used to be assiduously drilled into him throughout grammar school. He turned the page.

"I commemorated my seventeenth birthday at the recruitment office. There I formally enlisted in the United States Army with the goal of doing my duty in the Great War in Europe. This book, the one that I now take pen to hand in, was given to me by my sisters Iris and Anne the day I left for camp. They made me promise to write my experiences in this book as a record for propensity [sic]. I'm not exactly sure if they wanted to read it after I came back, or against the chance that I didn't come back. I don't know how much time I will have to write. I expect they keep you

pretty busy in a war. I will try to record as best I can what I see and what I do for as long as I can until 'It's Over, Over There.'"

This diary must hold the secret so dark Alexander felt compelled to hide it from his own son. But what could it be? Had he been more than an ordinary soldier? His medals and decorations attested that he had gone beyond the call of duty. Had Alexander Potoski been a blood-thirsty killing machine in the bloodiest conflict in recent history? Was he later ashamed of his actions? But why would he hide those facts from his son, but entrust them to his daughter?

He read on.

The first pages were interesting for the insight it provided into his grandfather. It was a glimpse into the character of the innocent boy who would eventually become the scarred and scary old man. He told, with almost mesmerizing dullness, of the drilling and routine employed to turn raw recruits into soldiers. As Chesney read, he learned that his grandfather was the smallest member of his unit, standing a mere five foot four inches tall. Chesney concluded that's where he got his own stature or lack of it. He didn't recall his grandfather as short, but then when you're three-years-old, all adults look big to you. Chesney was five foot six. The only difference was that in addition to being short, Alexander was also skinny, a trait which his grandson never shared.

Being the smallest member of the company, there were anecdotes about the kidding Alexander Potoski received from his mates. These all seemed good-natured, or at least that is how they were received by the person relating them. Still, none of what Chesney read was in the least bit shocking.

He skimmed ahead until reaching the point where his grandfather arrived in France. It was April 1918. After a short time back behind the front, the company was sent forward for its first taste of action. Chesney read of his grandfather's baptism in combat. The First World War involved long stretches of boredom only relieved by horrible flashes of carnage and death. The writing tone became more terse and mature, reflecting the experiences that his grandfather witnessed but had not been able to capture in words. Then, after taking part in several battles, Alexander's company was relieved and sent for a month's rest and recuperation.

The entries had now reached July 1918, the same month referenced in the commendations. That didn't make sense, thought Chesney. He was being moved away from the front. How could he be a hero on leave?

"The boys are putting on a show," began the first entry in July, *"something to keep us busy and stave off boredom. The Captain chose our platoon to put it on, mainly because Corporal Wright knows how to play the piano and knows most of the popular songs. They want me to be in it as well, saying my voice will be just right."*

The next day's entry struck the first sour note.

"Nothing doing! I joined the army to fight the Hun and to defend liberty. I didn't enlist to make a fool of myself in some silly show. I told them there was no way on Earth I was going to play a chicken in their Follies! I'd volunteer to go back to the trenches first. Nuts!"

They wanted Alexander to play a chicken in a camp show? That seemed an odd choice, but hardly as ignominious as playing the back end of a cow. He read on to the entry on the following page.

"Got chewed out but good by the 2nd Louie. Ordered to volunteer for that show. Given a lot of banana oil about morale and company spirit and 'all in good fun,' but in the end, it was an order. Went over and reported for rehearsals. NUTS!!!"

And the diary ended there. The remaining pages were all blank. Chesney closed the book and stroked his chin. He couldn't understand his grandfather's outrage at being asked to play a barnyard animal. After all, Alexander Potoski, by his own admission was the smallest member of his company. Was playing a chicken in a camp show an affront to his manhood? If so, Chesney didn't understand why his grandfather would have to be ordered to participate.

Then, just as Chesney was about to give up his search for the family mystery, he discovered the missing piece. As he was returning his grandfather's diary to the large envelope, Chesney noticed a smaller envelope inside. He pulled it out. It was addressed to his Aunt Elinor at her address in England. The postmark was upstate New York and was dated a few months after Alexander Potoski's death.

"Dear Miss Potoski," the letter began, *"first let me express my sympathy for the loss of your father. Alex was a good soldier and a fine man. I'm proud to have commanded him back in the days of the AEF.*

"I'm not surprised that your father never explained the details of that day back in 1918 when he saved the lives of his comrades. Aside from being modest about his own bravery, the circumstances of that day were disconcerting to your father. But as one whose life was saved, I only recall it with the greatest admiration for him.

"Knowing how he felt about all of it, I hesitate to tell you. But as he is gone now, your father can no longer feel any shame from the incident, and I believe that he never had any cause to anyway. So here goes.

"As you said in your letter, your father's diary ends with the mention of him having to play a 'chicken' in the show we were putting on. As you also rightly guessed, that was popular slang at the time for a girl or a pretty young woman."

Chesney looked up from the letter. That made more sense. As the smallest member of the company, Alexander Potoski would have felt such a request was an affront to his manhood. It was hard enough proving his masculinity without having to do so while wearing a dress. He continued reading.

"He was practically spitting bullets over the idea. As you know, your father wasn't a big man. Like a lot of smaller fellows he had a chip on his shoulder about his size. He was always volunteering for anything that would prove his bravery, and he never backed down from a scrape. So the suggestion that he should play a woman in our company show didn't sit well with him. When he was ordered to do it, that made it even worse, especially when it was pointed out that he looked the part more than any of the other men!

"I'm sure you're a very lovely young lady, and I'm sure you take after your beautiful mother, but even if you took after your father, that wouldn't be so bad either. I only mention that to say that your father made quite a good looking young lady when he was all done up in his costume and the makeshift wig. Again, I'm not detracting in the least from your father's manliness. He was all man, but also a pretty one under the right circumstances. But I'm getting off the track.

"As you mentioned, according to your father's diary, we were back of the lines for what was supposed to be a month of recuperation. During that time we were putting together that show. It seems like a silly thing to do in the middle of a war, but it wasn't that uncommon, nor was what your father was asked to do. We didn't have any women around, and men had to play those parts. We were part of the U.S. 42nd Division stationed near Champagne when it started.

"In was the fifteenth of July (you tend to remember the date you think the world is ending). The Germans were making their last big attack to try and break through and end the war. The units at the front were caught by surprise at the strength of the attack, and they quickly fell back. We were about ten miles behind the lines, but that rear position soon became the front before we knew it. We had been running through our show rehearsal when our company was suddenly in the thick of it. I recall all of us rushing to get out of our costumes and back into our uniforms. I remember an artillery shell going off, hitting the building that housed our stage. Soon after, we were overrun by the advance units of the German army. A good part of our company was taken prisoners. We were held there for a few hours and were told that we would soon be marched back behind the German lines.

"While we were there as prisoners, your father appeared. He apparently had suffered a glancing blow in the initial artillery barrage. He had been knocked out still in his costume of a French farm girl. Not only was he in costume, but he was still in character! As I said before, and with no impugning of his manhood, he made a presentable young lady, especially to soldiers who had not had much in the way of female company!

"To this day, I don't know how he did it, but your father played his part to the hilt and was accepted as what he appeared to be by the Germans. He behaved

very demurely and waited on the soldiers who were guarding us. He brought them wine and some food and even cast a flirtatious eye to several of our captors. He was so convincing that one of the Germans pulled your father down on his lap and kissed him at one point. Your father pretended to be surprised but wisely gave the man a peck on the cheek before scurrying shyly away. Fortunately, he had picked up enough French lingo to pretend not to know either any English or German. This helped in his disguise.

"When he could, he tipped us the wink on the side, so we didn't think he had gone off his head. In any event, he kept the guards distracted enough, that when, after a few hours, he found the opportunity and took it catching the Germans completely by surprise. He grabbed one of the officer's sidearm. That was the signal the rest of us had been waiting for. A fight broke out. Thanks to your father plying the Germans with drink and lulling them into a false sense of security, we were able to gain the upper hand and our freedom.

"I hesitate to mention to a lady such as yourself the details of how your father lost his leg. Suffice it to say, he received that wound during the fight. I'll just say that when Alex started shouting out to the rest of us in English and his normal voice, the Germans were stunned that he was not the little French maiden they had taken him for. The officer who had kissed and been kissed by him, went after your father and with a long knife. He pinned your father and was about to cut something else off in revenge. Fortunately Alex was able to dodge the blade at the last minute resulting in the wound that eventually resulted in his leg being amputated. I say 'fortunately' for had he not avoided the German's intended target I would not be writing to you or any of his offspring. I think you will understand that without a more detailed explanation.

"I think that's the only missing parts of the story. You have the commendations. The attack was repelled. Your father spent the rest of the war in the hospital recovering from his wounds suffered that day. I think I can speak for all of us that were there that day and say that Alexander Potoski was one of the bravest men we had the honor and privilege to serve with and know.

"Yours truly, William Dodd, (former sergeant)."

Chesney folded the letter and placed it back in its envelope. He returned the items to the trunk and locked it up again. He stared at the trunk for several minutes. Chesney understood his grandfather's embarrassment over how he became a hero. For a man who felt the constant need to prove his manhood it was a bitter irony that he would do it disguised as a woman. Chesney doubted if his own father would have thought less of Alexander Potoski for how he managed to save his friends. After all, he hadn't planned things that way. Those circumstances presented themselves to his grandfather. He used his brains and his bravery to play the hand that had been dealt him.

Looking at the clock, Chesney saw that it was late, and he realized he was exhausted. He brushed his teeth and climbed into bed and quickly fell into a deep sleep. Several hours later, in the middle of the night, he awoke with a start and sat up.

"That's it!" he cried and jumped out of bed.

– 60 –
How to Spoil a Rainy Sunday

Valerie Fierro loved rainy Sunday mornings. They forced her to stay in bed listening to rain on the windowpane. She would languish in comfort until she was forced to stir by a greater desire: either a cup of coffee or a need to pee.

She was between boyfriends, or at least between sleep over boyfriends. She liked the latest one, but she wasn't sure yet if she could deal with the sight of looking at him with nothing but 24 hours of beard stubble to adorn him. He was good in bed, at least the first two times, but until she was sure about a guy, Valerie was loath to have them spend the night at her townhouse. If she found she didn't like him that much, it was difficult to get rid of them. Then they went from a nighttime lover to an all-day pest. Still, if Bob were there now, he could fetch her first cup of coffee. The boyfriend had not been invented yet, however, who could pee for her. Once that technological impediment was conquered, Valerie would never have to leave her cozy bed on rainy weekends.

She rolled over and glanced at the clock. It was 10:55; another hour of sleep would be perfect. Valerie buried her face in her pillow, took in a deep breath, and then slowly exhaled, fully expecting to be asleep by the end of that sigh.

Before the last bit of air could escape from her lungs; however, the doorbell rang.

"Oh, shit," she muttered into the pillow, "go away. Whoever you are, go away."

Ten seconds of blissful silence followed, which was shattered by the bell, rung twice in short, insistent bursts.

"Get lost, just get lost," growled Valerie flopping over in bed and hiding her face in the other pillow.

318

This time her wishes only received five seconds of fulfillment. Now the creature, the interloper, the asshole was rapping on her brass doorknocker. She cursed the person knocking even more severely.

"It's no use," she spat, throwing off the covers. "Even if they left now, I'm too awake to get back to sleep!"

Valerie reached for her robe, covered her silk nightshirt, and then crossed to the window. Her car was in the driveway. She couldn't pretend she wasn't home, not with her Nissan contradicting her. Out on the street was a Honda Civic. Her sister, Rose, didn't have a Honda, did she?

By the time she made it to the front door, Valerie had gone through at least a half-dozen people she knew that may have had a Honda, but whom she doubted actually did. As a precaution against intruders who drove economy automobiles, Valerie put the chain on her door and then opened it a crack.

"Valerie!"

It was a horrible looking person. And although he seemed to know her, she had no idea who he was. The man was ragged-looking, he had long brown hair, matted by the rain, and he had the oddest looking beard, but only in spots. In other places, his face was quite bare. She had never heard of male-pattern baldness on the face. And he was almost emaciated, but then that effect may have been heightened by the fact that he wore a raincoat at least two sizes too large.

"Valerie, it is I!"

She turned her head to the side and smiled, while at the same time backing away from the door in anticipation of slamming it shut.

"It's Chesney," said the man.

Valerie gasped and shut the door.

The person on the other side began knocking and ringing the bell simultaneously.

"Valerie, it really is Chesney, let me in," he cried. "I need your help."

Chesney Potts? She hadn't seen him for months, not since she helped him decide Peter Liverot was the person to blame for Martina's death. After that, it was like Chesney had dropped off the face of the Earth.

She heard about how Chesney practically accused Peter Liverot of throwing Martina in front of that bus. Valerie expected him to call after that. For weeks, she held her breath every time her phone rang, but he never called. It was just as well, she thought. Chesney needed a fresh start. He needed to go away. As for her, with Martina dead, and Albrecht Eckner transferred to Gibraltar, Valerie's stock at work had risen considerably. She was finally getting the recognition she wanted, and more importantly, deserved. Now, this…

Valerie realized she couldn't leave him out there on her doorstep in the rain, banging away. What would her neighbors think? She opened the door a crack. She could see by the pitiful look in his eyes that it was Chesney.

"What do you want?" she said.

"I need your help," said Chesney.

"Did your car break down?"

He looked over his shoulder. "No, my car's okay," he said. "No, I need your help in something else."

"What?"

"Justice," he said, stabbing the air with his index finger.

"Justice for who?"

"For whom, and for Martina, of course," said Chesney, "I figured it all out. Can I come in?"

"Just a minute, let me undo the chain," she said and closed the door. What did he mean, he figured it out? If he really figured it out, and was talking about justice, that could only mean one thing. Chesney was there looking like a scrawny bum to settle the score with her. Still, she reasoned, he didn't seem angry, and he did say he needed her help. She would let him in, but she would be on her guard.

"Sorry," she said, opening the door, "the chain was stuck. Come on in."

Chesney entered and removed his raincoat. Underneath it, he was even thinner than she imagined.

"You... uh..." she scanned his gaunt frame, "you look...good."

Chesney looked down at his own body and nodded.

"Yes, I've lost some weight," he agreed.

"Well, you could stand to lose a little bit," she said.

"A little bit?" he laughed. "I'd say a lot..."

"Yes, well, I never look at that sort of thing," said Valerie. She never looked at Chesney's weight, or anyone's for that matter, at least not for very long. Fat was repulsive and just plain icky.

"I'm down to 135 pounds," he proclaimed.

"What?" Valerie weighed that, and she was only an inch shorter than he was. "Have you been sick?"

He smiled and waved his hand. "Not at all. In fact, I've never been in better shape. I do a lot of cardio."

Valerie looked at his thin arms. "You should add some weight training to that."

"Oh, no, that would be counter-productive to the plan!"

Valerie sighed and gestured in the direction of her kitchen. This was obviously going to take some time. "I'm making some coffee. You want some?"

"Could I have some tea?" he asked.

Valerie shrugged and led Chesney to the kitchen and then pointed to a chair at her table.

"Sorry if I came over too early," he said. "Only I saw your car out front, and I thought you'd be up."

Valerie looked down at her robe. "Oh, yes, I've been up for hours," she said. "I was just doing the wash." He cocked his head, as if to hear evidence of a washing machine or a dryer. "Oh, it must have just stopped," said Valerie.

"Do you need to go take it out?" he asked.

"Take what out of what?"

"Your clothes out of the dryer."

"Uh, no, it's just towels," she said. Valerie turned on her coffee maker and then started boiling water for his tea. "I can get them later." Valerie finished making Chesney's cup of tea and set it in front of him, poured her coffee, and sat down.

"Now, what's all this about," she asked.

"I've figured it all out," he said.

Valerie took a slow sip of her coffee while studying him over the rim of the cup. She wondered if Chesney finally cracked up. Even if he had, she didn't think he'd be violent, but even if he was, she figured she could beat him up, especially in his present state.

"And what have you figured out, exactly," she said, lowering the cup. "You still haven't told me what you're talking about or why you're here. I haven't heard from you in months."

Chesney lowered his eyes and stared into his tea with a guilty expression. "Yes, I know, I'm sorry about that. You must have been very worried."

Valerie smiled slightly. Actually, she hardly thought about his whereabouts, but apologies were always nice.

"But I've been very busy," he said. "I figured out Martina's death."

Valerie froze. Had he figured out that she was responsible for sending Martina to Chicago? Maybe that's why Chesney looked like a deranged lunatic, because now that's what he was. Valerie rose slowly, as not to make any sudden moves. She wanted to be standing, standing over near the counter, near the drawer where she kept her knives. To cover her movements, she opened up the boxed cake on the counter.

"Piece of cake?" she asked.

"No, thank you."

"No?" Valerie was surprised. Chesney Potts had never turned down baked goods before. He *had* gone crazy. She slid open the drawer containing the knives.

"I've got to watch my figure," he said.

Valerie's brow furrowed. Figure? Some guys, watched their weight. They didn't watch their figures.

"I know who's responsible for Martina's death," he continued, "and more importantly, how to deal with him."

"You did," said Valerie. Without looking down she felt her fingers close around the handle of a carving knife. One sudden movement from Chesney, and she'd plunge it right into his chest. It would be self-defense. She stopped. What had he just said? "Him? You said, 'deal with him.'"

"Yes, him," said Chesney, "Liverot is a him, isn't he?"

"Liverot? Oh, yes, he's a him, he is."

Valerie's fingers relaxed from the handle of the carving knife. Instead, she took out a small knife, cut herself a slice of cake, and sat down.

Chesney nodded his head. "Oh, I know what you're thinking, that I blamed myself. When I confronted Liverot he told me that the only reason that he hired me was because Martina had insisted on it. He needed her."

Valerie nodded.

"So you knew," he said.

She stopped. "Uh…yeah…"

He stared at her. She wished she was back standing next to the drawer with that big knife. Now all she had to defend herself was a half-eaten slice of crumb cake. She reached for a handier weapon and one she was much more skillful using: she lied.

"He made me promise," she said.

"Liverot?"

"Yes," said Valerie. "I didn't want to lie to you, but Liverot threatened me if I told you."

A sympathetic look overspread his face.

"You didn't lie to me," said Chesney. "I never asked you. Why would I? You must have felt a tremendous burden carrying around that secret and being sworn to keep it. What did he do, threaten to fire you?"

Sure that sounded good, Valerie thought. She nodded.

"He's beneath contempt," said Chesney. "That's another reason to settle the score with Peter Liverot. It's like he's some flesh-eating bacteria, a virus, a plague, everything he touches he infects. He had me convinced that I was responsible for Martina's death because she wouldn't have been working for the bank if it wasn't for me."

Valerie hadn't thought of that defense. Still, she didn't need it now. Liverot was a big enough target to hide behind.

"And I almost believed it," said Chesney. "I almost…well, it doesn't matter what I almost did. What matters is what I'm going to do."

"Are you going to get back at him?"

"Yes," said Chesney, "but, not revenge, justice. I'm going to bring him to justice."

"Are you going to call the cops?"

"No, he's too clever for that. Besides, it wouldn't surprise me if he and his compatriots have bought off half the police force. I'm going to get the goods on Liverot. I'm going to get the evidence on all the shady things he's doing and share it with the appropriate parties."

"What shady things?"

"You know, all things he's been doing: his crooked deals, his cooked books, anything he's been up to."

"Who told you about that?"

"You did," he said.

Valerie thought about it. Yes, she may have intimated it to Chesney. And she heard Albrecht brag about some deals and some connections that were probably shady. If she had to lay odds on it, she'd bet that Liverot and his partners were up to their eyeballs in illegal shit. But, now, Chesney was taking all that as gospel truth.

"Didn't you tell me all that?" he asked.

Valerie looked at him a moment. He was giving her that trusting, searching expression. Okay, thought Valerie, she could agree with what he was saying. It was probably true. Then Chesney could go after Peter Liverot, and that would be that. Or she could tell him it was a mistake, and that Liverot wasn't the villain she had made him out to be. In which case, Chesney, being the obsessive person he was, would start looking for another person to bring to justice. Besides, Martina had forgiven her, so it really wasn't her fault any more... if she only had that letter. Still, she was basically a good person, wasn't she? And Peter Liverot was mainly a snake, wasn't he?

"Uh...yes," said Valerie, "I did tell you all that."

"But?"

"I just don't want you to...get hurt," she said.

Chesney patted her hand. She looked down. She hadn't noticed it before, but his fingernails needed trimming.

"You're a good sister," he said. "And don't worry about me. I'm going to get all the evidence on Liverot and all his crooked deals and secret partners."

"How do you expect to do that?"

Chesney tapped the side of his head. "With brains, and from the inside."

"But you're not on the inside of the bank anymore," she reminded him. "The only person you know..." Valerie stopped in mid-sentence. That's why he needed her help. Her mouth hung open.

"Relax," said Chesney, "I wouldn't do anything to put you in danger. I've lost enough people I, well, that I... love."

"Well, then the only other person, is.... Patsy?"

Chesney smiled. "No, Patsy's too sweet, too innocent. She's probably been looking at the evidence on Liverot for years and doesn't even realize what it is. No, I need the right bait. I need someone with your brains, with Patsy's access, and who is attractive enough to be distracting to Liverot."

Valerie smirked. "So, you need a good-looking woman with a good body, smart, and one to take Patsy's place."

"Exactly," he said with a smile. "And I've got her."

"And who exactly is this wonder woman?"

Chesney's smiled broadened.

"I am!"

– 61 –
The Tweezer Initiation

Well? Say something," said Chesney.

Valerie opened her mouth, hoping something intelligible would come out, but so many thoughts were running through her head. They were all caught somewhere between her brain and her vocal chords. Finally, they started to dribble out.

"A woman...you?"

"Yes, me," said Chesney as if he had always been a woman.

"Attractive?"

"Well, that's where I'll need your help," he said. "You said it yourself to me once."

"I said what? I said you were an attractive woman?"

"Not in so many words," said Chesney.

"There aren't enough words..."

"We were at the Hotel duPont. You pointed out some woman's makeup. And then you said you could make anyone attractive, and said that you could make me an attractive woman."

"So?"

"So, make me an attractive woman."

Valerie threw up her hands. "You're out of your mind."

"Not at all," said Chesney. "It's been done before. My grandfather did it."

"I think you're confused. A grandfather that's an attractive woman is called a grandmother."

"No, he...well, that's a long story. But I know it can be done."

"But takes more than a pretty face to be an alluring woman."

"That's why I lost all this weight," he said. "I'll soon be thin enough. Then I'll just need a little padding in the right places. That's why I grew my hair."

She studied his face. "And that beard? That's a mess! You look like a dog with the mange."

"Laser hair removal," he said, pointing to the bare spots. "It's not quite done, but you can't be an attractive woman with five o'clock shadow."

"No, that's true," said Valerie. "You really did all that? I mean, the hair removal, the hair growing, and the weight loss?"

Chesney's expression grew dark. "I'd do that and more to bring Liverot to justice."

Valerie studied his face. "Yeah, well, you do have pretty good bone structure, I guess."

Chesney pulled out a photograph. "That's what I thought," he said. "Well, maybe not about the bone structure. You're the beauty expert. But under all that fat, look what I found…"

He handed Valerie a picture of an attractive woman.

"That's my late Aunt Elinor."

Valerie studied the photograph and then held it up to Chesney's face for comparison.

"I definitely see the resemblance," she said. "She's pretty."

"Can you make me look that good?"

Valerie scrutinized the picture. The woman didn't have on much makeup.

"Better," concluded Valerie. "You've got the same raw material as your Aunt, but with the right cosmetics and a good beauty regimen, with my skills, you'd be fabulous."

"I knew you could do it," he said.

"It might be fun at that," she said aloud, but mainly to herself, "a real challenge."

"You'll teach me what I need to know about makeup and hair and all that?"

"'All that' is right," said Valerie. "You'll need to know how to walk, talk, think…"

It was like having a life-size Barbie, she thought, albeit with a slightly large nose, but still, one she would control.

"I've thought of all that," he said, "but of course, you're the expert, you're the teacher."

Valerie nodded. She was the expert. She looked at his face again, and she noticed the first item that bothered her.

"Get up," she said. He did so. She grabbed his hand and led her into her living room. "Lie down on the sofa…"

He wore a puzzled expression, but he did as he was told. She ran upstairs and returned with her makeup case.

"Now lie still," she ordered, pulled out her tweezers, and yanked the first clump of hair from his shaggy eyebrows.

"Ow!" cried Chesney.

A satisfied smile overspread Valerie Fierro's lips. "Welcome to my world!"

– 62 –
Okay Rules for an
Industrial Strength Innis

fter that," explained Lorraine Innis, "it was a lot of hard work. I had to learn everything a woman learns over years of growing up, except instead of years I did it in months."

Lorraine sat up on the couch, rubbed her eyes, and looked at Clodagh Clott.

"It sounds like a second puberty," observed Clodagh, "only from the other side, and in much less time. What about the voice, the walking, the mannerism?"

"Valerie coached me in all that," said Chesney. "The voice was the hardest until I realized that I once had a voice similar to a female voice. When I was a boy before my voice broke. Then it was a matter of going back before the break and learning to use that voice again. The rest of it was just a matter of practice and getting used to it all. Plus, I had to invent a history for me, for Lorraine. I had to know where I was born, where I went to school, all of it."

"And the name?" asked Clodagh. "Where did that come from? How did you become Lorraine Innis?"

She smiled. "It's an anagram of Aunt Elinor's name…Elinor Iris Anne… Lorraine E. Innis."

"And the 'E?' What is your middle name?"

"Elizabeth," said Lorraine softly. "The same as…"

Clodagh nodded. "Verity Elizabeth Goodhue."

Lorraine looked down at her hands. "The body and the makeup is Valerie's doing. But I like to think there are little bits of all the girls around me in what Lorraine turned out to be. Aunt Elinor, Martina, and, you know…"

"I know," said Clodagh. "You do them proud. Not many women have a living memorial as fine as Lorraine Innis."

Lorraine shrugged.

"So," said Clodagh after several moments of silence, "when shall we do it."

"Do it?" said Lorraine. "You mean, you will? You'll help me forget about Chesney?"

"Temporarily," said Clodagh.

"Yes, of course, only temporarily," said Lorraine.

"Yes, I can do that," said Clodagh. "Now that I understand it all, and why you did it, and how you got here, and where you hope to go with it."

"Chesney got it all wrong," said Lorraine as if she were talking about another person. "He thought it was Peter Liverot who was to blame for Martina's death. Liverot did a lot of bad things, including using the charity to launder money. Still, he wasn't responsible for Martina being in Chicago. I'd like to figure out that, and sort out the charity mess, so I can stop being Lorraine once and for all."

Clodagh smiled. "Don't want to join our team permanently, eh?"

"It's lovely sex," said Lorraine, "and womanhood is a nice place to visit, but I wouldn't want to live here."

"It's ironic. You have to be a more complete woman so you can stop being a woman at all. And you're convinced that Lorraine is the only person who's smart enough to get you out of being Lorraine."

"Yes," said Lorraine. "Now, what do we have to do?"

"Well, put simply, I just have to put you into a deep trance, and we'll make you forget, temporarily, that there's a Chesney Potts. You'll be all Lorraine Innis, all the time."

"And how do you bring me out? How do you make Lorraine go away, and Chesney come back?"

"I'll give you a trigger word to bring you out of it, to make you remember who you really are."

"Will it be jarring coming out of it?"

"Oh, I imagine so," said Clodagh. "When you come out of full Lorraine, it will be like shaking the foundations of her world as she believes it to be. We'll be establishing Lorraine Innis as the basis of all you believe, your starting point in life, as it were. She is the person upon whom your world and worldview will be built. When she's taken away, it could be quite traumatic."

Lorraine nodded and recalled the previous year when Valerie had jolted her out of her Lorraine mindset and made her remember Chesney. Lorraine freaked out and nearly ran through a glass door.

"That's why," continued Clodagh, "we will need to select a word that you're not likely to hear in casual conversation. And I will be the only person who knows it. When you need to come out of Lorraine, we want to do it in private, just you and I, so as not to cause any harm to you."

"What should we use?"

"I know exactly what we need to use."

Lorraine looked at Clodagh and searched her eyes for a moment, and suddenly realized it. "Yes, I think you're right," she said. "I've rarely heard it, except in that context…"

"Verity …" said Clodagh.

Lorraine winced but nodded in agreement. "Yes. It's not a very popular name, especially in the United States. And as a word, it's almost archaic in use."

"And no one knows about her? I mean, no one around you, Patsy or Valerie, for example?"

Lorraine shook her head. "No, not by name. They know there was a girl in England, but I never could say it aloud. Aside from you, the only one around here who knew was Martina."

"Then 'Verity Goodhue' is the phrase," said Clodagh.

"The magic phrase," said Lorraine softly. She thought for a moment and then looked up. "What about sex?"

"Sex? In what respect?"

"I suppose in all respects," said Lorraine, "most pressing would be my sex. Can you make me ignore what I see when I'm naked?"

"Ignore? Hmm, let's just say we'll have you accept it, much like a birth defect that only you know about. I can have you look at it and believe you're perfectly normal."

"What about doctors?" asked Lorraine. "If I have to go to a doctor, we can't very well hypnotize them, can we?"

"I'd avoid doctors, as best you can. Think of me as your primary physician. If you get sick, call me first, and then we can deal with it. If the condition warrants it, I can bring you out, and we can decide what to do from there. Okay?"

"Right," said Lorraine. "What about relationships: personal relationships?"

"Don't have any," said Clodagh. "That is if you're talking about romantic relationships, not unless you plan on letting your partner in on your secret. You were essentially in this situation before. How did you handle it then?"

"I supposedly had a husband then," said Lorraine. "I was committed to Martin Innis. Only the media went out and found a 'Martin,' and he turned out to be a bigamist. So, now, I'm available. Poor Nikolai Kropotkin is still carrying a torch for me. I want to appear to be a normal, healthy woman, but not *that* normal and healthy."

Clodagh looked closely at Lorraine. "Yes, you're attractive, and your fame only adds to your desirability. I could see a lot of men wanting to bed you just to say they had."

Lorraine buried her head in her hands. "I wish I had my imaginary husband back."

"There are several approaches. We could put you in a committed but secret relationship, or you could declare you've decided to become celibate."

"This is getting complicated," said Lorraine.

Clodagh laughed. "Getting? Look, why don't you just refuse any intimate relationships. I can give you a standard list of excuses. When a girl doesn't want to be with a guy, it doesn't have to be a good excuse. Anything else we need to cover?"

Lorraine thought for a few minutes. "No, I think that should do it. Oh, wait, how will I know when I can stop being Lorraine if I don't know I'm anything else?"

"Hmm, that's a good question," said Clodagh. "You and I can have regular appointments. We'll make up some pretense why Lorraine would need to see me. Then, when we're alone, I'll say the trigger word, and we'll let you have a look around from the other side, see how everything is progressing, and how much longer you'll need to continue."

"That sounds like a good plan," said Lorraine.

Clodagh reached into her purse. "Here's my business card," she said, handing it to Lorraine. "Put this in your wallet. I'll include in your suggestions that you'll call me if Lorraine feels things are getting out of control in between our regular visits. You won't know exactly why you need to call me, just that you do if you're in a crisis situation that you can't handle. Okay?"

"Oh," said Lorraine, "and don't forget my mission, you know what I want to accomplish as Lorraine."

"You want to find out who is responsible for Martina's death, bring them to justice, and sort out all of the charity's entanglements."

"Yes, but I don't want to discuss those with anyone," said Lorraine. "I want to be like a secret agent, even to myself."

"Got it," said Clodagh jotting down a final notation on her legal pad, and then looked up. "Is that everything?"

"Yes, I think we've covered everything."

"Okay, lay down."

Lorraine looked up at Clodagh. "You mean right now, this minute?"

Clodagh shrugged her shoulders. "Why not? Is there something Chesney needs to do?"

"No, I don't think so," said Lorraine, a noticeable waver in her voice.

Clodagh looked at her sideways. "You don't have to do this."

"No, I do," said Lorraine. "It was my idea, it's just..."

Lorraine embraced Clodagh.

"Wish me luck, Clo," said Lorraine.

"Best of luck," said Clodagh with a reassuring smile.

"And you won't forget me?"

"I never did."

"And you'll come and see me?"

"I'll always be here when you need me," said Clodagh.

"Thank you," said Lorraine as she lay back down, "for everything." Lorraine nestled into the cushions of her sofa and closed her eyes.

"I'm ready," she said.

"You're sure you're not afraid," asked Clodagh.

"Chesney is," said Lorraine, "but I'm not."

– 63 –
Industrial Strength Innis Rules, Okay?

"Another day with this f**kin' cast," muttered Valerie Fierro.

"Don't think of it that way," said Mike Valvano as he parked outside Fourth Fiduciary Trust. "Think of it as another day closer to getting it off."

"Yeah, right," she said.

Mike flashed a sympathetic smile, and Valerie sighed inwardly. He thought her mood was down to PMS. Mike was like every other guy she had ever known, ascribing every sour mood to her monthly cycle. Dumb guys. Whenever she tried to attribute her problems to Lorraine, Mike would tell Valerie what a nice lady Lorraine was. No, most of Valerie's problems were Innis-centered, and no one would ever understand that except Valerie. And she couldn't explain Lorraine to anyone without landing herself in even deeper trouble. The only way of dealing with Lorraine was with Lorraine herself.

Mike leaned over to kiss her. Valerie wasn't in the mood, so she turned and gave him her cheek.

"Thanks," said Valerie, climbing out of the car and reaching back in for her purse and her briefcase.

"Have a good day, I'll pick you up later," he said and then drove off.

A good day? That all depended on whether Lorraine finally decided to show up at work, and if she decided to finally speak to Valerie. They hadn't spoken for almost two weeks. Not since that horrible day back in Washington when Valerie broke her arm, and her car was totaled. Oh, yes, that was also the day that Peter Liverot and President Merton were blown up. Since then, according to Patsy, Lorraine had been meeting with some private consultant. Who was that consultant? A lawyer? A detective? Or even worse, an accountant? It all depended on what Liverot had told

Lorraine on his deathbed. And that was what she had to force Lorraine to tell her.

Valerie exited the elevator and trudged past Patsy's desk on the way to her office. Valerie kept her head down and pretended to be reading her newspaper.

"Good morning, Valerie," she heard Patsy say as she walked past.

"Morning," said Valerie, not looking up.

"Valerie, Lorraine would like to see you when you're free."

Valerie stopped.

"Lorraine is in?"

"Yes," said Patsy, "She came in this morning, bright and early. She was here before I came in."

"Alone?"

"I always come in alone."

"I meant was Lorraine alone?" asked Valerie. She wondered if Lorraine was fortified by a platoon of her private consultants, or lawyers, or cops.

"Yes, she's in her office," said Patsy.

Valerie hurried to her office to put away her briefcase and bag. Then she checked her appearance in the mirror and steeled herself for the confrontation. She would have it out with Lorraine, no matter what. Valerie would reach through that woman she had created and grab Chesney Potts by the neck and make him tell her everything she wanted to know.

"Ready," she said, and then walked to Lorraine's office. The door was open. Lorraine was standing behind her desk. Valerie rapped once on the doorframe.

"Valerie," said Lorraine looking up and smiling, "come in."

Valerie walked in and closed the door without asking for permission.

Lorraine walked over to meet her. There was something in the way she moved, thought Valerie, an air of confidence, of self-assurance. Shit, thought Valerie, she knows something. This was going to be it, at least Valerie promised herself she would go out swinging.

"Valerie, dear," Lorraine came over and hugged Valerie, affording extra care around her broken arm. Then, in an unfamiliar act, she gave Valerie a very feminine peck on the cheek. "How are you feeling? How's your arm?"

"Uh, okay...I guess?"

"Good," said Lorraine, "if you need any more time off, or if you need a car and driver..."

"Mike brought me to work," said Valerie.

"He's very sweet, isn't he? Come, let's sit down and let's chat..." Lorraine gestured to the sofa. Valerie sat down, and Lorraine sat next to her. There was something so odd, yet familiar about the way Lorraine was behaving. Still, it could be a tactic. Valerie decided to go on the offensive.

"Chat, eh?" she said.

"Yes," said Lorraine with a smile.

"So, you're talking to me again?" said Valerie.

Lorraine looked confused.

"You didn't speak to me all the way back from Washington," said Valerie.

Lorraine looked at her for a moment with a vacant expression before a concerned looked replaced it.

"That was a horrible day," said Lorraine. "I don't think any of us were at our best. Please forgive me if I was preoccupied."

"It didn't have anything to do with Liverot?"

"Liverot?" repeated Lorraine. "Of course it did. I watched poor Peter Liverot die. And to think they were there to honor me. We can't be responsible for the acts of a deranged individual, but still, it was a tragic day."

"Yeah, okay," said Valerie, "but what did Liverot tell you?"

Lorraine looked at her a moment. "He told me some very upsetting things, but I don't want you to worry about those."

"I can help you. I can do whatever you need me to do," blurted Valerie. Mainly, she thought, I need to know if Liverot told you about his private deal with me.

Lorraine smiled. "There will be time for all that later. Right now, I just need my cousin and best friend to get feeling better."

That was it, thought Valerie. She couldn't take any more of this phony sympathy, especially when it sounded so real.

"All right, let's stop playing games," snapped Valerie. "We're alone. You can knock it off, Chesney!"

A concerned look crossed Lorraine's face. "I don't understand, Valerie. Knock what off, and who's Chesney?"

"Chesney...Chesney Potts," said Valerie, barely restraining her fury.

Lorraine shook her head. "Do I know him?"

Valerie opened her mouth to speak, and suddenly stopped. She looked deep in Lorraine's eyes. They were clear and bright.

"Are...are you feeling okay?" asked Valerie.

"I feel wonderful," said Lorraine. "Personally, I've never felt more energized, more alive."

"Oh, shit," said Valerie.

"What's wrong? Is it your arm?"

"No, no," said Valerie. "Have you been hit on the head recently?"

Lorraine looked at her askance. "Never, as far as I can recall. Not even as a girl."

"A girl..."

"Yes, you know, as a child?"

"And you were a girl?"

Lorraine laughed. "What else would I have been?"

"Oh, no..." said Valerie.

"I was a little girl, you were a little girl, now we're grown women." She said it calmly and with conviction.

Valerie looked at Lorraine and suddenly recalled that expression. It was the same one Lorraine had worn the previous October when Lorraine thought she really was Lorraine. Now apparently, somehow, Lorraine was back again in industrial strength. That wasn't good. Valerie always had some leverage against Chesney. He had a weak spot that Valerie could exploit. Though she was more loving, more feminine, Lorraine was also smarter and tougher. This was not good at all, what could…

A thought occurred to Valerie. Back then, she had jolted Lorraine from her Lorraine-osity by showing her a photo of Chesney. She had one in her desk.

"Are you okay, Valerie," asked Lorraine. "You're acting very strangely."

"Yeah, I'm fine. I need to show you something, okay?"

"Of course…"

Valerie leaped to her feet. "I'll be right back," she said, starting from the room, before stopping and pointing at Lorraine. "Don't move, okay?"

"All right," said Lorraine.

Valerie rushed from the room, down the hall, and into her office. She grabbed the photo and ran back into Lorraine's office. She started to sit and then jumped back up to close the door.

Lorraine looked puzzled.

"Okay, hold on," cautioned Valerie. "Here it is."

"What?"

Valerie breathlessly held up her palm. "I want you to brace yourself."

"If you say so," said Lorraine calmly.

"What I'm going to show you is going to upset you."

"Oh?"

"Yeah," said Valerie, "but don't freak out, okay?"

"Freak out? Me?"

"And don't throw anything, or tear out your hair, or run through the window…"

"Valerie, we're on the ninth floor. I'm not likely to run through any windows."

"Okay, okay, I just want you to be calm, control yourself, and look at this…"

Valerie handed her the photograph of Chesney Potts and braced herself for the reaction. Instead of shouts, tears, or anything nearing violence, Lorraine looked at the photo passively for a moment. She then looked up at Valerie with an expression that, if anything, asked: "so what?"

"That," said Valerie, "is Chesney Potts."

"Oh," said Lorraine, and took a second look at the photograph before handing it back to Valerie.

"Is that all you can say?"

Lorraine shrugged. "Does Michael know?"

"Michael?"

"Your boyfriend, does he know about you and this man?"

Valerie rolled her eyes. "Do you think I'm seeing... that guy... romantically?"

"Aren't you?"

"As if!" said Valerie, forgetting that in insulting Chesney Potts, she was also insulting Lorraine Innis. "I mean, no. That's not why I showed it to you."

"Well, then," said Lorraine, "why did you show me his photograph?"

Valerie pursed her lips and pointed at the photograph again. "Because....you've had a good look at the picture?" Lorraine assured her she had. "Do you notice anything about him?"

Lorraine looked intently at Valerie and then motioned to see the picture again. Valerie handed it to her. Lorraine studied it carefully for over a minute and then gave it back to Valerie with a sage nod of her head.

"Very nice eyes," said Lorraine, "but he should lose some weight. He doesn't look very healthy. Was that okay?"

"Just great," muttered Valerie, "couldn't have been better. Welcome back, Lorraine."

"Thank you, dear," said Lorraine with a smile. "Now, let's get to work. There's a lot I need to get done."

THE END

of

THE GIRL IN THE SAFFRON ESPADRILLES

The Story of Lorraine Innis will continue in Book 6:

"The Girl in the Blood Red Stilettos"

Visit www.iLorraine.com

for more information on news, products, and giveaways